For Scot

Hue

Hope you enjoy the next
installment!

John R. Gentile

OFFWORLDER
Book II of the SOFAR Trilogy

A Novel

by

John R. Gentile

1663 LIBERTY DRIVE, SUITE 200
BLOOMINGTON, INDIANA 47403
(800) 839-8640
WWW.AUTHORHOUSE.COM

First published by AuthorHouse 12/05/05

ISBN: 1-4208-7233-8 (sc)
ISBN: 1-4208-7232-X (dj)

Library of Congress Control Number: 2005906368

Printed in the United States of America
Bloomington, Indiana

This book is printed on acid-free paper.

© Cover art by Jason Pedersen
© Cover design by Jason Pedersen and Katie Iverson
© Author photo by Katie Iverson

ALSO BY JOHN R. GENTILE

Blue Planets: Book I of the SOFAR Trilogy

Acknowledgements

I am deeply grateful to the following individuals who have not only believed in my writing, but have also encouraged me to see this project through to its completion.

First, an apology is in order for an omission in Blue Planets: Book I of the SOFAR Trilogy to George Thomasson. His valuable insights and experience training marine mammals during the Viet Nam conflict helped define the character of Cooper Ridley. Thank you, George, for your insights, generosity and time.

To my wife and chief editor, Katie Iverson, whose patience and never ending red ink helped to shape my story telling and yield a much more compelling manuscript: thank you for keeping me honest. I love you.

You can self-edit and self-critique your own work for only so long. I am deeply indebted to the following friends and family members for their tireless enthusiasm, good humor, and solid critique. For content and line edits, I wish to thank Michael Barwick, Randall and Susie Claybourn, Chris and John Clifford, Dr. Timothy Fagan, Steve Iverson (The Undisputed King of the Yellow Sticky Tab), Stirling Iverson, Paul Maseman, Jason Pedersen, Dr. Thomas Strong and Joia Wheeler.

Thanks go to Lucinda Davis (The Web Master) for her great website design and Jason Pedersen, illustrator extraordinaire, for the fantastic front cover design.

I wish to acknowledge the support of Antigone Books, Catfish Books, Changing Hands Bookstore, Greenfire Bookshop,

Reader's Oasis, Tohono Chul Giftshop, the University Of Arizona Bookstore and other independent booksellers who have promoted my writing.

And a special note of thanks to Melissa Miller, Assistant Program Director, KUAT, for helping me get my foot lodged in several well placed doors.

Finally, a heartfelt thank you to my readers from Mrs. Anderson's Fourth Grade Class in Limon, Colorado and to the wonderful residents and staff at Mountain View Retirement Village in Tucson, Arizona. Your enthusiasm and support has made the arduous journey of writing and publishing a book well worth the toil.

For Katie: wife, best friend, artist, scientist, mentor, and muse, who wields a sharp, but wise red pen.

In time, even the deepest of oceans will reveal its secrets.

-- Fourth century Delfinian proverb

CHAPTER ONE

Azrnoth-zin stood up from the navigation console and stretched. His senses dulled from the lingering effects of post cryo-sleep, he felt as if he were dwelling in the gray world between sleeping and waking. In a vain attempt to alleviate the stiff joints and muscles, he assumed several unusual and uncomfortable positions with his neck and torso. He was surprised the soreness was still present after three cycles.

The ship's computer had awakened from stasis after a navigational error in the auto-piloting system had caused them to miss the next wormhole jump. With the jump sequence out of sync, the ship was forced to take a longer way home. Azrnoth-zin did not mind this major inconvenience in their flight plan. He would arrive back with the Delfinian fleet all too soon. He knew what was waiting for him.

A computer-enhanced voice came over the ship's communication network, interrupting his thoughts.

"Commander of the Third Order, the human is coming out of stasis. You are requested to report to the medical-surgical bay."

"Update on vital signs," said Azrnoth-zin, punching a set of coordinates onto the flat bluish-green console.

"Core temperature is at ninety-two point four, Earth standard measurement in Fahrenheit degrees. Heart rate is thirty-two. Respirations are at nine. Encephalographic readings are within normal limits, but are erratic. Alpha patterns are not

1

stabilized at present. This could be due to the inducement of increased cortical activity from the neural assimilators."

"Keep monitoring his life signs," said the alien. "I want him observed even after he comes out of stasis. I am returning the ship to auto-pilot mode."

Azrnoth-zin moved his hand reluctantly over the flat screen once more. The ship's controls were now guided by the computer system. He wanted the chance to pilot the long-range transport himself for a while. He knew it would be the last flying he would be doing.

"I am on my way to med-surg now," he said. Turning clumsily, he walked through the passageway and descended to the lower deck.

He had never been this cold before. It was the coldness of the ocean abyss, the vacuum of space, the endless antarctic ice fields. All he wanted to do was to curl into a fetal position and sleep forever. He groped for the blanket he thought lay somewhere near his bare and frozen feet. But the blanket was not there.

He stood on a vast, frozen tundra. As far as he could see, everything appeared a muted and opaque white. Land and sky fused together into one blinding entity. Snow swirled around his naked feet. When he looked down at his feet, all he saw were leathery flippers. Holding his hands in front of him, he witnessed the transformation: his fingers were fusing into paddle-like appendages.

He shuddered. Strange creatures appeared out of the swirling white. Dream creatures. A large yellowish animal resembling a slug slithered across his path. It possessed appendages that appeared and then withdrew into its gelatinous body, only to reappear in another location on the torso. Small furry creatures that walked upright with bulging black eyes milled around him, then disappeared into a swirl of snow.

Walking down the dimly lit corridor, Azrnoth-zin's footsteps reverberated on the metal floor grating. The ship was utilitarian, designed for long-range reconnaissance and recovery missions. Due to space constraints and great distances between star systems, Azrnoth-zin placed himself in cryostasis to conserve much needed resources. Before going under, he had reviewed the logs that were imprinted into the computer from the Water Council. Upon his return to the fleet he was to be met by a security detail. He suspected incarceration prior to his arraignment before the Council.

In seventeen cycles, they would rejoin the Delfinian fleet. The armada was in a completely different quadrant of space since he had left. That was not surprising. Their enemy was perpetually on the move. Azrnoth-zin's mood further darkened as he wondered how many of his former comrades were still left.

The *Kren-dahl* was unmanned except for a skeleton crew of "metallics," sophisticated robots that maintained the ship's navigation, life support, and emergency medical treatment as it traversed the great void. Azrnoth-zin knew no Delfinians would be spared from the war effort to bring him back.

He looked down on a blue and green planet from space. He desperately wanted to reach its surface. He wanted to go where it was warm. He would give anything to feel the sun's warmth again. The planet looked like Earth. But it was not Earth. It was completely covered in water. Where were the continents?

He found himself moving underwater, the fluid chill enveloping him, sapping his body heat. His arms and legs were of no use. The current was too strong.

Two large blue dolphin-like creatures swam alongside him. They turned their heads ninety degrees to look at him, revealing eyeless sockets that stared at nothing. The dolphin-creatures possessed fins that looked like some bizarre hybridization of a flipper and a hand. The digits moved independently of one another. The alien dolphin-beings gestured to him, beckoning him to follow.

The dolphin-creatures spoke to him in a language he had not heard before. Yet on some level, he vaguely understood the high-pitched rise and fall of their dialect. He tried to speak

3

back to the creatures but no sound escaped his lips. The strange nektonic beings faded into the blackness, powered by their heavy trident-like flukes. Caught in the wash from the flukes, he began to tumble uncontrollably. The strong current dragged him down into the cold blackness. His struggling became feeble as the abyss enveloped him.

Azrnoth-zin entered the med-surg section of the ship, which also housed the cryo chambers. Four cylindrical chambers about ten feet in length fanned out from the center of the room. All of the elongate sleep tubes were empty except one. Over the farthest pod a metallic hovered, monitoring the life signs of the occupant floating in the cylinder.

The metallic possessed an ovoid central body for data processing and mechanical functions. Two multi-axial hinged appendages with flexible finger joints and opposable thumbs were capable of performing the most intricate digital manipulation. Above the central body, a sensory disc processed tactile, visual, and audio information. Below the alloy body, three hinged legs were retracted into grooves that would distend and act as a tripod when the metallic rested on a fixed surface.

Azrnoth-zin approached the pod and peered inside the transparent portal. Inside the cylinder, the naked form of Ridley was bathed in a viscous, cobalt-colored solution. Synaptic leads were attached to Ridley's body, with the greatest concentration placed on his head, chest and around the wound sites.

Azrnoth-zin checked the monitors located at the top of the pod. Scrolling across the screen in Delfinian characters, readouts of all of Ridley's physiological systems were being displayed.

"I do not like the readings from his diencephalon." he said.

"I have experienced difficulty in stabilizing the hypothalamus. This could explain the erratic changes in core temperature," said the metallic, adjusting the settings with one of its mechanical hands. "Most of this procedure is experimental. We have no records of human physiology. The parameters of the neural reorganization are set for Delfinian brains."

"I was operating on the assumption that Delfinian and human brains were more similar than not," said Azrnoth-zin.

"In basic structure, they are similar," the metallic said. "The frontal, temporal, and parietal sections are more developed in Delfinian tissue. Observe here at the central sulcus." The robotic medical unit pointed a mechanical finger to an area on the monitor screen. "Do you see the activity here?"

Azrnoth-zin nodded.

"This area is one-third as developed as the Delfinian equivalent. From my analysis, another major difference is the speed of axoplasmic transmission. The rate of nerve conduction in Delfinians is faster than humans."

Ridley's body went into a series of convulsions, causing his body to writhe in the thick fluid. Several times he bumped against the walls of the cylinder. The readings on the monitor jumped off the screen.

A great chamber lay before him. There was something sinister and foreboding about this place. Cold fear invaded his being as he walked through a room like none he had seen before. All around him, as far as his eyes could see, large glass-like cylindrical chambers stood shrouded by a ghostly mist. Inside the chambers, a greenish-yellow gas swirled. Someone or something was inside the capsules, but the sickly looking fog obscured the occupants.

His dread grew ever deeper as he walked among the chambers. Suddenly, he felt an uncontrollable urge to get out of this place, to flee from the coldness. Here was a different type of coldness: the coldness of dead things.

With a hiss, the chamber in front of him opened, pouring the yellowish cloud onto the floor. It crept toward him, enveloping his feet and moving up to his knees. Another tube opened, then another, all unleashing their poisonous vapors. He saw movement inside the chamber.

He needed to find the door. He needed to get free of this place. Something was emerging from the chambers.

"What is happening to him now?" said Azrnoth-zin.

"The humanoid is experiencing extreme neural overload," stated the metallic matter-of-factly. "The seizures have been growing progressively more intense and lasting longer the closer he gets to what is considered his normal levels of basic metabolic function." The metallic performed more adjustments on the monitor. Ridley resumed floating in the suspension, the turbulence from his seizures causing his body to rock from the rebounding eddies.

"Will he survive?"

"At this time, that is difficult to ascertain. As you will recall, he had no life signs when he was brought on board. Our medical database has very little information on the rate of human tissue degradation following trauma. The other unknown is that these tubes were designed for Delfinian reorganization, not Earth human."

He was staring at a dark and barren landscape, the only light being the diffuse glow from two distant moons. He felt the chill of cold desolation. He saw a figure, alien to him, hunched over something. In two large claws with three digits ending in rapier-like nails, it grasped an object of prey. The alien-being squatted on powerful segmented appendages. It was tall. A creature like that shouldn't be that tall. And it was - feeding. Its oblong head looked up at him revealing large yellow serpent-like eyes and a mouthful of bloodstained silvery fangs.

He could not pull his gaze away from what the creature was feeding upon. The body was mutilated, but the face appeared to be humanoid. The creature opened its mouth and emitted a scream that chilled him deeper than the barren landscape. The hideous creature bounded toward him.

Ridley's body was shaken with another full-body convulsion causing the bluish liquid to swirl and roll inside of the chamber. The metallic attempted to dampen the seizures by performing another series of adjustments to the chamber's controls.

Ridley's convulsions escalated. His body slammed against the inside of the cylinder.

"The humanoid will experience complete neural shutdown in ninety-six seconds," said the metallic.

"Terminate neural reorganization," said Azrnoth-zin. "We will just have to wait and see the residual effects of the damage once he comes out of stasis."

"The Reorganization procedure cannot be terminated at this time due to the time lock placed on the chamber at the initialization of the process. The procedure will not be completed for thirty-two hours, seventeen minutes and nine seconds."

"What? There is no manual override on the cylinder for this procedure?" said Azrnoth-zin.

"It was a pre-existing program, used for severe trauma to Delfinian brains. Apparently, the human brain withstands much less than we anticipated. Neural disintegration in twenty-two seconds."

Azrnoth-zin ran over to the far wall, activated a disc on the wall, and a small plasma pistol appeared from behind a panel. He checked the charge, then ran back to the chamber. He fired a short blast into the control unit residing above the cylinder. Instantly, a white gas erupted from the cylinder as the glass door slid back. The bluish ooze erupted forth, spilling onto the metal decking. Azrnoth-zin dodged the viscous fluid and moved quickly to the other side of the chamber.

"Ten seconds to neural disintegration," said the metallic.

Azrnoth-zin ripped the leads from Ridley's head and then went after the leads still attached to his torso. The remainder of the fluid drained out of the cylinder, exposing the deathly white form of Ridley curled in a fetal position, convulsing slightly. Azrnoth-zin looked up at the overhead monitor. The time on the display read 0:00.04.

"His core temperature must be raised or he will terminate from hypothermia," said Azrnoth-zin.

Ridley's body was covered in a gelatinous, blue ooze. Azrnoth-zin and the metallic transferred Ridley's stiff, inert form with considerable difficulty to another reorganization chamber.

7

Immediately, the metallic adjusted the controls to increase the core body temperature. Ridley's uncontrollable shivering subsided after several minutes.

Ridley saw himself swimming upward from a deep well. It must be a well. Only a well could be this dark and cold. He could see a circle of light above him, but it still appeared a long way off. Somewhere overhead, he was aware of voices, but he could not understand the context of the conversation. How had he come to be in this cold dark well? Damn. There was going to be hell to pay when Uncle Jake found out he'd fallen into a well. Jake had warned him time and again about stepping too close to holes in the ground. He desperately wanted to reach the surface. His lungs felt as if they were full of cold, foul tasting water. He still had no feeling in his arms or legs.

A face appeared above him leaning over the edge, peering down at him. He could not tell who it was but the face seemed vaguely familiar. Jake? The circle of light and the face grew larger. His vision cleared slightly. He recognized deep cerulean eyes, like two large beacons guiding him to the surface. He felt the overwhelming sensation of suffocation from the fluid trapped in his lungs. The icy grip of the water pulled him downward into the blackness.

Ridley vomited violently, ejecting thick bluish-white fluid from his mouth. Azrnoth-zin was not fast enough to get out of the way and ended up wearing the slimy effluent down the front of his tunic. Ridley wretched again, but not before Azrnoth-zin turned him on his side. Another fit of coughing and the last of the cryo-fluid was forced from his lungs. The spasms gave way to more uncontrollable shivering.

The chamber's window slid into place and the metallic adjusted the environmental controls. The chamber slowly pressurized until ambient conditions were achieved.

"Core temperature is reaching ninety-six point two," said the metallic.

"Continue to adjust the temperature and pressure," said Azrnoth-zin, "until you have reached ninety-eight point six degrees."

Several hours passed. Most of the severe spasms and shivering had dissipated, but Ridley's gaze remained unfocused. The metallic continued to hover over its patient, monitoring life signs and relaying any significant changes in Ridley's condition to the command center of the ship. Azrnoth-zin was completing the calculations on the next worm jump when the message came through from the med-surg section.

"Commander," said the metallic over the com-link system. "The human's vital functions appear to be stabilizing. Visual systems are becoming more utilized, heart rate is increasing, and voluntary movement appears to be occurring in the distal extremities."

"I will be there momentarily," said Azrnoth-zin.

When Azrnoth-zin walked into the med-surg section and gazed into the pod containing Ridley, he was not prepared for what he saw. Inside the pod, all of the color appeared to be washed out of Ridley's face and body, giving him a gaunt, wraith-like countenance. Ridley's eyes were milky and all around the sockets a purplish discoloration had set in. The wound sites were an angry pink and raised well above the skin. Ridley turned and faced Azrnoth-zin and attempted to mouth something.

Azrnoth-zin looked up at the monitor, then turned to the metallic. "Can we open the capsule now?"

"His life signs are stabilizing. Except for the continued erratic cortical impulses. Yes, I believe the human can be examined out of the chamber now."

"The *human* has a name. He is called Ridley."

"Ridley," repeated the metallic. "I will correct."

The metallic moved its mechanical hands deftly over the control panel and with a loud hiss, the transparent panel slid back. Ridley gasped as the ship's air greeted his aching lungs. He flinched from the brightness of the light in the room.

"Ridley, it is I, Azrnoth-zin. Do not attempt to speak yet. You have experienced severe trauma. I believe you will survive. When you are feeling better, we will speak."

"C-c-c-cold," Ridley stammered. "C-c-can't see."

Azrnoth-zin nodded. "Rest now. We will increase the pod temperature to reduce the chill. Try to get some sleep. You have been through a great deal. Your vision and all of your other system's functions will return soon."

"Commander, I would like to begin infusion of nutrients with your permission. We would begin by re-establishing fluid balances based on the hu - Ridley's physiology."

"I will leave Ridley in your capable care," said Azrnoth-zin. He turned and walked back to the command center of the ship. "Keep me apprised of any changes."

Ridley awoke alone in a sterile room. He lay in a semi-recumbent position on a table and was covered by a fine transparent film that appeared to shimmer with his every movement. He touched the layer with his hand and felt warmth pulsating from it. To one side of the bed was a table containing various odd looking vials and objects. Something wasn't right about the table, but Ridley's addled brain could not register what it was. After several moments, he realized the table had no legs; it appeared to be floating - hovering next to the bed he was in. Ridley closed his eyes and drew several ragged breaths. Upon opening his eyes again, he saw the image was still there.

Ridley caught glimpses of quick, erratic movement in his peripheral vision. At first, he thought he was experiencing "floaters" and tried to blink them away. The objects were small and multicolored, shaped like oversized paramecia. They appeared to be moving across the walls of the infirmary only to dissolve into the wall itself. He squeezed his eyes shut, but upon opening them, the images scuttled around another section of the med-surg section.

He tried to shake his head but the attempt sent a white-hot pain through his skull behind his eyes. He lay there for what seemed an eternity, eyes closed, teeth clenched, until the sensation subsided.

Ridley's joints felt like they were encased in glue. Any effort to move his arms and legs resulted in spasms and the return of the headache from hell.

The airlock door slid open and the metallic unit floated into the infirmary. Ridley kept his eyes closed, fearing that opening them would bring on the stabbing pain behind his eyes. The metallic now hovered beside Ridley's bed.

"Can you hear me, Ridley?"

"I can hear you," Ridley said hoarsely. He opened up his eyes to a squint and gazed at the apparition suspended in the air. Ridley's eyes grew wide. He tried to back off the opposite side of the bed, disrupting the floating table. Vials clattered loudly to the floor.

"Do not be afraid," said the metallic. "No harm will come to you."

"Where am I?" said Ridley, his voice choked with fear.

"You are aboard the ship *Kren-dahl.* It is a light reconnaissance, long-range flyer."

"Who - what are you?"

"I am META IV, medical-surgical robotic. You have been in my care since your injury."

"What injury? I don't remember anything."

The metallic extended one of its multiaxial arms toward Ridley. In its fingers it held what appeared to be some type of hypodermic.

"It is time for your neural dampener. Please remain still while I administer the medication."

"I don't think so."

Ridley backed away from the metallic and tried to swing his legs to the other side of the bed. An exquisite wave of pain rolled over him. He cried out and lay on the side of the bed gasping.

META IV contacted Azrnoth-zin through the ship's com system.

"Commander, Ridley is conscious. His sympathetic nervous system responses are sending him into neural overload. I require your assistance."

Azrnoth-zin arrived in the infirmary quickly and assisted Ridley to the semi-recumbent position once more.

"Try not to move for a while," said Azrnoth-zin. "Your muscles have not been used in almost six weeks. You are still suffering the effects of prolonged cryo-sleep and trauma."

"Six weeks? Cryo-sleep? What in the hell are you talking about, Arn? And what's that oversized cuisinart doing with that needle?"

"META IV is responsible for saving your life. If it were not for this med-surg unit, your life functions would have ceased weeks ago back on the volcano."

Ridley's eyes wandered from the metallic back to Azrnoth-zin, registering a combination of confusion, fear and pain. The metallic continued to hover with only slight shifts in movement, accompanied by a quiet whirring sound with each subtle change.

Azrnoth-zin drew a deep breath. "For all purposes, you were left for dead back on the crater. You were shot three times by Jenks' agents and the soldiers."

"Shot? I was dead?"

"Please try not to speak until I have finished," said Azrnoth-zin. "I will answer all of your questions then."

Azrnoth-zin continued. "The first projectile almost severed a large artery next to your heart. You call it the aorta. The second projectile entered the nerve plexus in your right shoulder. The third shattered your large thigh bone that you refer to as the femur, severing the femoral artery."

Ridley felt over those places on his chest, shoulder and thigh, feeling the raised, tender areas under his fingers. "How come I don't remember any of this?"

"It is common following a serious trauma that no recollection of the injury exists. I was monitoring these events from my ship. When I saw you fall, I disengaged the auto drive and came back to retreive you."

Ridley closed his eyes and breathed deeply. Azrnoth-zin watched the rise and fall of his chest. If not for the deep furrow in his brow, he would have surmised that Ridley had drifted back into sleep, the events from the last few minutes too much for his already overtaxed system.

"Wait. I think I'm starting to remember. I remember you disappearing in a blue light. Then, I remember looking up at a similar blue light," said Ridley.

Azrnoth-zin nodded. "What you saw was the molecular transfer beam. You were brought on board the *Kren-dahl* and immediately placed into the cryo-stasis chamber to prevent further tissue degradation. META IV went about the task of replicating your blood and serum types, then performed the repairs on your damaged tissue. Because your brain waves had ceased to function, it was necessary to have you undergo neural reorganization."

"Neural reorganization? I'm sorry, Arn. But you lost me."

"It is a procedure that re-establishes collateral pathways in the Delfinian nervous system following severe trauma. Encoded into the assimilation are motor and sensory programs as well as implantation of electrical signals to the frontal portion of the brain where memory and learning reside. Because the Delfinian brain processes almost three times faster than a human's, you were at risk for sensory overload while the new pathways were being established. On several occasions over the past six weeks, you were close to termination."

Ridley stared dumbly at Azrnoth-zin. "So, let me get this straight. I was basically dead until I went through this reorganization procedure?"

"Essentially, yes."

Ridley winced and rubbed his temples in a vain attempt at ridding the gnawing pain within his skull. "So what is this? A post mortem hangover?"

"Unfortunately," said Azrnoth-zin, "no other species has undergone the procedure. There are no records of outcomes following neural reorganization other than in Delfinians. It was . . . the only way to keep you alive."

"I wish this ringing in my ears would quit," said Ridley gently rocking in the bed. "Maybe staying dead wasn't such a bad idea after all."

Through blurred vision, Ridley thought he saw a shadow of sadness pass across the face of Azrnoth-zin.

"You should rest now, Ridley. And please cooperate with the META unit. It will help you recover your strength."

"Please hold still and try to relax," said the metallic.

"Yeah, right. Relax," said Ridley tersely.

META IV moved in close and Ridley felt a pressure against the base of his skull. The room began to spin and then went to black.

CHAPTER TWO

The following thirty-six hours had to be the worst in Ridley's life. He suffered a series of seizures that required META IV to place a containment field around him so he would not throw himself out of the bed. During his conscious moments, Ridley's headaches became so intense that the infirmary had to be darkened. Any light at all would send searing flashes of pain through his head. A continuous state of nausea prevented all but some forced liquids to stay down.

On several occasions, out of painful frustration, Ridley had hurled the nearest object available at META IV. The metallic dodged the missiles with ease, quickly resuming its normal routine in the infirmary.

Compounding the headaches were the dreams. Ridley could not slip into deep sleep. The constant state of REM sleep beset him with a myriad of strange and often ghastly images. Alien creatures, battles on unknown worlds, mathematical formulas, words and phrases strange to him all floated behind his eyes in a continuous jumble. Intermixed were images of Earth, Enrique and the Seris, Jake and Marjorie, his mother and father, and dying dolphins. The dreamscapes attacked his senses until he lay on the bed, bathed in sweat, too exhausted to move.

One recurring nightmare was particularly disturbing. It always began the same way. Ridley was in a large darkened building that resembled a laboratory, but which was the size of several airplane hangers. The building was filled with dark, fluid-filled chambers. When the first tube hissed open, Ridley started to run. The chambers spewed out deadly yellow gas blocking his path wherever he turned. Something menacing waited just beyond the yellow fog, waiting to pounce. A hideous creature sprang from the cloud. All Ridley could see were malevolent yellow eyes and teeth. Horrid, dripping teeth.

Ridley screamed himself awake. He could not stop shaking. He lay there for what seemed an eternity, attempting to breathe deeply behind clenched teeth and praying that the gnawing pain in his skull would abate.

He squinted his eyes open enough to let in some light and to keep the pain in check. Glancing down at his torso, he saw several of the "floaters" again. He could see them more clearly this time. They were several different colors - iridescent purple, pink, green and yellow. They moved rapidly about his chest, arms and legs, mainly around the wound sites, propelled by the tiny ciliary projections on their bodies. For a brief moment, Ridley thought he was back in freshman biology class, looking for the first time at pond water under the microscope. Though not painful, their presence made Ridley's skin crawl.

One of the creatures slid over to his chest and began to make tiny slurping noises around the raised pink wound on his chest. Ridley lifted his head to get a better look at the protistan-like alien. He blinked again to see if the floater would disappear. Ridley's panic overtook him as three smallish, impassive red eyes blinked back.

He screamed again, his body writhing violently. The protistoid disappeared in a blur, emitting a tiny squeak as it found a place to hide under the floating bed. The other tiny aliens disbursed as Ridley's struggling intensified.

"Get them off me! Shit! Get them off!

META IV entered the infirmary and moved quickly over to where Ridley lay. The metallic administered another in a series of neural dampeners. It then adjusted the parameters on the medical computer monitors, watching as Ridley's muscles relaxed and the tremors subsided.

Azrnoth-zin entered the infirmary and walked quickly to Ridley's side. Ridley opened his eyes and looked up at Azrnoth-zin plaintively. The alien saw tears forming in the eyes of his Earth friend.

"I can't take it anymore," Ridley said, his voice breaking. "I don't know what's real and what isn't. Do whatever you have to do to stop the dreams. Kill me if you have to."

"What happened?" said Azrnoth-zin.

"He was dreaming. His alpha state became elevated. When he awoke he saw the detritophages," said META IV. "All of his systems are overloaded. Even after removing him from the chamber, his brain functions continue to change. His physiology cannot keep up with the neural reorganization."

"Is there anything that can be done for him?"

"I have been analyzing his brain chemistry," said the metallic. "There is an enzyme that his brain produces that inhibits the neurotransmitters. The neural reorganization overrode this center. Perhaps if we were to administer a significant dosage of the enzyme to stimulate it, we could retard the effects of the uncontrolled neural overload."

"What are the negative possibilities?"

"It is not known how the manufactured enzyme will react with his altered tissue. It could cause severe cerebral hemorrhages in various places in his cortex. He could terminate."

"Caught between a rock and a hard place," said Azrnoth-zin heavily, casting a concerned look at the prostrate human.

"I do not understand," said the metallic. "Please clarify."

"Earth idiom I learned from Ridley. Translated, it means neither of our choices are optimal."

Azrnoth-zin turned to Ridley. "I believe this must be your decision, Ridley. META IV has a hypothesis. We have no way of knowing if this procedure will work. It may kill you."

"Do it! Anything's better than this." Ridley slumped back in the bed. "Just do it."

"Prepare the dosage," said Azrnoth-zin.

The metallic floated over to a control center in the infirmary and began to key commands into the medical computer.

After several moments the robotic returned to Ridley's bedside with a 3 inch, thin-gauge hypodermic needle in one of its mechanical hands.

Azrnoth-zin handed Ridley a small white, cylindrical object, which resembled some type of high-density foam.

"Here. Bite down on this. It will prevent you from severing your tongue."

Ridley placed the soft cylinder in his mouth and nodded weakly to proceed. META IV held the hypo just at the level of Ridley's right frontal-temporal area and injected the mixture. The man from Earth was thrown into an immediate seizure that overtook his entire body. His muscles tensed into tetany, jaws clenched against the pain. Sweat soaked onto the floating platform, the body's reaction to a sympathetic nervous system overload. Azrnoth-zin and META IV could do nothing but watch Ridley's body fight with his last reserves.

Suddenly, the seizures stopped, leaving Ridley drained and breathing heavily. Azrnoth-zin gazed up at the overhead monitor and saw that Ridley's neural functions had dropped within the tolerance range. The brain waves registered that he was now in a state of deep sleep.

"Can you assess for any residual damage?" said Azrnoth-zin.

"It is too early to tell," replied META IV. "But, for the present, his systems appear to have stabilized. There is still reorganization occurring in the frontal portion of the cortex. The cerebellum continues to demonstrate collateral development."

Azrnoth-zin walked over to the corner and activated a floating cushion that was lying inert against one wall and sat on it. The cushion transported him to the bed of Ridley. He maneuvered the cushion so that he could lean against the bulkhead.

"Now we wait," he said, folding his arms over his chest and settling in.

When Ridley came to, the first thing he noticed was the headache. It had gone from a searing pain to a continuous dull throb. Tentatively, he opened his eyes to slits, fearful of the blast of pain that lurked behind.

The pain did not intensify. Although his vision was still blurred, he recognized the face that was near his.

Azrnoth-zin's face was impassive. The only indication that gave away his emotions was the large blue eyes. Ridley thought he saw a hint of worry there.

"Hey, Arn," Ridley said weakly.

"Hey to you, Ridley."

"How long have I been out?"

"The first time or the second?"

"The last time."

"Twenty-nine hours, thirty-seven minutes, fifteen seconds by your Earth standard time. But who is counting? How do you feel?"

"Pretty good for a dead guy, I guess. The jackhammer in my head is still there, but it's operating on low power. My body feels like I just went ten rounds with a Kodiak bear."

"Do you desire nourishment yet?"

Ridley winced. "I don't think so," he said. "Food is the last thing on my mind at the moment."

"Then you are not hungry for the Mexican food I had META IV replicate for you?"

Ridley stared at Azrnoth-zin with a narrow gaze. "You're kidding, I hope."

Azrnoth-zin smiled. "I enjoy this thing you call humor, Ridley."

"Funny guy. Don't give up your day job." Ridley looked at his friend. "Thanks, Azrnoth-zin. Thanks for pulling me off that crater and saving my life. There was a time back there when I didn't think saving my bacon was such a good idea."

Azrnoth-zin became pensive. "You may be premature in your gratitude. I might have done irreparable damage to your nervous system. You are the first non-Delfinian to go through the Reorganization. For the moment you are stable, but we do not know what the long-term effects will be. Essentially, your body has been sensorially and motorically reprogrammed. Think of the reinstallation of a computer hard drive to your brain."

"Do you mean to tell me that with all of your technology, you don't know the effects of this reorganization on other species?"

"Please understand, Ridley. The reorganization process not only repairs and restores damaged neural tissue, but it also serves another function. It is used in the event of severe neural trauma, and only as a last resort. It provides the memories, histories and culture of the Delfinian people. Essentially, I have placed in your cortex information that no offworlder has access to. To my people, this makes you an extremely dangerous entity, and I have progressed from mere desertion and cultural contamination to treason."

Ridley lay back on the bed and closed his eyes, his chest rising and falling rhythmically. Azrnoth-zin thought he was dropping off to sleep again when Ridley's eyes fluttered open.

"So what's going to happen to you? And to me?" he said.

"I do not know what your fate will be. There is no prior record of this occurring in any of the databases I have scanned. The Water Council may want your memory erased. I fear that would be fatal for you. You might be relegated to the Displaced Work Force that maintains our battle cruisers, but that is highly unlikely."

"The Displaced Work Force?"

"Yes. They are the survivors of civilizations that we have rescued from the Trochinid onslaught. They have been incorporated into the Delfinian system as laborers to maintain the inner workings of the great battle cruisers. Unfortunately, you lack even the most rudimentary skills to be put to work there. Although you are not that dissimilar in appearance from the Delfinians, you would be viewed as different."

"Some choice. Have a mixmaster taken to my brain or I become the new Delfinian poster child."

"I am sorry, Ridley. Perhaps I acted rashly, bringing you aboard and restoring your functions. At the time, I did not even think. I just reacted."

"I guess that's what you get when you shoot from the hip," said Ridley. "That seems to be a nasty trait you and I share."

"Sadly, that is true."

"This doesn't sound like I'm going to enjoy myself in the near future."

Ridley closed his eyes and smiled thinly. After a moment, he reached out and grabbed Azrnoth-zin's arm. "You sure know how to show an out-of-towner a good time."

The med-surg section was quiet except for the distant thrumming of the drive engines. Ridley reopened his eyes, the rims still swollen and angry. "So, what's in store for you?"

"That," said Azrnoth-zin, "is difficult to say. I could find no information on other Delfinians who have deserted their posts or breached the tenets of secrecy. It is probable that I will have my memories erased and be prevented from verbal or mind-link communication with any other Delfinian. For Delfinians, this is the worst fate. If I am fortunate, they will terminate me. But hopefully, not before I inform them about your world and the Delfids."

Ridley closed his eyes heavily and took a deep breath. He blew out his cheeks and exhaled. "Will I get to speak my piece to this Water Council?"

"Offworlders are not permitted to speak to the Council. When negotiations with other cultures are called for, the Water Council sends a delegation of sub-commanders."

"Sounds like they're pretty well insulated."

"Very little is known about Delfinian culture and societal structure on outer worlds. The Water Council has kept it that way for hundreds of years."

Ridley swung his legs over the edge of the bed and gingerly placed his feet on the floor. META IV, sensing the humanoid's increased activity, moved quickly to intercept Ridley.

"Just what do you think you are doing?" said Azrnoth-zin.

"Please get back into the bed," said META IV. "You are still too weak to be moving around."

"I need to get up for a minute," said Ridley. "My back is killing me." He took a few halting steps, then stopped to regain his equilibrium. With his next step, Ridley's legs buckled beneath him. He would have crumpled to the floor had it not been for Azrnoth-zin's quick reaction catching him from behind.

"Ridley, you have not used most of your systems for six weeks. Some of your bodily functions will take weeks to return."

Ridley felt drained again. He lay his head back on the bed, breathless. "Bad patient. Bad patient," he said.

META IV interjected. "Perhaps if I prepared some Celesian soup for him, it would help to increase his strength."

"Sounds like a culinary adventure," said Ridley.

"Consider it the "chicken soup" of space travelers," said Azrnoth-zin, a faint smile etching his lips. "I must get back to the control center to program the computer for the next jump sequence. We rendezvous with the main fleet in eleven cycles. I will return soon."

Ridley looked at Azrnoth-zin. "Eleven cycles? What the hell is a cycle?"

"I apologize, Ridley. A Delfinian cycle is the equivalent of your Earth's rotation around its axis. However, the Delfinian day is one-third longer than an Earth day. To be exact, a Delfinian day lasts thirty-two point four hours."

"I'll bet upper management can wrap their brains around that work schedule."

Ridley gazed out the portal across from him. Outside, points of light trailed off into the void. It reminded Ridley of the light shows he used to see at the planetarium as a child. The stars appeared to be swept into the wake of the speeding ship.

"How fast are we going?" said Ridley.

"By Earth's standards, fifteen times the speed of light."

Ridley closed his eyes and smiled. "I guess that makes me the first human to go this fast and this far."

"I believe you are correct."

"You know what sucks?"

"No. What sucks?"

"I can't brag about it to anyone."

"Is it important to boast of your accomplishments to other humans?" said Azrnoth-zin.

"Damn straight."

"If it will make you feel any better, you may boast to me and META IV."

"Right. Are there any stars out there that I would recognize?"

"We passed out of your system almost six weeks ago," said Azrnoth-zin.

Ridley stared at Azrnoth-zin, his look an undeniable "you better not be bullshitting me." When the alien's expression did not change, Ridley forced a short laugh, which ended up in a coughing spasm. When he was able to catch his breath, he looked up at Azrnoth-zin and smiled weakly.

"You know, I used to think of myself as a man without a country."

"And now?"

"It's worse," said Ridley. "Now I find I'm a man without a planet."

Azrnoth-zin looked at META IV. "I believe he will survive." He turned to walk away and was almost through the airlock door when Ridley spoke again.

"Hey, Arn?"

Azrnoth-zin turned around. "Yes?"

"I saw them. In my dreams."

"You saw who?"

"The Trochinids. I saw them devouring Delfinians, and others. Earth doesn't stand a chance, does it?"

"Get some rest," Azrnoth-zin said. He turned and walked through the airlock.

CHAPTER THREE

The soup didn't taste half-bad. Ridley was surprised his stomach allowed the contents to stay down. META IV brought him a second steaming bowl, placed it on the bedside tray table and moved quickly out of the way.

"I'm not going to bite you," Ridley said between spoonfuls.

"Perhaps not," replied the metallic. "But I have already experienced your ability to target projectiles a short distance. I do not wish my memory banks or servo motors to suffer damage from your agitated state."

"Oh. Uh, sorry META. I haven't been myself lately."

"Are all humans this irrational?"

"Only after we've been shot, frozen, packed into a big test tube and shipped halfway across the galaxy."

"We were only trying to restore your life functions."

Ridley swore that if he did not know better, something like a sigh emanated from the bizarre robot.

"You're right, META. I'm sorry I behaved the way I did toward you and Arnie. I hope you will accept my deepest and sincerest apology."

"Why do you call the Commander of the Third Order "Arnie"?"

"Oh, that." Ridley scratched his head. "It's kind of a nickname, a term of endearment. I called him that because on Earth, well, not a lot of people go around calling themselves names like Azrnoth-zin. Unless, of course, you're a famous rock star."

"Are these pseudonyms common on Earth?"

"Yeah. Sure. Lots of people have nicknames. Some aren't so nice."

"What do they call you?"

"Just Ridley."

"Just Ridley," the metallic repeated after processing this new information. "Is that how I should address you, "Just Ridley"?"

"No," said Ridley smiling. "My full name is Cooper Mathias Ridley. Call me Ridley."

"Very well, Ridley. Apology accepted."

Ridley spooned more hot Celesian soup into his mouth. A large drop of the mixture dripped down his chin and splashed unceremoniously on the floating tray before him. In an instant, an irridescent purple detritovore was on the dollop, emitting faint sucking noises as it cleaned up the spill.

"I guess there's no need to tell you that you have an infestation on the ship," Ridley said annoyed, lifting the soup bowl above his head. Once the area on the tray was clean, the protistan-like alien looked up at the bowl suspended above it.

"Forget it. This soup is mine. META! What the hell are these things anyway?"

"These gellatinoids are not infestations, Ridley. They are simple organisms that eat and digest detritus, dust and bacteria. They are utilized by the Delfinians to maintain sanitary conditions on the ships."

"If they're supposed to be used to maintain cleanliness on the ships, then what were they doing crawling all over me when I woke up?"

"They were sterilizing your wounds and removing necrotic tissue. Their saliva is highly toxic to bacteria and even most viruses. The red detritovores even possess a clotting factor in their saliva to control bleeding."

"Where did you pick up these little beauties?"

"They were created by the Delfinians, the result of many years of biologic engineering," said META IV.

"Great. Interstellar leeches. What's next?"

"Ridley, you should finish your soup. It is getting cold."

Ridley lowered the soup bowl to the tray. When the purple gelatinoid approached the bowl, Ridley lowered his face to the tray and growled menacingly. The frightened creature squeaked loudly and shot off the tray.

"META, what can you tell me about the Delfinians?"

"I can tell you no more than you already have present in your cortex."

"I'm still having a lot of trouble pulling all of this information together. Most of it comes to me when I'm sleeping, in bits and pieces. I can see events that have taken place, but I have no reference point for them. And the equations and formulas that I see are enough to give me the mother of all headaches. I have no clue what any of that is all about. What I mean to say is, what are the Delfinians like as a race of people? Are they compassionate? Fair? Do they possess a sense of humor, an appreciation for beauty and the arts? My only contact has been Azrnoth-zin. I can see these qualities in him, but for all I know, he could be the Delfinian equivalent of Groucho Marx."

"Commander Azrnoth-zin is looked upon as different. He does not follow the traditional lines of Delfinian doctrine and philosophy. The Delfinian system is quite regimented and strictly controlled. The commander has been brought before the Water Council on two prior occasions for disciplinary matters. Only his combat record has kept him from being demoted. I fear this time the Water Council will deal with him severely."

Ridley smiled. "So, ol' Arn is a bit of a loose cannon, eh? Your Water Council sounds like a bunch of tight asses to me."

"I beg your pardon?"

"Nothing," said Ridley. "Go on."

"The Delfinian's ability to wage war diminishes," META IV continued. "They have been depleted in available combat warriors, ships and resources. The enemy's numbers continue to increase, impairing our fleet's effectiveness in stopping them. Although Commander Azrnoth-zin and Fourth Order Porin-fah were the first Delfinians to walk away from the war, there has been unrest among the people for a long time. The Water Council fears more will follow Azrnoth-zin's example. That is why he will receive the harshest of penalties."

"You like Azrnoth-zin, don't you?" said Ridley.

"I have served with him since he became a starship commander. It was he who sought my promotion to Medical-Surgical Technician, level IV."

"Metallics can move up the ranks?"

"To a certain degree, yes. As long as it is in an ancillary position and it is a function the Delfinians cannot or will not assume. There are two hundred and eighty-three META units currently operating between all of the great ships. My creators felt that the implementation of metallics would free up more of Delfinian personnel to actively participate in the war effort."

"At the rate things are going, from what you and Azrnoth-zin tell me, it may not be all that long before you'll have no masters to serve."

"Unfortunately, I believe you to be correct, Ridley."

Ridley studied the metallic for a moment. "It's amazing," he said. "If not for the fact that I'm looking at your mechanical body, I'd swear that I was having a conversation with another person."

"META units achieved a sentient state hundreds of years ago. Our creators installed in our data banks the ability to evolve over time, especially in the areas of free-form thought. But I thank you for the compliment."

"So, META," Ridley said, pushing the soup bowl away. "What's the connection between the Delfinians and the Trochinids?"

"What do you mean, Ridley?"

"Well, Arnie told me the Delfinians have been fighting these things for something like nine-hundred years. You would think that after nine-hundred years of getting your asses kicked, you'd know when to call it a day. Why don't they just cut their losses?"

"I do not think you understand, Ridley. The Delfinians have been trying to prevent the Trochinids from spreading to other systems. They are the best equipped, with the greatest technology to deter the invasions. Most civilizations fall under their countless numbers in days, perhaps weeks if they are resourceful. The problem lies in the adaptability of the Trochinids. Their genetic composition allows them to withstand extreme atmospheric changes in temperature, pressure, and toxicity. Just as the finest minds in the Delfinian fleet have come together to discover a means to eradicate this plague from the solar system, the Trochinids quickly adapt to new weapons and strategies."

"Surely they possess an Achilles's heel somewhere," said Ridley.

"I'm sorry. I do not understand your choice of words," said META IV.

"I mean a weak spot. A hole in their armor, so to speak."

"The only one we have observed - and it has not proven to be a weakness," said the metallic, "is that they have a tendency to avoid planets with large bodies of water. However, these planets are few in number."

"Is that what's kept them away from Delfinus?"

"No one is sure. That theory has never been truly tested."

Ridley's headache was coming back with a vengeance. He winced once, then kept his eyes closed. He leaned back against the inclined bed. "I don't get it. Why haven't the Delfinians warned my planet that the Trochinids are out there? Don't you think Earth has the right to know, the right to at least try and mount some sort of defensive countermeasure?"

Ridley turned abruptly to look at the metallic. "I want some answers, damnit!"

Instantly, he grabbed his head as a bolt of pain bored through his skull.

"Ridley, your cortical readings are beginning to accelerate again. I believe it would be better for you if we continue our conversation later, after you receive your scheduled dosages and rest."

Ridley laughed bitterly. "Your masters programmed you well. Just when I get to the good questions, you change the subject."

"I am not the one to provide you with the answers you seek. For now, you must rest. When you awaken I will inform Commander Azrnoth-zin of your request for additional data."

"I still think it stinks." Ridley watched as his vital signs were showing a rapid increase on the monitor above him. "My world is about to become extinct and you guys are talking like insurance salesmen."

"There is a possibility," the metallic stated, "that the Trochinids will bypass your system completely. Since your civilization is not advanced, they might not pick up on your crude level of transmissions."

"What are the chances of that?"

"There is ninety-one percent probability they will detect your planet's presence."

"Looks like the house loses," said Ridley.

CHAPTER FOUR

Two members of the Delfinian Water Council walked slowly down the long corridor, talking quietly. The forward section of the sixteenth level of the immense star cruiser, *Delfon-quah*, flagship for the Delfinian fleet, was unusually deserted for this time of day. Passing by one of the large starboard viewing ports, the rest of the fleet became visible to the two Delfinian leaders. Outside, the command ship was flanked by sixty frigates and warships, all moving at sub-warp speed. The two Council elders paused by the viewport.

"Azrnoth-zin's ship will arrive in less than four cycles," said the younger of the two council members. Although his hair was graying at the temples, he still carried some of the features of a Delfinian just passing out of his prime. Their long white robes were a stark contrast to the drab tunics worn by the other Delfinians who passed them in the wide corridor. Occasionally, a Delfinian officer would pass them and salute, his tunic bearing the muted coloration of rank.

"Have the other members of the Council been informed?" asked the older of the two. His hair had long since turned white and was braided to the middle of his back. His white beard, reaching down to his chest, was equally magnificent. The face was accentuated by a sharply defined nose, uncommon among most Delfinians. Both had the piercing blue eyes that stood out like blazing lanterns.

"Yes, the others have been briefed," said Phon-seth. "I have received and reviewed the latest of Azrnoth-zin's transmissions. It seems there is a new and unexpected development."

"And what is that?" said Quillen-tok, without taking his eyes off the ships outside the viewport.

"Azrnoth-zin has brought with him an offworlder, a humanoid."

Quillen-tok turned to face the younger Council member. "Did you say humanoid?"

"That is the information we received," continued Phon-seth. "He did not provide details, but said it was of the utmost urgency that he be able to address the council before sentence is passed. All we know is that the offworlder is injured or sick."

Quillen-tok's brow furrowed. "Where did Azrnoth-zin find this humanoid?

"His initial report states the humanoid hails from the third planet in the Sol system," said Phon-seth, trying to read the emotions of the Delfinian elder. "We could find no record of this planet called Earth in any of our navigational computers or archives. Evidently, Azrnoth-zin and Porin-fah accidently encountered the planet after emerging from an ion storm."

Quillen-tok heaved a great sigh. He turned his gaze back out the portal, watching the formation of ships. "Before Azrnoth-zin is taken before the Water Council, I want to speak with him. Bring the offworlder to me as well."

"I will bring the two as you requested," said Phon-seth. "First Order, you have far greater experience in these matters than I. How do you think the rest of the Council will decide?"

"That is uncertain," said Quillen-tok. "The other First Orders will vote for separation. Bahrin-fahl will cast his vote for the harshest sentence. He is bitter over Azrnoth-zin allowing his only son to accompany him. In the eyes of Sarn-ula, Azrnoth-zin is a dissident and a deserter. The others will follow her ruling."

"It is bad enough that Azrnoth-zin deserted his post and caused the death of a young impressionable warrior, but now it is obvious that he has contaminated a less developed world by bringing this offworlder," said Phon-seth. "There is but one way to balance the scales of justice and send a message to those who would contemplate desertion."

The old Delfinian sighed. "I have been a witness to this war far longer than you, Phon-seth. I want you to tell me that you have not had similar thoughts pass through your mind. We have been fighting the Trochinids longer than I care to remember. I know in your heart you realize it is no longer a battle we can win. The other members of the Council, in their rigidity, will not admit to defeat. Do not pre-judge Azrnoth-zin for his actions unless you can say that you have never had such thoughts of leaving."

The other Delfinian looked down at the floor, then gazed into his mentor's eyes. "I have had the same thoughts many times," he admitted.

"I make no excuses for Azrnoth-zin. He has brought upon himself the harshest of punishments dictated by Delfinian law. He must answer for the death of Porin-fah. But I think it is time to continue discussions in earnest with the other members of the Council. Perhaps it is time to return home and prepare for the inevitable. It will take all of our available resources to defend our home world. Azrnoth-zin is held in high esteem for his feats in battle among the other commanders and warriors. His sentence will not bode well among the Third through Ninth Orders."

"I fear that you will meet with great resistance," said Phon-seth. "I support you, Quillen-tok, but as the most recent First Order, my decision does not carry as much weight with the others."

"Bring them to me as soon as they have docked," said Quillen-tok. "We will develop a strategy before going in front of the rest of the Council."

Phon-seth bowed slightly and strode off down the corridor, leaving Quillen-tok alone with his thoughts. What was it that finally pushed Azrnoth-zin into deserting? Quillen-tok knew that Azrnoth-zin had lost Resar-dan, but that was several years ago. Everyone had suffered such losses in this madness. And what could have possessed Azrnoth-zin to convince Porin-fah to go along on such a fool's mission?

Quillen-tok pondered the most recent development. Why did Azrnoth-zin bring back an offworlder? A human from Earth,

Phon-seth had said. He had succeeded in committing the worst
infractions possible for a Delfinian warrior. And finally, the
question that gnawed at him most was why did Azrnoth-zin decide
to come back at all knowing fully the fate that awaited him?

Quillen-tok stared out the portal at the remainder of the
Delfinian fleet. One hundred and twelve ships. At one time, the
Delfinian armada was the most impressive in the system. Their
culture and civilization were unparalleled. Now, a diminished and
battered fleet of ships was all that stood between the Trochinid
advance and Delfinus and the rest of the systems. The ships at
dock outside the portal were but drops of water against a tsunami.

The older Delfinian's thought turned to his own mate. She
had just wanted to surprise him. Five years of separation had
been a very long time. But, they both had their duties to perform.
Quillen-tok got the news of her transport being intercepted by a
Trochinid warship. Several days later, he found his mate's name
among the missing.

Some painful memories, he thought, do not soften with
time.

META IV had decided the best way to develop Ridley's
strength and endurance was by altering the gravity forces in the
chamber: diminished G's at first to allow pain free movement
of joints, with a gradual progression to full weight bearing in a
positive gravity environment. The chamber was mainly used for
the storage of materials that could not be transported in normal
gravity. During Ridley's recovery, the anti-grav chamber now
functioned as an exercise room for his rehabilitation.

Azrnoth-zin entered the chamber where META IV was
taking Ridley through physical rehabilitation. Because of the
decreased gravity environment, Azrnoth-zin had to place special
anti-grav discs on his boots to keep his feet firmly on the floor.
Ridley was engaging in a series of exercises with which Azrnoth-
zin was not familiar. The exercises involved precise movements
performed slowly with arms, legs, and torso. Clad only in a pair of
shorts, Ridley's skin was glistening from the exertion. Droplets of

sweat leapt from Ridley's body and floated all around him like tiny
jewels as he executed a series of choreographed kicks and punches.

"This is not the protocol for neuromuscular re-education,"
said Azrnoth-zin, standing next to the metallic.

"It was not by my choosing either," said META IV. "He
became bored with the standard protocols two cycles ago and
said there was something he wanted to attempt. He has been
performing these exercises for over three hours. It is remarkable
how quickly his motor patterns are returning."

Azrnoth-zin noticed that some of the color had returned to
Ridley's face. He appeared less gaunt than a few days earlier. The
wounds were healing nicely, the scars beginning to fade. Ridley,
sensing the presence of Azrnoth-zin, spun quickly in the air, and
kicked, his foot missing Azrnoth-zin's face by inches. Azrnoth-zin
did not flinch.

"You appear to be feeling better," said Azrnoth-zin.

"The headaches still kick me in the butt, but at least I'm not
tottering around the place anymore," said Ridley. He picked up a
towel, wiped his face, and threw it over his shoulders.

"What is that form of exercise that you were doing?"

"I'm not really sure," replied Ridley. "Some of the moves
I thought were from Tai Chi, a form of martial arts from Earth.
It's used as a form of hand-to-hand combat and energy centering
through movement. Played around with it a bit as a kid. Got more
instruction in Tai Kwon Do when I was training to be a Navy
SEAL. What's weird is that all of a sudden, I have these moves -
these steps that I don't ever remember having learned."

Azrnoth-zin looked concerned. "META IV, is there any
record in the archives of a form of combat training such as this?"

"I have searched the available data bases and there are no
such recorded training techniques."

"Perhaps the neural reintegration has enhanced the motor
learning centers as well," said Azrnoth-zin.

"I believe that to be true," META IV said. "The portion of
his brain, the cerebellum, has shown a seventeen percent increase
in motor neuron activity since he came out of cryo-sleep. He
may be undergoing the unlocking of motor memories from earlier

experiences. Or perhaps we may be witnessing the result of dormant genetic patterns activated by the reorganization."

"How does the rest of you feel, Ridley?"

"I don't know how or why, but I am beginning to understand some of the things I'm seeing on the ship, although I've never seen them before. Is that from the neural reorganization?"

"Possibly. Although I am not sure where some of these other memories are coming from."

"Ridley's cortex has made an adjustment in the past twenty-four hours," said META IV. "He is no longer in danger of neural collapse. The cortex has begun it's own dampening process."

Azrnoth-zin noticed that META IV's voice was different. It took on an almost lilting quality to it.

"META IV, is there something wrong with your audio actuators?" said Azrnoth-zin.

"No, they are working within acceptable parameters," said the metallic. "It was Ridley's idea. He thought that I had a distinctly gender specific quality and thought I should adjust my actuators accordingly."

"You sound vaguely like a human female," said Azrnoth-zin, staring at Ridley.

Ridley shrugged. "I was just trying to help META discover her inner metallic."

"I do not think it wise to tamper with Delfinian technology," Azrnoth-zin chided. "As it is, we have much to explain to the Water Council when we arrive in less than nine cycles."

"I thought the METAs were sentient," said Ridley.

"They are, to a certain degree."

"Then why don't you let META IV choose for herself."

Azrnoth-zin turned toward the metallic. "Well, META IV, what is your preference?"

"The timbre of this new voice is most pleasant," replied the metallic. "If it does not offend you Commander, I wish to retain it for a while."

Azrnoth-zin appeared genuinely agitated. Shaking his head, he said to Ridley, "Try not to make any more modifications to personnel or equipment on this ship for the remainder of the voyage." Turning back to META IV, he said, "Please have Ridley fitted with clothing suitable for presentation to members of the Water Council."

"Shall I fit him in the standard Delfinian issue?"

"No," said Azrnoth-zin. "That would be viewed as an insult to the Council. Ridley, assist META IV and it . . . she will fabricate appropriate clothing. As the representative from Earth, you should be clad in your native garments or at least a reasonable facsimile."

Over the next few days, Ridley's strength and endurance continued to improve. Particularly bothersome, the headaches at times were so severe that Ridley had to find a dark and quiet place to rest until the storms inside his head subsided.

Once he fell asleep, Ridley was subjected to another type of maelstrom. This one was an assault on his psyche in the form of confusing and terrifying dreams. Many parts of the dream sequences continued to repeat themselves. Azrnoth-zin and META IV encouraged Ridley to audio-record his dreams into the Krendahl's medical data banks. For some reason that he was unable to explain or justify, Ridley thought it best to keep the information to himself for the present.

Invariably, he would awaken, sweating and emotionally drained. Ridley found the only way to staunch these nightmares, even if only slightly, was to exercise himself into physical exhaustion. This proved to be a point of contention with META IV, continuously monitoring Ridley's neuro-muscular patterns for signs of system overload.

On the morning of the eighth cycle, Ridley awoke early after a triple feature of horrific nightmares. Swinging his legs over the side of the sleeping platform, Ridley activated the small overhead light. He still slept in the infirmary - META's orders. As he dressed, he wondered if the great horror writers on Earth went through this kind of hell to get their stories down on paper. He remembered from his high school English class that Edgar Allen Poe wrote his fantastic stories under the influence of some very serious drugs. Opium or heroin, he thought, but could not recollect for sure. If he made it back to Earth in one piece, maybe he'd get some of this down on paper. Ridley shook his head. They'd just lock him up and throw away the key.

A metallic form appeared in the soft light from the shadows. META IV hovered next to Ridley.

"Ridley, you have only been asleep for four hours, twelve minutes and forty-seven seconds. According to my data base on human physiology, your species requires six to eight hours."

"Can't sleep. Goddamn dreams are making me nuts."

"Would you like a neural dampener?"

"No, thanks. Got any specials on lobotomies?"

META IV hovered momentarily, silent except for the whirring of her servomotors, as she considered Ridley's question.

"Ridley," META IV said, "I believe a cranial lobotomy would be an extreme measure."

"Joke, META. It's a joke."

"What is a joke?"

"I'll tell you what's a joke. I'm a joke. You're a joke. This whole thing is a joke. A really bad joke."

"Ridley, your agitation levels are elevating. Please allow me to administer a sedative."

"Forget it. I'm going to work out."

Ridley stormed out of the medical-surgical unit and instantly felt remorse at being so angry at the metallic, an assembly of circuitry, wiring and alloys. As he walked down the dimly lit corridor to the anti-gravity chamber, Ridley thought he was truly losing his sanity. *Who am I going to go off on next*, he thought sarcastically - *the food processors?*

Arriving at the anti-grav chamber, Ridley stepped through the circular portal and closed the door. Ridley stretched and warmed up for several minutes. He donned a vest with a large red disc on the chest and on the back. He then walked over to the wall and activated a button on a small keypad. Four small doors slid open around the chamber and four cylindrically shaped objects hovered into the chamber. The metal cylinders, roughly two feet in length were oriented vertically and coated in a clear, thick, plastic gel coating. Ridley keyed more commands into the keypad, then stepped to the middle of the chamber and assumed a defensive stance as the cylinders encircled him.

From behind him, one of the cylinders broke ranks and charged. Ridley spun and kicked it effortlessly out of the way. Another cylinder moved through the air quickly, aiming for the red disc on his chest plate. Ridley's hand caught the cylinder in the soft gelatinous outer coat and deflected it easily. From behind, the third cylinder shot forward and connected with the red disc on his back. Ridley yelped as the connection delivered a strong electric charge.

As the four cylinders orbited around him, Ridley once again assumed a defensive position. Two cylinders came at him at once. Ridley was up in the air, spinning, kicking the cylinders away. The next two rushed in. Ridley batted them away with quick forearm blocks.

Over the next two hours, Ridley was stung eight times, the last four in the final ten minutes of his workout. Bathed in sweat and breathing heavily, Ridley deactivated the makeshift fight simulators and opened the portal to exit the anti-grav chamber. Azrnoth-zin stood in the doorway, his face impassive.

"Couldn't sleep again?" said Azrnoth-zin.

"Not much on late night TV, so I decided to blow off a little steam," said Ridley, wiping his face with a towel.

"That is a use of the metalloids that I am not familiar with," said Azrnoth-zin, his own agitation growing. "Normally, their primary function is to manipulate objects in zero gravity environments. I will speak to META IV about the unauthorized reconfiguring of equipment."

"META didn't reconfigure them. I did."

Azrnoth-zin's eyebrows shot up.

"You? How did you accomplish this?"

Ridley shrugged. "I don't know. I just kinda changed the program. Oh, META provided the gel coat to keep them from getting banged up in the simulation. So, no worries there."

Azrnoth-zin gazed critically at the contact vest. "And I suppose you altered the grav-vest, too?"

"Just switched polarities. Makes for a killer video game."

Azrnoth-zin sighed deeply. "In the future, I would appreciate all equipment modifications to go through me first."

"Sure, Arn. Whatever you say."

Ridley and Azrnoth-zin walked down the corridor toward the med-surg section, their footsteps clanging off the grated floor. Ridley had removed the anti-grav vest and now carried it at his side.

"META IV informed me you were quite agitated when you awoke. It - she informed me you are unwilling to undergo psychological profiling. Is there a reason for this?"

"I don't need to be shrunk," Ridley said testily. "I'm just having some hellacious nightmares lately."

"Perhaps if you were to discuss these nightmares with me, I could help you determine their meaning."

"Same stuff I told you about earlier. Trochinids eating Delfinians - and others. Then I'm in this place full of green and yellow gas tubes. The tubes open and *viola!* Little Trochinids spill out. They seem to be interested in Ridley *au tartare*. And lately, I'm seeing a lot of these big blue dolphin things. They're not so scary, but they keep wanting to show me something and I can't figure out what the hell it is."

Azrnoth-zin's face grew lined. "Tell me about the blue dolphins."

Ridley stopped wiping his face and looked at Azrnoth-zin. "They're big, blue, and have hands instead of flippers. Something is wrong with their eyes - they're sightless. But they keep speaking to me in this weird singsong voice. Like they want me to come with them."

"What else can you tell me?"

"That's it. Weird."

Azrnoth-zin stopped, then grabbed Ridley by the forearm.

"Ridley, it is extemely important that I perform the water-link with you. I believe your dreams may be significant."

"No way, José. I already told you how I feel about the invasion into my head without an invitation."

"Ridley, please. This could help alleviate the dreams."

"I said no! I've already had enough tampering with my circuitry to last me a lifetime. I'll just have to figure something else out."

Several moments of uncomfortable silence ensued as Ridley and Azrnoth-zin continued to walk the length of the corridor. Ridley stopped abruptly in front of the door to med-surg and keyed a series of complex commands into the screen before him.

"I suppose you figured out the entry code to med-surg on your own as well?" said Azrnoth-zin suspiciously.

"Nope. Those META gave me."

Ridley turned and tossed the towel to Azrnoth-zin. "See ya later, Arn. I've got an apology to deliver to a slighted medical-surgical robotic."

Ridley sat in the second command chair, staring at the immense ship they were approaching. Smaller, almost imperceptible ships hovered around it, like worker bees attending their queen. Ridley realized the "tiny" ships were three to four times the size of the *Kren-dahl*.

To Ridley, the vast ship appeared at first to resemble an aircraft carrier. But, five or six aircraft carriers could easily fit inside the flagship. The ship was almost half a kilometer in height; the front portion culminated in a series of right angles. On closer inspection, these angularities appeared to be landing bays for other ships. All along the superstructure, the landing bays were busily receiving incoming traffic while others handled the outgoing shuttles and supply vessels. Interspersed between the landing bays were weapons of gigantic proportions. Phase cannons, Ridley thought, then wondered how he knew that. Along the upper decks, more armament placements became evident, giving the great ship the impression of one giant pincushion. The flagship's upper decks were layered, almost as if Ridley were gazing on a huge floating metropolis. Thousands of multi-colored ovals of light indicating viewing portals made the sight even more spectacular.

"That is one big ship," said Ridley, unable to hide the awe in his voice.

"That is the *Delfon-quah,* one of our last great battleships in the fleet," said Azrnoth-zin. "It serves as central command and most of the Water Council reside there."

"It looks like a miniature country on the fly."

"It is impressive. But it is dwarfed by the Trochinid battle cruisers. They are easily three times that size."

Ridley looked at Azrnoth-zin increduously. "You're kidding?"

"I wish I were," Azrnoth-zin said. "The Trochinids not only absorb organics, but they have become skilled over the last nine centuries at taking the best of each civilization's technology and using it for their own applications. Their current use of large ships can be traced back three hundred years ago when they overran the Osendjii system."

"How do you defend against something like that?"

"The Trochinids are not tacticians. They rely on their vast numbers. The larger ships act as colonies for the Trochinids. Think of them as floating cities. They can launch hundreds of ships from one of these star cruisers. One of our only advantages is that these ships are much slower than ours."

Azrnoth-zin maneuvered the *Kren-dahl* past the frigates escorting the flagship. Ridley noticed hull damage on many of the battleships, some quite extensive. Charred and blackened areas were visible. Several ships did not appear to be space-worthy. In places where the outer hull was missing, the framework underneath lay exposed like a giant metal ribcage. Repair crews, like tiny insects, moved over the hulls. Suddenly, Ridley felt a slight jolt as the ship's controls moved forward automatically.

Azrnoth-zin removed his hands from the console. "The flagship has locked onto us with a magnetic tractor beam. It will bring us in the rest of the way."

A series of flashing colored lights appeared on the console. Azrnoth-zin moved his hand over it and in the next instant, a series of shrill whistles and clicks filled the cockpit of the recon vessel. Ridley winced at the high frequency barrage to his ears and attempted in vain to adjust his translator.

"Commander Azrnoth-zin, this is security on deck twenty-seven. You are being delivered to landing bay A-7. Is the humanoid secure?"

"I have received your transmission," said Azrnoth-zin in his native language. "The human is here with me. There is no need for further security measures."

"What did they say?" said Ridley.

"We are to be met by a security team upon arrival. I will see if META IV can adjust your universal translator before we dock."

The ship was being pulled toward one of the landing bays on the upper decks of the flagship. Ridley watched the rectangularly shaped port grow larger until he noticed figures moving about within. As the ship drew closer, the personnel in the landing area moved away from the designated landing pad.

"We will be passing through an ion curtain," said Azrnoth-zin. "It maintains the atmosphere within the landing bay while allowing us to pass through."

The ship settled smoothly onto the middle of the landing bay floor. The large hangar-like room, bathed in red light, turned to a soft blue-green when it was safe to enter once again. Instantly, the room became filled with bustling Delfinian personnel.

Walking down the ramp from the *Kren-dahl,* Ridley felt like the rube who had just gotten his first look at the big city lights. Everywhere Delfinian men and women engaged in the business of the hour. As their eyes fell upon Ridley and Azrnoth-zin, many stopped their activities and stared.

Azrnoth-zin turned to Ridley and said, "Remember. Do not speak unless you are spoken to. Keep your gaze focused ahead of you. And above all, tell no one about your memories."

"What memories?" Ridley said, a grim smile etched on his lips.

Try as he might, Ridley could not help himself. His head turned from side to side to take in all of this new sensory information. At the base of the ramp stood six armed Delfinian guards at attention in two lines of three. None of them looked particularly happy to see either Ridley or Azrnoth-zin.

"Commander of the Third Order, Azrnoth-zin, you are to accompany us to the decontamination area before you are to appear before First Order Quillen-tok," said the lead Delfinian guard. "The humanoid will be escorted to the primary med-surg section for screening of foreign microbes."

"That is not necessary," said Azrnoth-zin. "I have been with him for seven weeks without suffering any ill effects."

"These are my orders, Commander. You and the humanoid will be brought before the First Order after you are examined. Consider yourself under detention."

Azrnoth-zin turned to Ridley. "It will be all right. Go with them now. We will join up later."

Ridley's tension escalated as he watched Azrnoth-zin ushered off to one of the airlocks at the far end of the bay by two of the security guards. The remaining four, including the lead guard, began walking with Ridley toward another airlock. The weapons held at the ready position were not pointed directly at Ridley, but he sensed they would be brought to bear on him with little provocation.

As they walked, Ridley could feel that lots of eyes were marking his progress across the floor. Conversations became muted or ceased completely as the stranger moved through the working Delfinians.

Ridley was led through a series of airlock doors to a small, sterile appearing chamber with a floating table in the middle of the room and monitors high and against the far wall. Large mirror-like panels that shimmered like water covered the wall opposite the monitors. The guards remained by the airlock as Ridley was left in the middle of the room.

"Please remove your garments and lie on the examination pad," said a voice that could have belonged to another metallic. Ridley could not tell where the voice was coming from.

"What for?" said Ridley nervously.

"It is necessary to scan your biochemical systems and screen for harmful or contagious microbes," said the voice. "No harm will come to you."

Ridley noticed that every time the voice was activated, the mirror-device shimmered, as if a disturbance was occurring on the surface of a pond from within. He reluctantly stripped down and lay on the reclining table. The room became bathed in a strange reddish light. A sudden flash followed by a sensation of instantaneous warmth enveloped him from head to feet. Ridley looked down to see a fine pinkish dust coating his arms, legs and torso. He noticed all of his body hair was now absent. He ran his hand along the smooth skin of his forearm. The ultimate exfoliation, he thought. This machine would be a big hit in day spas and salons on Earth.

Suddenly, the floating table began to hum. Ridley felt himself pulled into the table, his arms, legs and head were restrained from some invisible source. From out of nowhere, hundreds of gelatinoids appeared and began to vacuum up the pinkish dust at Ridley's feet. En masse they swarmed up his legs, probing and cleaning everywhere, in his mouth, nose, ears, and other orifices he didn't want to think about. Ridley attempted to brush them away, but found he could not move. He had no choice but to endure the onslaught of maddening crawling sensations all over his body. Just as quickly as they appeared, the detritivores vanished.

A metal door slid open from the wall on the far side and a metallic floated across the room toward Ridley. It was similar to META IV in its basic structure, but the sensory disc atop was different. This one had what appeared to be a series of glass cylinders stacked upon it, each with different colored liquids within.

The metallic held an odd shaped device in one of its mechanical hands that looked a little like Azrnoth-zin's horseshoe.

"Please remain still," said the metallic in a tinny voice. "It is necessary to obtain a tissue sample."

Ridley surmised that this must be a less sophisticated metallic from the voice patterns and servo movements.

The metallic placed the device against the base of Ridley's neck and he felt a burning sensation at the site. The robotic technician removed the small vial from Ridley's neck. Ridley attempted to bring his hand up to scratch at the area on his neck, but found he was still unable to move either his arms or legs. From an unseen source, the examination pad was restricting his movement.

More tests were performed, most of them painless. One particular test brought on one of his dreaded headaches, causing Ridley to shun the overhead lights. A small scanner passed over his body from head to feet, creating an unpleasant vibrating effect. The vibrations continued until Ridley thought his joints had shaken loose. By the time the machine finished its final pass, Ridley felt like he had just driven over the worst washboard road in Mexico in a car without shocks.

Ridley lost all concept of time in that room, the minutes passing agonizingly slowly. When the hum of the recliner pad finally ceased, Ridley discovered he could once again move his arms and legs. His headache had returned in earnest. Near the entrance to the chamber, another metallic held folded clothing for Ridley to put on. The tunic and leggings were an off-white color, made of light, yet unrecognizeable fibers.

The team of armed guards led him to a small, unfurnished cubicle with a platform extending out from one of the walls. The guards walked him into the enclosure and then stepped out. The lead guard touched the wall outside of the cubicle and a blue flash covered the entrance, followed by a stream of flashing red lights arranged in an asymmetrical pattern across the doorway. Two of the guards walked out of his line of vision, leaving two standing guards at either side of the entrance. He knew he wasn't going anywhere for a while.

"Excuse me," said Ridley. "But I'd like to speak to someone in charge, please."

"You are to remain silent, offworlder," said the lead guard. He was a stern faced individual, roughly the same height as Azrnoth-zin, but more stocky in build. Ridley thought his demeanor was that of someone who enjoyed doling out punishment.

"What's this? No one phone call? You guys ever heard of a lawyer?"

The guard spun and faced Ridley, only inches separating their faces, the force field barrier acting as a thin no-man's land. "I said silence! You will be arraigned before the Water Council when they are ready to see you."

Ridley met the cold stare of the guard. Neither one wavered for several seconds. The guard gave Ridley a contemptuous look and then returned to his post, facing away. Ridley walked over to the platform and sat with his back resting against the bulkhead. He closed his eyes, trying in vain to ease the pounding in his head. If this was the Delfinian's idea of alien hospitality, he wondered what lay in store for Azrnoth-zin.

CHAPTER FIVE

Quillen-tok sat at the elliptically shaped table, studying the readouts from the navigational logs of the *Kren-dahl.* The outside sensor detected a visitor at the entrance to his chambers.

"Enter," he said.

Phon-seth strode into the First Order's chambers and half bowed before the senior Delfinian. Straightening up, he said, "I bring disturbing news."

"What news?" queried the Delfinian leader.

Phon-seth slid a small crystalline disc across the table to Quillen-tok. "The offworlder has completed the medical examination. He shows three distinct and recently healing wounds. Based on his terran physiology, these wounds would have proven fatal had not some sort of intervention taken place. If the META unit had not intervened, the offworlder would have been terminal."

"On whose orders did the META unit act?"

"Azrnoth-zin's orders. There was no malfunction in the metallic."

Quillen-tok's brow furrowed. "Is there more?"

"I am afraid so, First Order. After performing a cortical scan on the terran, it was evident that he had undergone a recent neural reorganization."

The older Delfinian's head snapped up, his angry gaze meeting Phon-seth's. "Azrnoth-zin must truly have a death wish. What could he have been thinking? He has gone beyond ordinary desertion and cowardice and advanced to treason against the people in one deft move. Are you sure of this information?"

Phon-seth nodded. "The scans revealed a twenty-eight percent increase in cortical activity, particularly in the areas of frontal and temporal function. There has been a thirty-seven percent increase in cerebellar activity. This is from comparison of data before the organization took place to the most recent scans. The bulk of the reorganization has taken place but collateral pathways are still being established."

"His brain waves appear to be similar to Delfinian brains," said Quillen-tok. "What did you find in the data banks about humanoids and this place called Earth?"

"I was unable to locate any information. It seems Earth is in a sector that is not filed in our database."

"It appears we bear some of the same physiological characteristics, but the human brain is at least five to six millennia behind Delfinian development," mused the elder Delfinian leader as he examined the scrolling disc. Looking up at Phon-seth he said, "Has this information reached the other members of the Water Council?"

"Your eyes are the first to see it," said Phon-seth.

"Bring them to me," said Quillen-tok, emitting a great sigh. "Quickly. I must speak with Azrnoth-zin and find out what he knows of this terran civilization. I desire to interview the humanoid, too. It is important that we expedite this as quickly as possible. I will explain my reasoning later."

Quillen-tok entered his personal code onto the disc and handed it back to Phon-seth. "This should release them into your charge."

"I will bring them here directly." Phon-seth turned and walked toward the airlock doors. Before his departure Quillen-tok spoke once more.

"Notify Commander Mara-jul. I wish her to be present when Azrnoth-zin and the Terran speak."

"Is that not irregular, having a commander present ahead of the other members of the Water Council?" asked Phon-seth.

"Mara-jul has the most reconnaissance experience of any of our warriors and pilots. She and her pilots have the most contact with off-world races. Her input could be valuable. Since there is no recorded history of this place called Earth, we must rely on conjecture and anecdotal evidence."

Phon-seth nodded, turned, and walked through the airlock.

Ridley walked between the two Delfinian security guards down a long and mostly deserted corridor. Even above the sound of his footfall on the metal flooring, Ridley heard the blood rushing in his ears. He rubbed his damp palms on his tunic.

Leading the group was a Delfinian, dressed in long, flowing robes. Ridley assumed him to be some sort of leader, judging by how the guards responded to his commands. They walked briskly, occasionally passing small groups of Delfinians at work. Each time was the same. The Delfinians would stop whatever task they were engaged in and stare at him. He began to feel like he was on display.

He could not explain it, but at some level he knew about the devices they carried, the weapons held by the guards and other warriors. It still seemed so strange, so disjointed. It was as if he was in a past life and had fallen asleep for a very long time, then awakened with someone else's memories. Ridley intuited that it would be prudent not to let on how familiar things seemed. He hoped the Delfinians knew nothing about poker.

Ridley arrived at the twenty-fifth level. The entourage was halted at a large metal door. The lead Delfinian passed his hand over the grid to the side of the door. Instantly, a three- dimensional holograph of the Delfinian guard's fingerprints floated above a small disc near the entrance.

A voice from inside spoke, "You are cleared to enter."

The door slid open and Ridley was led into a circular room. In the center of the room was a half-moon shaped table that looked like polished obsidian. From behind, Ridley recognized Azrnoth-zin, who was seated facing the two Delfinians at the table.

The Delfinian who delivered Ridley to this room took his seat to the right of the elder Delfinian. Ridley thought he was looking at the incarnation of Father Time himself. The Delfinian had intensely white hair that cascaded around his shoulders and down his back. An equally impressive white beard reached to the middle of his chest. He was dressed in long, white flowing robes that gave him a misty, ethereal appearance. His deep-set eyes were the piercing blue of an arctic glacier.

To his left sat a strikingly exotic Delfinian female. In the muted light of the chamber, she bore a resemblance to Earth women, but there was something more otherworldly about her appearance. Her eyes were blue-green, like the water above a tropical coral reef. Her shiny black hair was braided and trailed down behind her shoulders. She wore a faded blue tunic that accentuated her fair, almost porcelain skin tones. With great effort, Ridley pulled his gaze from hers and looked forward.

"Please sit," said the senior Delfinian as a floating cushion materialized from one of the walls and hovered just behind Ridley. Ridley looked over at Azrnoth-zin for some reassurance, but his friend was staring straight ahead. The older Delfinian turned to the guards. "Leave us now."

After the guards had departed, the white-haired Delfinian spoke. "I am Quillen-tok of the First Order. You are called Ridley?

"Just Ridley, sir."

Quillen-tok indicated the woman to his left. "Just Ridley, this is Commander Mara-jul, Third Order."

Mara-jul met Ridley's gaze as if she were examining some invertebrate life form under a microscope.

"And on my right is Phon-seth, First Order."

"We've met," said Ridley. "And the name is Ridley, sir. There is no just."

The three seated Delfinians looked back and forth at each other in confusion.

"We are here to determine," Quillen-tok said, "the accuracy of Azrnoth-zin's statements and to verify them with our data base. I have asked Commander Mara-jul to be present for these proceedings. We wish to separate the facts from the perceptions. This dissemination of information will likely determine your fate and that of Azrnoth-zin."

The Delfinian called Phon-seth looked at Ridley, then at Quillen-tok. Ridley noticed that his temples were vibrating slightly. Quillen-tok nodded.

"Azrnoth-zin has given an extraordinary account of his encounter with you and your planet Earth," Quillen-tok continued. "He informs me that you are responsible for saving his life. Is that true?"

"I just helped him get to his ride on time, sir."

The white haired Delfinian frowned. "The data base from the *Kren-dahl* indicate you underwent a procedure that is forbidden to offworlders, the reorganization."

"I don't remember much about anything, sir. I remember seeing Azrnoth-zin's ship leaving, the blue light, and then I woke up in a test tube covered in blue gunk."

"In the data base, there is record that you requested the META unit and Azrnoth-zin to terminate you," said Phon-seth. "Is that correct and to the best of your recollection?"

"I'm not exactly sure what I said when I first woke up, sir. I was pretty out of it."

"You said, "Kill me if you have to." Do you remember saying this?"

Ridley shook his head. "No sir, I do not. All I know is that if it wasn't for Azrnoth-zin and META IV, I would be a faded memory by now."

Mara-jul spoke next. "Azrnoth-zin has spoken of the Delfids who inhabit your oceans and how a group of them assisted you. Can you describe your people's relationship with them?"

Ridley noticed the three Delfinians sitting before him periodically inserting small, colored crystals into a receptacle on the table. On a flat screen before each, small holographic images appeared, then were erased.

"Relationship? I'm not sure I understand your question," Ridley said.

The Delfinian female slid several cystals into the slots on the table.

"To rephrase the question," she said, the testiness in her voice evident. "Do your people worship these Delfids as deities?"

"No. They are the most successful mammalian species in the oceans, but they are not viewed as deities."

"Do you communicate with these beings?"

"Only on a rudimentary level," said Ridley. "It is only in the past few years that humans have begun to recognize the Delfids as sentient beings. On Earth, we call whales and dolphins cetaceans."

"Azrnoth-zin informs us that many of these Delfids, especially the larger ones, are slaughtered by your people - for food and other products derived from their bodies," said the female Delfinian.

Ridley fidgeted in his chair, then looked around for some support from Azrnoth-zin. Azrnoth-zin's posture remained rigid, his gaze focused straight ahead. He didn't like where this was going. "Our awareness for other species continues to evolve."

Quillen-tok intervened. "Ridley, is there a record on Earth of encounters with offworld travelers?"

"You mean extraterrestrials? Every culture has myths or legends about visitors from space. To my knowledge, there is no actual hard evidence of anyone visiting Earth. But I can't speak for my government - or any other nation, for that matter. They have ways of concealing information from the general populace."

Ridley noticed Phon-seth and Quillen-tok exchange a brief glance. Mara-jul inserted another crystal, studied it briefly and said something under her breath to Quillen-tok. The white- haired Delfinian turned his attention back to Ridley.

"How old would you say your civilization is, Ridley?"

"Civilization or human beings?" said Ridley.

"Human beings."

"I remember something about two or three million years. There are new theories popping up each year about our origins. As for civilizations, in Australia, a continent in the Southern

Hemisphere, it is said the Aboriginal people who were native to that place were one of the oldest races on the planet."

"How old are these people called Seri?"

Ridley shot Azrnoth-zin an angry look. "I couldn't really tell you how long the Seri people have been around. Thousands of years ago it is thought that most of the native Americans migrated over from Asia on a great land bridge that connected the continents."

Mara-jul looked up from the images on the table and spoke. "Why did you assist Azrnoth-zin? I find it strange that you would risk your life for a complete stranger. Is this a common activity among your species? Were you not fearful of reprisals from your government?"

Ridley might have been smitten by her incredible beauty had it not been for the feeling that he was scared half to death and was now forced to defend his own existence to these strangers. And now it looked as if he was going to have to make a case for the rest of Earth's inhabitants. A very twisted irony indeed, he thought. Ridley considered himself one of the most cynical people he knew and now fate had placed him in the role of primary advocate for the very humanity he disdained in so many ways.

"I don't know. I guess I've always pulled for the underdog."

The three Delfinians looked at each other, then back to Ridley. "Please explain underdog," said Mara-jul.

Ridley looked around at the gathering, extending his gaze to Azrnoth-zin, then to the ceiling to gather his thoughts. Proper word selection was going to be very important if he planned on living through the next few days.

"Well, we define an underdog as the guy who has the odds stacked against him. It was just by chance that I was led to Azrnoth-zin by the dolphins - er, Delfids. I just happened to be in the vicinity when his ship crashed. There are certain factions of my civilization that will, for greed , profit or power, do anything to acquire new technology. He didn't stand much of a chance on his own against these factions of Earth's governments."

"The database reveals you served under one of these agents," said Phon-seth. "You are not loyal to your ruling body?"

I have no ties to any aspects of my government," Ridley said. "I acted of my own free will."

Phon-seth frowned, then leaned across to Quillen-tok and conferred quietly. Ridley didn't wait to be asked again.

"If we didn't make a break for it, Azrnoth-zin would have wound up in some hidden laboratory with some misguided scientists taking a bone saw to his head after they relieved him of his technology."

Mara-jul looked disturbed. "They would have dissected him?"

"They would do whatever they thought necessary to gain access to his technology and physiology."

Mara-jul fixed her gaze on Ridley. "Is all of human society this barbaric?"

Ridley's last shred of resolve fractured. "Oh, I don't know, Commander. I don't think we're any more barbaric than the Delfinians allowing entire civilizations to be wasted by those overgrown cockroaches you call the Trochinids." Immediately after he said it, he cursed himself for reacting without thinking.

Quillen-tok, Phon-seth and Mara-jul were all now staring at Ridley, surprise registering on their faces.

"You know of the Trochinids?" said Quillen-tok. "How is this?"

Ridley realized he had just painted himself into a corner. Any answer he gave would not be favorable for Azrnoth-zin. Ridley drew a deep breath before he spoke.

"I have dreams," he said. "I see them every time I close my eyes. There isn't a night that goes by that I don't wake up in a cold sweat, scared shitless, if you'll excuse my French. If the Trochinids are heading toward Earth, why don't you at least warn my people. Give them a chance to fight back. The people of Earth will fight if given half a chance. This way, you might just as well paint targets on the whole lot of them."

"The affairs of the Delfinian people are of no concern to an offworlder," said Mara-jul angrily.

"This human could present a serious security threat to our people," said Phon-seth, under his breath. "I fear that he possesses much more knowledge than we first believed." Phon-seth glared at Azrnoth-zin. "Azrnoth-zin has perpetrated the worst form of treason against our people."

Quillen-tok held up a hand. "Wait," he said. "I did not summon you here to cast judgement. Azrnoth-zin's culpability will be decided by the Water Council. What I require is that we have all of the facts. There are circumstances here that have never before been encountered."

"The data banks were destroyed when Azrnoth-zin's ship exploded," said Phon-seth. "All we have to go on is the testimony of a traitorous deserter and an offworlder." Phon-seth spat out the last word contemptuously.

Ridley was beginning to get the idea that the word "offworlder" was not a term of endearment among the Delfinians.

"Enough!" Quillen-tok said sharply. The older Delfinian turned back to address Ridley. "I understand the concern for your people. Ours is a very complicated society. For reasons that I cannot disclose to you, we are forbidden to interfere in less technologically developed civilizations than our own."

"Then, that's it?" said Ridley. "Sorry that you're about to be dished up as the next intergalactic smorgasbord, but we can't get involved with your pitiful little civilization. Rules are rules, is that it?"

"First Order, I do not understand why you are tolerating this offworlder's insolence," said Mara-jul. "He has offered us nothing useful."

Quillen-tok looked tiredly at Mara-jul. "Neither one of you see it, do you? Is it a coincidence that we have in our presence another humanoid form, not all that different from ourselves? He comes to us from a sector of space of which we have little knowledge. Leave for a time the fact that Azrnoth-zin deserted his post and led Porin-fah to an untimely death. He was there, on this planet called Earth. He was with these Delfids or what appear to be Delfids. Is there a connection between the Delfids of Earth and the Revered Ones? For all that he is accused of, Azrnoth-zin is not a liar. I believe we can verify his account through a mind-water link. This could be one of the most important discoveries in our recent history. It is necessary that further investigation into this matter be brought before the Council."

Regaining his composure, Phon-seth spoke. "First Order, I will support your stand on this issue. However, I fear that your requests will fall on deaf ears once they find out the extent of the humanoid's knowledge of Delfinian secrets."

"I believe the human is being truthful," said Quillen-tok. "I do not think his cortex has the capacity to absorb all of the inputs he has received." The Delfinian leader turned back to Mara-jul. "Commander, do you think the human Ridley can be incorporated into the Displaced Work Force?"

Mara-jul studied Ridley with an air of scientific aloofness, then turned back to address the elder Delfinian. "I do not know enough of the social structure of humans to make that determination yet, First Order. I suggest that before he goes in front of the Water Council, he be put through a battery of tests to assess his level of technological skills. This would also give the Council the information regarding how much the offworlder truly knows of Delfinian society."

Quillen-tok nodded. "Agreed. Ridley, it is unfortunate that circumstances have brought you to us. Delfinian society is closed to outsiders. Because this is a time of war, your fate lies in the decision of the Water Council. They will decide between one of two resolutions to the problem you present. The first solution is to have all of your memories erased. You would have no knowledge of your past life on Earth. It is a dangerous and possibly fatal procedure."

"Taking a mixmaster to my brain is not at the top of my list," said Ridley. "What's behind door number two?"

Quillen-tok pondered Ridley's use of language for a moment before he spoke. "The second choice would be to assimilate you into the Displaced Work Force, a contingent of alien races that have survived the Trochinid invasions. Perhaps there is a way for you to become a contributing member to the Delfinian war effort."

"If I'm being called upon to enlist, you have a strange way of talking up the obvious benefits."

Quillen-tok turned to the Delfinian woman. "Commander, I would request that Ridley and Azrnoth-zin be sequestered here aboard the *Delfon-quah* until the Council convenes. The rest of the Council members are scheduled to arrive from Delfinus in three cycles. I feel confident that you can oversee the testing on the human and bring the results directly to me."

"I will carry out your wishes, First Order," said Mara-jul. "And what of Azrnoth-zin?"

"Once he leaves this room, he is to be placed in an isolation chamber until the information is extracted from the mind-water link. There is to be no verbal or non-verbal communication. After the Council renders their decision, I will inform you what to do next."

"May I speak?" said Azrnoth-zin.

Quillen-tok nodded. Azrnoth-zin faced the three seated Delfinians, his back straight. He looked at Ridley then directly at the two members of the Water Council and Mara-jul.

"Ridley poses no threat to the Delfinian people. I have come to know him. He is a brave and capable warrior. I would trust him with my life. Even though his people lack the technology to participate in space exploration and advanced defenses against the Trochinid onslaught, it would be unwise to dismiss the planet Earth prematurely. There is evidence that we have been there before. The significance of the artifact must be investigated."

"That is no longer any concern of yours," said Phon-seth. "The Water Council will deal with this matter now."

"I would request the death penalty be levied for my crimes against the Delfinian People," said Azrnoth-zin, matter-of-factly. "I do not wish to continue to live through this madness any longer. But, I respectfully request that Ridley be returned to his people. He has done no wrong and should be allowed to warn them of the impending invasion."

Ridley turned his gaze from Azrnoth-zin back to the threesome seated at the table. He thought he saw a fleeting disturbed look cross the face of Mara-jul and Quillen-tok.

"You know that is impossible," said Mara-jul. "We are conducting full scale warfare with a quarter of our former fleet.

Since you left, three more of our star cruisers have been destroyed.
All ships, no matter how limited their function, are needed for the
continued war effort."

"As for your termination request," said Quillen-tok. "I will
take it under advisement and state your case to the other members
of the Water Council."

"I stand in your debt," said Azrnoth-zin.

Mara-jul nodded solemnly to the leader. Quillen-tok and
Phon-seth stood, followed by Mara-jul. The two older Delfinians
turned and left the chamber, leaving Ridley staring after them.
Once the airlock doors slid shut, he shifted his gaze back to
Azrnoth-zin and Mara-jul.

"That's it?" said Ridley. "That's where we're leaving this?"
He stood and turned to Azrnoth-zin. "Arn, did I miss something
back there, or does it look as bad as it sounds?"

"I am sorry, Ridley. I regret deeply that I have pulled you
into this situation."

Mara-jul came from around the table and stood before
Azrnoth-zin. She did not speak, nor did Azrnoth-zin, yet Ridley
knew communication was taking place by the slight contractions of
the muscles at their temples.

*"I choose to speak this way because the humanoid need
not hear what I have to say to you. Why did you come back?
They will render the harshest punishment on you, to set you as an
example."*

"I had to come back," Azrnoth-zin projected. *"There
are too many coincidences to dismiss Earth as purely an isolated
phenomenon. The indigenous people have a long history of stories
about visitors from the sky. I believe they are describing us. And
what of the Delfids? Mara-jul, there are many forms of Delfids on
Earth, all sentient. The ones that saved my life were not unlike the
Delfids on our homeworld centuries ago."*

"Even so," she projected. *"You do not make a good case
for yourself by placing this offworlder in a restoration chamber.
What were you thinking?"*

*"What was I to do? Ridley saved my life more than once
on that planet. He is . . . a good friend."*

"You should have left him to die back on his homeworld. It would have been a much kinder fate."

Mara-jul's gaze softened. "We have fought alongside one another in more engagements than I can remember. Your mate, Resar-dan and I attended the flight academy together. I was there when she put herself between the Trochinid ships and our fliers. She believed in you, Azrnoth-zin. I suppose I should as well. I will speak to the Council on your behalf."

"And his, too?" said Azrnoth-zin.

Mara-jul gave Ridley a long, hard stare. "Yes, him too," she said reluctantly. Turning quickly, she departed through the airlock, giving the guards instructions on the other side. A moment later, the four guards appeared and marched toward Azrnoth-zin and Ridley.

"I'm probably not going to like what happens next, am I?" said Ridley, as they fell in step with the guards.

"Probably not," said Azrnoth-zin.

CHAPTER SIX

The pounding headaches had returned. Ridley was not sure how long he was in this holding cell. He felt suspended in time. He lay on the platform in the cell with his back to the entrance to block out as much light as possible. He was brought food in the form of greenish wafers or a gruel-like paste. Both were barely palatable. Whether it was from the headache or his predicament, Ridley was unable to force down more than a few bites. No wonder Azrnoth-zin couldn't get enough of Earth food.

When he was able to sleep, Ridley continued to be barraged with images that had plagued him since the reorganization. He tried to force himself to see the dream sequence to its conclusion. He had heard that the best way to diffuse a nightmare was to see it through to its finality, to take control of the images.

The large birthing room, as Ridley now called it, was the focal point of his nightmare. Even though the scenarios changed, the outcome was always the same: Trochinids leaping out of the fog after him. Once, he even tried to read the inscription on the cylinder, but the odd hieroglyphics became obscured by the yellowish cloud.

In the dream, Ridley saw his Seri friend Enrique standing at the far end of a great room, beckoning to him through the mist. Ridley ran toward Enrique trying to warn him to get away. Just before Ridley reached him, a Trochonid leapt out of the putrid yellow haze and bit down on Enrique's neck, before dragging him off into the fog.

Something new to the dreams had started in the last two days. Ridley would be asleep, but could feel a probing presence. On several occasions, his mind's eye registered a face, an ancient face obscured by shadow. The face drifted in front of him, leaving him feeling a dreaded sense of weakness. That face wanted to control him, wanted to possess his mind.

Ridley rolled off the wall platform and fell onto the cold metal floor, yelling at the top of his lungs. Realizing he was awake, he turned onto his back and stared at the ceiling, breathing heavily and trying to regain his focus.

He had the feeling someone was watching him. Propping himself up on his elbows, he saw the two security guards standing outside of the barrier, staring in at him.

"The Water Council has reached its decision," said the lead security guard. He was the same one Ridley had encountered when first coming off the *Kren-dahl.* "You are to accompany me to hear their ruling."

"What?" said Ridley, standing up slowly, still trying to clear the images from his head. "What do you mean ruling? Don't I get a chance to state my case?"

"Your case has already been decided," replied the guard. "Move to the front of the chamber."

"I don't believe this. I want to talk to Quillen-tok."

"It is not wise to keep the Council waiting," said the guard.

Ridley was ushered into a large, circular room. Except for seven upright cylinders filled with a faint bluish liquid, the chamber was dark. The light source emanated from below and within the cylinders. The clear tubes were arranged in a semi-circular formation. A curved table was positioned in front of the water chambers. At the table sat seven figures, shrouded in shadows.

Ridley, flanked by the guards, stood directly in front of the table. Suddenly, he found himself immersed in a harsh light. He blinked painfully and urgently pressed the palms of his hands to his temples as the light instantly aggravated his headache symptoms.

61

He squinted in an attempt to make out the facial features of the Delfinians seated at the table. Once his eyes adjusted to the low light, Ridley recognized the outline of Quillen-tok and to his left, Phon-seth. They were just to the right of a central figure.

A light beam that appeared to come from nowhere cast the central figure's face in an eerie glow. It took Ridley a moment to realize that he was looking at the severely lined face of a Delfinian female. An extremely old Delfinian female. Ridley's breath caught in his throat. He was looking at the old woman from his nightmares. She looked a lot worse in person.

If Quillen-tok was Father Time, then this one had to be God's mother. Her elliptical eyes blazed with a ferocity that made Ridley want to cower in the dark.

"Ridley-of-Earth, I am First Order Sarn-ula, Magistrate of this Council. You have been brought here to receive our edict. Do you wish to make a statement?

Ridley swallowed hard. "Yes, ma'am. I would like to say a few words on Azrnoth-zin's behalf. And then plead my own case, if I may."

"The fate of Azrnoth-zin is of no concern to you," Sarn-ula said sharply. "He will be dealt with according to our system of laws that have been in place for thousands of years."

"Well, then, do I get a chance to tell my side or has the Council already made up their minds?" said Ridley, unable to hide the anger in his voice.

"Impertinence will not be tolerated by this Council," said Sarn-ula.

"Excuse me. I apologize for my outburst."

"It is commendable that you saved the life of Azrnoth-zin and assisted him to reach his retrieval ship. The council also understands that you sustained serious injuries from your own people while attempting to get Azrnoth-zin to safety. Through the reorganization process, you have been given access to Delfinian matters of state that present a potential security threat to our people."

The ancient Delfinian woman looked to either side of the table at the other assembled members of the Water Council.

"Normally," Sarn-ula continued, "possession of Delfinian secrets is just cause for termination. There were those on the Council who voted to have you undergo a memory cleansing to remove the input knowledge. Our scientists have assured me that your brain is unable to handle the information at a conscious level and a memory cleansing would probably terminate your higher functions. A unanimous vote from the Council members was required to make this so."

"I did not ask to be reorganized, or whatever you call it," said Ridley. "This whole thing has been a huge mistake. I don't even know any of your secrets to divulge. I don't even know what my dreams mean. If you will kindly drop me off back on planet Earth, I'll forget I ever met any of you."

Sarn-ula regarded Ridley with a gaze that he associated with someone examining a strange blemish that had erupted on her skin. "You speak as if Earth is in proximity to us. Your planet is hundreds of light years away. We will not spare our already thinned forces to provide you with transportation home."

"So, you going to brainwash me?"

"We refer to it as memory cleansing. In your case, Ridley-of-Earth," Sarn-ula said, casting a brief sidelong glance toward where Quillen-tok and Phon-seth were seated, "The Council was unable to reach a unanimous decision regarding your fate. Your physical and mental profile has revealed you can be trained for rudimentary functions. Therefore, the Water Council has decided that you be integrated into the Displaced Work Force, with regular monitoring of your neural functions. These will be performed by our med-surg units."

"I guess I don't have any choice in this, do I?" said Ridley.

"No. You have no choice in this matter. Remember, Ridley-of-Earth. You have been given a reprieve because of circumstances that brought you here against your will. You will now have the opportunity to serve the Delfinian Fleet and to perpetuate our ongoing war effort. Any infraction by you will be dealt with quickly and severely."

"Sounds more like a prison sentence than a job offer," Ridley said, meeting Sarn-ula's stare.

John R. Gentile

"This meeting of the Water Council is now concluded," Sarn-ula said. The faces became dark once again, the eerie glow from the bottom of the seven tubes being Ridley's only indication there was anything else in the room. Strong hands gripped both of his arms and Ridley was led away in the darkness.

CHAPTER SEVEN

Azrnoth-zin walked between two Delfinian guards down a long corridor toward the psy-detention section of the *Delfon-quah.* Beside him, Mara-jul kept pace, her features solemn. She and Azrnoth-zin communicated temporally while the guards remained stolidly focused ahead, intent on the delivery of their prisoner to his destination in permanent isolation.

"I am sorry that Sarn-ula overturned your request for termination," Mara-jul projected.

"I am to be made an example before the other orders and warriors," replied Azrnoth-zin. *"Sarn-ula views my potential termination as an event that might elevate my status among the lower orders to that of a martyr. She wants to set my desertion as an example to all who would follow in my steps. I believe Boren-fahl insisted on the psy-deprivation."*

"Why did you allow Porin-fah to accompany you? You knew he was loyal to you. He would have obeyed had you ordered him to remain."

"Porin-fah had made his mind up long before I had decided to leave. He refused to disembark from the ship, even after I threatened him."

"You have taught your warriors too well."

"I regret Porin-fah's death. I do not regret taking him with me."

"You could have appealed the decision," Mara-jul projected.

Azrnoth-zin turned toward Mara-jul and attempted a wry smile, catching Mara-jul completely off guard. She broke the mind-water link.

"Since you have returned from this place called Earth, your mannerisms are different," said Mara-jul. "Perhaps you could appeal to the Water Council once more . . . tell them you have become infected from human-Earth culture."

"Mara-jul, I understand what you are trying to do, but it is too late for me. I grow tired. Tired of war and dying and of lost hope. This sentence is only a prolongation of my initial request. Either way, the end result is the same."

"Once the guards secure you inside the chamber, that is the last time you will speak or transmit thoughts to another individual. I can delay your sentence for a few moments if there is someone you would like to speak with."

Azrnoth-zin paused. "Yes. There is one I wish to speak with."

Mara-jul stopped in her tracks and looked at Azrnoth-zin. "I am not sure I can arrange that."

"On Earth, the condemned are granted a last request."

Mara-jul and Ridley, along with a Delfinian guard escort arrived at the entrance to the psy-detention block. The Delfinian female had said little on their long walk to level twenty-three. The only thing she told him was that Azrnoth-zin wished to speak with him and there was not much time.

The guard passed a disc on to the psy-detention guard manning the entrance. Ridley peered down the dimly lit corridor, noticing the circular doors. From what Azrnoth-zin had told him, this section was reserved for the worst of Delfinian society to be confined to an existence of complete emptiness. The thick walls were wired with electromagnetic circuitry that prevented the transmission of any form of communication, verbal or telepathic. Monitors were placed on the occupants to insure there were no violations. An intensely painful shock was administered to those who thought they could defy the system. Eventually, the offenders were driven mad by the silence of sensory deprivation.

Ridley and Mara-jul were led to the end of the long walkway to the last cell. The large, circular metal door was at least a foot thick and was open. Inside, Azrnoth-zin sat on a small platform. Sensing movement, he turned his head to face the visitors. Ridley noticed an orange ring encircling Azrnoth-zin's head, which flashed to green upon seeing his friend at the entrance to the chamber. The device hummed slightly.

"He has only a few moments," said Mara-jul. "Do not waste what little time he has."

Ridley stepped into the small chamber. Casting a quick glance around, he noticed a series of conduits that channeled vertically throughout the cell. Small receptors imbedded in the wall at varying heights glowed the same colors as the ring fitted to Azrnoth-zin's head.

"I love what you've done with the place," Ridley said, taking a seat on the platform next to Azrnoth-zin.

Azrnoth-zin looked at Ridley and smiled. The ring glowed a deep blue.

"Yes. I believe your homies of Earth would say "nice crib.""

Ridley forced a smile, then looked down at the floor.

"Shit, Arn. What the hell are we going to do now?"

Azrnoth-zin looked at Ridley, his face a sea of calmness. He drew in a deep breath and let it out slowly. The color of the ring turned to a deep green.

"Ridley, there is nothing to be done for me. I am at peace. Except for one last and important matter."

Ridley looked searchingly at Azrnoth-zin.

"I want you to survive. Do whatever you need to do to get back home. Remember. You are stronger than them all. You have the knowledge of two worlds locked in your brain. Use this knowledge to find your way back to Earth."

Ridley looked at up at the sensor system terminating on the ceiling in a series of small rotating colored globes and bit his lip.

"I'm lost, Arn. And I don't know how to find myself."

Azrnoth-zin turned to face Ridley. The ring's color faded into a deep purple.

"You must promise me this one and only request."

"You don't ask much, do you?"

"I ask everything. Do you promise me you will do this thing?"

Ridley swallowed hard. "Yeah. I promise."

Azrnoth-zin leaned back against the bulkhead and closed his eyes. "Good." After a moment, he opened them and turned to look at Ridley. "I am proud to have fought by your side, Ridley."

"The same goes for me, Arn."

Mara-jul stepped through the circular entrance to the cell. "It is time."

Ridley and Azrnoth-zin stood and faced one another.

"Anything I can do for you?" Ridley asked.

The disgraced Third Order Delfinian Commander smiled broadly. "You already have."

Azrnoth-zin extended his right hand outward. Ridley took his hand, and hugged Azrnoth-zin.

"See you around, Ridley."

"Yeah. See you around."

Ridley stepped out of the cell and was escorted to the end of the detention block. Mara-jul looked at Azrnoth-zin. He noticed a great sadness in her face.

"Do not grieve for me, Mara-jul. I am free at last from this madness." Looking wistful, Azrnoth-zin said, "I want to savor the sound of your voice and mine intertwined in conversation for the last time."

He gazed around the circular chamber as if familiarizing himself with each sensor that would soon pervade each of his senses. "I have heard that the longest anyone could withstand the psy-detention is two and a one-half extended cycles." He forced a weak smile at Mara-jul. "Perhaps, I will break this record."

"Know that you will be in the thoughts of many, mine included," said Mara-jul. "I never thought this is how it would end for you,"

"It matters not." Azrnoth-zin looked at Mara-jul. He gently grabbed her shoulders. "Do not waste your life, Third Order. Do not let it end for you out here in some unnamed sector of space."

"It is all that I know."

Azrnoth-zin sighed. "Then you must seek what you do not know."

Mara-jul nodded.

"I have two requests. Call them the indulgences of a condemned warrior."

Mara-jul looked at Azrnoth-zin suspiciously. "So long as it does not involve subversive activities."

"No subterfuge. I would request that the human, Ridley be looked after. He did not deserve his fate. He is ill-equipped to handle assignment to the Displaced Work Force. I fear he will meet a very untimely and violent end."

Mara -jul looked disturbed. "That is a request that I am afraid will be difficult to honor. Ridley is to be monitored by a contingent chosen by the Water Council to determine if his cortical development poses any threat to Delfinian security. Any interference on my part will be viewed as insurrection in the eyes of the Council."

"I understand."

Azrnoth-zin reached inside his tunic and produced a small blue crystalline disc. Handing it to Mara-jul he said, "As my final request, I ask you to give these instructions to META IV."

"Azrnoth-zin, you know that I cannot issue orders to META IV that defy the judgement of the Water Council."

"You must trust me, Mara-jul. The META unit cannot defy the Council. That would go against her programming."

Mara-jul's gaze lingered on the disc. Returning her eyes to Azrnoth-zins' she said, "I will make sure that META IV receives these instructions."

"Thank you."

Two psy-detention guards appeared at the doorway.

"I am ready," Azrnoth-zin said.

Mara-jul stepped out of the cell, turned and faced Azrnoth-zin one last time. He smiled again and raised his hand to Mara-jul. Mara-jul did not understand the facial expression, but the hand gesture was unmistakable. She raised her hand in a return gesture.

At the entrance to psy-detention, Ridley winced from the sound of the heavy circular door swinging closed with a hollow finality.

CHAPTER EIGHT

Not his wildest dreams, nor his imagination's most vivid wanderings, could have prepared him for his descent into the bowels of the great ship. Ridley stood staring, mouth agape. Around his neck, he wore a translator similar to the one he had seen in Azrnoth-zin's possession back on Earth.

Ridley was looking at a vast room. It was hard to believe that this was the underbelly of the star cruiser *Delfon-quah.* Metal catwalks, lit from below, connected huge turbine-like structures, which seemed to rise several levels toward the ceiling. The temperature and humidity in this place were almost tropical, the air heavy with moisture. Ridley felt the sticky wetness on his skin, and when he breathed, felt like he was back in the Amazon Basin. Instead of staring at an impenetrable canopy of trees, he now gazed upon immense polished metal structures. He didn't remember the rain forest smelling this foul either.

Stranger than the impressive display of Delfinian technology were the residents of the dimly lit room. Small, furry creatures with bulging black eyes scurried about. They walked erect and many of them carried objects that resembled tools. They appeared to possess the ability to produce these tools from within folds of skin on their bellies. The dream creatures! Ridley thought they resembled a cross between an Australian wombat and a small black bear. The diminutive beings scampered from machine to machine at a frenetic pace, chattering loudly.

A large creature lumbered from out of the steamy mist on its hind legs and down the catwalk toward Ridley. With a long fleshy neck that supported a large, flat crocodilian head, the alien being stood well over seven feet. The reptilian eyes were rounded, moving independently of one another. The skin was a greenish hue, with purple striations on the horny scales. A thick tail covered in spikes swung to and fro as the lizard alien waddled toward Ridley.

"What in the hell is that?" said Ridley.

"That," said the guard, "is a Drolong. His name is Gort. Your new supervisor."

"I'm working for an iguana?"

The saurian-like creature stopped in front of Ridley and regarded him first from one yellow eye, then turned its head to size him up with the other.

"Is this the new one?" said the creature. Its voice possessed a burbling quality as if it were speaking through a thin veil of water.

"Yes," said the guard. "Human. Male." The guard handed the reptilian alien a disc. "Your instructions from the Water Council."

With surprising dexterity, the Drolong grasped the small disc between two of its digits, pinning the small disc between two large and serrated black nails. It grunted in agitation.

"It looks weak. Can it work?" the green alien rasped.

"The human's medical status is stable. It can perform the necessary functions."

"Functions?" said Ridley. "Functions of what? What is this place? What's that smell?"

"Welcome to waste processing," said the guard, prodding Ridley forward. He then turned and walked briskly to the airlock.

The Drolong motioned with a long nailed foreclaw for Ridley to follow. It turned and lumbered down the dimly lit catwalk. The overwhelming humidity coupled with the stench and noise made Ridley nauseous. He put his hands on his knees. It had been almost twelve hours since he had last eaten. All he could do was force a dry heave.

Ridley heard a strange gurgling sound. He looked up between spasms and saw Gort emitting a series of barking noises and gesturing for him to move along. If he wasn't feeling so ill, the sight of an irate overgrown lizard might have been humorous. For a second, Ridley thought of the popular kid's show back on Earth, the one with a large and friendly purple dinosaur. One thing was for sure and for certain: the alien leading him down the catwalk was no Barney.

Ridley followed Gort down several levels of catwalks. More of the small furry creatures scurried in and out of the light. They all appeared to be in fast motion. Ridley grew fatigued just watching their frenetic pace. The catwalk emptied into a large area with several catwalks leading away. An enormous piece of machinery of unknown function stood in the center of the room. Ridley stopped and stared at the superstructure in amazement.

A large, yellow gastropod-like creature moved back and forth in front of the machine on a pseudopod. A gelatinous slime trail formed in its wake. As the creature moved back and forth in front of the great machine, arm-like appendages emerged from the slug creature's body. The gelatinous arms were withdrawn into the body cavity, only to reappear when it needed to adjust the controls of the large machine from another location on the panel. Two small eyes protruded from the end of eighteen-inch stalks.

Ridley also remembered this creature from his dreamstate. He wanted to stop and ask Gort about it, but a sharp bark from ahead made him change his mind.

After descending two more levels, Gort stood in front of a series of small cubicles. The metal door slid open, revealing a room that couldn't have been more than eight feet square. Ridley made a conscious effort to breathe through his mouth standing this close to Gort.

"These are your quarters, human. Your work schedule is posted in the computer located on the wall. Times for nourishment and rest periods are also noted." The lizard-like alien eyed Ridley from one side of its head, its fetid breath bringing on a new wave of nausea. "Do not be late for your duties. Discipline will follow any infractions."

"Just what is my job description anyway," said Ridley.

"Organic waste disposal. You will receive instruction on the operation of the reactors and transfer the pellets to the reprocessing center. It is time for your rest cycle, human. Your shift begins in six hours."

"Wait a minute. I'm not sure I . . ."

Gort turned and lurched back down the catwalk. Ridley stared after him.

"I don't believe this. Someone slap me and wake me up."

Ridley entered the small cubicle that was to be his new home. The room was empty except for a shallow dish-like object on the floor in one corner. Another one just like it was suspended directly above from the ceiling. Ridley walked over to the wall-mounted computer and studied the strange characters on its face. After several moments, he was able to discern the discs on the floor and ceiling were a combination ion shower and toilet. He wasn't in any great hurry to try out his new plumbing quite yet. Tracing his finger over one of the cryptic icons, he was almost knocked over as a sleeping platform materialized out of the rough metal wall. Ridley attempted to sit on it but found he was suspended over the bed by two or three inches of air. He lay down on the platform. It was an odd sensation lying on a cushion of air. It was as if the sleeping platform pushed back at his body weight. When Ridley shifted his weight, the platform readjusted and provided support.

Ridley figured out how to retract the bed and once he familiarized himself with the basic functions of the computer, was able to activate a small table and what might have passed for a rudimentary chair. Apparently, the last resident's anatomical makeup did not require an ergonomic surface for sitting. Or maybe this was designed for the last occupant. There was no way the bed and the table could fit in the tiny cubicle at the same time. At last Ridley was able to locate the icon that activated a small rectangular opening. He figured this to be a food and liquid synthesizer. God only knew what foul tasting concoctions passed for food down here.

Ridley realized how exhausted he was. He located the controls for the airlock door and the heavy door slid shut with a loud hiss. The room was plunged into silence, the outside thrum of the giant reactors gone silent. Ridley fell onto the air platform face first and passed out.

CHAPTER NINE

Mara-jul stepped into the large Command Center ready room. The chamber was unfurnished except for an array of chairs facing a central curved dais, reserved for members of the Water Council. Against the far bulkhead, First Order Quillen-tok stood with his back to her, gazing out at the stars.

"Please come in, Commander," said Quillen-tok, without turning around.

"Thank you for seeing me, First Order," Mara -jul said as she performed the formal salute signifying a Water Council member.

"How go the plans for the next offensive?" Quillen-tok asked.

Mara-jul thought she detected a note of weariness in the elder Delfinian's voice. Quillen-tok turned slowly and faced Mara-jul.

"Our scout-probes have identified three large battle cruisers heading for the Barhziul system. There are two inhabited planets in the system. We are determining their defensive capabilities presently and will reach a decision as to whether we can risk an engagement."

"How many inhabitants on the two planets?" Quillen-tok said softly.

Four billion on Iso Prime, the larger of the two. It has the least developed technology. Ciamebeta has sixty-three million with moderate defensive capabilities."

"The Trochinids will attack Iso first."

Mara-jul nodded. "Yes. That is what we have surmised. We are still running the battle scenarios to determine our effectiveness with a full intervention compared to peripheral skirmishes."

Quillen-tok turned to face Mara-jul. His brother's daughter bore roughly equal resemblance to her father and mother. Her eyes were the same eyes as his brother's: fiercely alive and defiant. The porcelain skin tones, delicate frame and intensely dark hair, thicker than most Delfinians, were her mother's traits. When Mara-jul was an adolescent, both of her parents had been killed, ambushed by a Trochinid cruiser.

Because of Quillen-tok's position on the Water Council, special favors or consideration bestowed upon kin was frowned upon. Mara-jul fought her way up the ranks through grim resolve, a natural talent for flying and leadership skills that could have only been imparted in her formative years. As Quillen-tok gazed at Mara-jul, the older Delfinian leader felt a pang for his long dead brother and sister-in-law.

"First Order, are you all right?"

Quillen-tok's focus returned. He nodded amiably. "I am just a little tired, Third Order. This business of war wears on an old man." His gaze sharpened as he looked into her eyes.

"What is it you wanted to see me about?"

"First Order, I wish to ask permission to speak of the non-existent."

"You heard Sarn-ula's ruling. It is final and irreversible."

"I do not understand why psy-detention was ordered for -."

Quillen-tok held up a hand.

" . . . instead of granting a warrior's release. He was a great warrior and a commander of the Third Order."

"It is out of my hands, Mara-jul. Sarn-ula carries more influence on the Council than I. These days, Boren-fahl seems to have her ear. He is bitter over the loss of Porin-fah. The Council ruled five votes to two during the Water link."

"There are many among the Third through Seventh Orders who believe this is no way to honor a brave warrior, given his service and sacrifice."

"Do not forget, Mara-jul, that the non-existent has done what no other Delfinian has in nine hundred years of battle. He deserted his post, his squadron, and the Delfinian people in a time of war. The end result of his sentence will be the same."

Mara-jul thought she caught a hint of bitterness in Quillen-tok's last statement. For a long time, she remembered Azrnoth-zin and Quillen-tok sharing an unspoken, yet strong warrior's link. When he was younger, Azrnoth-zin had been interested in the ways of the ancient ones, and on more than one occassion, badgered Quillen-tok to reveal to him aspects of Delfinian history that seemed inconsequential or minute. She remembered sitting around with him on the flight deck before engagements and Azrnoth-zin ruminating, sometimes to her heightened levels of agitation, about why the ancient ones had decided to abandon the People. Azrnoth-zin had always thought and acted a little differently than most Delfinians. Perhaps that was why she respected and admired him. For Mara-jul, every tenet of the code of conduct was to be carried out to the letter, no questions asked.

"You are still troubled, Third Order. Illuminate please."

Mara-jul shifted her weight, assuming a more formal posture.

"What of the offworlder, Ridley?"

Quillen-tok turned and looked out the portal into space, his robes swishing softly in the quiet of the chamber.

"Unfortunately, there is little that can be done for the Ridley-human," said Quillen-tok. "Sarn-ula and her personal guard have assumed responsibility for monitoring the offworlder's progress and life functions. She alone assigns and receives the medical updates and reports from the META units."

Mara-jul hesitated a moment before she spoke, weighing her words accordingly.

"Azrnoth -"

Quillen-tok spun and faced her. "You must not speak of the banished again, Third Order. I do not wish to bring you before the rest of the Council. The punishment for breach of the banishment tenet is severe. You know this."

Mara-jul persisted. "I was asked by . . . I was asked by the non-existent to make sure Ridley was treated well and to watch out for him. It was believed that the offworlder's life was in danger by placing him in the Displaced Work Force."

Quillen-tok stared at Mara-jul for a long moment, then sighed.

"How did he propose to accomplish this?"

"By arranging to have the META IV unit become part of the medical rotation."

"How will this be justified before Sarn-ula?

"META IV has the most extensive medical data base on Ridley. It would be a logical choice to continue. If I may remind you of your words when the offworlder was first brought before you, First Order Phon-seth and me. You said we had a unique opportunity placed before us."

"I remember what I said in those chambers. I may be old, but my memory still serves me well."

Mara-jul cast her gaze to the floor. "I did not mean to offend, First Order."

Quillen-tok touched Mara-jul lightly on the shoulder. "You do not offend. Sometimes, we all need to be reminded that the shortest path to a goal is not necessarily the optimal path."

Quillen-tok turned and faced the large portal, their faces outlined in the clear window against the backdrop of streaks of light in the blackness. After a moment's silence, the elder Delfinian spoke.

"It is admirable your loyalty to Az -, to the non-existent. Dissemination of data that Sarn-ula has deemed restricted could be viewed as a treasonous act. I do not want one of my commanding officers placed in such a position."

Quillen-tok's brow furrowed as he scratched his chin. When he looked up, Mara-jul saw the deep blue intensity of his eyes.

"Inform the META IV unit that I wish to speak with it."

CHAPTER TEN

The next four weeks seemed like two years. Ridley had to adapt to a schedule of work and sleep that seemed to operate on six-hour shifts. In the short intervals between shifts, when he was not passed out on his bunk, Ridley kept his mind active by meditation and martial arts practice, both of which he performed in the privacy of his tiny quarters. He studied schematics of his work area on the computer and labored over the garbled messages that were transmitted back and forth between the various species sequestered aboard the *Delfon-quah.*

From the chatter on their computer, Ridley figured there to be at least eight to ten species of displaced aliens working in the bowels of the Delfinian vessels. For some reason beyond his comprehension, the Delfinians had installed the Drolongs, a race of warm-blooded saurians as supervisors over the rest of the work force. Ridley found them to be ill-tempered, dull-witted bullies, using force and coercion to maintain their control over the others. Even in space, Ridley thought, the concept of The Peter Principle held constant.

Ridley's first week as a waste-processing technician turned out to be a lesser circle of hell. Provided with only basic instruction, he had to rely on intuition and deeply imbedded memories to discern the function of the strange machine. The job was hot and dirty and the stench from the processors lingered in his nostrils long after his shift was finished. Ridley was unable to hold down much of the barely palatable food. As a result of the poor working conditions and lousy food, Ridley lost the rest of any fat stores he carried from earth.

He received unlikely assistance from the little bear-like creatures. Ridley must have conveyed a sense of hopelessness. Two of the furry aliens began to come around and when they found the strange, hairless alien could not understand their rapid-fire vocalizations, which ranged from sharp barks to staccato chattering, they finally settled on a form of rudimentary sign language. Within a few days, Ridley was operating the waste unit on his own.

With difficulty, he was able to figure out the small aliens were called Mawhrbahts. They appeared to be a subterranean race of engineers. They seemed adept at all types of mechanical manipulation and invention. Each one carried an odd assortment of tools tucked into a pouch near their bellies.

Two weeks after his arrival, Ridley stood in a long line of displaced aliens to receive his food credits after a particularly long and hot shift. His clothes, hanging loosely on his frame, were soaked with sweat and grime. He knew he smelled rank, but right now, he couldn't care less. He was dizzy from the humidity and loss of appetite. All around him were the disjointed and unfamiliar sounds of alien dialects. Ridley looked ahead at the ragged line of bizarre creatures, arguing and jostling each other, waiting for their disgusting ration of God-knows-what. Ridley seriously considered dropping out of line. The effort didn't appear to be worth the reward at the front of the line.

Someone pushed him out of line. Ridley looked up and was face to face with an alien that resembled a walking tadpole, glaring at him. Even though these were creatures unfamiliar, Ridley knew the universal sign of an impending confrontation.

The alien's four beady eyes were out of proportion to the fleshy head. The skin was warty and peppered with ugly brown blotches. The mouth was wide and filled with short, serrated teeth that reminded him of certain shark species he had encountered on the research vessels back on Earth. Where were Darcy and Theresa when he needed them the most? Ridley looked down at his arm and felt minor revulsion at the coating of mucous on his arm where the alien had pushed him. Two other similar aliens jostled their way into line.

"It's okay, fellas," Ridley said tiredly. "There's enough of that slop to go around." He wiped his arm on his pant leg. "I doubt if anyone would go back for seconds here anyway."

"It is beyond offensive," stated the first alien to his cohorts, "that the bastard seed of some perverted Delfinian tryst be allowed to eat with us."

"It is ruining my appetite, the smell it gives off," said the second one.

The first alien turned to Ridley. "You disgust me. Go to the back of the line so I do not have to smell your stink."

"I'm too goddamned tired to go through the line again, ace. So, just close your nostrils, get your food pellets, and stay out of my face."

The three amphibian-like aliens turned and faced Ridley. Suddenly, the line parted, leaving the three aliens and Ridley standing in the middle of a circle of jeering extra-terrestrials.

"This human not only stinks, but he has no manners," rasped the first alien.

Ridley saw that the other two aliens were moving to either side, attempting to gain a flanking advantage.

"C'mon, guys. I don't want to fight you."

"Ho! The offworlder is a coward, too," retorted the third alien.

The taunts from the crowd grew louder and more emphatic. Ridley's shoulders slumped as he resigned himself to his fate.

He barely had time to straighten up when all three aliens attacked him simultaneously. Punching him with their soft arms and webbed hands, Ridley felt like he was being slapped by a barrage of wet towels.

Ridley blocked and counterpunched, but found there was no effect when hitting the aliens any place on their torsos. His fists seemed to disappear into the gelatinous bodies. It was like punching jello. He was almost slapped silly before he realized the only place where a blow was effective was on top of the amphibian

alien's heads. This was made even more difficult by the fight
stance the aliens assumed with their bulbous heads tilted back.

Ridley managed to put some space between him and the
three circling aliens. One of the aliens lunged at Ridley. He went
to the ground and swept the legs out from under the attacking
amphibioid. The alien hit the floor, presenting its head briefly.
That was all that Ridley needed.

With a quick jab he punched the only solid place on
the alien's body, the crown of its head. The alien went limp.
Ridley was up and shifting his position to keep both remaining
amphibioids in his line of sight.

The leader of the aliens lurched after him, slapping Ridley's
legs as he attempted another sweep. Quick learning curve, Ridley
thought. Reddish welts were forming on Ridley's arms, legs, face
and back from the barrage of slaps.

Ridley feinted one way as the amphibioid sailed past him.
He spun and landed a kick to the first alien's head from behind.
The alien toppled over backward, grunting in pain.

Ridley turned to face his last attacker when he felt a searing
lash fall across his back. He yelped in pain. When he looked up,
the third alien was backing away into the crowd, its face pulled into
a mask of fear.

Ridley turned slowly to see the source of the burning on his
back. Gort stood several feet away, a sinister type of whip in one
of his claws. The blue whip buzzed and crackled with the distinct
smell of a lightning stike.

"You are in violation of the codes of conduct, human.
Fighting is not permitted among the workers," Gort gargled. "It is
punishable by the tase whip and solitary confinement."

Ridley grimmaced at the burning sensation that worsened
with each passing second. It was as if his back was on fire from a
thousand stinging nettles.

"I didn't start the fight," Ridley said between gritted teeth.

"I saw you striking the Ventans," replied Gort. "That is
enough evidence for me."

Gort barked a series of commands and two smaller Drolongs emerged from behind the crowd of onlookers. They grabbed Ridley by each arm, dragging him to his feet.

"Tie him to those pipes," commanded Gort.

Ridley attempted to break the grasp of the two Drolongs, but their grips were like iron. He was quickly tied to two vertical conduits. One of the Drolongs ripped away Ridley's blood- and sweat-soaked shirt. The saurian rolled up the shirt and held it to Ridley's mouth.

"Bite down on this, so you do not sever your tongue," the Drolong rasped.

Ridley bit down as the first lash tore across his back. Tears formed in his eyes as he felt the burn of the whip and the electric shock combined. After the second strike, Ridley could feel something warm running down his back. From an agonized haze, he heard the taunts of the crowd growing more distant. He looked down to see droplets of blood pooling on the floor around his feet.

Gort brought the tase whip to bear on Ridley's back again and again. Ridley did not remember anything at all after the seventh lash.

Ridley was having another nightmare. Trochinids were after him, chasing him down a long, darkened corridor. He could hear the clatter of their talons on the steel floor, their fetid breath smelling of carrion. Ridley felt his flesh tear as the Trochinids ripped at his back. He dared not turn around or stop. He felt the repeated agonizing stabs from behind as the slow evisceration continued.

He had to keep running. There was something at the end of the dark corridor. A door? Drawing closer, the lines and shadows began to coalesce. A face materialized out of the blackness. As if moving in slow motion, Ridley advanced a few more steps.

The face belonged to an ancient woman. It was the face of Sarn-ula. Ridley grabbed his head and screamed as the pain shot through his head.

"Get the fuck out of my head!"

Ridley's eyes flew open but something was wrong. He could not see. He blinked several times. Then, he attempted to move. He screamed. Searing pain shot throughout his body, the intensity of which he had never experienced before. He lay on the dirty, cold metal floor, gasping for breath, yet fearful to draw a breath for the wave of pain that would follow.

He must have passed out. When he again opened his eyes, a diffuse light was coming from somewhere overhead, dimly illuminating a patch of flooring in front of his face. His back felt raw and tight. His mouth was dry and he felt sick to his stomach. Ridley noticed he was lying in a congealed pool of his own vomit.

Something moved just beyond the square of light. Having difficulty focusing with one eye, Ridley could barely make out the two yellow pinpoints of light that moved horizontally, back and forth. He tried to raise his head, but thought better of it when the fire on his back flared.

Suddenly, three red and black-segmented legs appeared in the light, then disappeared back into shadows. A squat crab-like creature re-entered the light. It was about a foot and a half in width. The little alien's carapace was covered in sharp, thin spikes, which moved as if fanned by a breeze. The yellow eyes mounted on thin stalks moved independently, watching Ridley's every move. He wasn't sure, but this crab facsimile appeared to have at least six pairs of jointed legs coupled with two pairs of formidable serrated claws, which it waved in circular fashion in front of its eyes.

The crab-creature moved sideways toward Ridley. When it got to arms length away, the creature's mouth plates separated, revealing row upon row of needle-like teeth.

Ridley rolled out of the way as the crab-like alien lunged for him. He scrambled on his hands and knees until he collided with the far wall of the cell. Ridley cried out in pain.

"Christ! Isn't there anything in this goddamn place that doesn't have teeth?"

He fought the urge to vomit again, regulating his breath until the pain subsided. After a time, Ridley's eyes adjusted to the dim light in the cell.

The room was roughly eight by ten feet. Floor, ceiling and walls were all unpolished metal. One portion of the cell opposite him was bathed in darkness. In another corner, Ridley thought he could discern some sort of fixture on the floor and the ceiling. Ridley's eyes traveled across the dark space once more. He was about to attempt to turn his body to see the light source when he caught movement in the dark corner. When he looked again, all he saw was black. Straining his eyes through the inky darkness, Ridley thought he could make out the outline of a large, yet misshapen form lying opposite him against the far wall.

Ridley closed his eyes and drew a ragged breath. When he opened them, his breath caught in his throat. Two large, ovoid pink eyes were staring at him from out of the darkness. The eyes blinked slowly, then held his gaze again.

"If you had not moved so suddenly, I might have caught us something to eat," said a voice.

CHAPTER ELEVEN

It took time before Ridley's eyes adjusted enough to the dimly lit cell to be able to make out the outline of its other occupant. The alien was strangely proportioned: an ectomorphic torso with an inordinately long and slender neck. The smallish head appeared to be out of proportion to the body. The arms and legs were long and delicate. In the gloom, Ridley could not see how many digits were on the hands the alien possessed. The large eyes were particularly disconcerting. The being would close its eyelids for minutes at a time, only to open them slowly, revealing pinkish eyes. He thought his cellmate must have been on one hell of an intergalactic bender and wound up here in the Delfinian version of a drunk-tank.

Ridley pulled himself to a sitting position with great effort. Unable to place his back against the wall, he leaned against it with his least injured shoulder and faced the alien. It took him several moments before he was able to speak.

"Can you understand me?" Ridley said hoarsely. He couldn't believe the voice escaping his cracked lips belonged to him.

The eyes fluttered open, regarding the new arrival with dispassionate aloofness.

"You are the hu-man," the alien said. "I heard you were here, working."

The voice was lilting, yet Ridley had a hard time understanding the cadence due to the implosive nature of the speech.

"I'm Ridley," he said, grimacing as another exquisite wave of pain washed over him.

"I am called Kelun of Yhrys," said the slender alien.

"Pleased to meet you." Ridley attempted to shift his position. "Godammit, that hurts!"

"I see you have experienced the tase-whip," remarked Kelun. "Compared to the others I have seen who underwent the punishment, you have held up remarkably well."

"I didn't know it was a competition," Ridley said. "I guess requesting medical assistance is probably out of the question."

"Perhaps your benefactors will take pity on you. After all, you bear a striking physical resemblance to the Delfinians."

Ridley thought he caught an air of contempt in Kelun's voice.

"The physical resemblance is about as far as it goes. I've got no use for any of the Delfinians."

They sat in the dark, silent for a time. Ridley closed his eyes and focused his breathing, trying to will the pain down. To his surprise, he was moderately successful. The pain abated somewhat.

When Ridley opened his eyes, he saw Kelun gazing at him.

"So what the hell was that thing that was sizing me up for lunch?" Ridley said.

"A Trimeria. It is a scavenger that is common in the detention sector. They live in the drainage systems aboard the ships. If you could have kept still for a moment longer, I would have snared it. If you peel back the carapace, the meat is almost palatable."

"Sorry to ruin your dining experience," Ridley said tersely.

"Perhaps you could again lie in the middle of the floor near that grate where I had dragged you before. If you lie quietly, I believe I can catch it next time."

Ridley was incredulous. "You dragged me over and dumped me in the middle of the floor to lure that thing out?"

"You are the only one in this cell that is currently bleeding," said Kelun, matter-of-factly. "It was the obvious choice."

"Forget it, Slim. I ain't bait for you or anyone else."

"That is a pity. We are fed food pellets once a day, water twice. Unless you can procure a means to supplement, you will grow weak and die."

Moments of silence passed as waves of pain washed over Ridley. He fought to maintain his ebbing state of conciousness.

Ridley sucked in a painful breath, then looked at the alien. "So, what's your story?"

The pink eyes fluttered open. "I do not understand."

"How did you end up in all this splendiferous decadence?"

Kelun blinked once, then fixed Ridley with an impassive gaze.

"I killed a Drolong."

"No kidding? I'm developing more respect for you with each passing moment. What happened?"

"I grew tired of the Drolong's beratings. Once, it attempted to beat me with the tase-whip. I stripped it from him and beat him with it."

"You killed him with a tase-whip?"

"No. I was incarcerated for that infraction for twenty cycles. After my release, the Drolong continued its relentless harrassment. They are not very intelligent creatures, if you hadn't noticed."

"Oh, I noticed. Go on."

"On my world, we develop the capacity to fashion weapons at an early age. I was able to fashion a blade a from discarded metals in the recycling section. When the Drolong next attempted to beat me with the tase-whip, I eviscerated him. Unfortunately, it was within the sight of many witnesses."

Ridley now closed his eyes, the pain in his back returning in throbbing waves. "Funny, you don't seem the type."

"What was your infraction?" asked Kelun.

"Three overgrown tadpoles with attitudes cut in front of me in the food line. They proceeded to insult me all the way back to my family roots. I finally got tired of listening to them. Problem was, Gort saw me hitting them, not vice-versa. So here I am."

They sat in silence for several minutes, the only sound the steady thrumming of the immense Delfinian thruster engines. Kelun was the first to speak.

"Impressive. You handled three Ventans without assistance?"

"Well, two actually. Gort showed up before I could take a shot at the third one."

"I am developing more respect for you with each passing moment as well," said Kelun.

Ridley nodded and forced a smile.

"So, how long are you in for?" Ridley thought if he didn't feel so bad, he would have laughed at the reference to the old prison movies he saw as a kid. Right now, that seemed like a very long time ago and a lifetime away.

"My sentence is for life," came Kelun's reply.

Ridley stumbled through the shallows only to collapse on a blistering beach. The brightness of the sun reflected off the water and the brilliant sand blinded him. His back was on fire; he had stayed too long in the sun. He attempted to crawl back toward the water. Suddenly, his skin felt as if thousands of tiny needles were piercing it. Portuguese man-o-war, he thought. He must have swum through them.

Out of the white light, a figure walked toward him. It was the figure of a woman. She was clad in a white tank suit. Her light brown hair appeared to be blown by a wind. But Ridley could feel not the slightest breeze stirring. She stood over him, smiling ethereally. As she drew nearer, Ridley recognized Liz, his former wife.

She kneeled and looked upon him. A faint smile crossed her lips as she gently brushed the back of her hand against Ridley's cheek. Her touch felt invigoratingly cool.

"You're red as a lobster," Liz said. "We need to get you inside."

"It's not safe here, hon," Ridley said. "We need to get away from this place."

She stood, looked down at Ridley in the shallows once more and offered her hand to Ridley. He reached for her outstretched hand, but found she was just out of his grasp. Liz then turned to leave, looking back at Ridley, beckoning him on. Ridley attempted to stand, but found his arms and legs mired in the white-hot sand.

Liz turned around to face him one last time, her image almost enveloped by the whiteness of the background. A sad look of resignation registered on the fleeting image of her face.

"You still don't know where you belong, do you?" she said dreamily.

Ridley thrashed madly to free his hands and feet.

"Liz! Wait! I'm sorry. Don't leave me here! Liz!"

Ridley stood in front of one of the deadly gas-filled cylinders. The contents of the tube swirled and roiled, obscuring the moving entity within. How did he get so close to the damn cylinder? Frantically, he attempted to crawl backward, but the floor was slick. Looking down, Ridley saw that he was sitting in a viscous mass of yellow-green ooze.

The large convex cylinder door slid open, spewing the yellow-green gas cloud. The tendrils crept along the floor and enveloped Ridley's feet. The smell was overpowering. Ridley felt like his lungs were going to ignite. He pulled with all of his strength to get away from this place. It was no use. The floor held him fast.

A form appeared out of the sickly fog. Ridley knew the Trochinid would see him. He was too close. The gas dissipated and Ridley looked at its face. But, it was not the face of a Trochinid. The placid countenance of Enrique Morales regarded Ridley benignly.

"Enrique! Get Maria and the children away from here!

"Hola, Amigo. Como Estas?"

"You shouldn't be in there, Enrique. They are worse than El Tiburon."

Enrique stood causing the yellowish gas to curl around his torso. The Seri shaman held something in his closed fist. Enrique extended his hand toward Ridley and opened his palm. In his brown and weathered hand he held a large blue and white marble. Ridley looked closer. He saw the patterns of blue and white change as if the patterns formed by the motion of wind and water. Ridley recognized the outlines of the continents. Earth rotated slowly in the Seri's palm. The large, slowly rotating marble proceeded to sink into the lined palm, like a moon dipping below a rugose horizon.

"What does it mean?" said Ridley, looking into the wizened eyes of the Seri man.

Enrique smiled, his white teeth a beacon in the brown face. "The answer lies within, my friend. You possess the key."

"Damnit, Enrique, I hate riddles. Just tell me. Please. There's no time."

"Less time than you think."

Ridley looked down at Enrique's palm. The marble-sized version of Earth had disappeared. When he looked up, Enrique was smiling again. The white teeth were gone. He opened his mouth wide, revealing a maw of blood-stained fangs. There was nowhere to run.

When Ridley opened his eyes, he was still slumped against the wall. The slender form of Kelun was motionless against the far wall.

Ridley attempted to stand up and cried out. The scabs on his back pulled and crackled as the movement broke them open. Ridley felt the stinging of fresh blood oozing. He leaned against the cold cell wall, breathing heavily.

"I could treat your wounds," said a lilting voice.

Ridley looked up through tear-hazed vision to see Kelun staring at him.

"I'll pass, thanks."

"Your wounds are beginning to fester. You will soon fall into a fever, then death."

"Boy, you're just full of glad tidings and sunshine."
Ridley's back burned. Come to think of it, the rest of him felt like
it was on fire as well. "What would you treat me with?"

The alien held up something shaped like a small vial in his
hand. "This salve will soothe the wounds and kill the infection."

"I don't recall seeing any medicine chests around here.
Where did you get this wonder antibiotic?"

"I produce it myself from small glands located at the base
of my wrists. It is a chemical that heals and regenerates tissue."

"Your tissue, maybe. In case you haven't noticed, Mr.
Kelun, you and I don't look too much alike. I doubt our DNA is
compatible either."

"It will suffice. At this time, you do not have another
option."

Ridley eyed the alien from Yhrys suspiciously. "So what's
in it for you?"

"I am hungry for something other than pellets. Due to the
chemical makeup of my body and these glands, the Trimeria will
not come near me."

"You want me to lie down on the floor and act like bait?"

"A fair exchange, would you not say? I will even share
some of the Trimeria meat with you."

Ridley stared into the darkness beyond the floor grate
where the Trimeria sought refuge. "Oh, hell." Ridley slowly got to
his hands and knees and crawled to the middle of the floor of the
cell. Grunting in pain, he lowered himself slowly to the floor.

"Make sure you get this right the first time," Ridley said.

When Ridley awakened, the first thing he noticed was the
pain - or lack of it. Whatever the secretion that Kelun produced
from his own body had the added benefit of acting as an analgesic
to Ridley's raw and festering back. The salve had a sticky
consistency, similar to petroleum jelly.

Ridley sat up tentatively, testing his muscles in anticipation
of the burning that followed movement. So far, only a deep
soreness across his back pervaded his senses. His breathing
relaxed. He looked across the cell to where Kelun sat obscured in

shadow, except for the large pink orbs, which continued to regard Ridley impassively.

"How is the pain in your back?" Kelun asked.

"Tolerable," said Ridley. "Thank you."

Ridley touched one finger to the salve, then rubbed it between his fingers. "What's this stuff made of?"

"Proteins, lipids, and a glyco-matrix. We are able to heal our own wounds, even regenerate lost limbs with the secretion."

"Really?" A horrid thought pervaded Ridley's brain. What if his body reacted to the salve and began to generate an alien from his back? Wasn't that what happened in that movie he saw as a kid? Ridley shook his head. "I'm not going to -?"

"Do not worry. The enzymes will adapt to your tissue's normal matrix," said Kelun, sensing the tension building across the cell.

The Yhrynen pointed a slender finger to the floor in another corner. Ridley could make out pieces of carapace and disjointed legs. In the lower carapace, segmented legs and meat were heaped.

"I thank you. That was the best meal I have had in a very long time," Kelun said. "What is there is for you. You should eat before it becomes rancid. I prefer to suck the meat out of the legs. Most flavorful."

For the first time he could recall, Ridley suddenly was very hungry. Scrambling over to the Trimeria carcass, Ridley quickly grabbed one of the legs and snapped it in two, pulling the stringy meat from the shell.

"Not bad," Ridley said between mouthfuls. "Could use some butter though." He crunched another leg ravenously.

Holding a piece of the Trimeria flesh in the light, Ridley saw that the meat was green. His stomach performed a triple somersault.

"That is the normal color," Kelun said, noticing the sour look on Ridley's face. "When it goes bad, the flesh turns black."

"Oh." Ridley looked at the piece of flesh in his hand, then placed it in his mouth, chewing tentatively. The hell with the color. Anything was better than food pellets.

Once Ridley was sated, he went back to his corner of the cell and sat, avoiding contact of his back with the wall.

"You don't come out into the light very often," Ridley remarked after a time. "Are you photo-sensitive?"

"My skin has adapted. It is the lack of pigment in my eyes that requires filters to block out ambient light," said Kelun. "You see, on my homeworld, Yhrys, or should I say my former homeworld, our planet dwelled in perpetual twilight. We adapted to this low light condition over the millenia."

"What happened to your planet?" Ridley asked, although he was pretty sure he already knew the answer.

"The Trochinids overran Yhrys in twenty-three cycles. I was informed by the Delfinians that my people held out longer than most races."

"I'm sorry about your planet," Ridley said. After a moment's uncomfortable silence, Ridley decided to risk asking another question.

"How many of your species escaped?"

The Yhrynen blinked slowly. "I do not know. To my knowledge I was the only survivor. The Delfinians intercepted my shuttle heading for Yhrys. I cannot help but believe there are more of my race out there, stranded, unable to go home."

Ridley felt a great sadness for the odd being with whom he was now sharing a cell and meals.

"Tell me of your homeworld, Ridley. What is it called?"

It's called Earth. It is the third planet in the Sol system, part of the Milky Way. My homeworld is covered by seventy percent water."

"Most interesting. Third planet from your star. It must be very bright there."

"That it would. It was a pretty nice place until we started screwing up the air and the water."

"The Trochinids have not attacked your homeworld?"

Ridley sighed deeply, feeling the throb in his back become more pronounced. "Not yet. I have it from someone who's good with numbers that it's only a matter of time."

"I would like to see this place called Earth some day," said Kelun, closing his large eyes.

"If we ever get out of here, I'll give you the grand tour myself," said Ridley. "The Ray Bans will be on me."

They sat again in silence. Ridley felt the pull of sleep, drawing him once again into oblivion. Just before he dropped off, Kelun spoke once more.

"When I was treating you, you were dreaming. You screamed in your sleep."

Ridley opened his eyes, shaking his head. "Sorry if I yelled. Lately, there's some strange things taking place inside my head."

"You mentioned an old woman. I believe you called her Sarn-ula."

"Yeah. Sarn-ula. Do you know her?"

"I have heard of this Delfinian on the Water Council, but we have never met."

"The dreams of the Trochinids scare the hell out of me. That's a physical fear. I can understand that. When I dream of Sarn-ula it's a different type of fear. More like a psychic horror. Like she's trying to steal my soul or something. Sounds pretty weird, huh?

"Dreams are what they are, Ridley," replied Kelun.

"I didn't start dreaming about her until I landed on this giant floating fun house."

Kelun stood slowly to his full height. Ridley was surprised the Yhrynen was almost three feet taller than he. The Yhrynen moved fluidly in two large steps to where Ridley lay against the wall. Ridley caught a flash of delicate, pinkish-gray skin that appeared to glisten. The last survivor from Yhrys gently turned Ridley to expose his back. Ridley felt the elongated fingers, surprisingly strong, grip his shoulder. He noticed the fingertips ending in flattened pads, like a gecko's. The pads were slightly sticky.

"When you were first brought to detention, the door was held open for a moment," said Kelun, inspecting the wounds and adding more salve. "Gort, the Drolong overseer stood near a diminutive humanoid, presumably a Delfinian. I could not see her face. She was hooded. The Drolong referred to her only as Master, but did not mention her name. She spoke to the Drolong."

"What did she say?" said Ridley.

"Break him down," replied Kelun. "That is what she told the Drolong."

CHAPTER TWELVE

META IV glided above the dimly lit floor grates. Her scanners projected a schematic for level thirty-eight, waste reduction and disposal. The metallic had never been down here before. META II units were employed to service the medical needs of the Displaced Work Force. The lower levels were presently a hive of activity with various species of aliens busily going about the maintenance of the flagship's internal workings. From somewhere below, the bio-signals from the human were registering. The metallic made a hard left at a junction of two catwalks and proceeded in her original direction.

META IV descended another level. She then make a right turn into a long, dimly lit corridor before entering an expansive room filled with machinery. A large central processing unit thrummed out a regular beat. Her scanners registered the human to be very close.

Facing the anterior portion of the unit, META IV's visual receptors almost did not register the darkened form crouching at the lower left panel. The shirtless human was on his hands and knees, his head inside a small circular opening. Tools and pieces of circuitry lay all around him in a state of disarray.

The bio readings confirmed this was Ridley. She had not seen the human in over five months, but the signature was unmistakable. But the Ridley-human did not look the same. His skin was darker, almost black. The body composition was different than when it had been measured aboard the *Kren-dahl*. Sweat glistened off the human's bare upper torso and appendages. META IV's visual receptors registered a series of recently healed scars crisscrossing the back.

Ridley turned and looked at the metallic, revealing a gaunt face covered in grime and several weeks beard growth.

"META IV? Is that you?"

"Ridley. Your physical features have been altered."

Ridley scratched his face. "Oh, yeah. Guess it's been a while since I looked in a mirror. How ya doin', META?"

"All of my functions are at optimal levels. It is time for your systems check, Ridley. The members of the Water Council require an update on your neural reorganization."

"Tell them to go pound sand," Ridley said. "I'm busy at the moment." Ridley turned back to the opening and began to adjust components in a relay box.

"I do not understand your response."

Ridley thought of chucking a tool at the metallic, but stayed his hand. "Tell them I'm getting along just peachy."

"My scanners reveal that your metabolic functions are accelerated based on the decreased lipid concentrations in your body. However, the scanners also reveal that you are remiss in your personal hygiene. By not taking advantage of regular ion showers, you expose yourself to a myriad of foreign bacteria which your human system may not tolerate."

"Thanks, META. I'm really touched that the Water Council is concerned about whether or not I wash behind my ears."

"Azrnoth-zin has requested that I check on your well being."

Ridley looked up from his work. "Arnie? How's he holding up?"

"He took a great risk to break his vow of silence by asking me to check up on you. It took some manipulating of the META II rotations to arrange to come here."

Ridley stood up and stretched his back. "How is he handling solitary confinement?"

"His life force grows weaker. Lack of neural stimulation to the brain eventually breaks down all of the systems."

"Tell him I'm doing just fine down here, META. I'm adjusting."

"He wanted me to convey a message to you, Ridley."

"What's that?"

"I do not understand the context but the message is in the form of a question. He stated, "Do I not know how to show an out-of-towner a good time"?"

Ridley blinked, then remembering, broke out into a laugh that reverberated in the room above the noise of the machinery.

"He's a lot more alive than he would lead you to believe," Ridley said. He shook his head and laughed again. "I can't remember the last time I had a good laugh. Thanks, META."

A tall figure entered the work area. META IV turned her scanners on the new arrival who regarded the metallic with mild interest in its large pink eyes. The being was tall and delicate appearing with long arms and a long, thin neck ending in a small head. The pinkish-gray alien pushed a floating sled loaded with small cylinders.

"A Yhrynen," said META IV, surprise registering in her audio actuators.

"You sound surprised," said Ridley. "META IV, meet Kelun of Yhrys."

"I have no record of a Yhrynen working among the Displaced Work Force," said META IV. "The ship's data logs state there were no survivors after the Trochinid attack on Yrhys."

"After my arrival, I became a guest of the penal system that has been put in place by your masters," said Kelun. "To what do we owe the honor of a META IV unit coming down here? It was my understanding that only META II units were to be utilized for providing medical care to the Displaced Work Force."

"The Water Council requires a periodic review and reassessment of Ridley's systems," said the metallic.

Kelun looked at Ridley. "The Delfinians appear to be worried about the offworlder."

"So it would seem," said Ridley.

Kelun unloaded several small canisters from the floating platform. "You said you required three?"

"If you have enough to go around, I'll take an extra one or two," said Ridley. "One of the pre-cyclers is touchy. I can waste a half cylinder just getting the mix right."

"Why were you incarcerated?" asked META IV, turning her sensors back to Kelun.

Kelun looked at Ridley, looked at the metallic, then back to Ridley.

"It's okay, Kelun. META IV is good people."

The Yrhynen stretched to its full height. "I killed my supervisor."

"Why did you do this?"

"For asking too many questions," came the Yrynen's modulated reply.

"Oh."

"If not for Ridley, we would not be having this stimulating conversation. Ridley was able to buy my freedom from the Drolongs with work credits."

Ridley shrugged. "The Drolongs seem to have a weakness for gambling and I was more than happy to relieve them of their credits. Kelun saved my life in the cell. I figured I owed him one."

"On Yhrys, once someone saves your life, your life is theirs and theirs is yours until death or release from the vow." Turning back to Ridley, Kelun said, "I must continue with my deliveries. Gort would like nothing better than to find me remiss in my duties."

"See you tomorrow night, then," said Ridley.

Kelun pushed the floating sled before him and disappeared around the corner.

Ridley walked over to a stack of green cylinders lying on their sides and sat, leaning his back against one. The metallic's sensors registered the economy of movement in Ridley's body. While Ridley sat back, META IV scanned him.

"Body composition, seven percent lipid concentration; temperature, ninety-eight point six; heart rate thirty-nine, pressure of vascular system is normal for human parameters. Respirations are twelve per minute."

"Don't even think about asking me to bend over and cough," Ridley said.

"It appears your reorganization patterns are stabilizing," the metallic continued. "There has been significant improvement in neuro-motor function since you were last scanned. Cerebral cortex patterns have slowed, but it indicates that tissue reorganization is still occurring at the cellular level."

"I still have the dreams. And the headaches that follow them are enough to make me commit acts of violence. But they seem to be letting up a little." Ridley shook his head. "What day is it?"

"By your Earth calendar, it is Sunday, February 26, the year two thousand twelve. You have been here for six and one-half of your lunar cycles."

"Six and a half months. What did you say? What year is this?"

"Two thousand and twelve, Earth date."

"META, last time I checked, it was two thousand ten."

"On Earth, time progresses linearly. In space, you have been traveling at speeds many times the speed of light."

META IV's visual sensors registered moisture forming around the human's eyes. He put a grimy hand up to wipe them away. "Just tell Azrnoth-zin that I'm getting along fine down here. Hell, you can even tell him I love my job as waste disposal technician at station Y-38. META, I can tell you more about Delfinian waste than your memory banks can hold. And no matter what anybody up there tells you, their shit does stink."

Something slithered out of the open portal and writhed on the floor in front of Ridley and META IV. The creature resembled an eight-foot purplish earthworm. Spiky, reddish hair-like structures protruded from each of its segments.

"Dammit! I should have closed that scupper," Ridley said, jumping off the cylinders and circling the wiggling alien. The worm-like creature reared one end of its body and opened a gaping mouth lined with a set of curved teeth in the front, a series of grinding plates behind.

Ridley feigned in one direction, then moved in the other, pouncing cat-like on the creature. With both hands gripping the head-mouth, Ridley walked the creature over to the portal. The giant worm wrapped its body around Ridley's legs. It took several moments before Ridley was able to stuff the wiggling creature back into the portal. He quickly affixed the panel back in its place.

"And that's another thing."

"What was that?" said META IV. "I am not familiar with that life form. The Delfinians are adamant about not allowing vermin on their ships."

"You mean you don't know? I call them politician worms. Gort says they're biologics, some concoction of the Delfinians to aid in waste disposal. They do a good job of chewing through the sewage, but don't let one of them get their sucker-mouths on you." Ridley rolled up his pant leg almost to his knee. On the backside of his calf muscle was a reddish circular scar almost eight inches in diameter. "This was a small one. I sent it on to parasite purgatory. Still took over two weeks to heal."

META IV scanned Ridley's leg, then moved up to the fresh scars lacing his back. "Azrnoth-zin is concerned for your welfare among the Displaced Work Force. Since you are the only one down here who remotely resembles a Delfinian, my former commander worries that you have been the target of misdirected aggression."

"Don't have a lot of contact with the locals except for Kelun and the Mawhrbahts." Ridley could see that the metallic was still processing this information. "They really do keep you all in the dark about what goes on down here, don't they?"

"All of this is new information to me, Ridley."

"Somehow, I get the feeling that our benefactors don't want the general populace to know what goes on in the guts of these ships."

"Why is it then that they want regular medical updates on you?"

"Because I'm a threat to them, META." Ridley pointed to his forehead. "I have things in here that make them nervous."

"Who are these Mawhrbahts?" said the metallic.

"They're the fuzzy little guys you see everywhere. Stand about yea high and look like nuclear hamsters with a thyroid problem."

"I find it disturbing that none of this information is in the Delfinian data banks."

"You should find it disturbing. Kelun may be the last Yhrynen alive. Down here reside the last vestiges of several civilizations. All from civilizations the Trochinids wiped out. What records of their cultures they have, they carry with them now in stories and anecdotes. The Mawhrbahts, well, they're just simply amazing. Damn near fix anything and faster than you can imagine. Before the Trochinids gassed them out, they were subterranean dwellers. Had mega-cities under their planet's surface. The ones that made it here were able to hide out in the catacombs. I can't say much for the way they're treated down here. It seems Gort, my supervisor, has a problem with them. He likes to kick them around a lot."

"And you?" asked META IV.

Ridley glanced at a freshly healed scar on his shoulder.

"We've had a few strained conversations. I think Gort gets his orders from someone up above, but I can't prove anything."

META IV examined Ridley's back more closely. "Why was a META II unit not sent down to treat these wounds? The healing process left permanent scar tissue."

"I guess the Delfinians believe "Offworlder heal thyself." ""

"Who appointed this Gort to a position of torture and incarceration?"

Ridley looked at META IV. "Gee, I wonder."

"This is unconcionable. Azrnoth-zin must be informed."

"Arnie's got enough on his plate already, META."

"Why has this Drolong targeted you?"

"Beats me. Why don't you ask the Water Council?" said Ridley.

META IV continued her assessment of Ridley, performing a full sweeping analysis of all of Ridley's systems.

"My analysis reveals numerous old contusions, lacerations and blunt trauma wounds. Are these from the Drolong?"

"Not all of them." Ridley sighed. "I don't care much for bullies, no matter what planet they come from. In the past six months, I've pulled solitary twice, been on decreased rations three times, and been ordered to work double shifts five times. I kind of get the feeling Gort doesn't like me much. Reminds me of some of my former bosses in the Navy."

Suddenly, two black, hairy creatures appeared out of the shadows and clambered upon the cylinders, each one flanking Ridley, chattering and gesticulating wildly. Their small hands possessed three stubby fingers and a large opposable thumb.

"Okay, Okay. I was going to return the tools as soon as I finished . . . I don't know why I'm so slow," Ridley said testily. "Why are you in such a hurry?"

So intent was their conversation with Ridley, the Mawhrbahts had not noticed the metallic hovering nearby. Leaping up, they scampered over to where META IV floated and began examining her. An excited exchange ensued between them. From out of nowhere, tiny tools appeared in their paw-hands.

"I don't think that's a good idea," warned Ridley

A personal force field enveloped the metallic in a shimmering blue haze. One of the Mawhrbahts touched the field with its tool. In the next instant, both were hurled across the floor, rolling like small furry basketballs. They unfurled after caroming off the front of the disposal unit. Shaking their heads, the Mawhrbahts stood and hurled a string of expletives at META IV.

"I am not programmed to understand their language," said META IV. "What are they saying?"

"I don't think you want to know. Probably be a good idea to keep your force field up when you come down here though."

"How is it that you can communicate with them and they understand you?"

"Shortly after I arrived they got a hold of my translator and modified it to their frequency," said Ridley. "It's okay, you two. Ryk and Tikah, meet META IV. META's the med-surg unit that saved my life, for what it's worth."

The Mawhrbahts exchanged glances and then spoke to Ridley. META IV recognized that the Mawhrbat's speech was accelerated. Ridley looked at META IV. "They apologize for any impropriety. They want to know if they could examine your circuitry. They've never seen a META IV unit before."

"Certainly not! I am to be serviced by META III technical units only."

The two furry aliens shrugged and fired off a staccato set of codas directed at Ridley. "Behind you, port two," he said. "I couldn't restart the primary cycler."

Instantly, the Mawhrbahts had the panel peeled off and were inside of the mechanism. While they worked at a furious pace, an equally strident line of conversation continued between them.

"Technically, Tikah is a female and Ryk is a male," explained Ridley. "I'm not well-versed in their biology, but it seems that they can change sexes if conditions necessitate. Back on Earth, we have lizards and fish that are able to reproduce this way, but none of the higher life forms."

"Does the Water Council know of the Mawhrbahts abilities?"

"Don't know," said Ridley. "But I'd bet a month's food credits that this ship would be dead in the water if it weren't for them."

"How many of them are working in the ships?"

"From what they told me, somewhere between one hundred eighty and two hundred, give or take a couple dozen."

"That would make them the largest contingent among the Displaced Work Force," said META IV.

"They used to number close to three hundred million before the Trochinids processed their homeworld. There are others down here, META, that literally, are the last surviving members of their race. Who knows? Maybe I'm to be the last of humanity. That's a sad statement for my race if I am."

The Mawhrbahts backed out of the portal and stood up. They spoke in truncated chirps and once again assumed seats on either side of Ridley.

"Thanks," said Ridley. "You guys got that fixed a helluva lot faster than I could." Turning to META IV, he said, "they want to know if you're in for poker tomorrow night?"

"I beg your pardon? What is this "poker"?"

"It's a card game popular on Earth. Down here we play for food or time off credits. You bet on your cards and try to bluff your opponent when your hand is lousy. Seems the Mawhrbahts have a taste for gambling." Ridley cast a sidelong glance at Ryk and Tikah. "And some of them cheat, too."

This last accusation produced a fusillade of sharp barks from the one called Ryk.

"I had a time of it trying to get the duplicators to come up with something that vaguely resembled a deck of 52 cards."

The furry aliens jumped from the cylinders onto the grate and turned to leave. A shadow passed between them and Ridley. Gort's thick, spiked tail swung out of the darkness and caught both the Mawhrbahts, catapulting them across the room. They slammed into the huge waste processor and fell limply to the floor. The follow-through of Gort's tail connected with one of the cylinders, causing the stack to clang loudly on the grate. Ridley was sent sprawling.

"Hey! What the hell are you doing?"

"These two are not at their assigned stations. They are in violation of the work code," Gort said.

Ridley stood and faced the saurian supervisor. "Look, asshole. I asked them here to help me. They fixed the primary cyclers."

"Then you are in violation of the code as well."

Ridley ran over to the fallen Mawhrbahts. "META! Get over here! I think they've got internal injuries."

META IV glided over and began to scan. Ridley turned and squared off in front of Gort again. "I think I've had enough of you. I wonder what you would do with someone who's a little bigger."

"You?" Gort snorted. "You are pathetic and weak. Your food rations are reduced immediately and you are to pull successive shifts for the next five work cycles." The lizard-creature turned its back and began to lumber out of the area. "Humans. Ha!"

"Back where I come from, they say your kind taste a lot like chicken."

The alien froze in its tracks, a low rumbling growl building in its throat.

"That did it," Ridley said.

"Did what?" said META IV.

The Drolong turned and the tase-whip cracked the air near Ridley's head. He felt the heat of the whip pass by his face, the electrical crackle sizzling in the humid room. Gort moved in.

"Your arrogant face will soon bear the force of my whip," the Drolong gargled.

Gort raised his arm and snapped the tase-whip at Ridley. In an economy of movement, Ridley tilted his head to one side, the tase-whip missing his face by inches. Quickly, the Drolong drew the whip and cracked it at Ridley's face again. Ridley feinted to the other side. Angered, Gort drew back his heavily muscled arm and prepared to lash out once more. Ridley grabbed one of the small pre-cycler cylinders and brought it up as the end of the tase whip arced toward his face.

There was a loud POP! A flash of electric blue arced across the cylinder. Gort's instinctive reaction was to pull the whip back. The whip and the cylinder snapped back, hitting Gort between the eyes. The Drolong roared in anger and pain.

Gort went into a semi-crouch position, its thick legs wound like steel springs. Its head swayed back and forth, jaws opening and snapping shut. Ridley realized that if he followed the head movements, he was dead. Focusing on the alien's midsection, Ridley faced Gort.

The Drolong leapt at Ridley, hind legs forward and mouth wide open. Landing on the grate heavily, the great tail flashed out suddenly from one side. Ridley was barely able to duck out of the way, the spiked tail grazing his left shoulder, missing his head by inches.

While stepping back to avoid Gort's powerful tail, Ridley lost his balance and slipped over one of the loose cylinders. Gort advanced, sidestepping the cylinder and wound up to deliver another blow. Ridley rolled to his right as the alien's spike connected with the floor grate. Ridley sprang to his feet before the Drolong could react.

Looking down, Ridley noticed a length of scrap metal he had removed from the processor earlier. He scooped up the metal bar and assumed a defensive position. This only served to further enrage the already out-of-control Gort.

The head continued its side to side undulation, in an attempt to distract Ridley. Ridley maintained his focus on the creature's midsection. He moved forward until he was straddling one of the fallen cylinders and waited for the Drolong to make its move.

Gort leapt at Ridley. Ridley rolled forward and came up under Gort's belly as the tail smashed into the empty cylinder. Ridley swung the metal bar and connected with the softer underbelly of the Drolong. Gort went down on his side, grunting in pain. Ridley rolled to his feet. The heat and humidity were making him dizzy.

The lizard-alien jumped up, snarling. It side stepped several cylinders and moved in toward Ridley. Ridley found himself near another cylinder. He kicked it lightly with one foot. This one was full. Straddling the cylinder, Ridley took one hand from the metal bar and gestured to the Drolong to come forward. Gort's tail twitched back and forth. Between the head and the tail, it was difficult to tell where the Drolong would strike next.

The legs went low into a crouch and the Drolong flew at Ridley. The spiked tail arced in a semi-circle like a mace and came down aimed at Ridley's head. Timing it to the last second, Ridley dove out of the way.

Gort's spike punctured the cylinder almost dead center. A blue-green liquid spurted forth covering the tail and Gort's belly. The Drolong screamed in pain. It tried in vain to wrench the spike free, but it was stuck fast.

The solvent stung Ridley's eyes and burned his nostrils. Avoiding the caustic liquid, Ridley moved in. Snarling, Gort turned his head and snaked his neck out toward Ridley. The metal bar landed heavily against the side of the Drolong's head. The lizard-alien crashed to the grating, its forelegs twitching involuntarily.

Ridley moved away from the solvent and collapsed to his knees. His breath came in gasps, sweat pouring off of his body. After several minutes, he was able to look around and survey the damage.

The work area was a mess. Toxic solvent dripped through the grates. Gort lay on his side, mouth open, a frothy, yellowish liquid oozing from it. Ridley used the bar to help himself stand and stumbled over to where META IV was attending to the Mawhrbahts.

How're they doing, META?" Ridley could hear whimpering coming from Ryk and Tikah.

"I have treated their internal injuries. I am not well-versed in Mawhrbaht physiology."

"Maybe you need to review some of the data files down here."

"There are no data files on most of the Displaced Work Force," META IV said.

"That figures," said Ridley. "So what happens when one of the Displaced gets sick or injured?"

"Again, Ridley, I cannot answer your question. I am sorry."

"I'm beginning to wonder who is the more advanced race here."

"Ridley, are you damaged?"

"I'm okay. Make sure that these two are all right."

"Should I attend to the Drolong as well?"

"Nope. Save your energy cells. Gort just left for the big iguana terrarium in the sky."

META IV continued her ministrations on the two ailing Mawhrbahts. Ridley sat and leaned against the processor panel, tilted his head back and closed his eyes.

"Is it always like this down here?" said META IV.

"Just another day at the office," Ridley said.

Ridley stood slowly, rubbing his shoulder and grimacing, then limped over to where the lifeless form of Gort lay on the grate. He walked over to the com-link located on a nearby support. Ridley input the codes while leaning his head on the cold metal column.

A moment later, the lilting voice of Kelun floated over the com.

"What is it, Ridley?"

"Better get down here, Kelun. I've got a waste disposal problem."

CHAPTER THIRTEEN

The briefing room was full. Mara-jul looked around the chamber, hoping her agitation was not showing. At the circular table, other Delfinian commanders and sub-commanders were engaged in varied states of excited conversation. Members of the Water Council were due to address the roomful of squadron leaders. In these chambers sat the officers who commanded the remainder of the Delfinian fighting force. Based on the gravity of the situation, the Council appeared to be taking its time.

Two cycles ago, the com link between the central command ship and the cruiser was broken after reports of heavy fighting with great damages. A mid-sized star cruiser and eight light fighters disappeared from scanners after encountering strong resistance from the Trochinid contingent. The remaining commanders were at odds as to why the Delfinian forces were caught unaware. Speculation ran through the command room like a fire being fanned by a stiff breeze.

Seventh Order Kirin-rah turned to Mara-jul. She appeared, by all standards, to be in her teens, but was already flying her own light fighter. "Third Order, do you believe the rumors of a shielding device the Trochinids now have in their possession?"

"I refuse to speculate until we have more facts presented to us. The Water Council will inform us of any new developments."

Mara-jul's confident tone belied her underlying feelings of uncertainty. The Trochinids rarely attacked by surprise. They depended on overwhelming numbers to subdue their enemies. If the Trochinids were utilizing some newly acquired technology unknown to the Delfinians, the already lopsided campaign would take another ill turn.

"That was Azrnoth-zin's former squadron," said Kirin-rah.

Mara-jul turned sharply to face the sub-commander. "It is forbidden to mention the name of the banished. It is also forbidden to relay your thoughts to another regarding the banished."

"I do not think they would have been caught by surprise if commander Azr-".

"Sub-commander! Once more and I will be forced to bring you before the Council for violation of the tenets of exile."

"Many humblings, Commander. I feel a great sense of loss when we lose our warriors from without and within."

"As do I, Kirin-rah. It is not for us to question the ruling of the Council." Mara-jul had wondered more than once over the past few days whether the squadron would have not been overtaken if Azrnoth-zin had been in its command. She wondered if the other commanders and sub-commanders in the chamber were having the same thoughts.

The metal doors slid open and into the room walked Quillen-tok, Phon-seth and Bharin-fahl. The room full of officers snapped to attention.

Bharin-fahl was the third eldest of the Water Council, with a smooth head and short beard. Mara-jul had heard he was Sarn-ula's primary supporter on issues decided by the Water Council. It was his influence that swayed Sarn-ula and the rest of the Council to issue the most severe sentence. The three Council members strode to the front of the room and sat at the apex of the curved table. Once seated, the other commanders in the room took their seats.

"As all of you are well aware, the Twenty-first Squadron was caught in a surprise attack by a contingent of the Trochinid fleet, two cycles ago," said Quillen-tok. " From the limited data transmission, our forces did not see the enemy until the last moment. I regret to say there were no survivors. We wish them peace on their journey to dwell with the Ancient Ones. We can only offer our regrets to those mates and family members left behind."

Phon-seth stood and addressed the roomful of commanders. "Judging by the swiftness of the attack and the complete element of surprise, our tacticians believe the Trochinids may have incorporated some stealth technology into their fleet. Scans of the last system where Trochinid activity was heavy revealed a planet that was once very technologically advanced. It is reasonable to assume they have acquired some of that planet's technology and are currently using it." He placed his hands on the table and leaned forward. "If this information is accurate, we now have an enemy that is not only vast in numbers, but nearly invisible."

A murmur went up among the commanders in the room. Kirin-rah looked at Mara-jul, hoping to see the confident gaze of her commander. Mara-jul tried her best not to give away her feeling of fading hope in her glance.

Bharin-fahl stood next. "All commanders will be issued a new set of scanning frequencies that will modulate the proximate space to within fifty thousand gelacs. Any anomaly in the scans is to be taken as a direct threat. You are to act accordingly."

Quillen-tok stood and before him, the holo-image of the Delfinian commander appeared. The commander was mortally wounded. His words came with great difficulty.

" - boarded us before we could fully deploy shields. . . " The image faded and then returned, weaker this time. " - many losses. . . unable to get to escape pods." The image blacked out, then reappeared, only as a shadow. " - most to command center. . . commencing self- destruct sequence. Tell my mate. . ."

The image in front of Quillen-tok went dark.

"He did not have time to complete the destruct sequence," said Quillen-tok. "We would have found evidence of their debris signature on our long-range scanners."

"What became of the attack force?" asked one of the commanders from the back of the room.

"We do not know," said Quillen-tok. "We can only assume the ships and all aboard were processed on one of the refinery asteroids."

A chill went up Mara-jul's back. If it came down to it, she would turn her phase weapon on herself before she would allow herself to be processed into food by those monsters.

"Do we have information on how many were in the Trochinid attack force?" asked Mara-jul.

"To the best of our information, it was a star cruiser, the largest ship in their fleet."

"I do not know of concealment technology that can incorporate a ship that size," said another commander to the left of Mara-jul.

"We are in a sector that is mostly unfamiliar to us. Our records of civilizations in this sector are incomplete," said Phon-seth. "Our last scouting report of this system is outdated. There was a planet that harbored an advanced civilization as recently as six extended cycles past. Scans reveal that the planet in those coordinates is now lifeless. I believe it is from there that the Trochinids acquired this technology."

"All commanders are to meet with third and fourth order sub-commanders immediately," said Bharin-fahl. "The Water Council awaits your new strategies."

As the roomful of Delfinians dispersed, Mara-jul approached the head of the table and stood before Quillen-tok. "First Order, may I have a word with you?"

Quillen-tok nodded. He gestured to Phon-seth that he wished to be left alone. Mara-jul led him into a smaller chamber off the main meeting room.

"What is troubling you, Third Order?" said Quillen-tok. "I was sensing your unrest from where I sat."

Mara-jul was slightly taken aback. "Forgive me, First Order. I did not think I was projecting that much."

Quillen-tok walked over to a view portal and gazed out into space. "I, too, have grown weary of this conflict. I am sickened each passing day with the losses of our young and strong. We are fighting a war that we can never win."

"Then why do we persist in this madness?" Mara-jul said. "We are already demoralized. Every day, I am sending members of my squadron to a certain death. With this new threat, it would be more humane to turn my own phase weapon on them than to ask them to confront the Trochinids."

Quillen-tok sighed heavily. "It seems we have forgotten everything except the war. Did you know there is a great hall on Delfinus that houses some of the most magnificent works of art our civilization has ever known? Antiquities that date back fifty thousand years?"

"I have never seen these things," Mara-jul said.

"That is because the Water Council has deemed it damaging for young warriors to think about art and culture. They have but one purpose. There are those on the Water Council who feel as I, that perhaps we should end this. However, because of our history, the other members of the Council believe that we must continue to take the battle to the enemy down to the last Delfinian."

"But that is nothing more than self-induced genocide. We are now sending our children to battle. In my squadron, one-third of the warriors are either too young or too old."

"Do not discount the old," Quillen-tok said, a slight smile etching his ageless face. "They still have much to teach, even in times of war."

"I mean no offense, First Order. It is just that I . . ."

Quillen-tok held up his hand. "It is all right, Mara-jul. I do not take offense from my most trusted commander. It is refreshing to hear someone speak with forthrightness. But you will not hear me speak like this in front the others. You are correct. Morale is at its lowest ebb. Each day there is more talk of desertion. Azrnoth-zin no longer claims the singular shame of insubordination. He is now in the company of an ever growing new breed of Delfinian."

"I did not expect him to desert," Mara-jul said, surprised at Quillen-tok's deliberate breach of the Tenets of Banishment. "Perhaps his squadron would be here today if it not were for his actions."

"Perhaps. And then, perhaps not. Azrnoth-zin was one of the greatest warriors in recent times. His accomplishments read like an odyssey of our mythical heroes. But his discord has been evident to me and other members of the Council for some time now. He had grown tired of the fight a long time ago."

Mara-jul thought she picked up a tone of sadness in the great leader's voice. Of all the members of the Water Council, she felt the closest to Quillen-tok. His fairness and sound judgement had smoothed the volatile personalities of the other members.

"How long will you be staying aboard the *Delfon-quah?*" said Mara-jul.

"Two to three cycles," repled Quillen-tok. "Until we have the new parameters incorporated into the scanners."

"As always, the ship and all of its crew are at your disposal, First Order."

"Thank you, Commander. I do have a request, however."

Mara-jul came to attention. "Your orders, sir?"

"Not orders, Commander," the old warrior said gently. "A request. I was hoping you would accompany an old man to take a meal."

Mara-jul's shoulders relaxed. "I would be honored, First Order."

CHAPTER FOURTEEN

META-IV hovered outside of the small chamber, waiting for the right moment to move in. Blocking her entrance were alien forms jostling to get into the already packed room. Retracting her sensory equipment into the ovoid disc, META IV was barely able to squeeze over the head of a large, gelatinous-appearing creature.

The room temperature was far higher than was deemed normal for most living beings. A pall of smoke hung in the air. The metallic attempted to scan the mass of the Displaced Work Force in the room. She was surprised that many were not registered in the main data banks at all.

In the center of the room, seated at a table with three Mawhrbahts and two unrecognizable aliens was Ridley. Behind Ridley stood the odd-looking Yhrynen, Kelun, passively watching the proceedings. The survivor from Yhrys looked placid, but the metallic sensed that Kelun was watching out for the smaller humanoid.

Ridley held in his hands small rectangular cards with numbers and pictures on them. Every time Ridley passed cards to the other participants at the table, a cacophony of sounds erupted from the gallery.

In the diffuse light, Ridley's skin glistened over the tight muscles in his arms and shoulders. Though he had removed the facial hair as recommended by Meta IV, his skin was now the color the metallic remembered from the *Kren-dahl*. Ridley must have figured out the operation of the ion showers. His hair was tied into a ponytail, which trailed down between his shoulder blades. From the deference of the representative alien species present, it was obvious Ridley commanded a great deal of respect.

Ridley looked up to see META IV hovering several feet away. "Hey, META! How ya' going? Care to be dealt in?"

"I prefer to observe for now, thank you," replied the metallic. "Is this the game called poker?"

"Five card draw, jacks and deuces wild. Okay, boys and girls, ante up!"

Almost simultaneously, the seated aliens produced various objects from below the table and placed the objects in front of them. The crowd noise increased by several decibels, especially when some of the "currency" attempted to run off the edge of the table.

"Easy guys. You may not want to shoot your wads all at once," Ridley said.

A squat, toad-like alien placed a writhing mass of tissue onto the table. The pulsating blob of protoplasm belched in tiny eruptions.

"No, Grelb. We're playing for credits here. No one is interested in a Gomalaspore aphrodisiac."

The toad-alien opened its mouth and emitted a series of deep bass croaks.

"I don't care how much it cost you. You know the rules. You already lost all of your credits two hands ago."

More vociferous protestations from Grelb.

Ridley rolled his eyes. He slid some of the credits that were stacked in front of him toward Grelb. "This is all I'm spotting you for. You lose it, you go home. I'm not starting a chapter of Gamblers Anonymous out here just because you can't control yourself."

With that gesture, the throng exploded into raucous catcalls and taunts. Ridley held a hand up to silence the crowd. "They're my credits. I'll do as I please with them." He turned to one of the Mawhrbahts. "Ryk, I believe it's your bet."

The furry alien slid five credits forward and indicated he wanted two cards. Ridley dealt him two cards face down.

119

Ryk studied his cards and turned to face several Mawhrbahts seated behind him. A moment's conference produced some loud chattering that could be heard above the din of the crowd.

"Hey! No conferences. This isn't Family Feud," Ridley said.

Ryk placed five more credits on top of the first five. The noise in the small chamber was deafening. "Tikah, what do you want to do?"

The smaller Mawhrbaht studied her cards intently, not allowing any of the others to peek at them.

"She plays by the rules," said Ridley, aiming the barb at Ryk and his assistants. Apparently, there wasn't a word in the Mawhrbaht vocabulary for cheating. Tikah cautiously advanced ten credits and then five more, shrinking at the renewed energy from the crowd.

The next Mawhrbaht folded his hand as did the alien next to him. It finally came around to Grelb. The toad-alien could barely sit still, a trickle of spittle forming at one corner of his huge mouth.

"C'mon Grelb, before we all drown in here. Put up or shut up."

The alien moved his entire stack of credit chips onto the table and croaked at Ridley for three cards.

"Never let it be said that you lack a certain style about you, Toady," said Ridley, sliding three cards across. The alien gazed at his cards and promptly closed his eyes as if sleep were instantaneous.

It was Ridley's turn now. Ridley matched the bet and drew two. The crowd went suddenly silent, waiting to see what the human would do. Ridley was looking at a straight, king high. He pushed fifteen more credits toward the pile, then gave a slight half smile to Ryk.

This caused great consternation among Ryk and his colleagues. After some deliberation, Ryk matched Ridley's bet and indicated that he was calling. Ridley laid his cards down and the crowd of aliens erupted once more. The Mawhrbaht across from him chattered and exposed a royal flush.

"I don't believe it," said Ridley. "Son of a bitch."

"And you won my freedom by playing this game?" asked Kelun.

"The little hairball with legs got lucky, that's all," Ridley said disgustedly.

Ryk leaned forward to scoop the pile of winnings toward him. Suddenly, a huge concussion rocked the chamber, sending everyone sprawling. The lights went dark as a second shudder passed through the great ship.

Ridley found himself on his back, a great weight pushing into his chest. All around him were cries of panic and pain. He felt something wet against his forehead.

The emergency light system activated and Ridley found himself staring into the distorted face of Grelb. The alien was not any the more pleasant the closer you got to him. Ridley realized that the toad-alien had been drooling on him.

Wiggling out from underneath the unconscious Grelb, Ridley checked for damages. Nothing broken here, he thought and tried to stand. The room was in pandemonium: a massive bottleneck of alien bodies scrambled to get through the door at once.

"META! Are you still in here?"

From against the wall the metallic moved from behind a jumble of bodies clawing toward the door. META IV floated over and around the panicked aliens, deftly picking her way through the moving forms like a running back through a defensive line.

"Ridley, are you damaged?"

"I'm okay. What happened?"

"We have come under attack. My emergency scanners have just been activated."

"Who? The Trochinids?"

"That is affirmative."

"We need to get the hell out of here!" Ridley looked down and saw that Ryk and Tikah were at his side looking up at him and chattering nervously.

"META IV says it's the Trochinids." Turning back to the metallic, Ridley said, "Where should we go, META?"

"Once I access the control center, I can determine the origin of the attacks. It is necessary that we leave this room."

"I'm with you," said Ridley.

The last of the aliens in the room scattered leaving Ridley and the others a clear path through the door. Kelun pulled a length of metal from the floor grate and stood by Ridley's side.

"This will do little against a Trochinid," said the Yhrynen.

Ridley looked at Kelun. "I'm not feeling real good about our abilities to defend ourselves so far," said Ridley.

Grelb lay face down on the floor, snoring loudly.

"What about him?" said META IV.

"You can't wake him and I can't carry him. He'll come around. Right now, we need to tap into the mainframe."

Ridley ran with the others along the catwalk, now illuminated in orange emergency lighting. He felt the panic rising in his chest. Muffled explosions from above shook the great ship, each one growing closer and louder. The next series of explosions sent all of them sprawling. META IV stopped abruptly, suspended several feet above the catwalk.

"Hurry up, META! They're getting close."

The metallic rotated to face Ridley. "I have just accessed the primary computer system. The Trochinids have attacked the ship in three places. One strike targeted the power source and crippled the main star drive generators. The second attack was directed forward of the command center. Those last explosions came from another group who have breached the battle cruiser amidships at level twenty-eight. They are advancing toward the first attack force, driving a large contingent of Delfinians before them."

How could they get close enough to board the ship?" said Ridley.

"I do not have access to that data yet," replied META IV. "The command section is in chaos."

"I'm open to suggestions," said Ridley. "Where's Azrnoth-zin?"

"Level twenty-three, psy-detention. The security force is badly outnumbered and pinned down by a Trochinid advance."

"Shit." Ridley looked around at the bizarre group of aliens gathered about him. "Is there a way for us to get to him?"

"It is doubtful that we can reach him and then access the stern landing bays before the Trochinids close off our avenue of escape," said META IV.

Members of the Displaced Work Force were running past Ridley and the group. Many of them were Mawhrbahts, panicked into a frenzy. Ryk and Tikah barked out a series of staccato sounds and the other Mawhrbahts stopped and then grouped together. Within seconds, a dozen of the small furry aliens gathered around Ridley.

"I have just pulled up the schematics for the ship," said META IV. "We can circumvent most of the Trochinid force by following the maintenance conduits. I do not think we will be able to reach him in time. The enemy is massing to overrun the security area."

"None of you has to do this," Ridley said. "META IV will give you the quickest path to the landing bays. I gotta go and see if I can help Arn." Ridley looked around, eyes wide. "I can't believe I'm doing this. "

"Ridley, you said you had no use for the Delfinians," interjected Kelun. "Yet you will risk your life for this one?"

Ridley held up a finger. "Just this one."

The Mawhrbahts chattered animatedly among themselves and then turned to Ridley.

"Ridley, you will require my guidance to get to the detention center," said META IV.

"I believe I will come with you also," said Kelun

"Okay, you guys. It's your funerals." Turning back to META IV, Ridley said, "Let's go find Azrnoth-zin." The metallic turned and sped off down the catwalk with Ridley, Kelun, and the Mawhrbahts following closely behind.

Quillen-tok, Bharin-fahl and Mara-jul were seated at the table facing the other Delfinian commanders and sub-commanders when the *Delfon-quah* was rocked by the first of three blasts. Everyone in the room was thrown to the floor. A section of bulkhead caved in, burying several of the commanders beneath a mass of twisted metal rubble.

A piece of flying debris grazed Mara-jul's cheek. Dazed, she reached up and touched her cheek. She felt the sticky flow of blood on her face. All around, the cries of the wounded and dying mingled with the concussive explosions of phase weapons. Recovering somewhat, Mara-jul looked around, and, locating Quillen-tok, crawled over to where he lay on his side near a collapsed bulkhead. She rolled the Delfinian leader onto his back. A small trickle of blood was forming around his mouth. His gaze was distant.

"First Order! Can you hear me?" Mara-jul gently shook Quillen-tok's arm. "First Order!"

After a moment, Quillen-tok's gaze cleared somewhat. "What has happened?"

"We are under attack. Judging by the location of the blast, the Trochinids have destroyed the command center."

"Gather the commanders and begin moving toward the rear landing bays," said Quillen-tok. "Take what wounded you can. Leave the dying."

"Can you walk, First Order?"

"I believe my leg is broken near the foot. I have internal damage. Leave me."

Mara-jul's gaze hardened. "If I have to carry you to the landing bays on my own back, so be it. I will not leave you."

"How is Bharin-fahl?"

More blasts were coming from the forward section. Now, Mara-jul could discern the report of small arms fire interspersed with the moans of the wounded and yells from the panicked. Mara-jul looked around the smoke-filled room and spied the other Delfinian leader propped against the bulkhead. Blood ran freely from a wound on his forehead. She limped over to him and kneeled down. After several attempts at gentle shaking, she was finally able to revive Bharin-fahl. Numerous plasma burns still sizzled on his face and hands.

Bharin-fahl looked up at Mara-jul, his eyes unfocused.

"Are you damaged?" she asked.

He stared at her mouth.

"Where are your injuries?"

Bharin-fahl attempted to mouth words, but managed only a guttural moan.

"Can you hear me?" said Mara-jul, above the din in the room. The First Order did not respond. He appeared to be in a state of shock. His hearing must have been shattered during the blast. Mara-jul put her head under the arm of Bharin-fahl and supported his back as she lifted him to his feet. With her first step, Mara-jul felt the white pain slash through her ribcage, taking her breath. She almost fell over Bharin-fahl but caught herself in one agonizing lurch. She managed, with great difficulty, to half-carry, half-walk the First Order over to where Quillen-tok lay propped against the bulkhead.

Mara-jul produced her com link and spoke into it. "Command center, this is Third Order Mara-jul. What is your status?"

Static. Then, " - heavy resistance on levels twenty . . ." More static was heard and then, " - uating command center . . . no warning." The command center link went dead.

"The Trochinids attacked the command center first. It appears the brunt of their attack is forward and amidships. They want to drive us toward the stern landing bays," said Mara-jul.

Through clenched teeth, Quillen-tok said, "They will try to cut us off from reaching the stern landing bays. You must move these people out of here quickly." He looked over to the other Delfinian leader. "And that means leaving us behind. We will only lessen your chances of escape."

Mara-jul motioned for several sub-commanders to come to her. The dazed and confused squadron leaders responded.

"Are any of you damaged?"

They all shook their heads.

"The First Orders are injured and require your assistance. I want them and all other wounded personnel moved toward the stern landing bays."

"And you, Third Order?" asked Kirin-rah. A gash on her shoulder was still producing a fresh stream of blood.

"A contingent of warriors and I will bring up the rear and discourage any pursuit from behind." Just as Mara-jul finished her sentence, another blast resounded from the direction of the command center.

"We are severely short of weapons other than small arms," said another of the sub-commanders.

"We will have to make do. Scavenge any weapons you find on the dead, Delfinian or Trochinid."

Discipline was restored quickly when Mara-jul began issuing orders. Any that could walk assisted those who could not. The group made their way to the airlock door, the able-bodied in front, the wounded behind them. Quillen-tok and Bharin-fahl were each supported by two Delfinians. It was going to be a slow retreat to the stern of the great battle cruiser.

Mara-jul stood in front of a semi-circle of Delfinian warriors. Other than their side arms, only one individual carried a plasma rifle.

"Kirin-rah, you are with me."

The young Delfinian Seventh Order nodded.

Beneath the nagging pain in her ribs, Mara-jul felt the mixture of fear and defiance.

Unholstering her phase pistol, she said, "Move out!"

The airlock doors slid open and the group of Delfinians pushed into the smoke-filled corridor.

CHAPTER FIFTEEN

Ridley was too preoccupied with keeping down his panic and trying to keep up with META IV to think about the familiar voice he heard at the edge of his mind. At first, he thought the voice was coming from up ahead. It was like a distant conversation just out of range of his hearing to be discernable. Suddenly, he recognized who was speaking.

"META! Azrnoth-zin's in trouble. The Trochinids are about to breach the security chambers."

"How did you access this information?" META IV said, spinning around.

"I don't know. I heard his voice in my head. Is there anything around here that resembles a weapon? What works on these things?"

"Plasma rifles at close range are marginally effective," said Kelun. "Enhanced with electromagnetic tracers, their performance improves by forty percent. Photonic pulse cannons are the most effective, but they cannot be operated alone."

The metallic engaged her servo-mechanisms, replaying the ships schematics once more. "There is a weapons locker on the next level. It appears to be undisturbed."

"Let's go!"

"I regret to inform you that three Trochinids are about to enter the storage area."

"Are there any other lockers nearby?"

"Negative. The next weapons storage area is located above that level and has already been secured by enemy forces."

"Dammit! Now what?"

Tikah stepped closer to Ridley and pulled on his arm, chattering rapidly. She was joined by several other Mawhrbahts.

"What are they saying now?" said META IV.

"It seems our engineering friends have a plan. They're going to distract the Trochinids. You and Kelun and I are going to break into the weapons locker."

"At this time, I feel it is necessary to inform you of the overall odds of success of such an endeavor."

"Save it for Las Vegas. It's the best idea I've heard in the last fifteen minutes."

Ridley and Kelun crouched behind a jumble of odd-shaped equipment that he guessed were spare parts for the drive engines. From the looks of them, they had been sitting there for some time. Against the adjacent wall, META IV lay motionless, giving the appearance she was part of the discarded machinery. From Ridley's position, META looked as if she had deactivated herself. He estimated the weapons storage locker was about thirty yards away, against the far wall. It was to be the longest thirty yards Ridley would run in his life.

Ridley was staring at his nightmare creatures. They crouched near a collapsed bulkhead to the right of the weapons locker. Three Trochinids appeared to be picking at something that was lying on the floor. Two of them began to squabble over something that they each held in their mouths. Ridley felt the bile rising in his throat as he realized they were having a tug-of-war over a dead Delfinian's entrails.

The third Trochinid extended itself into full erect posture. Standing almost eight feet tall, its skin appeared to have a metallic sheen to it. The segmented carapace reminded Ridley of a beetle's exoskeleton.

The elongate heads were exceptionally large compared to the body size. The creature scanned the room with enormous elliptical yellow eyes, the eyes of a viper. In their heavily clawed hands, each of the Trochinids carried sinister looking weapons that were attached to a pack-like apparatus on their backs. The air in the room reeked of a sulphur-like smell.

The standing Trochinid turned and fixed its gaze where Ridley crouched. The other two stopped eating and stood as well.

"Oh, shit," Ridley said.

The panels from the ceiling caved in. Large fuel cylinders crashed to the floor, their contents exploding into a cloud of white gas that obscured the Trochinids from view. Somewhere overhead, Ridley could hear the excited chattering of the Mawhrbahts. Another volley of cylinders fell through the opening in the ceiling. Tracers from the Trochinid's weapons arced upward through the smokescreen.

Ridley sprang to his feet and sprinted across the room with Kelun several feet behind. META IV was just in front of him leading the way to the locker. Overhead, a Mawhrbaht screamed in agony.

Reaching the locker, META IV overrode the security sequence and the doors slid open. The smokescreen was beginning to lift. An array of unfamiliar weapons were arranged in rows in the locker. Ridley grabbed two of the smaller side arms and stuffed those into the waistband of his trousers. He tossed two more to Kelun.

"Which ones?" he yelled.

"That one. No! Not that one. The plasma rifle. The cannisters are to the left."

Ridley hefted the rifle. His fingers fumbled over the workings of the alien weapon. Then, as if he had been around a plasma rifle all of his life, he snapped a canister into place, activated the weapon and released the safety.

A tracer came out of the lifting haze and impacted the locker. Ridley and Kelun were flung to the floor. When Ridley looked up, two Trochinids were alternately squatting and leaping toward him. Ridley rolled away from the locker just before the next tracer tore into the weapons cache. A series of small explosions rolled outward from the wall as the cannisters ignited, sending molten plasma outward. As the molten substance

connected with bulkhead and superstructure, the plasma burned
through, turning the metal into slag. The Trochinids attempted to
shield themselves from the blast and flying debris.

Out of the fog, the first Trochinid stepped forward. It was
yanked backward as a white stream of concentrated plasma caught
it full on in the chest. It landed against the far wall in a sickening
splat, a greenish-yellow cavity smoldering where its chest once
was. Ridley looked at Kelun who nodded calmly, then continued
firing away.

The second Trochinid went into a crouch and aimed at
Ridley. Its head disappeared in a mist of exploded tissue. Ridley
came to a half kneeling position and searched the dissipating fog
for the third Trochinid.

The remaining Trochinid was still firing blindly through
the ceiling. Ridley could make out the silhouette of the creature
through the lifting smoke. He leveled the weapon and fired. The
impact spun the hideous alien around to face Ridley. The next shot
slammed it into the far wall.

The Mawhrbahts dropped from the ceiling and scurried
to where Ridley stood, holding the recharging weapon. Ridley's
breath came in a series of short pants. He looked at the dead
Trochinids. He turned to speak to the metallic. Where was META
IV?

Ridley spied what was left of the metallic halfway across
the floor. One entire side of META's sensory disc was a charred
mass of twisted metal. One of her mechanical arms was missing.
Ridley ran over to META IV and knelt beside her.

"Can you still move, META?"

"- sta - bil - i - zers dam - aged. In - op - er - a - ble."

"Ryk, see if you can locate META's other arm. It's got to
be around here somewhere. Ridley removed his belt and fastened
it around the metallic. He removed the sling from the plasma rifle
and attached it to the metallic, forming a makeshift harness. He
slung META IV over his shoulders, immediately feeling the jagged
projections from her ruined sensory disc jab into his back. Soon
after, Ryk returned with META IV's mechanical arm.

Ridley discarded the used plasma canister and snapped
another one into place. The small band of survivors continued their
advance through the charred superstructure.

Ridley's senses were not ready for what greeted them on
level twenty-three. The corridors were laid waste with debris
and collapsed superstructure. Small fires were everywhere.
Scores of the dead littered both sides of the corridor. None of
the dead Delfinians had any weapons on their mutilated bodies.
Choking haze and smoke hung heavily about the corridor, causing
Ridley's eyes to tear. That gut-wrenching smell of sulphur was
overpowering.

Rounding a corner, Ridley almost ran into a solitary
Trochinid. It was hunched over a dead Delfinian woman. The left
side of her neck and shoulder were gone. The Trochinid turned, it's
silvery fangs outlined in crimson. The creature screamed, a sound
straight from hell - and lurched for its weapon. Ridley brought up
the rifle and fired. The head and chest of the Trochinid exploded
in a stain of gore. Its carcass flew backward against the wall and
slumped into a heap.

"How much farther?" said Ridley.

"- next sec - tion."

Another curve in the corridor and Ridley saw two
Trochinids firing into an open section. They were hiding behind
part of a collapsed wall. Firing intermittently, they attempted to
leap-frog ahead, but were thwarted by small arms fire erupting
from within the security section. From this position, Ridley didn't
have a clean shot.

"Az - r - noth - zin there," said META IV.

Ridley felt a tug on his pants leg. Looking down, he saw
Ryk and Tikah hefting the Trochinid weapon in their furry hands.
Two other Mawhrbahts supported the large recharger.

"You guys figure out how to use one of those things?"

The Mawhrbahts nodded.

"Okay. Step on up here then."

The Mawhrbahts stepped forward even with Ridley. Tikah
balanced the weapon while Ryk aimed. Ryk pulled the trigger.
The Trochinid weapon belched a fireball, throwing the four

Mawhrbahts backward. Ridley's eyebrows were singed off and his
hair was burning. He swatted out the small fires that had ignited
on his clothing and rubbed frantically at his smoldering hair.

The Trochinids were nowhere to be seen. A great pile
of smoking rubble lay where a bulkhead was a moment ago.
Cautiously, Ridley advanced, his weapon held at the ready position.
He sidestepped a few nondescript body parts, which lay scattered
about. The Mawhrbahts scurried up behind Ridley, dragging the
Trochinid weapon.

"Nice shot, guys. Next time, give me a chance to get
behind you, okay?"

Ridley peered into what had been the psy-detention section.
Several Delfinian guards lay sprawled in grotesque positions of
rictus. Ridley recognized one of the dead as the head guard who
had brought him before the Water Council. The walls were awash
in blood.

"Arnie! Are you in there?"

Seconds ticked by. No response.

"Arn, if you're in there, answer me, dammit!"

"Ridley? Is that you?" a voice spoke from beyond the
rubble.

"We're coming in. No friendly fire."

"We have wounded, Ridley."

Ridley clambered over the debris and came face to face
with Azrnoth-zin. It was a toss up as to which one of them looked
worse. They blinked at each other in the diffuse light. Azrnoth-
zin's tunic was torn and singed. Blood oozed from a wound in his
right shoulder and thigh. The man from Earth and the man from
Delfinus hugged each other fiercely.

"Saved your skinny Delfinian ass again, didn't I," said
Ridley, a crooked white smile lighting up his soot-blackened face.

"Almost didn't recognize you," said Azrnoth-zin. "That is
a new look for you, is it not?"

"Yeah, well you've looked better, too." Ridley turned
around. "I brought META IV."

Azrnoth-zin ran his hand over the metallic's pockmarked metal skin. Kelun and the Mawhrbahts arrived, clambering over the debris pile, lugging the bulky Trochinid weapon.

"What have we here?" said Azrnoth-zin.

"A little advantage for the home team," said Ridley. "Just make sure you're well behind it when it goes off. Azrnoth-zin, meet Ryk and Tikah. Bringing up the rear is Gya and Ielel. I haven't been formally introduced to the rest of the Mawhrbat contingent."

Azrnoth-zin nodded at the Mawhrbahts. His eyes fell on Kelun.

"My stars. You are Yhrynen?"

"I am Kelun of Yhrys."

"I thought you were all dead."

"Not yet."

"Guys, we don't have time for this," said Ridley.

"What is the status of the ship?" Azrnoth-zin said, turning back to Ridley.

"Don't know for sure," said Ridley. "Forward section and command section are toast. META said to head toward the stern landing bays." Ridley looked around at the six other survivors from psy-detention.

"Can you all walk?"

The Delfinians nodded grimly. Ridley turned to Azrnoth-zin. "How about you?"

"Don't ask me to race you right now. I can walk."

Ridley took a long ragged breath. "Which way?"

"There. Down that corridor to the next staging section. Then drop down two levels to twenty-five."

"I came from that area," said one of the Delfinians. "The Trochinids were everywhere."

"Then let's make for the level below that," said Azrnoth-zin. "Are we in agreement?"

"No argument from me," said Ridley. "Let's get the hell out of here."

Azrnoth-zin and Ridley took the lead. Azrnoth-zin's limp was noticeable, but he matched Ridley's pace.

"You realize," said Azrnoth-zin, "that we are most likely walking into a trap."

Ridley handed Azrnoth-zin a phase pistol. "There you go again, Arn. The glass is always half empty with you."

Mara-jul checked her supply of plasma cannisters. She was down to her last two. The pain in her side and left thigh were constant reminders of the firefight they faced to get to the star drive relay center.

They were cut off; sensing their escape route, the Trochinids had trapped them in one of the large staging areas. They were now hemmed in from three sides. The primary route to the stern landing ports was all but blocked. Of the twenty-one commanders and sub-commanders that left the airlock during the initial attack, only eleven survived. Three of the eleven were wounded and could barely shoulder weapons. The Delfinians that had been carrying Quillen-tok were cut down by Trochinid fire.

Quillen-tok took a fragment of shrapnel in his chest. Mara-jul ran back through the fire to retrieve the elder Delfinian. She felt a burning pain in her leg, causing her to drop to one knee. Struggling back to her feet with Quillen-tok leaning heavily against her, she stumbled the last few feet to the protection of a collapsed bulkhead.

Mara-jul had no chance to get back to Bharin-fahl and the two Delfinians assisting him. A Trochinid cannon vaporized them and several other stragglers. At least they died quickly.

Mara-jul crawled down the ranks of Delfinians lying against the rubble pile and scraps of the once majestic star cruiser. "Weapons status?" she said to each one as she went.

Kirin-rah held up her plasma rifle. "I'm empty," she said.

Mara-jul handed her one of the cannisters. "That's all there is. Make your shots count."

"I have a contingency plan, Commander," said the young officer. "After this I will begin hurling scrap metal at them."

Mara-jul touched the Seventh Order's shoulder and moved on down the line. She finally came to where Quillen-tok lay propped against a large metal plate.

"How are you faring, First Order?"

"It is not too bad as long as I do not move much." He was having difficulty breathing. "Mara-jul, you have handled yourself in the highest fashion of Delfinian warriors." Quillen-tok paused for several seconds to catch his breath. "It fills me with great pride to see how the others follow your lead. I have often thought you would be an excellent choice for ascension to the Water Council. The people need wise leaders like you."

Mara-jul looked at the First Order and then cast her gaze to the others. "I feel as if I have failed them, First Order. Everyone on this ship. I should have been more aware."

Quillen-tok coughed. A frothy, pink sputum gathered around the corners of his mouth. "You did all that you could. This ship was continually on an alert status. We had no knowledge of the Trochinid stealth technology."

The First Order lay quietly for a moment. "I have another request," he said. "If the Trochinids break through -."

Mara-jul nodded and touched his shoulder. "Yes, it will be done, First Order."

Dozens of Trochinid carcasses were piled near the three entrances to the large chamber. Under Mara-jul's direction the small group of Delfinians defended their position fiercely. They had almost made it. One more section and they would have accessed the stern landing ports. Now, it seemed a galaxy away.

She knew Quillen-tok would be dead soon if he didn't receive medical attention. The signs of shock had already set in. In the panicked attempt to reach the rear landing bays, not much thought was given to securing a med-surg unit.

For the past twenty minutes the near corridors had been quiet. Mara-jul could still hear distant explosions in other parts of the ship. She suspected the Trochinids were massing just beyond those three airlocks for one final, all-out attack on their position. The group of Delfinians with their meager armaments would not be able to withstand another onslaught.

The room shuddered from a resounding blast that occurred just beyond the ruined airlock. The fireball leapt outward from the corridor, blowing Trochinids and debris through the opening.

The Delfinians ducked for cover as metal and body parts rained down on their position. Mara-jul rolled to one side and peered over the top. Several Trochinids stumbled into the opening. Mara-jul leveled the plasma rifle and dropped all three in the rubble.

Another explosion ripped through the center airlock. As the smoke cleared, Mara-jul saw figures crouching, then running toward them. She raised the plasma rifle and targeted the lead figure. They were carrying something between them. It was a Trochinid cannon. If they were able to get it into position, the entire group of Delfinians would be gone in the first detonation. Mara-jul's finger increased the pressure on the trigger.

"Hold your fire! We're coming in!"

Mara-jul thought she was hearing things. That sounded like Azrnoth-zin. She raised her rifle again and sighted on the running figures. The two figures sprinted across the room. They weren't moving like Trochinids. Others were now following out of the haze. The two lead runners reached the fortification and dove over the top of the rubble pile, landing in a tangle of arms and legs at Mara-jul's feet, her weapon still trained on them. Ridley and Azrnoth-zin got up slowly and faced Mara-jul.

"You! And You! How did you get here?"

"Ridley and the Mawhrbahts liberated me from psy-detention," said Azrnoth-zin. "We were trying to reach the aft landing ports."

"As were we," said Mara-jul. "The Trochinids had us pinned down from three sides. We were unable to go any further."

"How many of your group can still fight?"

"Seven. Bharin-fahl was vaporized along with two sub-commanders who were assisting him. Three are severely wounded. One is Quillen-tok. He has gone into shock from blood loss. We have no med-surg units."

"We have one," said Ridley. "At least what's left of one." He signaled the Mawhrbahts who brought the wrecked META IV before them.

"This metallic is damaged beyond field repair," said Mara-jul. "It would take our best technicians days to make it functional to perform intricate surgical procedures."

"The Mawhrbahts can fix just about anything," said Ridley. "Let them have a go at META IV."

"They have no working knowledge of Delfinian technology."

"The way I see it, Commander, you don't have a lot of options here. Quillen-tok will be dead soon if you don't let them try."

Mara-jul glared at Ridley. She nodded her head without breaking eye contact. "Proceed."

Ridley spoke to the Mawhrbahts and they set to work on META IV.

"We must move the group to the landing bays quickly," said Azrnoth-zin. "The Trochinids know we are here."

"We are still blocked from the landing bays," said Mara-jul. "The only corridor leading there is under guard by several Trochinids. We will have to fight our way through."

Azrnoth-zin looked at Ridley. Ridley looked at Azrnoth-zin, then shifted his gaze to the corridor. Again his gaze fell on Azrnoth-zin. He shook his head.

"I know what you're thinking, Arn. And frankly, between you and me, I think the whole idea sucks."

A slight grin crossed Azrnoth-zin's face. "Have a better idea?"

"That's what sucks."

"Mara-jul, give us five minutes to clear a path through the corridor. The Trochinids will not be expecting to have one of their own weapons used on them. Move the rest of the group as quickly as you can."

Mara-jul looked at Azrnoth-zin, then to Ridley and back to the remainder of the survivors.

"Proceed, Azrnoth-zin. I will have them ready."

Ridley noticed the Mawhrbahts had already reattached META IV's arm. They were gathered around what would equate to the metallic's head, chattering animatedly.

Kelun approached Ridley. "I am sworn to protect you, Ridley. I will cover you."

Ridley looked up at the tall Yhrynen.

"Kelun, I appreciate it, but I think you would be better served bolstering the defenses here. They could use another crack shot. And besides, this is a job for . . . ah . . . someone of slightly smaller stature."

Azrnoth-zin looked at Ridley. "Ready?"

"Don't ever pop off again about my half-baked plans. Ready."

"This time, you carry the recharger," said Azrnoth-zin"

They exchanged components and peered over the rubble pile. There was no movement at the last airlock.

"What say we warm them up a little?" said Ridley.

"Let's."

Azrnoth-zin targeted just beyond the entrance, steadied himself and pulled the trigger. The large weapon bucked, almost throwing Azrnoth-zin back into Ridley. The explosion belched from the airlock, flames erupting into the room.

"Gotta leave now," Ridley said, turning to Mara-jul. Together, they rounded the rubble pile and ran into the blackening smoke. Tracers laced the haze as Ridley and Azrnoth-zin crashed against the remains of the bulkhead.

"Don't do anything heroic," Ridley said. "Remember, we're attached and you need to think about your partner."

Azrnoth-zin glanced around the corner. "Ready?"

"Go."

They stepped into the corridor and went into a half-kneeling position, just below the smoke level. Ridley heard the weapon recycling from the generator on his back. When it completed the recharge, he slappped Azrnoth-zin on the back and yelled.

"Now!"

Azrnoth-zin fired the weapon directly down the corridor. In the ensuing flash, Ridley caught a glimpse of Trochinid body parts and the grotesque creatures in flames. Behind them, Ridley heard the sound of small arms fire. They were up and running through the carnage and debris.

There was another blast from the weapon at the end of the corridor and the last of the Trochinid guard was dispatched.

Ridley and Azrnoth-zin emerged into the great landing bay and dove for cover as a single tracer hit above their heads. A lone Trochinid bounded toward them, firing and leaping simultaneously. Azrnoth-zin could not fix his sights on the Trochinid with the photon cannon.

"I can't get a shot!"

Ridley pulled the sidearm from the back of his trousers and fired. The first shot caught the Trochinid high and left, spinning it to the floor. It stood up and two more blasts opened gaping holes in its thorax and head. It collapsed to the floor with a sound like a wet sack of cement.

Azrnoth-zin looked at Ridley. "Not bad."

"Not bad? Just once I'd like to hear you say, "Hey, Ridley nice job!" You Delfinians are really a bunch of tightasses."

Standing up, Azrnoth-zin and Ridley looked around the smoke-filled chamber. Ridley's heart sank as he gazed around the landing bay. Every transport and fighter had been destroyed where they sat. Some were still burning. All of Mara-jul's fighters were now charred skeletons.

"Shit," said Azrnoth-zin.

A moment later, Mara-jul and the other survivors emerged from the corridor. Ridley saw the look of hope fade in all of the Delfinian's faces. Ridley stared at the twisted hulks in mind-numbing despair.

Ridley's eyes were drawn to the far corner of the landing bay. Sitting at an odd angle was a derelict cargo freighter, still intact. Along its squat hull, blackened scars from an earlier attack appeared like cancerous lesions. A large, gaping hole like a grievous wound, was located just behind the port amidships.

"What about that?" said Ridley, pointing to the freighter.

"I don't think it has been space worthy in a long time," said Mara-jul. "We salvaged it from deep space after it had been left derelict."

"Looks like the Trochinids didn't think it was worth wasting photons on."

Ryk and Tikah came over to Ridley and fired off a stacatto burst of chirps.

"You think?" said Ridley. He looked at Mara-jul and Azrnoth-zin. "The Mawhrbahts say they may be able to get this thing spaceworthy."

"It won't fly," said Mara-jul. "It's flotsam. And even if they could make it fly, the Trochinids will be on us before we can launch."

"I've seen these guys work. I say it's worth a shot. Hell, it's about our only shot."

"How much time do they need?"

Ridley turned to ask Ryk, but the diminutive furry alien let loose with a barrage of angry chattering. Ridley turned back to Mara-jul. "You don't want to know what he just said. To paraphrase loosely, he said he didn't know."

Azrnoth-zin looked around the landing bay. "We need to set up a defensive perimeter. Anyone who can still fire a weapon is on the perimeter. Under the nose of the ship is a suitable place to secure the wounded."

"How is Quillen-tok?" said Ridley.

"The META unit has his systems stabilized for the present. He requires a reorganization chamber in order to repair his wounds," Mara-jul said.

The Mawhrbahts sprang into action and descended upon the freighter's drive engines with a fury. The dozen of the diminutive aliens looked like thirty, moving about like bees in a hive. Parts began to move in and out of the blast hole. The Mawhrbahts scurried between the wrecked fighters and transports and searched for pieces of salvageable machinery that might be utilized.

Azrnoth-zin and Mara-jul organized the able-bodied Delfinians in establishing a barrier between the freighter and the airlock. Ridley assisted the others moving anything into place that would act as cover. He noticed one of the Delfinians crouched behind several pieces of scrap metal. Ridley thought of the Trochinid canon.

Ridley straightened up. "Hey?"

Azrnoth-zin worked with several Delfinians to finish moving a metal plate into place and standing it upright. Now limping badly, Azrnoth-zin was barely able to put weight on his leg. "Now what?"

"I think we should blow that airlock. You know, collapse the next level onto the corridor."

Azrnoth-zin blinked. "It could buy us some more time." He looked at Mara-jul. "Can you still rig those cannisters like you did on Solex Four?"

A fire returned to Mara-jul's eyes. "Create a chain reaction with the plasma cannisters at specific points in the corridor. It just might work. We do not have many cannisters left. There won't be anything left for a perimeter defense if we set a chain reaction detonation."

Azrnoth-zin looked around at the scrap piles forming around them. "These won't hold them for long once they reach the landing bay. We have to make it so they don't reach the airlock."

Mara-jul nodded. "I like this plan."

They gathered up the remainder of the plasma cannisters. Mara-jul gathered up all of the com links from the Delfinian officers. "We'll set the com links to a time delayed frequency. There will be one per canister. When the first one blows, there will be a five second interval between detonations. We can trap the Trochinids in the corridor and bury them in the superstructure."

Azrnoth-zin held up his hand. "They will be scanning for devices. There will need to be a diversion."

"I will stay behind at the entrance to the airlock," said Mara-jul. "I'll lay down fire to distract them and move down the corridor in front of each blast."

"I think I should be the one to lure the Trochinids," said Azrnoth-zin. "I am expendable. You are needed by the others and the fleet."

Ridley had been silent for the past few moments, watching the exchange between the two Delfinians. "Hell," he said, finally. "Neither one of you could make it down that corridor in time. I'm the only one among us that has two working legs. I'm going."

"Ridley, you don't have to do this," said Azrnoth-zin. "It's not your fight."

"It is now. Besides, I can't fly that ship. It'll take all of you to get that thing off the deck. Give me two plasma pistols. Keep the big blaster here for anything that gets through."

Mara-jul and Azrnoth-zin were staring at Ridley. "Well," he said, "what are you waiting for?" He picked up the satchel of cannisters and walked toward the airlock.

Mara-jul and Azrnoth-zin shouldered their weapons and limped into the airlock after Ridley.

Ridley marveled at the skill and dexterity Mara-jul exhibited as she set the timers on the detonation devices. She and Azrnoth-zin had leap-frogged to different positions in the corridor to set the charges. Ridley carried one of the plasma rifles and the two sidearms, standing guard while the timers and explosives were rigged. Azrnoth-zin and Mara-jul each carried a plasma rifle and sidearm.

Ridley peered around the airlock into the chamber they had fought through earlier. It was against everything considered natural in the universe to return to the carnage. A deathly silence hung in the air along with the acrid vestiges of smoke and burned flesh. For the moment, there was no movement from the other side of the large chamber.

Ridley turned back to see Mara-jul holding a piece of wiring in her teeth while she attached the charge to the weak point on the corridor wall.

"All this, but can you cook?"

Mara-jul shot Ridley a disgusted look and set the frequency on the detonation device. "There. I believe the last charge is in place. As the ship's commander I am well aware of the ship's strong points. I also know where the structural weaknesses are."

"Time for you to get back to the landing bay, Commander."

"We should go over the strategy one more time."

"I think I have it wired," said Ridley. "Once the Trochinids get past this first charge, I blow it by activating my com link to the frequency you set. Then it's a Michael Johnson down the corridor, blowing the other charges as I pass them."

"You must understand Ridley. You have less than five seconds after the signal is activated. If you hesitate at all . . ."

"Don't worry, Commander. I have a strong desire to keep all of my body parts connected and working." Ridley nodded down the corridor. "Better get moving."

Mara-jul started to walk back toward the landing bay. After two steps, she stopped and turned around. "Good luck, Ridley-of-Earth." She disappeared into the gloom of the corridor.

Ridley found a place to hunker down just inside the airlock. It would give him a good first shot. His heart pounded in his ears. His body was slick with sweat. The seconds languished into minutes.

His mind raced over the events of the past few months. Earth seemed a faded memory. If he hadn't been so frightened, he might have found humor in the fact that he, Cooper Ridley, had just volunteered for a suicide mission to save a race of people that had little or no sympathy for the inhabitants of his home planet.

Serves you right for the company you keep.

Ridley smelled the Trochinids before he saw them. The acrid smell assailed his nostrils, causing his eyes to tear. Somewhere beyond the pile of debris on the other side of the chamber, he heard a faint scratching sound, like metal on metal.

Venturing a look around the side of his blind, Ridley still didn't see anything in the darkness and haze at the other end of the chamber. The scratching grew louder.

Out of the darkness, at least a dozen Trochinids, all armed, advanced in their crouch - leap - squat - crouch style. There was no definitive pattern to their movements, obviously a strategy designed to make them difficult targets.

The smell caused Ridley to gag. It was the odor of putrefying flesh. Ridley swallowed back the bile rising in his throat. He counted to three, came over the top of the metal blind and fired.

Two Trochinids went down. The rest scattered in different directions, each varying the lurch-hop to avoid being hit. They opened fire on Ridley's position, tracers thudding into the bulkhead. Ridley came over the top once again and fired another burst. A Trochinid had taken two large leaps and landed fifty feet away. It saw Ridley and fired. The tracer ripped a section of the metal away. Ridley rolled to the side and came up to see the Trochinid at the apex of a jump, its claws coiled to land on him. He fired a full burst. The Trochinid exploded in mid-air.

Ridley was up and running. He zig-zagged down the corridor. Tracers arced and impacted the bulkhead at his feet, churning up clouds of debris.

He reached the next airlock. The Trochinids were cautiously entering through the first airlock. He needed to lure them further into the corridor. The nine or so Trochinids concentrated their fire on Ridley's position, never giving him a chance to return fire. Ridley hunkered down as flying pieces of metal rained around him. The plasma rifle beeped as the last of the canister was spent. Ridley tossed the plasma rifle aside and drew the phase pistol.

A lull occurred in the volley. Ridley peered around the airlock and saw the Trochinids were now inside of the corridor. More tracers arced toward him. He activated the signal on his com link. He blindly pointed the phase pistol around the corner and laid down a series of bursts. Then he hit the corridor running.

Ridley heard a concussive whump behind him, then the sound of collapsing superstructure. Looking over his shoulder, he saw the Trochinids advancing rapidly, matching his speed. They had caught on to the trap.

Five Trochinids cleared the second airlock. Three - two - one. Another explosion ripped through the corridor, this one closer. Ridley was in a full sprint down the center of the corridor. He felt the prickling sensation in his back, knowing that the Trochinids had him in their sights.

A hail of tracers landed all around him, caroming off the ceiling.

The sounds of the blasts became muted. He could hear the beating of his heart in his deafened ears.

A tracer exploded into the wall to his left. Ridley felt hot pain in his shoulder and forehead. He kept running.

Ahead, Ridley saw the light from the landing bay. He pumped his arms and legs. Forty yards. He felt the heat of a tracer as it narrowly missed his head. Thirty yards. The Trochinids poured a fusillade at the running Ridley.

Twenty yards. Ridley's lungs were on fire. A tracer hit near his feet, the concussion sending him sprawling. He scrambled to his feet, stumbling the last ten yards through the airlock. More tracers arced out from the corridor.

Something lifted Ridley off his feet and threw him forward. He landed on the floor, face down, sliding into a pile of debris. A great concussive wave passed overhead, like a giant low flying plane. The next sensation he felt were hands on him; someone was carrying him by his arms and legs.

Ridley rolled over onto his back. He couldn't see. Something was in his eyes. Someone was wiping his face. Through a blur he saw Mara-jul's outline standing over him.

"How'd we do?" he said hoarsely.

"I think we got them all," Mara-jul said, wiping more of the blood from Ridley's face.

"What?"

Mara-jul realized Ridley had lost his hearing. She squeezed his hand.

"Boom," said Ridley.

CHAPTER SIXTEEN

A series of muffled concussions emanated from beyond where the corridor once was. From where Ridley lay propped against a landing strut, he noticed all eyes turn toward the far end of the landing bay. Although he couldn't hear the explosions, the vibration passing through his body and the look on the Delfinian's faces told him more than he wanted to know.

"It seems we are about to have a visitation," said Azrnoth-zin. "How much longer?"

"How would I know?" said Mara-jul. "I cannot understand the Mawhrbahts. Every time I approach the main drive unit, they make the most unpleasant sounds."

Ridley tried to stand up. The great room began to spin and he sat back hard. Tikah scurried up to Ridley and began to chatter at him. Ridley leaned toward the Mawhrbaht and listened intently.

Turning to the others he said, "They've brought the basic drive on-line." He was almost shouting the words. "She said forty-five minutes, maybe an hour to get the navigational systems to function."

"That is welcome news," said Mara-jul.

"What?"

"I said that is good news!"

"Not so fast, Commander. Tikah tells me we have no shields. That hole in the side can't be protected. They'll try to seal it from the airlock connecting the chamber."

Another concussion shook the floor. The Trochinids were getting closer.

"We don't have an hour," said Azrnoth-zin. "In about fifteen minutes, the Trochinids will blast their way into the landing bay."

The little Mawhrbaht nodded and ran back into the ship. Mara-jul looked at Azrnoth-zin. "Tell everyone we are leaving in fifteen minutes. I will program the *Delfon-quah* to undergo the self-destruct sequence in seventeen minutes."

Azrnoth-zin went to the cockpit of the freighter while Mara-jul limped over to a wall computer access. She keyed in her command code and initiated the countdown for self-destruct. When she got back to the perimeter, Ridley was recharging the large Trochinid cannon.

"What do you think you are doing?" said Mara-jul. "You are in no condition to fire that weapon."

"I'm sorry, Commander. My hearing went south on me."

A blast shook the landing deck. The Trochinids were on the other side of the rubble pile that blocked the corridor now. Behind him, Ridley heard the firing of the freighter's initiators.

"Seems your timetable got moved up, Commander. I suggest you get everyone on board and buckle your seat belts."

Mara-jul made a movement toward Ridley, but found herself looking at the business end of a phase gun. "It's never a good idea to argue with a guy from Earth with a headache. Get going, Commander. Just keep the hatch down."

Mara-jul looked like she wanted to say something, then turned and limped to the gangway. The Delfinians who could walk carried those who couldn't into the ship. A moment later, Ridley heard the roar of ignition.

The blast blew debris outward into the landing bay. Behind him, Ridley heard the initiators die. Out of the smoking haze, several Trochinids lurched, firing tracers toward the ship. Ridley took aim and fired. He caught two Trochinids with the initial blast, the third going down from a rain of shrapnel.

The initiators fired, then died again. From his position, Ridley could see two Trochinids with a weapon similar to his setting up behind a pile of scrap. Two more ducked behind the rubble pile. He knew where they would be aiming.

The initiators fired once more. This time they held. Ridley raised up and fired a burst from the Trochinid weapon. The weapon bucked in his arms and sent out a white-hot stream of photons that caught the Trochinids behind the scrap pile. When he turned his sights on the ones behind the mound of debris, he realized the weapon had lost its charge.

The Trochinids were leveling their weapon and aiming for the cockpit of the derelict freighter. Ridley set the Trochinid cannon on the deck, raised the phase rifle and aimed. He had one shot. He took a breath and activated the firing mechanism. The burst missed the two Trochinids and connected with the fully primed weapon. An explosion ripped into the two Trochinids, sending pulverized body parts across the landing bay.

Ridley was up and sprinting across the floor to the open hatch. The ship began to lift from the flight deck. Photonic tracers arced all around him, but he focused only on the squarish opening of the freighter's cargo bay. He hit the ramp and scrambled into the hold of the ship. The freighter shuddered, rose off the deck and began moving slowly out of the flight bay. As the hatch closed, Ridley watched the Trochinids pouring onto the floor.

Stumbling to the cockpit, Ridley saw that Azrnoth-zin and Mara-jul had their hands full. Kelun was firing from the rent in the hull. The Mawhrbahts were back with the drive engines trying to boost the plodding acceleration. Tracers from the Trochinid weapons thudded into the unprotected hull of the freighter.

"How much time?" yelled Azrnoth-zin.

"Thirty seconds," said Mara-jul.

"We don't have enough acceleration to clear the blast."

"I'm more concerned about them targeting the reactors at the moment."

"Does this p.o.s. have any useable defense system?" said Ridley.

The derelict freighter cleared the landing bay and moved out away from the *Delfon-quah*. Ridley turned and gazed out the rear port of the command center to see the immense Trochinid vessel hovering over the dying Delfinian battle cruiser.

"Sensors indicate they are powering up weapons and have a lock on us," said Azrnoth-zin, his voice grim.

"Ten seconds," said Mara-jul.

All Ridley could do was stare at the Trochinid warship, waiting for that white beam of concentrated photons to blind him and then the final, instantaneous heat of vaporization.

Ryk stuck his head through the floor grate opening and barked loudly.

"Stomp on it, Commander!" yelled Ridley.

Mara-jul activated the drive and the freighter lurched forward. Ridley was thrown into the bulkhead, but was able to see the once great *Delfon-quah* begin seething with internal explosions, which spread to the outer reaches of the ship. The core from the Delfinian drive erupted vertically, engulfing the Trochinid warship whose vulnerable underbelly was sitting just above the *Delfon-quah*. The first explosion was quickly followed by a second as the two ships lit up space, pieces of debris blossoming out like a supernova.

The pressure wave from the twin explosions caught the derelict freighter on its starboard side. The impact drove the ship along in the wake of the detonation wave like a piece of driftwood. Inside, Ridley lost his balance and was thrown against the bulkhead, hitting his head and slumping to the floor. The last thing he remembered was the feeling of being pushed along at an odd angle.

The mass of debris and blast residue swept past the heavier freighter leaving it drifting in space. Azrnoth-zin wiped his face with his hand and looked over to Mara-jul. She sat, rubbing her shoulder and peering at the sensor array.

"Are you intact?"

"Yes," she said, her voice distant.

One of the Delfinians came up through the floor hatch. "Is it over?

"It's over," said Mara-jul.

"We sustained more injuries down here. The META unit is attending to them now."

"See if there are any medical supplies on board that can be salvaged and utilized by META IV," said Azrnoth-zin. He turned to see Ridley sprawled out near the bulkhead. "I will attend to Ridley's injuries myself."

Mara-jul turned around and saw Ridley's limp figure. "It appears all of this has proven to be too much for your terran friend," she said.

"Do not underestimate him, Mara-jul. He may surprise you."

"He already has," she said softly.

The fleet located the derelict freighter drifting in space after nearly three cycles. Two of the severely wounded Delfinians had died before the ship was picked up. Ridley had heard that Quillen-tok was still in the restoration chambers. For a while, it didn't look like the elder Delfinian would pull through.

META IV was restored quickly to her former levels of function by META III technicians and was able to attend to most of the survivors from the freighter. Azrnoth-zin had sustained wounds from flying shrapnel in his thigh and back. Mara-jul had received a neck wound and lower leg injury along with several broken ribs. The wound to her neck had left her with loss of sensory function to the right hand. META IV had assured her that function would return in time with healing.

Ridley sat shirtless on one of the floating platforms. Between the scars on his back, the fresh lacerations to his head, and the multitude of bruises covering his body, it was hard to locate any undisturbed tissue on his torso. META IV hovered behind him, tending to a large and particularly colorful bruise on Ridley's ribcage.

"You realize, don't you," said META IV, "that patching you back together is becoming somewhat of a vocation for me."

Ridley winced as the metallic probed his still tender shoulder. "Ow! Dammit, META. Where's your bedside manner anyway?"

"Please do not squirm. I have not yet completed the assessment of the injury to your rotator cuff. The plasma burns are healing nicely, however."

"They still itch like crazy."

"How is the ringing in your ears?"

"Almost gone, but my left ear still feels like it's underwater. I sure wish I'd stop getting hit in the head."

"It will take some time for your ossicles to adjust to your new tympanic membrane." META IV's servomotors hummed as she took another position hovering just above Ridley's forehead. "Are you still having the dreams?"

"That's what's weird. I haven't had them since our escape from the *Delfon-quah*. Not that I miss them, mind you, but maybe going against the Trochinids triggered something in my psyche."

"Sometimes your fears become lessened after you confront them," said META IV.

"How'd you get so smart? You know, sometimes I think the Delfinians would be a whole lot better off if they let the metallics call the shots around here."

"Complimenting me will not get you through this exam any faster. But, thank you, Ridley. There. Your examination is complete."

"When can I check out of here? No offense, but I'm getting a little bunchy staring at the walls of the infirmary."

"I will make my recommendations to the Water Council. I believe you are able to return to quarters."

Ridley hopped down off the floating gurney, ambled over to the wall computer and keyed in the sequence for the synthesis of Omect tea, something he had acquired a taste for while working with the displaced aliens. He heard the hiss of the airlock door behind him.

"Ridley! Does META IV know that you are on your feet?" said Mara-jul. Her gaze wandered momentarily to the latticework of scars criss-crossing Ridley's back. "As I recall, you were to be on bedrest for several days more."

"META IV informed me that your brain waves were still aberrant," said Azrnoth-zin. "You suffered a significant concussion."

"My brain waves have always been aberrant, Arn. Nice to see you both." He nodded to Mara-jul. "Commander."

"I believe he is recovering nicely," said Azrnoth-zin.

"Well, I've got to say that you both are looking better than you did on that pregnant pickle we limped across the system in."

"Ridley," Mara-jul began. "It is difficult for me to express -."

"It's okay, Commander. You're welcome." Ridley saw the look of frustration change to irritation in Mara-jul's face.

"You have a most annoying manner about you," she said. "Are all humans on your planet this way?"

"You will get used to it," said Azrnoth-zin. "Actually, it is one of Ridley's more endearing qualities."

"Remind me never to visit Earth," she said.

"Ridley, Mara-jul and I have come to talk with you. A special meeting of the Water Council has been called. The three of us are to go before the Council."

"Great." Ridley took a sip of tea. "I remember what happened the last time. You guys go and send them my regards."

"It is not what you think," said Mara-jul. "The Water Council plans on honoring you and Azrnoth-zin for your bravery back on the *Delfon-quah*. Quillen-tok has requested the other members of the fleet to be present."

"I heard Quillen-tok was still undergoing reorganization."

"He just came out," said Azrnoth-zin. "He made the request of Phon-seth from his recovery chamber."

"What about you, Commander? I didn't hear you include yourself in this fiesta."

Mara-jul's eyes broke away from Ridley's gaze. Her proud posture faltered slightly. "I am to be disciplined for my negligence in allowing the *Delfon-quah* to be destroyed and the loss of so many Delfinian lives."

"You do not know that," said Azrnoth-zin. "You had no means of knowing the Trochinids were poised to attack the ship."

OFFWORLDER

"Commander, in my humble opinion, if it weren't for you, no one would have made it off that ship. You had tough choices to make. Choices I would never want to have to make. You made them without faltering. Hell, if I were ever to serve under anyone, which I wouldn't, thank you very much, I would consider you a fine commanding officer."

Mara-jul straightened up. She looked into Ridley's eyes for any hint of insincerity. "Thank you, Ridley." She smiled slightly. "I hope that never comes to pass."

"Touché, Commander." Turning to Azrnoth-zin, Ridley said, "How are the Mawhrbahts?"

"By your request, we have kept them out of maintenance and repair sections. They have undergone extensive physical examinations and the com links are being modified to incorporate their language into the universal translators. Presently, they are dismantling and reassembling all of the machinery in the ancillary chambers on deck twelve. I believe they have grown bored with their present accommodations. It is interesting to note that all of the systems in the ancillary chambers have improved performance by as much as twenty-eight percent."

"I'm here to tell you, Arn, the Delfinians are wasting a lot of exceptional talent there. Those little guys have greater designs to them than just being intergalactic custodians."

"Those are issues you can bring before the Water Council."

"I already told you. The Water Council can kiss my ass. I don't feel like going on trial again. If I hear another person call me "offworlder" again, I'm liable to go postal."

Mara-jul stared at Ridley, then back to Azrnoth-zin. "What did he say?"

"Earth colloquialism. Translated, it means he will be moved to a violent, irrational act."

"That's right," said Ridley. "Hell, the only one of those guys that cut me any slack was Quillen-tok and he's drawing workman's comp right now."

"Ridley, this is different," said Mara-jul. "You are not to be judged. You are to be honored."

153

"You are the voice for the Displaced Work Force," said Azrnoth-zin.

"Oh, no you don't. Don't lay that on me. I have no interest in being the union representative for a bunch of homeless aliens."

"You can deny it if you like, Ridley. But the fact of the matter is this: the Displaced Work Force looks up to you. You can be their greatest advocate in front of the Water Council. With your voice, they can be moved into positions that would provide them more freedom."

Ridley was silent for a moment. "Damn you, Arn." He peered at his friend. "You know I can't say no when you put it like that."

Azrnoth-zin laughed, a sound that caught Mara-jul off guard. She regarded him with a look like he just taken on a terminal virus.

"Azrnoth-zin, are you ill?"

"Mara-jul, one of the other endearing qualities about our friend Ridley is that he will always side with the disadvantaged, the "underdog" as the Earth people call it."

"Okay. I'll speak for the Mawhrbahts, the Graellon, Yhrynen and the Arkoanians and any others I don't yet know about. Even the Ventans. Just don't ask me to go around kissing any of their babies."

"Ridley, you have a rare opportunity before you," said Azrnoth-zin. "This is the first time that an off - sorry, a non-Delfinian has had the ability to address the Water Council."

"Enough already. I said I'd speak. Keep pestering me about it and I might change my mind."

"If you will excuse the interruption," said META IV. "I have a few final tests to run on Ridley before his release from med-surg."

"The Water Council will make their announcement for the gathering soon. We will talk before then." Azrnoth-zin turned to leave.

Mara-jul turned on her heel but not before giving Ridley the slightest of lingering looks. Ridley thought he saw a flash of something in her brilliant blue-green eyes. He smiled at her. She cast her eyes downward and walked out of the room.

"The room just got a little chillier," said Ridley watching her depart through the airlock.

"The ambient temperature in this area remains stable," said META IV.

Ridley grinned at the metallic. As META IV performed the final test series, Ridley was apparently lost in thought. After several moments, Ridley snapped out of his reverie.

"META, do you dream?"

"Not in the same sense that you dream, Ridley. We experience a type of system artifact. Even after our main circuits are inactivated, sensory information still passes through the primary processors."

"What do you dream about?"

"Quaternary systems, mathematical models, phase mechanics. It is more like my central processor is scrolling through all available systems, something akin to rest and rejuvenation in humans."

"Wow. So that's what it's like to be a sentient metallic?"

"I do not believe that achieving a dream state is the only criterion for sentience. There should be other factors present. Emotions are a large component of sentience."

"Do you feel emotions, META?"

"I have - an affinity toward Azrnoth-zin. So, I surmise that you could say those are emotions. I have even grown fond of you, Ridley."

"What do you think of Azrnoth-zin's and Mara-jul's proposal?" said Ridley. "Do you think the Water Council will listen to me about the Displaced Work Force?"

"From my observations, there is no one more qualified to represent them. I was able to record how they reacted to you, both in times of non-danger and when the situation became critical."

Ridley sighed heavily. "All right, then. Guess I better get to thinking about what I'm going to say to the Water Council."

The metallic retracted her mechanical arms and moved around in front of Ridley.

"Ridley, may I ask you a question?"

"Shoot."

"Excuse me?"

"Go ahead."

"How did you and Kelun dispose of Gort's body? I am surprised there were no repercussions. Surely, someone must have known the Drolong was missing."

Ridley stepped off the floating gurney and gingerly slipped his shirt over his shoulders. With difficulty, he managed to fasten the buttons on the shirt. The Delfinian synthesizers still had not worked out the intricacy of button fasteners and cross-stitching.

Ridley looked up at the metallic, his face showing no emotion.

"Even politician worms need to eat."

CHAPTER SEVENTEEN

The chambers of the Water Council were full. Present were Delfinian Second Orders through Eighth Orders, warriors, support personnel and other non-combatants. The only members of the Displaced Work Force in the great room besides Ridley were Ryk and Tikah. The two Mawhrbahts stood on either side of Ridley, closely pressed to his legs. The quiet murmurings ceased as the six members of the Water Council entered from a side room and took their seats before the seven columns of water. An empty seat near the other end of the table was the grim reminder of the loss of Bharin-fahl.

Ridley was glad to see Quillen-tok among the six. Other than a mild limp, he showed no obvious signs of the near fatal trauma he had survived.

Mara-jul and Azrnoth-zin and the other surviving members of the *Delfon-quah* were dressed in the dark blue and gray tunics befitting Delfinian commanders. META IV had a difficult time coming up with an appropriate mode of attire for Ridley. Since he held no position among the Delfinians, Ridley could not wear a tunic of rank. A compromise was finally reached whereby he was issued a light gray tunic. By Ridley's suggestion, META IV synthesized a pair of Levi's 501 facsimiles. These he wore tucked into a pair of leggings that almost came to his knees.

Ridley's face was clean-shaven, his hair trimmed short, almost to the length he wore in the Navy. Even though he felt the wetness of nervous perspiration, the strange clothing wicked all of the moisture away from his skin.

His eyes met the penetrating gaze of First Order Sarn-ula. Ridley sucked in his breath as he felt the dissecting countenance all the way down to his core. He felt an odd discomfort in his brain begin to grow into a raging primal fear.

No! Get out! Get away from me!

You will tell me your mind! Give me your thoughts!

Ridley closed his eyes and concentrated. He focused all of his mental energies on blocking the Delfinian woman's invasion of his psyche. Random images appeared behind his eyes. Ridley squeezed his eyelids even tighter. An image coalesced in his mind. Instantly, the image of an enraged Sarn-ula dissipated like a soap bubble.

Ridley shuddered, then opened his eyes. Beads of perspiration formed at his forehead. He looked up at Sarn-ula, who now was speaking with another member of the Water Council. She did not meet Ridley's gaze.

Ridley felt two more sets of eyes studying him. He looked to either side and saw Mara-jul and Azrnoth-zin staring at him askance.

"Are you all right?" queried Mara-jul.

"Uh, yeah. I'm fine," Ridley replied, still shaken.

"You look as if you just awakened from a very unpleasant dream," said Azrnoth-zin.

"I'm fine. Really."

Azrnoth-zin and Mara-jul continued to stare at Ridley.

"What?"

Phon-seth rose from his seat next to Quillen-tok and spoke. "This Water Council is now joined." He sat down and all eyes turned to Sarn-ula. She remained seated.

"This Council has deliberated extensively over the attack on the cruiser *Delfon-quah*. After reviewing the information salvaged from the data logs leading up to the ship's destruction, we have reached the following conclusions. We, the members of the Water Council find that there was no indication of negligence on any part of the Third Order Mara-jul or any of her sub-commanders. We have concluded that the Trochinid force employed a new covert system that jams the frequencies of our defense scanners, rendering their ships nearly undetectable. There will be no disciplinary action."

Ridley noticed Mara-jul's shoulders relax.

"Of the twenty-two hundred warriors, support personnel and displaced work force," Sarn-ula continued, "only those before you today survived. With great courage and perseverance, they were able to evacuate the ship and cause the destruction of the Trochinid battle cruiser."

Sarn-ula cast her gaze at Mara-jul. "Commander of the Third Order, Mara-jul, step forward."

Mara-jul took three steps forward and performed a half bow, with a slight sweeping gesture of her right hand. She then resumed her rigid posture.

"By your direction and courageous leadership, Quillen-tok and several other high ranking Delfinians were saved from the Trochinid onslaught. Your quick decisions were pivotal in the destruction of the Trochinid warship. Members of the Water Council and the Delfinian people praise your actions."

The room erupted with the stomping of Delfinian feet in a loud cadence, which built to a crescendo. After the din subsided, Sarn-ula spoke again.

"Third Order, it has been brought to my attention that you no longer wish to continue as a starship commander. Is this your request?"

Mara-jul looked directly at the old woman. "That is correct, First Order. With the permission of the Water Council, I would request to step down and assume the role as tactical fighter squadron leader. I feel I would be more of an asset to our fleet if I were on the forefront of the battle."

Azrnoth-zin started to shake his head, but a glaring look from Sarn-ula stopped him. Ridley could see that Mara-jul was taking the loss of her ship pretty hard.

"Are you sure of this decision, Mara-jul?" spoke Quillen-tok.

"Yes, First Order, I am. I am bound by the warrior code. In order to be the most effective for the Delfinian people, I should be at the controls of a light fighter."

"Your request is granted," said Sarn-ula. "You will be reassigned to lead the fighter squadron based on the *Mentor.*"

"I thank the members of the esteemed Water Council." Mara-jul bowed once more and stepped back within ranks.

"Former Commander of the Third Order, Azrnoth-zin, step forward."

Azrnoth-zin took three steps forward, bowed and saluted.

Sarn-ula gazed at Azrnoth-zin, a scowl waiting to twist her face. Ridley could see the old woman wasn't enjoying this.

"Azrnoth-zin. This Council was divided as to dealing with you. There are those among the Water Council who felt, in spite of your heroic rescue of your fellow Delfinians, that your prior behaviors far overshadow your accomplishments. Treasonous behavior is still treasonous behavior."

Azrnoth-zin remained stolid, facing straight ahead.

"However, the Council has decided that all punishments be waived."

A thunderous roar from the stomping of feet deafened the large room. Ridley was glad to see that Azrnoth-zin was well liked among the Delfinians.

"I will have order in these chambers!" Sarn-ula cast a baleful look to the gathering. "The Council has also decided that you will be reinstated to a sub-command level, under the supervision of Commander Mara-jul. Your ranking will be that of Sixth Order."

Murmurings arose among the gathering of Delfinians. Ridley was just beginning to understand the military hierarchy of the Delfinians. Azrnoth-zin had been reinstated with a severe demotion.

Azrnoth-zin bowed slightly and saluted once more. He stepped back in place and gave Ridley a sidelong glance. If Ridley hadn't been so nervous, he would have found humor in the fact that of all the Delfinians that could have landed on Earth, he had befriended the rogue.

"The human called Ridley, step forward." Ridley did the same as Mara-jul and Azrnoth-zin before him. He assumed a military posture, his eyes fixed ahead. The two Mawhrbahts stood just behind him and flanked to each side.

The ageless woman looked at all members of the Council before she spoke. Ridley could feel a thousand eyes staring at him.

"Ridley of the third planet in the Sol system," began Sarn-ula. "You have presented this Council with a most perplexing situation. What has come to pass here has never before been recorded, therefore we have no precedents on which to rely. However, because of your bravery and selfless acts during the attack on the *Delfon-quah*, coming to the aid of those to whom you owe no allegiance, this Water Council and the Delfinian people are grateful."

The chamber floor vibrated from the stomping of hundreds of feet. Ridley felt a sudden swelling of pride in his chest.

"Since you have no status in Delfinian society, it is difficult to elevate your position. You have proven to be an able and tenacious fighter. The Council recommends that you be incorporated as a warrior, Tenth Order."

Ridley was pretty sure that Tenth Order meant the hamburger detail.

"May I speak?" said Ridley.

"You may address the Council." The room was hushed. Everyone wanted to hear what the offworlder was going to say.

"Excellencies, I have a proposition for you."

Sarn-ula looked at Quillen-tok and Phon-seth. They continued to focus their attention on the man from Earth.

"What is this - proposition?"

"The Delfinian fighting force is brave and perseveres beyond measure. I mean no offense to the Delfinian people or the esteemed Water Council." Ridley took a deep breath. "Your fighting force is being depleted by the Trochinids. They are chipping away at your resources, your defenses. What I would propose is to contribute to the war effort in my own way."

"And how would that be?" Sarn-ula looked at Ridley suspiciously, her blue eyes taking on an arctic gaze.

"With the Council's permission, I would like to establish a fighting force within a fighting force. I propose to train a specialized group of fighters, to strike guerilla-style at the heart of the Trochinid war machine, employing a series of hit and run strategies."

"And where will you draw these elite troops from? No Delfinians can be spared from our primary effort. I have doubts that any Delfinian would serve under an offworlder."

Ridley bristled, trying to maintain his composure.

"Well, your Excellency, as a matter of fact, you have a large contingent of willing participants. I would like to recruit the Displaced Work Force for this team."

The murmurings in the crowded room grew. Sarn-ula silenced the chambers with a wave of her hand.

"There are three hundred sixty-eight of the Displaced Work Force living and working in the holds of your ships, mostly performing custodial duties."

"And what makes you think that you can organize them to fight?"

"They lost their homes, too, Excellency. I know they will fight."

"What will you fight with? We have no ships to spare. Our weapons arsenals are dedicated to our own warriors."

"Let me have the derelict freighter we escaped in. I'll have it restored to battle ready status in six weeks."

Azrnoth-zin and Mara-jul stared at Ridley, their mouths open. Azrnoth-zin shook his head, mouthing the word "No."

"That freighter is almost scrap," said a First Order seated next to Sarn-ula. "How will you get it operational?"

"May I present to the Council, Ryk and Tikah," said Ridley. The two Mawhrbahts peered around Ridley's legs. "If it weren't for them, we would have never made it off the *Delfon-quah*. They performed the necessary repairs on the freighter."

"These creatures have been assigned to routine maintenance tasks in the absence of META units," said another First Order.

"Their talents are being wasted," said Ridley. "If you would venture down into the lower portions of your ships, you would find that all systems they maintain have been significantly improved for efficiency. The Mawhrbahts are a race of engineers. Their mechanical capabilities are boundless."

The voices of the observers rose in the room until the chamber was full of noise.

"Silence!" said Sarn-ula. "I will not hesitate to clear these chambers and finish this meeting behind closed doors."

She turned her attention back to Ridley and the two Mawhrbahts. In the strange light of the chambers, the wrinkles on her face stood out like crevasses on a moonscape.

"You claim you can, with the assistance of these - Mawhrbahts, not only restore the freighter to flight condition, but make it battle worthy as well in six weeks?"

"Six weeks, Excellency. All I request is access to any and all scrap materials and armaments that you feel are not salvageable."

"The Water Council will, as is convention, confer in closed chambers. This situation will be taken into consideration and our answer will be forthcoming."

Now it was Quillen-tok's turn to speak. He rose slowly and placed his hands on the table, moving like someone who had been debilitated for a long time. He looked at Ridley and the Mawhrbahts, then to the other members of the Water Council. His gaze came to rest on Sarn-ula.

"I think we owe Ridley an answer to this now. I have witnessed the mechanical ability of the Mawhrbahts. If not for them, we would have perished on the *Delfon-quah*. They enacted repairs to the med-surg unit necessary to provide me needed life support. I believe they can be better utilized for the war effort. We can no longer claim the luxury of time."

Sarn-ula glared at Quillen-tok, then looked to the other members of the Council. "Do all others agree? Should the vote be taken now?"

The six members of the Water Council nodded once.

"Very well." The six joined hands and closed their eyes. Ridley could swear he felt a warm wave wash over him from his position in front of the Council members. As if on cue, all of their eyes opened simultaneously and they released their grips.

"This Council has agreed to your request, Ridley-of-Earth. Four votes to two." The crowd erupted into a clamor of foot stomping and shouting. Ridley looked over to Azrnoth-zin and shrugged. Azrnoth-zin just shook his head.

Sarn-ula raised her hand once more and the crowd went silent. "The Water Council wishes to know how you will select crew members."

"I'll interview them myself, Excellency."

"What criteria will you use?"

"At this time," said Ridley, "I haven't hammered out the details. I plan on forming a crew of the most able, the most ambitious, and the hardest working. All who apply will be given consideration."

Sarn-ula's gaze could have bored a hole through Ridley's skull. "You have six weeks."

CHAPTER EIGHTEEN

Quillen-tok and Phon-seth stared at the crude placard tacked to the bulkhead. It was written in several languages, the only one recognizable to them being the Delfinian characters. Quillen-tok rocked back and forth on his heels as he read through the strange message.

"Why did he not utilize the ship-to-ship com link to convey this message? This seems an inefficient and antiquated means of sending a communication."

"Apparently, he felt that not all of the Displaced Work Force have the ability or desire to interact on the shipwide com link," said Phon-seth. "I understand that he is worried about our monitoring their communications."

"Not very trusting, these terrans." Quillen-tok read over the message once more.

- **LOSE YOUR HOME TO THE TROCHINIDS?**
- **MAD AS HELL, BUT FEEL HELPLESS?**
- **DON'T GET MAD - GET EVEN!**
- **LOOKING FOR QUALIFIED PERSONNEL IN THE**
  FOLLOWING POSITIONS:
      TACTICAL
      WEAPONS
      ENGINEERING
      NAVIGATION
      COMMUNICATION

CULINARY
- **EXPERIENCE PREFERRED BUT ATTITUDE GOES A LONG WAY.**
- **INTERESTED PARTIES SEE RIDLEY, CARGO BAY 17, MENTOR.**
- **LET'S KICK SOME TROCHINID ASS!**
- **WE ARE AN EQUAL OPPORTUNITY EMPLOYER.**

"What do you suppose that last statement means?" said Quillen-tok.

"I do not understand much of the idioms the offworlder speaks. Perhaps you need to ask Azrnoth-zin. It seems he has become the expert on Earth culture."

"This Ridley is turning out to be a most interesting individual." A slight smile etched Quillen-tok's craggy face.

"It has been four weeks since Ridley began recruiting and rebuilding the freighter," said Phon-seth. "He supplies the liaison with only the barest of details. His progress reports are not forthcoming. All he will say is "not bad for a bunch of rookies." We cannot find the term "rookie" in the data banks. He has refused the inspectors entry to the ship. He states that they will be able to go over every inch of the ship only after the work is complete. Sarn-ula does not trust this Ridley."

"See that the security inspectors do not interfere with the project."

"First Order?"

"I do not want unnecessary interruptions impeding their progress," said Quillen-tok. "I will speak with the other members of the Council."

"It will be done." Phon-seth heaved a sigh. "That is not all," he continued. "Recently, there have been reports coming in from all ships concerning the disappearance of certain pieces of equipment. Each item by itself does not amount to much, and most of the missing pieces are either scrap or stored. But when you look at the total number of missing items, from medical supplies to parts utilized for propulsion, a pattern begins to emerge. It is as if some entity is fitting out a ship. Shall I have a security team search the flight deck and freighter?"

Quillen-tok raised a hand. "No, Phon-seth. If anyone asks by whose authority the supplies and equipment have been requisitioned, tell them that I have assumed full responsibility. I want to see this to its conclusion."

Phon-seth noted an odd look in the eyes of the elder Delfinian.

"He has begun training in a form of personal self-defense. Several of our Third, Fourth and Fifth Orders are enrolling in these classes."

Quillen-tok turned away from the bizarre sign. "Phon-seth, I believe it is time we paid a visit to our terran friend and his project."

Sweat ran into Mara-jul's eyes but she dared not wipe it away. The four attackers slowly circled her on the large spongy mat. Each carried a stun stick, the end of which could deliver a painful jolt.

The assailants wore soft helmets, which were equipped with one-way eye visors in order not to reveal their intentions through eye movements. Mara-jul's head moved back and forth in a rhythmical motion that seemed to be disconnected with her body.

One of the attackers lunged at Mara-jul, the stun lance aimed at her chest. She dropped to a crouch and then feinted to one side. As the assailant moved past her, she used his momentum and sent him skidding off the mat.

The second attacker came at her from her blind side. He thrust the stun stick at her throat. Mara-jul's hand came up and blocked the shaft of the stick. At the same time with one leg, she swept the feet out from under attacker number two, disarming him and delivering a zap to the chest. The attacker yelped in pain.

With the stun stick in hand, she faced attacker number three. They parried, the stun sticks discharging every time they connected. The third assailant left his trunk area vulnerable; Mara-jul blocked his thrust and spun. With a deft move she landed a reverse thrust kick to number three's solar plexus. Number three went down to the mat.

Mara-jul rolled out of the way as the stun lance from number four burned into the mat, near her head. She brought the stun stick to bear, only to have it knocked out of the arena. She attempted to roll to her left, but was stopped by another thrust from the stick. She came up and tried to land a kick to the kidney region of the last attacker, but number four blocked her leg with the stun stick and Mara-jul crashed onto her back. The attacker held the stun stick inches from her throat, his breaths coming in near gasps.

"Hold it, hold it," said Ridley walking onto the mat. "Commander, you are very dead. You handled the first three bad guys okay, but you weren't centered when you threw that last kick. You had no momentum from your hip. What have I been telling you?"

"Load the cannon," Mara-jul said between breaths. She stood slowly and put her hands on her knees. Sweat droplets spattered onto the spongy mat.

"Right." Ridley turned to the other onlookers. "People, you need to remember this. All of our power comes from the hips. We have large muscles in our butts for a reason. It's hips and focus. Hips and focus. The idea here is to build a body count on the enemy without getting yourself vaporized or eaten."

Ridley turned to walk away, then launched himself at Mara-jul. She reacted with a side thrust kick and Ridley went down hard on his back, the wind driven from his lungs. She was on top of him instantly, her dagger inches from his throat.

"Now, you are dead." Her eyes blazed fiercely.

She stood up and assisted Ridley to his feet. "Better," he said trying to catch his breath. The crowd gathered around the mat broke into applause. Ridley looked around the crowd, his face taking on a crimson hue.

"Any questions?" Ridley dusted himself off. He looked up to see Quillen-tok and Phon-seth standing just beyond the fringe of the participants and onlookers.

Walking up to where the Delfinian elders stood, Ridley performed the salutary bow and right hand gesture. "Excellency, it is good to see you. How's the leg?"

"Mending, Ridley. That was quite an impressive demonstration Mara-jul provided. This is by your instruction?"

"Yes, sir. The commander is a quick study."

"Where did you learn these techniques? Some of this form of self defense looks vaguely familiar to me."

"I have no memory of this style of combat," said Phon-seth.

"I'm not sure, sir. After my reorganization, my body remembered the movements. Oh, I had a smattering of martial arts instruction back on Earth, but I was never very good at it. In fact, I knew just enough to get the living daylights kicked out of me. This new stuff - well, I can't explain it. I guess it came with the new Ridley."

"This is most disturbing, First Order," said Phon-seth. "I cannot help but wonder what other secrets he keeps from us."

"I have memories of an ancient fighting technique," said Quillen-tok. "It has not been used by our people in a very long time."

"I have no such memories," Phon-seth said indignantly. "That disturbs me greatly."

"The commanders and sub-commanders are picking up the instruction quickly," said Ridley trying to ease away from the topic of his brain.

"Indeed, they are," said Quillen-tok. "How progresses the restoration of the ship?"

Quillen-tok noted that there were at least two dozen Delfinians working on the ship while another two dozen milled about. Everywhere, aliens of all shapes and sizes moved in and out of the transforming freighter, now propped in the center of Cargo Bay 17. The ship rested on a myriad of metal supports while the refit progressed. In many places, large portions of the outer hull were missing, revealing the underlying supporting structures. Beneath was a tangle of conduit and circuitry. Sparks flew off the hull in various places from the tiny engineer's welders.

"It's going about as well as can be expected, Excellency. The hardest part is making parts fit that don't belong in this ship. We've had to resort to a great deal of make-it-up-as-you-go technology. Right now, the outer hull is being reinforced to carry some small shuttles and light fighters."

"Have you completed your crew selection?"

"We're not through them all. I mean - we haven't interviewed all the applicants yet. Some of the Work Force are suspicious of outsiders and, to be frank, have been a little hesitant to throw in with the Delfinians. Originally, this ship was designed to carry a crew of 250. But whoever flew this rig before was a little on the vertically challenged side of the scale. We had to modify bulkheads and airlocks to accommodate some of our own. By the completion of the project, the ship will comfortably hold 146."

Quillen-tok's gaze took in the bow section of the ship. Characters he did not recognize splashed across the nose section. Under the large symbols was the English word:

ZOO

"*Zoo?*" said Quillen-tok, raising an eyebrow at Ridley.

"Uh, yes, sir. A few weeks ago we came out and found someone had tagged the nose of the ship with some type of paint. It was written in Galtaen. It took some doing to get those symbols translated. We were going to whitewash it down, but decided after a while that the name fits."

Mara-jul approached, a towel draped around her neck. She bowed twice before the elder Delfinians. "Excellencies, I am surprised to see you here. Are you feeling well, First Order?"

"Quite well, Commander. I am even more surprised to see you here, Mara-jul. That was a most impressive demonstration you put on moments ago."

"Thank you, First Order. At times it can be very difficult, maintaining that level of concentration. I believe it will improve my reaction time in battle. I have ordered my squadron to undergo the training."

"I notice there is a large number of Delfinians about," said Phon-seth. "Some of them appear to be engaged in working on the ship. I hope their duties are not being neglected."

"I assure the First Order that all of us are here on our own time. If you will check the flight records, you will notice that our efficiency has improved by twenty-one percent. The Mawhrbahts have been most effective in repairing and maintaining our fighters." She cast a hard stare at Phon-seth. "After all, it is for the Delfinian fleet."

"You may continue, Commander," said Quillen-tok. "As long as schedules for patrols and duties are kept."

"Thank you, Excellency."

"I do not suppose Azrnoth-zin would be somewhere about," mused Quillen-tok.

"Oh, yeah. Sure," said Ridley looking toward the *ZOO*. "Last time I saw him, he was up in the cockpit, working on the drive unit. Hey Arn!"

Azrnoth-zin poked his head out from one of the forward hatches, looking irritated at being disturbed. When he recognized the two Delfinian leaders standing next to Mara-jul and Ridley, he tried to extricate himself.

"As you were, Sub-commander," said Quillen-tok. Azrnoth-zin attempted a partial salute, then disappeared down inside the ship.

The older Delfinian turned back to Ridley. "Would it be possible to take a tour of the inside of the ship?"

Ridley fidgeted. "Your Excellency, I know it's a lot to ask, but can you give me two more weeks? Two weeks and I'll give you the grand tour myself. By then we'll be fully manned and fully operational. I'll have a complete ship's manifest for your inspection at that time."

"Very well, Ridley. I look forward to our meeting again in two weeks."

Ridley was glad that a Delfinian week was one and one-third times as long as a week on Earth.

Phon-seth produced a computerized tablet from beneath his flowing robe. "Recently, all ships are reporting missing items from various departments." He handed Ridley the tablet. "Do you recognize any of these items?

Ridley scratched his head as the list scrolled through. "Gee, First Order, no, I don't. But if any of that contraband shows up around here, you can bet I'll get on the horn to security."

Phon-seth eyed Ridley suspiciously. "The Delfinian security force is thorough and relentless. If these items are on this flight deck, they will be recovered."

"Would you excuse us for a moment, First Order?" Quillen-tok said.

"Yes, of course." Perturbed, Phon-seth turned and walked over to a group of milling Delfinians. Once Phon-seth was out of earshot, Quillen-tok addressed Ridley.

"If there is something that you require, contact me on a closed com link. Commander Mara-jul knows the frequency." Turning, he limped after Phon-seth.

A group of Mawhrbahts pushed a large cylindrical device used in the navigational systems in front of Quillen-tok and Phon-seth. Stopping and watching the Mawhrbahts roll the array up a cargo ramp and into the belly of the *ZOO*, Phon-seth said, "I suppose I did not see that, either."

"See what? Come, Phon-seth. I feel a sudden strong desire for a tall vessel of Markanian ale."

Ridley watched as the two Delfinian leaders made their way across the busy cargo bay floor.

"I'll be damned," he said.

CHAPTER NINETEEN

Over the past few weeks, Ridley had come to look forward to Mara-jul's visits to the cargo bay. He found himself checking up on her frequently, sending covert glances in her direction. Several times, Ridley looked up from what he was doing and met Mara-jul's gaze directly. Ridley felt the blood rush to his head and quickly averted his gaze.

Still, the tension between them felt like one of his old climbing ropes, stretched to the breaking point. He worked himself to the point of exhaustion, yet still lay sleepless on his floating platform between shifts, staring at the ceiling.

Ridley rubbed his eyes. The meeting between the Galtaens, Markanians, and the Yhrynen had been stressful. None were used to cooperation and teamwork with alien races. Instead of formulating the best design for the new weapons array aboard the *ZOO*, Ridley had acted more as a referee to keep the three parties talking. He hoped that by providing the groups with a general idea, they would come together and hammer out the details. Now it looked like he was going to have to walk them through the entire process.

To look at the Yhrynen, one would not suspect that, at one time, Yhrynenian armies were the scourge of their system. Their delicate pinkish-gray bodies gave the appearance of placidity, not ferocity. Ridley marveled at Kelun's knowledge of weapons systems and battle tactics. He could understand why the former inhabitants of Yhrys were so formidable. Until they met the Trochinids.

Unlike the Yhrynen, the Galtaen maintained an erect posture with the greatest of difficulty. Galtaen ships were designed so that all control functions could be set up on the floor. Their large heads were encased in a bony skull that was one-third the size of their bodies. Huge band-like strap muscles attached the base of their skulls to the bony plates of their shoulders, creating a shroud-like appearance. They constantly complained to Ridley that all instrumentation on the ship was designed for bipedal members of the Displaced Work Force. They were not used to working in the vertical world. Based on their bizarre anatomy, Ridley wondered if chiropractic could have been the most profitable venture on Galtar.

On the Markanian homeworld, the inhabitants were adapted to an arboreal existence, their arms evolved to move quickly through a dense canopy or a busy metropolitan superstructure. Brightly colored with yellow bodies and heads and purple appendages, the legs were considerably shorter than the arms and a prehensile tail enabled them to sleep upside down. More reptilian than primate in appearance, Ridley thought the sleeping arrangements for the Markanians could present some logistical problems on the *ZOO.*

Unable to sleep, Ridley went back down to cargo bay 17 and looked over the weapons schematics one more time. He needed to find a point of common ground between the three arguing groups soon. They were less than two weeks away from deadline. Ridley did not fancy another meeting with Sarn-ula.

Work continued around the clock on the *ZOO.* Everyone drew six-hour shifts, working their schedule around their regular duties. Presently, a skeleton crew of Mawhrbahts was working on one of the nacelles.

Walking toward the stern of the metamorphosing freighter, Ridley examined the aft weapons placements once more. He stopped to admire a newly refurbished phase cannon. The weapon, like the rest of the ship, wasn't pretty, but was an amazing feat of Mawhrbaht engineering and innovation.

A sound behind him caught his attention. Turning, he saw Azrnoth-zin approaching.

"How's it going?" said Azrnoth-zin. "I thought I would find you still down here. META IV has informed me that you have developed some erratic sleep patterns."

Ridley barely noticed Azrnoth-zin's speech any longer. His use of Earth idioms and slang were nearly flawless. He also noticed that Azrnoth-zin spent hours regaling the other Delfinians about the strange, but unique language and customs of Earth. Ridley found it interesting that there was always a contingent of Delfinian females present when Azrnoth-zin performed Earth talk.

"I can't believe this shit," said Ridley, sitting down and leaning back on a stack of plasma cylinders. "I'm no arbitrator. All I want to do is get this bloody piece of space junk ready. But, no-o-o-o. Instead, I get to play referee to a group of aliens that would rather vaporize each other when the first back is turned."

"Negotiations between the Galtaens, Markanians, and the Yhrynen are not proceeding according to plan?" said Azrnoth-zin, flopping down beside him, while perusing the schematics of the *ZOO's* drive engines on a hand-held computer.

"They'd just as soon blast each other before they sit down at a negotiating table. Kelun complains the Markanians know nothing of advanced weapons technology and the Markanians think Kelun shouldn't be allowed to have so much input, since he's the only Yhrynen around. And the goddamn Galteans are just arbitrary. It's like trying to negotiate with a bucketful of red ants."

Azrnoth-zin ceased his calculations, caught up in some thought. His eyebrows raising in a sudden revelation, he keyed in more information to the pad.

"No one said being the leader of the Displaced Work Force would be easy," he said absent-mindedly.

"Thanks for the sympathy, Arn. This was your damn idea."

Azrnoth-zin smiled. "No thanks are necessary, Ridley."

"I'm beginning to worry that we won't make the deadline in two weeks. I do not look forward to Sarn-ula's looks of disdain, nor her disparaging comments about the inbred weakness of offworlders."

"Perhaps you should try a different approach." Azrnoth-zin said distractedly, while his slender, webbed fingers flew over the keypad.

"Like what? Since when have you taken up politics?"

The Delfinian turned his head and looked at his terran friend. "Ridley, I have a lifetime of exposure to alien races. Sometimes, it is necessary to assert your superiority."

"That may work for you Delfinians, but it doesn't fly here in the cargo bay. I said equal opportunity and that's the way it goes."

"You do not understand. The Galtaens, Markanians and the Yhrynen need you to delegate to them what your wishes are. I do not think they are races that have ever cooperated with other life forms before. They respect you. They will listen to what you dictate."

"That simple, huh? Just tell them, this is how it is?"

"Try it. You may surprise yourself."

Ridley sighed heavily. "Do you think this whole idea is nuts, Arn?"

"When you first proposed it to the Water Council with most of the high ranking Delfinians also gathered in the room, I thought we would be laughed out of the chamber. And as you have noticed, Delfinians are not quick to laugh. I too, had my doubts. But now, as I look around and see what we have accomplished in four weeks, I believe this could work. Even among many of my fellow Delfinians, I notice a change. They appear. . . hopeful. And that is something I have not seen in a very long time."

"I hope they're not disappointed by the outcome," said Ridley.

"I have put in a request to Mara-jul," said Azrnoth-zin. "I have asked that I be permanently assigned to this unit as a tactical fighter pilot."

"What did she say?"

"She said she would confer with Quillen-tok. I suppose I should ask your permission as well."

"Nope. I don't want a tactical fighter pilot."

Azrnoth-zin shot Ridley a stunned look.

"I need a pilot, first seat, for the *ZOO*, Arn. And that's you."

"Ridley, this is your project. You should be first seat."

"Look. Sure I can fly that thing, but I can't fly it with the style that you have. I'll never be the pilot that you are. Second seat suits me just fine."

"The Water Council may disagree with your choice."

"Let them. The bottom line is I want what's best for the *ZOO*. They can't bitch if your kill ratio goes up, no matter which boat you're on."

Azrnoth-zin contemplated this for several moments. "I would be honored to serve aboard the *ZOO*."

"Another thing. I've had some requests from some Delfinian officers and warriors. Some of them want to sign on. What do you think the Water Council would say to that?"

"Which officers?"

"Kirin-rah, the young sub-commander. Seventh Order, I think. You remember her from the *Delfon-quah?* She's green, but she's got *chutzpah*. Also Duhon-yar and Tran-dol from the *Mentor*."

"This is getting more and more interesting each day," said Azrnoth-zin, bemused. "I am not surprised. I have noticed over the past weeks, many of the Delfinians speak of you with great respect. Which is something not easily achieved."

"For an offworlder, you mean?" Ridley grinned.

"That is not what I was going to say."

"Speaking of going to say. I've been meaning to ask you. Back there on the *Delfon-quah*, when we were trying to find where you were holed up, I could swear I heard your voice inside my head, giving me directions to the security section. Now what's that all about?"

Azrnoth-zin looked at Ridley, this time a mixture of surprise and concern lining his face. "You received my thoughts?"

"Yeah. Loud and clear. What does that mean?"

"It means that you will speak to no one else of this. If the Water Council finds out that you are a receptor, there is no telling what action they will take."

Now it was Ridley's turn to contemplate this new twist. After several moments of silence, Azrnoth-zin spoke again.

"Four weeks ago, when we were honored at the ceremony, you were acting strangely. Was someone attempting an unsolicited mind link with you?"

Ridley turned to look at Azrnoth-zin, his eyebrows raised.

"How did you know that?"

"You appeared outwardly frightened, like you had just experienced unpleasant images in your mind. I believe you call them nightmares. It is not dissimilar to the looks on Delfinian children when they are learning the mind-water connection."

Ridley drew a deep breath, closed his eyes and leaned back against the cylinders once more. For a moment, Azrnoth-zin thought Ridley had decided to avoid answering the question by falling asleep.

"Sarn-ula."

"What did you say?" Azrnoth-zin sat up abruptly.

"Sarn-ula's been attempting to dig through the dusty attic of my mind. She's looking for something, but I'm damned if I know what it is."

"How long has this been going on?"

"Since I got here. I think she set me up for a rough time with the Drolongs."

Azrnoth-zin grew angry. "We must bring this before Quillen-tok and the other members of the Water Council. Psychic assault on another individual is a punishable offense."

"Forget it, Arn. There's too much riding on this project."

"But they must be told!"

"It stays between you and me. You need to promise me you won't tell anyone else."

Azrnoth-zin glared across the cargo bay floor, his webbed hands alternatingly clenching and unclenching.

"As you wish. I will abide by your request."

"Besides," said Ridley, "I think I finally figured out how to keep Sarn-ula out of my head."

Azrnoth-zin was suspicious. "How did you manage to do that?"

Azrnoth-zin thought he saw Ridley's face turn a slight reddish hue.

"Well, if you must know, whenever she tries to burrow into my head, I just kind of form an image of her in my mind's eye."

Azrnoth-zin looked at Ridley suspiciously. "And that stops her? What kind of image?"

"A naked image."

"What?"

"I'm not proud of it, okay? But it was the best I could come up with at the time."

Azrnoth-zin shook his head slowly. "In your mind, you imagine Sarn-ula naked."

"Okay, so I'm an intergalactic perv. At least she's staying out of my head for the time being."

Ridley and Azrnoth-zin sat staring ahead for several moments. "That is most disagreeable," Azrnoth-zin said finally.

"Tell me about it."

A strange sound emanated from Azrnoth-zin's chest. Ridley thought at first the alien was wheezing. Only when he recognized the transformation to that high-pitched Delfinian sound he remembered from the Dutchman's cabin, did Ridley realize that Azrnoth-zin was caught up in a fit of uncontrollable laughter.

"That's not funny, Arn."

Azrnoth-zin rolled off the cylinders, clutching his stomach. In the next moment, Ridley was laughing as hard as Azrnoth-zin. So loud were their carryings on, the Mawhrbahts working on the scaffolding above them looked at the Terran and the Delfinian with a mixture of apprehension and annoyance.

When Ridley looked up, he noticed that Azrnoth-zin's eyes were producing a thick, viscous fluid at the corners. His eyes appeared to be clouded over. Azrnoth-zin dabbed at his eyes and rubbed the sticky substance between his fingertips as if he hadn't experienced tears before. The Delfinian broke into fresh gales of laughter.

"Ridley, I'm worried about you. I think you have been among the Displaced Work Force for too long."

After a time, the two were able to return to their original positions leaning against the plasma cylinders. Azrnoth-zin finished his calculations, set the small computer down, leaned back and closed his eyes.

"You know who surprised the hell out of me?" said Ridley. "Old Quillen-tok. Who'd have figured he would be the one to get Sarn-ula's flunkies off our backs?"

"I have known Quillen-tok a very long time," said Azrnoth-zin. "His reputation for savagery in battle is renowned among Delfinians. But he is a fair leader and believes in the People. Something he saw in you, Ridley, gave him cause to trust you and this project."

"Well, it sure helps to have connections in high places."

"Do not become complacent with Quillen-tok, my friend. He can mete out as severe a punishment as any other member of the Water Council."

"Don't worry. The last thing I want to do is alienate the only supporter for our project."

"How is Mara-jul?" Azrnoth-zin said, suddenly changing the subject.

"Now, what's that supposed to mean?"

"Ridley, you may be an alien species, but you are not that difficult to figure out. I have observed, as have others, how you look at her. I have also noticed her looking at you in a similar fashion."

"Look, Arn, I assure you that -."

"Mara-jul and I have known each other since our early instruction in Academy. She was Resar-dan's closest friend. I never cared that much for Mara-jul's choice in mates. I thought it was a poor match. Still, I shared her grief as she did mine when our mates were killed."

"I don't know what the hell I'm thinking. Delfinians don't mix with other races. It seems to be one of your society's greatest taboos. Even if we could get through all the other stuff, like figuring out how to bridge the space-time communication gap, we'd have no shot in front of the Water Council."

"You don't know unless you try," said Azrnoth-zin. "Besides, I would think her image is preferrable to that of Sarn-ula."

Ridley turned his gaze on Azrnoth-zin, regarding him through squinted eyes. "You're enjoying this, aren't you? One more burr to put under the Water Council's robes."

"No one has ever attempted to develop a relationship with an off-world species. The possibilities are endless."

Ridley turned back to watch four Mawhrbahts push a floating transport platform loaded with armaments across the cargo bay floor. "It's a moot point anyway. Every time I get around her, I just wind up pissing her off. And I've already told you about my track record on Earth."

"She too does not know how to proceed. I think if you are both interested enough in each other, none of the other things will matter."

"She has a lot more to lose than I do."

"We all stand to lose everything if things do not change. My people are a dying race. We are systematically exterminating ourselves to fight a pointless war. Perhaps it is time to shed the ways of the old and focus on rejuvenating our society. Even though I regretted bringing you here initially, I have witnessed the changes you have effected not only with the Displaced Work Force, but with the People as well."

"I still can't get it out of my head, Arn. That someday in the not-too-distant future, the Trochinids are going to be knocking on Earth's door. That thought scares the hell out of me."

"Would you go back now - if you could?"

"I don't know. Something inside my head tells me I need to see this through to the end. Don't ask me why. It's just a premonition, just beyond my conscious mind that I can't quite figure out."

"If things turn for the worse, I will make sure that you get back to your homeworld. That, I promise you."

They sat for several minutes, each absorbed in their thoughts. Ridley broke the silence by chuckling softly.

"What do you find humorous?" said Azrnoth-zin.

"It's funny," said Ridley. "I always fantasized about falling in love with the girl next door."

"And?"

"I never figured I'd fall for the girl from a distant galaxy. Hands down, I think this could take the prize for most geographically undesirable relationship."

Azrnoth-zin pondered this for a moment. "Yes. This relationship could be challenging in many ways."

CHAPTER TWENTY

Mara-jul placed her hand on the security screen outside the Water Council's chambers. Another sensor at eye level scanned her retina and the chamber door slid open with a soft hiss. Mara-jul entered the dimly lit room and allowed her eyes to adjust to the darkness.

The only light present emanated from the seven large fluid filled tubes arranged vertically in a semi-circle in the center of the chamber. A series of steps wound their way around the cylinders to a small platform on top. The light source did not appear to come from one location, but bathed each cylinder in a soft, yet pervasive bluish cast. Although she had been here many times before, the sight of the mind-link tubes still sent a shiver down her spine. Here was the seat of the Delfinian Fleet and for all intents and purposes, the governing body of Delfinus.

A figure stepped out of the veil of darkness from behind one of the cylinders and approached Mara-jul. Shrouded in long, flowing robes and partially hidden in shadow, the silhouette was unmistakable. Sarn-ula appeared to float across the floor.

"Ah, welcome Third Order Mara-jul," said the ancient Delfinian. "Come and sit with an old woman." She motioned Mara-jul toward the elliptically shaped table in front of the Water-link cylinders. Mara-jul sat uneasily.

"You wish to speak with me, First Order?"

Mara-jul had never been comfortable in the presence of Sarn-ula. The supreme head of the Water Council wielded a great deal of power and had no misgivings about letting the those around her know who had the final say in matters of state.

"Yes, my child. I have not had the opportunity to speak with you since the Ceremony of Honor. How are you faring?"

Mara-jul did not like the direction the conversation was going. Never before had the Delfinian First Order asked about her well being.

"I am well, First Order."

"Good." The old Delfinian's arctic blue eyes shone in the low light. "I was . . . concerned for you after the loss of the *Delfon-quah* and so many of those warriors under your command."

Mara-jul blinked, her only response to the less than subtle inference about her dereliction of duty. The light in the room accentuated the thousand wrinkles on Sarn-ula's face, giving her the countenance of a twisted mask.

"I am in a better position now to serve the Delfinian people," said Mara-jul, maintaining her composure.

"You were meant for greater things than a mere commander of a light fighter squadron," spoke the old woman. "Quillen-tok has recommended to me and the other members of the Council that you would be the next logical choice for ascension to a seat on the Water Council. The Council is faced with choosing a new First Order, after the death of Bahrin-fahl." Sarn-ula narrowed her gaze at Mara-jul. "Are you the one to take his place?"

"It would be the highest of honors, First Order. Many pardons, but I do not think I am ready."

The Delfinian elder waved a robed arm dismissively. "To take a seat on the Water Council means all of your personal desires and agendas are left behind. To serve the Delfinian people is your primary directive. Are you ready for that?"

"I will serve to the best of my ability, First Order."

Sarn-ula turned and walked toward the nearest water cylinder, her cylinder, and faced the blue-green column of liquid. Her frail figure was outlined by the gently swirling water, giving Mara-jul the perception that the old woman was floating through liquid space. After a prolonged pause, Sarn-ula spoke.

"Are you aware of the insurrections that are taking place among our People with regular occurrence?"

"I have heard of dissension among the warriors," said Mara-jul cautiously. "Those that have deserted the fleet have been captured and subsequently punished."

Sarn-ula turned back to face Mara-jul. "I have great concerns about the offworlder, this Ridley. The dessertions have increased since he arrived among the People"

"I have not heard of this, First Order."

"This human cannot be trusted. I believe he will be the cause of more insurrection among the People. You can see yourself the influence that he wields with that band of rabble which populate the holds of our ships."

"Ridley is organizing the Displaced Work Force to help in the war effort. I do not believe he is planning any insurrection."

"That is where you can, once again, prove your loyalty to this Council and the Delfinian People. I wish for you to get next to this Ridley-human. Find out his motives. Learn his mind. Use whatever means necessary to expose him."

"You want me to spy on Ridley?"

"It is no secret that the offworlder holds you in high esteem. If his intentions are benign, then there is nothing to worry about. But if he was brought here to infiltrate our society, to cause unrest or worse, then think of what that could mean to the people of Delfinus."

"But, Quillen-tok believes -."

"Quillen-tok is a sentimental old fool!" Sarn-ula said sharply. "He yearns for days that are long since past. You will speak of this to no one, especially Quillen-tok."

"Respectfully, First Order," said Mara-jul. "I do not feel comfortable carrying out this request."

Sarn-ula's look was predatory. "You are a brilliant leader and warrior, Mara-jul. However, after losing a battle cruiser to the Swarm, perhaps you are losing your edge. If it had not been for Quillen-tok, the verdict may have been reversed. Instead of being honored by the Council, you could be indicted for negligence and held responsible for the death of thousands."

185

"I was exonerated by the Council," Mara-jul replied, her anger evident even through the steadiness of her voice.

"One never knows if new, incriminating evidence may turn up."

Mara-jul heard the veiled threat, yet Sarn-ula's face remained impassive.

"Think of your future as a commander and a First Order on the Water Council," said Sarn-ula. "What is this offworlder to you that you would risk such a bright future?"

None of us have any future, Mara-jul thought, but regretted it immediately. The elderly First Order glared at Mara-jul, indicating she had received her unshielded thought.

"The offworlder means nothing to me, First Order,"

"Then, you will have no difficulty monitoring his activities and intentions. It should prove to be a simple matter. Humans are a primitive species. Think of it as your patriotic duty to the Fleet and the Delfinian People."

Mara-jul looked away, staring at the mind-link tubes.

"I will do as you wish," she replied. "But I feel no honor or sense of patriotic pride in this undertaking."

CHAPTER TWENTY-ONE

Cargo bay seventeen could not hold any more occupants. Most if not all of the Displaced Work Force were present as well as any Delfinian not pulling reconnaissance or watch duty. The two groups mingled freely around the *ZOO*. No one was allowed inside until after the Water Council had performed its inspection.

Ridley was not comfortable in the gray Delfinian uniform. The strange fibers itched and out of nervousness, he found himself sweating more than usual. The collar felt constraining and he wanted to leave it open. The synthetic, knee length boots pinched his feet. No wonder the Delfinians did not laugh much. He couldn't wait to get out into space and change into comfortable clothes.

Looking at the *ZOO*, Ridley could hardly believe the transformation in the derelict freighter. Although still possessing a cylindrical body, stabilizers now curved outward, their smooth lines giving the *ZOO* the appearance of a gigantic manta ray. Since a substantial amount of the metal alloys were salvaged materials, the skin of the refurbished ship varied in a patchwork of silver and coppery hues. The Mawhrbahts had worked a minor miracle. Gun ports were exposed for all to see. The command center's blast shields were down, revealing a large viewport in the blunt nose section. Technicians from the Displaced Work Force moved freely in and out of the cargo hatches and loading ramp, making final adjustments and delivering last minute ordnance.

Mara-jul and Azrnoth-zin strode up to where Ridley stood. Both of them were in the Delfinian uniforms befitting their ranks.

"The ship is ready," said Mara-jul. "Sub-commander Kirin-rah has called the crew to order."

"There was a time that I didn't think we were going to make it," said Ridley, admiring the ship.

"I did not think this undertaking was possible either," said Mara-jul. "You have surprised many here, including me."

"Well, it ain't over yet. We still have to go through a shakedown flight. Am I to understand that we will be monitored by the fleet during the demonstration *and* during our first mission?"

"That is correct," said Azrnoth-zin. "Sarn-ula's insistence."

"Of course," said Ridley. "Any word on your request to join the *ZOO* crew, Arn?"

"I understand the Water Council has been conferring on this matter prior to the inspection. I suspect we will know soon."

"I have sent my recommendation for Azrnoth-zin to be a part of this crew," said Mara-jul. "I believe the Council will approve."

"We'd better queue up with the others," said Ridley. "It's almost showtime."

Azrnoth-zin noticed the Galtaens, Markanians and the Yhrynen, Kelun, standing next to each other in formation. They were discussing something but without that air of animosity that was always present in prior exchanges.

"So, what did you say to them?" Azrnoth-zin said.

"I just did what you told me," said Ridley. "I told them it was my way or the highway. I was amazed to see how fast they could cooperate."

No sooner had they found their place in the lineup when the atmosphere suddenly changed in the cargo bay. All conversation died as the Water Council was led into the great room by twelve of the elite Delfinian security team. The stern looking guards moved with an air of arrogant precision.

"They were chosen to guard the Water Council because they are the quickest, deadliest Delfinian warriors in the fleet," said Mara-jul.

"Oh yeah?" said Ridley. "They haven't met up with you and the others yet." Ridley smiled as he watched the approaching entourage.

Mara-jul looked at Ridley, waiting to see if he was speaking in the manner of humor which she was barely able to grasp. Satisfied that Ridley was not making a fabrication, she turned her gaze back to the procession.

Behind the security team walked Sarn-ula with Quillen-tok keeping stride with her. He was flanked by Phon-seth with the other Council members falling in behind. All wore the impressive white robes that flowed along the floor.

The Displaced Work Force snapped to attention as the Water Council passed in front of them. The procession stopped in front of Mara-jul, Ridley, and Azrnoth-zin. All three of them bowed deeply to the council members and gave the salutary right hand gesture. Ridley noticed a slight scowl cross the face of Sarn-ula.

She spoke. "It appears you have completed your task. The Water Council is impressed by your perseverance." She gazed at the transformed ship, then turned back and looked directly at Ridley. "Remarkable. I still find it hard to believe that this entire restoration was carried out using only cast off equipment and materials."

"Thank you, Excellency." Ridley did not falter from her hard stare. "As I said before, the Mawhrbahts are engineers without equal."

"Yes, quite remarkable. Can we now, at last, be granted a tour of the inside of the ship?"

"Absolutely, First Order. I will give you the grand tour myself."

Sarn-ula and the other members of the Council stepped off the ramp and once again were standing on the flight deck floor. Ridley, Mara-jul, and Azrnoth-zin followed behind the security team. During the inspection, Ridley held his breath more than once when the delegation would stop and inspect a particular piece of equipment or weapons placement. Once, Ridley turned to observe Phon-seth who had a visible scowl on his face after he recognized a part of the holo-emitter, which had recently disappeared from his quarters. Still, the First Order said nothing.

"Well done, Ridley," said Quillen-tok. "It seems you and your team have not only reconfigured the freighter, but your crew appears to be adequately staffed as well."

"I assure you, First Order, they are much more than adequate."

"We will see," said Sarn-ula. "They have not been tested in a combat situation yet. Only when the battle is joined will we witness the true effectiveness of your training."

"Excellency, may I ask a question?"

"Proceed."

"About the transfers -."

"Yes, yes." Sarn-ula waved a hand in dismissal. "Against my better judgement, the Water Council has approved Azrnoth-zin's transfer to the *ZOO*. Incidentally, Ridley, you are now a representative of the Delfinian fleet. I want you to find a more suitable name for your ship."

"Thank you, Excellency. I'll start working on that after our shakedown flight."

Sarn-ula turned to Mara-jul. "Commander, your request has also been granted. Quillen-tok and Phon-seth had a difficult time in convincing me and the rest of the Council to grant you away status. You will pick the elite warriors from your squadron and accompany this assemblage of . . . sympathizers, through their first mission. I want a first hand account of their behavior when the enemy is engaged."

"It will be done, First Order," said Mara-jul.

"As for the others," said Sarn-ula. "Seventh Order Kirin-rah, Ninth Order Tran-dol, and Tenth-Order Duhon-yar are denied transfer status. They are needed in other functions at this time. Once the initial demonstration flight is complete, they will be reassigned to their former units."

"But, First Order, they have incorporated into the crew quite well. Their functions are necessary for our operation," said Ridley.

"Their functions are required elsewhere," Sarn-ula snapped. "Do not test my patience, Ridley. It is only under the lightest veil of acceptance that are you allowed to proceed at all."

"I seek the First Order's forgiveness," Ridley said, feeling the heat at his temples. "I did not mean to speak out of turn."

"You will be monitored by the Water Council on your mission. We will then determine if your band of volunteers are worthy to fight along side the Delfinian fleet."

"We will not disappoint you, Excellency."

Sarn-ula leaned in close and spoke in a low tone. "Be sure that you do not, Terran."

The Water Council, flanked by the security elite moved across the flight deck floor and filed through the airlock. No sooner had they left than a team of metallics carrying sensory equipment came through the crowd and moved up the ramp into the ship.

"Well, it looks like Big Brother will be riding along with us," Ridley said.

"Very diplomatic," said Mara-jul. "You went from a position of honor to contempt in less than five minutes. How do you do it, Ridley?"

"Call it a gift."

The test flight was considered a success. The *ZOO* deftly performed a series of maneuvers based on simulator programs supplied by members of the Water Council. Small target drones were released to simulate Trochinid fighters. Several larger frigates assumed battle positions and attempted to outflank the refurbished freighter. Even Sarn-ula was forced to admit the *ZOO* performed beyond the Council's expectations. But, she reminded Quillen-tok, it was only an exercise. Things were different in a real battle.

Upon entering the enlarged cockpit after the final meeting with the Water Council, Mara-jul noticed Kelun's delicate neck and head curved over a small console studying a readout on the *ZOO*'s weapon readiness. In another corner of the cockpit, nestled against the bulkhead was Trahg, the Galtaen navigational officer, inputting jump routes. Although the console was raised to the levels of the others in the command center, a special chair had been implemented to accommodate Trahg's unique posture.

Ridley sat in the second command seat next to Azrnoth-zin. They were poring over the readouts from the *ZOO*'s drive.

"Ryk said he could give us QS-20," said Azrnoth-zin. "Peak speed during the demonstration was no greater then QS-18."

"They're working on it. By the time we reach the Syntha system, the Mawhrbahts will have this box o' bolts flying faster than anything else in the Trochinid or Delfinian fleet," said Ridley.

Mara-jul sat in the third command chair. Ridley started to stand up to relinquish his seat, but she waved him off.

"You and Azrnoth-zin belong in those seats," she said.

"But you outrank us both, Commander," said Ridley.

"I am here to provide fighter support and to report back to the Water Council regarding the performance of this ship during a combat situation."

Trahg punched a series of coordinates into the computer relay on his adapted console.

"So, Commander, what do you think the Water Council thought of our shakedown demonstration?" said Ridley.

"I have received no feedback from them as of yet."

"I got the feeling they were not real impressed," said Ridley. "Of course, flying a few maneuvers and blasting a couple of pieces of space junk out of the sky wasn't something that would impress that bunch."

"I believe you are right, Ridley. The true test of this ship and crew will come when we engage the enemy."

Azrnoth-zin looked up from his calculations. "I've got it. Based on our long-range scanners, there appears to be a contingent of Trochinid battle cruisers located around the fourth planet of the Syntha system. The planet appears to be in the final stages of processing." He transferred the coordinates over to Trahg's astrometrics computer.

"That means they're going to be too busy to pay a lot of attention to us. As good a place as any to give them a kick in the ass."

Trahg looked up from the coordinates that began scrolling across the blue screen. Even though the Galtean's extremities were clumsy in appearance, resembling cloven hooves more than hands, the dexterity was remarkable as they moved across the pad.

"Commander, I believe I can save us twenty-two hours of flight time," said Trahg. "if we can reach these jump coordinates within fourteen hours."

"Good. Recalibrate to new coordinates."

Azrnoth-zin memorized the new numbers on his screen. He looked out the cockpit window, then checked the visual sensors one more time before activating the *ZOO's* launch sequence.

Are all ground personnel clear?"

"Clear for takeoff," replied Trahg.

Ridley felt the vibration deep within as the star drive engines came to life and powered up. He remembered how exhilarated he felt as the remodeled *ZOO* went through the exercise at speeds he would never have dreamed of months ago. The ship shuddered as the engines' force increased. Ridley felt the *ZOO* lift gently off the deck of Cargo Bay 17.

"Ion shields have been deactivated," stated Mara-jul.

The newly outfitted ship moved out of the landing bay and into the darkness. Ridley gazed out the blast window and marveled at the number of stars. Employing thrusters, the *ZOO* moved away from the *MENTOR*.

"Ridley," said Azrnoth-zin. "We must have those drives at maximum output."

"Don't worry, Arn. Ryk and Tikah will have it wired by the time we get to Syntha. Commander, are your people ready?"

"They await your final briefing and review of the assault plan. At this time, Ridley, it is no longer necessary to continue to address me formally. You may call me Mara-jul."

"Okay, Commander Mara-jul." Ridley was grinning. For the first time, Mara-jul smiled back. Ridley thought he was going to fuse into the seat.

"I must say that I was impressed with the new weapons array," said Mara-jul. She nodded toward Kelun. "The combined technology of the Yhrynen, Galtaen, and the Mawhrbahts have produced a formidable arsenal."

"Thank you, Commander," said Kelun. "I look forward to turning the array on our enemy."

"If you think that's something, wait till you see what they're cooking up for us in the way of personal assault weapons. We're all about to become very dangerous," said Ridley.

"I am still curious why Quillen-tok is supporting this project," said Mara-jul. "Azrnoth-zin, what do you think?"

"I think Quillen-tok is as tired of the war as we are. I believe that he knows the Delfinian forces cannot go on much longer. He sees this as a chance to change the course of the war. He has seen the change in the People."

"I am curious, Ridley. Did you say anything in particular to convince him to lend his support to this endeavor?" Mara-jul said.

"No. I said nothing to him. Maybe he just read my mind."

"I doubt that very much," said Mara-jul. "Unless he would be interested in a vacuum." Now, it was her turn to grin. Azrnoth-zin stared at Mara-jul, then broke into a high pitched laugh.

"I think I liked you better when you were just body slamming me to the mat," Ridley said, feigning disgust.

Mara-jul looked at Azrnoth-zin. "This humor thing. It is not so difficult."

"She learns quickly," said Azrnoth-zin.

"I guess so," replied Ridley. "What else is Azrnoth-zin teaching you?"

"I have been studying the data logs from the *Kren-dahl*. Azrnoth-zin is filling in the missing information. This concept in your language you refer to as slang, is difficult for me to grasp."

"It was probably a bad idea for Azrnoth-zin to pick up some of the idiomatic phrases first," said Ridley. "That's my fault. Stick to the proper English for now. That's hard enough as it is."

"I am finding the study of Earth's cultures fascinating. I have never taken the time to study another race in depth."

"Remember, Mara-jul. Azrnoth-zin's version of Earth is somewhat skewed, given the company he was keeping during his visit there."

"Do you mean that you are not representative of your species?"

"Well, I am a Caucasian or white person. Collectively, we make up less than a quarter of Earth's population. I'd bet the cultures of Earth are as diverse as any planet you may have encountered in your travels through space."

"That is correct, Mara-jul," said Azrnoth-zin. "Earth culture is rich and multi-layered. We could learn much from the Terrans."

"I am curious about the food there. The data logs speak of strange and wondrous sensations on the tongue and in the nostrils."

Ridley laughed. "Hey, Arn. Do you think Mara-jul would like Mexican food?"

"I don't know. Perhaps, if she has a mind for a different type of adventure."

Kelun, who was up until now engrossed in his calculations, looked up and spoke in his soft, lilting voice. "I look forward to sampling this Mexican food as well, Ridley."

"Well, based on your anatomy, Kelun, we may have to make a few modifications. But we'll get a reasonable facsimile of some chicken enchiladas for you to try. At any rate, it beats raw Trimeria any day."

The long necked alien nodded. Over in the navigational seat, Trahg spoke up in a guttural, rasping voice. "First jump in two hours, fifteen minutes, forty seconds. Twenty-nine hours until we reach the outskirts of the Syntha system."

The pitch of the SD engines increased. Ridley braced himself in his padded chair. Suddenly, the *ZOO* shot forward and disappeared into the vacuum of space.

CHAPTER TWENTY-TWO

The Trochinid battle cruiser moved slowly through the floating debris field, scanning for salvage. After the initial engagement of Synthas Prime, space all around the dead planet was a vast suspended junkyard of ruined ships and metal fragments. The Trochinid ship was to perform one last scan before joining up with the already departed assault force.

The huge ship detected the odd shaped derelict freighter floating in space only on a final sweep. It seemed strange that the lifeless freighter was still intact at all. The parts may be useful. The cruiser adjusted its course to intercept the disabled ship from above. Once the ship assumed a position over the disabled freighter, a tractor beam was activated and began to draw the salvaged freighter into the large, central opening located underneath the great ship.

The Trochinids operating the controls were so preoccupied with manipulating the freighter they did not notice the power signatures from a dozen light fighters flare on. Only too late, did the Trochinid command center realize that the fighters had been lying in wait, disguised as pieces of space flotsam. Like angry hornets, the fighters swarmed over the Trochinid cruiser.

Inside the *ZOO,* Azrnoth-zin and Ridley sat in the dimmed blue light of the command center. Kelun and Trahg stood ready at their stations. The navigational computations were input, the weapons sequences keyed in. All eyes were on the immense Trochinid cruiser, which filled the view screen.

"Just a little bit closer," said Azrnoth-zin as he watched the great ship looming overhead.

"They get much closer and we'll be able to see what they had for breakfast," said Ridley.

"Commander Mara-jul's squadron has engaged the Trochinid ship," said Kelun. "The Trochinid fighters are powering up. Their shields have been activated."

"Are we inside the shield?" said Ridley.

"Yes.

"Activating all ship-wide systems. Charge weapons to full power," Ridley stated.

"Weapons are charged and ready," said Kelun.

"Commander Mara-jul reports heavy resistance from all ports," replied Trahg.

"Tell them to put some distance between themselves and the cruiser. Fast!" said Ridley.

"They're breaking off the attack now," said Trahg.

Ridley checked the readouts one last time. "It's now or never, boys."

"Fire weapons!" said Azrnoth-zin. "Pulse cannons to full burst."

A concentrated burst of energy arced into the belly of the Trochinid cruiser. The tractor beam was severed as a series of explosions rocked the inside of the ship. The *ZOO* was jolted by the first series of explosions. Ridley grabbed hold of the console to steady himself. Loose objects flew around the command center as the ship pitched violently.

"Get us out of here, Arn!"

Azrnoth-zin actuated the maximum drive sequence. The *ZOO* bucked, then shot away from the cruiser just as the belly of the Trochinid warship exploded outward.

Through the rear visual scanners, Ridley could see the Trochinid ship begin to pitch to starboard and descend toward the planet's surface. Another explosion tore the ship in half. A squadron of fighters that had just lifted off from the ship, were engulfed in the maelstrom, many tiny explosions like afterburners from a fireworks display.

Ridley picked up the com link. "*ZOO* to Skeeters. Are you receiving this transmission?"

"We receive loud and clear," Mara-jul's voice came over the com. "That was a beautiful sight. Nice shooting."

"Thanks for the cover. Anyone hurt?"

"No injuries reported. Two of the fighters sustained damage. I am afraid they are no longer spaceworthy."

"Can they get back to the *ZOO* under power?"

"Yes, we can." It was the voice of Kirin-rah. "Do not expect a smooth docking."

"Nice job, you all. Hurry up and get back here so we can go home." Ridley switched the com link to the *ZOO*'s general bandwidth. "Great work, you guys. Any damages down there?"

A litany of barks and chirps emanated from the com system.

Ridley turned to Azrnoth-zin. "They said to -."

"I heard them."

"Most impressive," said Quillen-tok after reviewing the flight logs from the *ZOO*'s mission. "A bold and daring campaign."

"A bit reckless, would you not agree?" said Phon-seth.

"Their plan was well conceived and flawlessly executed. I think the fleet needs to rethink some of our battle tactics and formations after witnessing this type of warfare. Think of it, Phon-seth, this type of strategy may give our people the advantage we have lacked for so long."

"It was highly innovative," said Phon-seth. "I will admit that. How do you think the rest of the Council will react?"

"How else can they react except favorably? A Trochinid battle cruiser was destroyed without incurring any loss of life and minimal damage to our ships. Even Sarn-ula will have to admire their tactics."

Phon-seth looked at the aged leader. "First Order, I cannot help but think that you are planning something else. You are withholding your deepest thoughts."

Quillen-tok smiled. "You are astute, my friend. I plan to go before the Council and recommend that the remainder of the Delfinian commanders and sub-commanders undergo the training that Ridley has provided. I will also request for a permanent contingent of Delfinians to be assigned to the *ZOO*. Commander Mara-jul will oversee this."

"What about Ridley? Do you think he will allow the interference from the Delfinian high command? Ridley's psychological mapping reveals a personality that has limited tolerance for authority."

Quillen-tok smiled again. "Ridley has already requested this of me. He asks for permanent assignment of what he refers to as key personnel to perform certain functions on the *ZOO*. Among these, besides Azrnoth-zin and Mara-jul, are Kirin-rah, Duhon-yar, and Tran-dol. They have meshed well within the crew of the *ZOO*. All of them wish to continue their assignments"

Phon-seth shook his head in wonder. "I find it strange that so much interest has been generated in this offworlder. We have encountered civilizations as we spanned the galaxy. Our people have always maintained a cultural distance, even as exchanges of information or commerce took place. It is different with Ridley."

"Perhaps it is because Ridley resembles Delfinians more than not," mused Quillen-tok. "Azrnoth-zin has embraced Ridley as his friend. Azrnoth-zin's exploits in battle have been recounted at length by young and old warriors alike. Ridley has a powerful ally in our recently disgraced Third Order."

"I have lost track of how many times he has been demoted. Should not he be equivalent in rank to Mara-jul?"

"I cannot remember all of his transgressions, either. But, I can tell you this, Phon-seth. Azrnoth-zin was coming before the Water Council long before you ascended to your present position."

Phon-seth was surprised to hear the latent affection in Quillen-tok's voice. It was as if he was speaking of a misbehaved, but greatly adored child.

"They should be arriving within the next hour. I would like to debrief them before they meet with the rest of the Council," Quillen-tok said, standing up and moving away from the com link.

"I think our terran friend may require a quick lesson on the best way to deal with certain members of the Council."

"I will make the necessary arrangements, First Order."

After the hearing with the Water Council, Ridley, Mara-jul and Azrnoth-zin stepped out of the chambers and started the long trek back to flight deck seventeen. Ridley felt the waves of fatigue, magnified by the stresses and cramped quarters of the past few days aboard the *ZOO*.

The rest period would be brief. The Water Council wanted the team back in action again the next day. The Council had requested a new battle plan and wanted details of the next attack on the Trochinids. None of them spoke for several minutes, absorbing all that transpired in the Council chambers.

Azrnoth-zin broke the silence first. "I think the Water Council was impressed with our initial effort. I was surprised that they voted to keep the Delfinians serving aboard the *ZOO*."

Turning to Mara-jul, he said, "and I was even more surprised that you had requested to remain with this crew. My impression was that you were only along for the initial mission."

"Someone needs to watch out for you and Ridley," Mara-jul said, the hint of a smile crossing her face. "The Water Council has voiced concerns over the two of you working together."

"What? Do they think I'm a bad influence on him? I think it's a little late for that."

"I would like to commend you on your civility during the meeting, Ridley. For the most part, the Water Council was impressed with the operation," said Mara-jul.

"Yeah, all except Sarn-ula. During the entire meeting she hardly spoke. But the look on her face was that of someone who had recently bit down on something very nasty." Ridley looked at Azrnoth-zin. "I get the distinct impression she doesn't like me."

"Sarn-ula is the Water Council," said Azrnoth-zin. "She usually sways the other members to her views. But there is dissension among the Council members of late. Quillen-tok and Phon-seth are openly opposing her. Some of the more reticent members are beginning to question her rulings. She thinks your arrival among our people has acted as a dangerous catalyst that could change the Delfinian way of life."

"It is wise for you to walk softly in her presence, Ridley," Mara-jul said. "Any threat to her authority, be it real or perceived, will be dealt with harshly."

Ridley shrugged his shoulders, then let out a ragged breath . "I guess that kinda makes me the first interstellar pain in the ass then, doesn't it?

"No," Mara-jul said. "Azrnoth-zin claimed that dubious honor long before you."

CHAPTER TWENTY-THREE

In the ensuing four months, the *ZOO* completed thirty-two missions. No loss of life occurred, but several members of Mara-jul's squadron had to be replaced due to injuries sustained in battle. Filling their position was not difficult; anxious Delfinian volunteers stepped up immediately. The successes of the *ZOO* spread throughout the Delfinian fleet. Mara-jul continued to update the growing list of hopeful candidates.

The Water Council approved Ridley's training protocol and Delfinian commanders, sub-commanders and warriors began the rigorous martial arts and weapons training regimen. Initially, Ridley tried to oversee the training and fly the missions as well. Seeing to the needs of his crew and his own growing physical exhaustion eventually forced him to turn the duties over to Delfinian trainers. The troops under the supervision of the Delfinians did not fare as well, although the success rate of the missions against the Trochinids improved significantly. Losses were cut in half, but they were still far too high.

A wave of hope began to grow within the Delfinian fleet. From Second Orders to technical support, the mood had changed. It was no single event that stood out from the others. Duties were carried out with renewed sharpness and clarity. Personnel moved differently, as if their purpose had been redefined. Efficiency on the flight decks improved. More Delfinian cruisers and fighters were making the return trip back to the fleet following successful sorties.

In Ridley's mind there was another wave growing. The more missions he flew the more he had to fight the feeling that they were spitting into a tidal wave. Even with the increased number of missions, the Trochinid swarm pushed onward, fanning out in all directions. Sooner or later, no question about it, they were going to home in on a signal from Earth. If the war took them anywhere near his homeworld, Ridley vowed to do all in his power to warn Earth of the impending destruction.

The *ZOO* had taken a considerable pounding during the months of engagements, requiring the Mawhrbaht crewmembers to constantly be on the ready to make repairs. Ridley was grateful the furry little engineers appeared to be so tireless. No longer was there a need to pirate parts for their ship. Ridley and Azrnoth-zin made the necessary requisitions from Quillen-tok and the parts were delivered to flight deck seventeen.

During their return flight from a successful raid in the Xerbyn sector, Ridley and the others were informed that the Trochinids had employed the stealth device once again and surprised a mid-class Delfinian cruiser. The entire battle took only minutes to conclude. There were no survivors. The loss appeared to further dampen any spirits within the exhausted crew aboard the *ZOO*. A pall hung over the rest of the fleet. The Trochinids had struck again, quickly and without warning. Everyone in the command section of the *ZOO* was quieter than usual on the return trip to the fleet.

Ridley trudged down the ramp, phase rifle and side arm slung over his shoulder. He was barely able to keep his head up. His eyes were red rimmed, sensitive to the lights in the hanger. After him shuffled Mara-jul and Azrnoth-zin, followed by the other members of the ZOO crew in varying states of fatigue.

"The Water Council wants us out again tomorrow," said Mara-jul, her voice bearing the flat tone of resignation.

"The hell with the Water Council!" Ridley snapped. "Look at us. There's no way we're going out again tomorrow. Bad things happen to you when you're this tired."

"It's because of the *Burok-gahn*," said Azrnoth-zin. "When it was destroyed, the Water Council viewed it as an opportunity to exact revenge and keep us focused."

"That's the most insane logic I've ever heard of. How'd those guys get their jobs anyhow?" Ridley said, his voice raising.

"We are in agreement with you, Ridley," said Mara-jul. "There is no reason to turn your anger on us."

Ridley stopped, looked at the deck and let his shoulder sag. "Sorry, y'all. No sleep for four months makes for one crabby offworlder."

"Perhaps we should request of the Council to grant the crew of the *ZOO* more time for repairs," said Azrnoth-zin.

"That would be special dispensation," said Mara-jul. "The Council would never agree to that."

"Hell, we should receive some dispensation," Ridley said sourly. "We've flown more damn missions than anyone else."

"Sarn-ula would like nothing better than to see us fail. She wants us to show weakness," replied Azrnoth-zin.

"I don't care what she thinks . . . or does. As of right now, this crew is on furlough for three days. I want to see to it that extra rations and drink are extended to all. If Sarn-ula has a problem with that, well, she can just shoot me!"

"Do not dismiss that as a possibility," said Azrnoth-zin.

At that moment, a Delfinian, clad in the distinct black and orange uniform befitting Sarn-ula's personal guard strode with purpose up to the exhausted Mara-jul. The look on his face was stern. When he reached Mara-jul, he snapped to attention and performed the salutory bow with sweeping right hand gesture.

"Commander of the Third Order, Mara-jul. You are to accompany me and appear before First Order Sarn-ula in the Water Council chambers. She desires a status report on the last mission."

"Can't it wait?" said Ridley tiredly. "The commander hasn't slept in two days."

The elite guardsman gave Ridley a deadly look. "Sarn-ula waits for no one, offworlder."

"Oh, yeah?" Ridley stepped forward, only to be restrained by Azrnoth-zin and Mara-jul. "Come on, I'll show you some offworlder."

The guardsman's hand went to the weapon at his side.

"Ridley," Mara-jul said evenly, "I will be fine. There is no need to lose control here and now. A few more moments without sleep will not harm me."

"We have fought too hard to lose this now," Azrnoth-zin said, looking directly at the haggard face of Ridley.

Ridley held up his hands. "Okay. Okay. I'm cool." Ridley and the guard glared menacingly at each other like two angry cats sizing the other up.

"Get some rest," said Mara-jul. "Everything will be fine."

Mara-jul turned and accompanied Sarn-ula's guardsman toward the far airlock, but not before the guard turned and gave Ridley a menacing glare.

"There will be another time, another place," Azrnoth-zin spoke quietly to Ridley, releasing his grip.

Mara-jul entered the private quarters of Sarn-ula. By far, these were the most spacious of any in the fleet. The room was almost in darkness, except for a floating table near one wall. Strange objects of various shapes and sizes, with equally bizarre heirogylphics, were arranged on the floating dais. The artifacts appeared to be very old, something from an alien culture. Mara-jul felt an odd sense of recognition, even though she had never beheld such objects before.

A pyramid-shaped object, which rose to a sharp point, beckoned to her. She reached out to touch a four-sided quadrilateral stone object. The weathered inscriptions were in the shape of crude, but unmistakeable Delfid-like creatures.

Something stirred behind her in the darkness.

"How fared the mission?" came the crackling voice of Sarn-ula.

Mara-jul spun around to see that the oldest member of the Water Council had been sitting in the darkness, her silhouette barely discernable.

"I beg forgiveness, First Order," Mara-jul apologized and performed the formal greeting salute. "I did not see you there." Regaining her composure, the Third Order Commander straightened her posture and attempted to disguise the waves of fatigue that washed over her.

"The mission was a success, First Order. We destroyed four Class M mid-size Trochinid cruisers at a processing station in the Xerbyn sector. However, we sustained more wounded this mission. Many of the light fighters require extensive repairs due to battle damage. It is my assertion the crew is functioning beyond normal levels of endurance."

The silhouetted figure of Sarn-ula did not move. A clucking sound escaped the old woman's mouth. "Their wounds will heal," Sarn-ula said disgustedly. "Every Delfinian must work beyond their measure during these times."

Mara-jul focused her thoughts to keep her anger in check.

Sarn-ula stood slowly and walked to where Mara-jul stood. She studied the face of the battle-fatigued commander.

"I can access mission details from the computer. Tell me about Ridley."

Mara-jul fidgeted slightly, enough for Sarn-ula to notice her discomfiture.

"I have observed Ridley for more than four extended cycles, First Order. I find no evidence of treason or subterfuge in his actions. Perhaps the First order has made a misjudgement of his character."

The old woman's gaze turned arctic. "What do you know of subterfuge? Or character? Such insolence that you question my judgement!

"I beg the pardons of the venerated First Order," Mara-jul said quickly. "I spoke with haste."

"I am wondering, Mara-jul, if you truly have the interests and well-being of the Delfinian people in your heart. Have you turned into a sympathizer for this offworlder?"

"I remain loyal to the Water Council and the Delfinian people," Mara-jul replied, meeting the gaze of the old woman with a cold stare.

"Ridley is an interloper. He seeks to undermine the Water Council from within. He carries in his brain information that could be damaging to our way of life. If he is not exposed for the dangerous entity he is, you will shoulder the responsibility for the repercussions our people must bear."

"What is it you wish from me?"

"Know his mind, Mara-jul. Perform the mind-water link with him. Bring the information to me."

"What will happen to Ridley if and when I recover this information?"

"Ridley's fate is of no concern to you, Commander," Sarn-ula snapped. "A traitor will be dealt with as the Council decides."

Mara-jul's gaze faltered. "First Order, to link with a non-Delfinian is a punishable offense which could result in a mind cleansing."

"Those edicts can be overruled in matters of state security. After all, I possess the power to overturn rulings. Especially if the accused is acting on behalf of the Delfinian People."

Mara-jul was barely able to control her anger. "If this is your wish, First Order -."

"It is."

"Then, for Delfinus, I will do as you command."

Sarn-ula looked smugly at Mara-jul, then gently touched her cheek. "Good."

Twenty-four hours later, Ridley stood at the entrance to Mara-jul's quarters. He placed his hand over the disc located to the left of the door and waited while the computer relayed the information into her quarters. It would be difficult to carry on a clandestine relationship under these circumstances, he thought.

The door slid open and Mara-jul stood before him wearing a floor length white robe. Her raven hair hung loosely about her shoulders and spilled down her back. For a moment, Ridley forgot why he had called on her.

"Hi. Hope I didn't wake you."

"No. I have been awake for several hours. I was studying."

"Mara, I have an idea that I wanted to run by you and Azrnoth-zin if you have a moment."

"Please come in." Mara-jul stepped aside and Ridley walked into her quarters.

The room was at least twice the size of the chambers Ridley occupied. There were two distinct rooms. They were standing in a spacious sitting room, spartanly furnished with floating furniture that materialized out of the floor. It was similar to the setup in his quarters below decks, yet considerably more elaborate. Geometric metallic sculptures adorned two walls. A second room was located off the central room. Although it was dark, Ridley assumed that was the sleeping area.

"Studying what?" Ridley said, surveying the room.

"Earth sociology."

"And?"

"And what?"

"What are you finding out about Earth?"

"Earth societies are very strange," said Mara-jul. "The cultures seem to be always in a state of flux. Especially, in your own culture. Certain ideas or principles persist for a time and then they are replaced by other ideas which may or may not have relevance to the culture overall. I find it most confusing."

"I'll let you in on a little secret. So do I."

Mara-jul motioned for Ridley to sit. "May I get you something to drink or eat? Is that not part of Earth culture, too? The proferment of beverages or food upon entering one's dwelling?"

"Well, I'd take a cup of tea if you have it, thanks."

Mara-jul stood and brushed by Ridley. He caught the briefest glance of the curves of her figure from the soft light source emanating from the floor and the walls. She padded over to the far wall and within seconds had synthesized a steaming cup of tea.

"Omeck tea is what you drink, is it not?"

Ridley smiled. "Thank you." He was pleased she remembered. He took a sip and made a smacking sound with his lips. "Yes, I believe you can cook."

"Don't be ridiculous," she scoffed, but a smile formed on the corners of her mouth. "The synthesizer made the tea."

"I'd like to be around when you get a taste of honest to goodness food," said Ridley. "I'd bet a month's credits that you'd be as big a fan of fine dining as Azrnoth-zin."

"What is it you wanted to discuss?" Mara-jul said.

She certainly wasn't one for small talk, Ridley thought.

"This is going to sound insane, but after what just happened to the *Burok-gahn,* I was thinking we should have one of those stealth devices for the *ZOO.* It would certainly even up the odds a bit. It doesn't appear the Trochinids are utilizing it at full scale presently. It seems to be used randomly and haphazardly. That tells me that they really don't have a good handle on the technology. All we need to do is locate one of their ships with the mechanism in place and steal it right from under their noses."

Mara-jul continued to stare at Ridley for several seconds after he finished speaking.

"Well, what do you think?"

"You are correct. It is an insane idea. Do you realize how heavily armored and guarded those warships are? There are thousands of soldiers on those ships. Hundreds of light fighters. Even if we were to locate a ship that carried the device, there would be no means to board it."

"I'm not talking in space," said Ridley. "I'm thinking of one of the planetary moons or asteroids where the Trochinids set up their processing and repair stations. Our scanners reveal there are several located throughout the quadrant. They'd never expect us to hit them on the ground."

"Those processing stations are transient facilities," said Mara-jul. "Finding one that was operational would be one thing. But the probability of finding a facility that has a ship with the stealth device is . . ."

Ridley held up his hand. "Please, you're starting to sound like META IV. Look, Mara, I know it seems crazy, but that's what we have long range scanners for. We put the word out to the fleet, tell them to keep a look out for Trochinid ships with the possibility of this technology. Hell, maybe even figure a way to tag one somehow. Then we follow the trail back to the nest."

"How would we mount this assault? By ground?"

"That's right! We create another diversion from the air. Utilize the light fighters that have been deployed from another spot on the planet or moon. While the Trochinids are straining their necks to see where the fighters are coming from, we slip in with a small group and lift the device. Simple."

Mara-jul shook her head. "It's not simple. It is a suicide mission. I doubt my squadron could provide the necessary cover for you to slip in undetected. It is most disconcerting , your lack of details in this proposal."

"I haven't worked out all the bugs yet. Sorry. Bad choice of words. I just want you to think on the idea for a while, that's all. Will you do that?"

Mara-jul looked away, staring off into space, alone with her thoughts. Ridley sipped the tea, draining the last from the cup and setting it back on the table.

"I will consider your proposal," she said finally. "Have you spoken of this to Azrnoth-zin?"

"Not yet. I wanted to get your feelings on it first."

Ridley noticed something change in Mara-jul's otherworld eyes. Somewhere deep within, a look of intensity and ferocity glowed like embers caught in a wind. Ridley's grip tightened on the chair, for fear he would be drawn into the depths of those blue-green eyes.

"Talk to Azrnoth-zin. We must have a detailed plan of attack or I will not commit my squadron."

Ridley got up to leave. "Thanks for the tea."

"You're welcome." She escorted him to the door.

Ridley stepped through the doorway and took two steps, then turned around. "Uh, Mara, I was wondering if I could request the pleasure of your company over dinner tomorrow evening in my quarters."

Mara-jul looked confused. "Do you wish to discuss the operation at length with Azrnoth-zin and me?"

"Well, we could do that, too. Actually, I was thinking of just having a quiet dinner for two and just . . . ah, you know . . . talk."

Mara-jul raised her eyebrows. "Can *you* cook?"

Ridley laughed. "I'll try my best. I've yet to fully understand all of the nuances of the food synthesizers. But if you're stout of heart and strong of stomach, I'll fix you a reasonable facsimile of Earth cuisine."

Ridley set a time that was agreeable to Mara-jul and he turned to go. As he walked away, she noticed a bit more spring to Ridley's step than before.

Ridley found Azrnoth-zin sitting in the command section of the *ZOO*. He was going through a systems check after the Mawhrbahts had enacted repairs. Two Delfinian technicians were completing repairs to the com link, damaged in the last mission. They acknowledged Azrnoth-zin with a small salute, then turned to Ridley.

"Commander Ridley, the communications array has been repaired," said one of the technicians.

"Thanks, guys. I appreciate the good work."

The two Delfinian technicians bowed and saluted in the fashion befitting an elevated level of warrior, then parted. Azrnoth-zin stared after them, then looked at Ridley.

"Commander?" Azrnoth-zin asked. "When did you receive the elevation in status?"

"Don't ask me." Ridley shrugged. "Guess they're not sure just how to address me."

"You look rested," said Azrnoth-zin. "I assume you have slept since I last saw you."

"Yep. Another two or three days and I might just start feeling human again. I guess it may take you a little longer."

"May I never truly feel completely human," Azrnoth-zin said, distracted.

He looked up to see Ridley grinning at him. "I have seen that look on your face on several occasions. And every time I see it, something is about to transpire that usually results in chaos and mayhem."

"You know, Arn, I've been thinking."

"A dangerous activity."

"As I said, I've been thinking of the loss of the *Burok-gahn*. It sure took the wind out of everybody's sails. I was thinking about a way to even up the odds a little in our favor."

Azrnoth-zin ceased his computations. He rubbed the bridge of his nose. "You realize, that Sarn-ula is most displeased with our overly long layover."

"Gotta rest the troops sometime. If we can pull this one off, Sarn-ula will be inviting us over for tea. Well, maybe not."

"You were thinking of stealing a stealth device from the Trochinids."

"Damn you, Arn. I told you no mind reading."

"I didn't have to mind-link with you, Ridley. I know how you think. It is just the type of ill-conceived plan that your brain would generate. In fact, I would wager a full cycle's credits that you really do not even have a plan at this point."

"Well, it's just a bit rough around the edges. But the rest of it will be there with your help."

"You are a very bad influence on me, Ridley. I would, under normal circumstances, tell you that you are as insane as a grooting verblach. Such an operation would be highly unlikely to be carried off successfully. There is high probability that none of us would return."

"But you like the idea, don't you?"

Azrnoth-zin sighed. "Tell me what you have."

Ridley roughed out the plan. Azrnoth-zin listened while he completed the final drive systems check. Ridley was mildly irritated at the appearance of the alien's lack of focus, yet he knew Azrnoth-zin had heard every word and was processing the information.

"So, what do you think?" Ridley leaned forward in the seat.

"I think I might be as crazy as you are. This could work."

"Arn, you're a prince among Delfinians."

"I suppose it's time to go speak with Mara-jul," said Azrnoth-zin.

"Already did."

Azrnoth-zin's eyebrows raised once again. "You did? What did she say?"

"She's in. She wants to see a detailed plan of operations down to the millisecond."

"Then, I think it is time we talked with Kelun," said Azrnoth-zin.

CHAPTER TWENTY-FOUR

Ridley was fretting over the dinner. He fervently wished to impress the solemn and dignified Mara-jul. Invading the galley of the *ZOO*, he attempted to piece together a representative Earth meal. This greatly chagrined the Arkoanians, who did not appreciate an interloper in their galley and food supply stores. Slender and bird-like, the Arkoanians' torsos were covered in large blue-green scales, which flared outward when they became distressed or angry. This, in effect, made them appear twice their normal size. Right now, the galley of the *ZOO* was colorfully crowded. Ridley could only conclude that all cooks throughout the galaxy were of the same temperamental nature.

The original plan was to have an Italian-type dish, somewhere along the lines of an eggplant parmesean or baked ziti. Ridley tried his best to describe the ingredients to the Arkoanians. It was nearly impossible to find any ingredients in the supply store that even vaguely resembled tomatoes, garlic, eggplant or pasta. The Arkoanians were horrified at Ridley's description of cheese.

The food preparation had to take place in the galley of the *ZOO*. Ridley's cramped quarters did not have facilities for cooking, and only a small synthesizer was available. The Arkoanians stood close, murmuring to each other in their almost Asian sounding dialect over Ridley's inept preparation.

Ridley tasted the sauce. It was definitely not red and was far too bitter to be palatable. Ridley requested something to sweeten the sauce. He hoped to find something at least slightly resembling sugar or honey. He forced down a feeling of revulsion when he saw that the sweetener the Arkoanian chefs added to the mixture kept trying to leap out of the pot of its own accord.

But the dinners under the transparent warmers actually did look appetizing when placed steaming on a fully set table. Two glasses of a dark liquid that Ridley hoped tasted like wine finished off the setting. If nothing else, it was an admirable presentation.

The computer announced the arrival of Mara-jul at the door. His stomach clenched when he realized she was one minute early. Ridley waved his arms over his head several times, an attempt to staunch the flow of perspiration under his arms, then checked himself over one last time. He wore a replicated pair of khaki trousers with a light blue long sleeve shirt with the sleeves rolled up. Ridley had decided against shoes.

Ambling over to the computer inset, he took a deep breath and activated the door. It slid open with a soft hiss, revealing Mara-jul standing rigid in a black cocktail dress with spaghetti straps and black heels. Her hair was pulled back off her neck and arranged in an intricate patern of tightly woven braids. Her porcelain skin almost glowed in contrast to the black of the dress. Ridley was almost too stunned to speak.

"Did I arrive at the correct time?" she said, trying to understand the look on his face.

"Mara, you look -."

"This was Azrnoth-zin's idea. He said that females on your planet wore clothing like this."

"No, no. You look great. I was just a little surprised, that's all."

Mara-jul attempted to walk into Ridley's quarters. Ridley noted that it was more like a series of lurching movements as her feet kept losing their purchase in the unwieldy pumps. Ridley could barely contain himself.

"I find it amazing that human females of Earth can walk at all. This footwear was not designed for humanoid use."

Ridley lifted the cuffs of his trousers, revealing his bare feet. "Why don't you make yourself more comfortable."

"I believe that Azrnoth-zin was enjoying himself at my expense," Mara-jul said, tossing the heels into a corner.

"You have to remember that Azrnoth-zin's view of Earth was somewhat myopic. Most of what little he actually knows he got from watching television at my friend's house. I tried to keep him away from it, but once he got hold of a channel changer at the Dutchman's place, we knew we had lost him."

"I remember the concept of television from the data files of the *Kren-dahl*. It is a one- way medium your people use for entertainment and to receive information."

"Well, your information is partially correct. The thing is that a great deal of television is not based in reality, even though some segments claim it is. It's all about an image that is being pushed onto the public. You are to look a certain way. You are to eat and drink certain advertised products if you want to be attractive or have vitality. A lot of it has to do with the sale of sex."

"I do not understand," Mara-jul said as Ridley pulled back the chair for her. "All of this has to do with the mating ritual?"

He noticed that she was wearing a scent, something that he could not recognize. It was faint, yet undeniable. It smelled all at once like the surf crashing on a beach and the desert during a rainstorm.

"That's what the sponsors and producers want you to believe."

"Then males on Earth are not attracted to females who present themselves in this fashion?"

"Please don't get me wrong, Mara. You look absolutely stunning. But I think Azrnoth-zin got the idea for your mode of dress from a beer commercial."

"I do not understand."

"These people on the television believe that they can sell more of their product, which in this case is some type of weak beer, by showing that if you drink this beer, beautiful women in cocktail dresses will be at your beck and call."

Mara-jul contemplated this for a moment, her face registering a mixture of irritation and confusion. "You come from a very strange society, Ridley." Then, looking down at the dress, she said, "I am sorry for the choice in garments. I did not mean to offend."

Ridley touched Mara-jul's arm. "No. I'm not offended at all. I'm flattered that you would think to wear the garments of my home world. Back on Earth, you would turn a lot of heads the way you look tonight. I just want you to be comfortable."

The evening wasn't off to the best of starts.

Ridley took his seat and raised the glass of wine-colored fluid. "A toast. To the success of our mission and the safe return of the *ZOO* and all her crew."

Mara-jul followed Ridley's lead by holding up her glass. Ridley clinked his glass to hers. "To the success of the mission." She took a sip of the liquid. Her eyes widened and she broke into a smile. "How did you get the ceremonial liquid? This is only to be used by the Water Council."

Ridley took another sip. It certainly was not wine, but the semi-bitter taste was palatable. It tasted like a cross between cough syrup and Dr. Pepper, with a hint of anise.

"A present from Azrnoth-zin. After I told him that you and I were to be having dinner, he thought there needed to be some wine for the occasion. He never told me where he got it."

"There would be serious consequences if the Water Council were to find out about this," said Mara-jul, and tilted the glass back for another swallow.

"Who's going to tell them? Not me. Besides, I don't think it's going to affect Sarn-ula adversely not to get her nightcap for one evening."

"The food appears . . . interesting," said Mara-jul. "Is this what you call Mexican food?"

"No," Ridley said. "I'm not sure what you call it. Let's say eggplant parmesan twenty-three thousand light years removed."

Mara-jul looked at the food, unsure as how to proceed.

"On Earth," Ridley continued, "this dish is from a region called Italy. It is a place known for its fine foods and wine, and its richness in art and history."

Mara-jul watched as Ridley manipulated the utensils, then copied his movements. She forked a small bite into her mouth and chewed contemplatively. She stopped chewing and stared directly at Ridley.

"I have never tasted anything like this. I have strange sensations occurring in my mouth."

Ridley leaned forward. "Are you all right? Is it too spicy?"

"No. It feels as if my mouth has . . . come alive. The sensations on my tongue are most interesting."

Ridley breathed a sigh of relief as he watched Mara-jul savor her dinner. Considering what he had witnessed in the galley earlier, the end result was a pleasant surprise.

"Were you of the warrior caste on your homeworld?" Mara-jul asked, helping herself to another serving of the main course.

"I served in a branch of the military called the Navy. But I was not considered a warrior."

"Would it be possible to have some more of the liquid?"

As Ridley stood and went to an alcove where a sleek carafe held more of the ceremonial liquid, he felt a slight buzz. He poured Mara-jul another glass and then sat down.

"What then were your duties?"

Ridley took a breath. Talking about his less than colorful past was something he had not wanted to engage in tonight.

"I was part of a special project that trained cetaceans for warfare. You refer to them as Delfids. I helped to train them to locate enemy infiltrators by water and to detect and set explosive devices."

Mara-jul's eyes grew wide again. "You trained Delfids for war? Terrans can communicate with Delfids?"

"Not like you would think, Mara. Azrnoth-zin was able to establish a link with them. Humans and Delfids communicate in only the most rudimentary fashion at present."

"On Delfinus, the Ancient Ones were revered. They were never used as pawns in a war."

"Not all of us wanted them to be utilized in that way," Ridley said defensively. "Unfortunately, there are those on my homeworld that believe all life forms other than humans are inferior and are to be used as a resource. I don't share that belief."

"Azrnoth-zin told the Council that your planet has many races of Delfids that live in all of the oceans. He said there are Delfids that achieve enormous sizes."

"That's right. The blue whale is the largest creature that inhabits the Earth. And Earth has had its share of big critters over the years. Did you ever see one of the Delfids?"

"No one has seen a living Delfid for a very long time. I could not even begin to describe them for you. It is told they left Delfinus after becoming dissatisfied with the People."

"I've seen them. Or what I would think to be a Delfid, anyway."

Mara-jul stopped eating and stared at Ridley.

"They're not all that different from the Delfids on Earth. Except that they have prehensile flippers with fingers, and they're blue. Their language is strange, but not all that different from Delfinian."

"Stop! What you are saying is preposterous. And blasphemous. No one has seen a Delfid. How could you, an offworlder, know what they look like?"

"I don't know how the hell they got in my head, but they did. When I dream I see them swimming. I see a lot of other stuff, too. Most of it doesn't make a damn bit of sense. It's all part of that stupid reorganization procedure. I can assure you that I don't want those images in my head either. Some nights, I wake up screaming."

"I do not wish to discuss this further," said Mara-jul. "The Delfids are deities and will be treated with the reverence they deserve."

They ate in silence for the next few minutes, both of them wondering how the conversation had soured so quickly. Ridley thought that all of his interactions with Mara-jul up to now had been in the company of other Delfinians, particularly Azrnoth-zin. Perhaps, without his well-timed mediation, Mara-jul and he would have become antagonistic a lot sooner.

"Azrnoth-zin told me you were removed from warrior status because you struck a superior," Mara-jul said following a protracted silence.

Ridley stopped chewing, his gaze narrowing. "What else did Azrnoth-zin tell you?"

"He said the superior was abusive with his power. Under his direction, two Delfids that you befriended perished. He said the superior was a human who enjoyed the act of killing for the violence." Mara-jul directed her gaze directly at Ridley, her blue-green eyes sparkling. "Are most of the humans on Earth like this?"

"No." Ridley didn't like her tone of voice. "Most of them are good people. There are some only interested in the possession of power or wealth, and will use it to inflict pain on others. I've noticed that your people aren't exactly what I would call the humanitarians of the universe, either."

"What is that supposed to mean?"

"Oh, come on, Commander. Surely you weren't blind to the conditions that the Displaced Work Force lived and worked under in the bellies of your star cruisers. It was more like a prison labor camp down there than a cooperative working environment."

"The Delfinians did not wish to intercede in the affairs of offworld races. There were appointments made to oversee the operations."

"I'd like to know what criteria you used to determine who would supervise. Most of the choices that I came across were big, stupid and mean."

Mara-jul had stopped eating. She sat straight-backed in the seat and glowered at Ridley. "You have no place to sit in judgement of Delfinian society. Just because you have undergone the reorganization does not mean that you possess even the slightest knowledge of Delfinian ways."

"If ignoring other cultures and subjecting their only survivors to a life of indentured servitude is your idea of an advanced society, then give me the Displaced Work Force any day. Where do you people get off being so . . .?"

Mara-jul stood up and tossed her napkin onto the table. "I don't know why I came here tonight. You are the most argumentative, narrow-minded species I have yet encountered - in

220

all the systems! At times I wish you were a Trochinid. Then I could just shoot you!"

Ridley caught himself. Taking a deep breath, he said, "Mara, I'm sorry. I feel like I'm the only one worried about what's going to happen to my planet. Everyone has this "oh, well" attitude. Just another link in the food chain. It pisses me off."

"Is that what you think? That no one cares? We have been fighting for hundreds of years, lost friends, family to the Swarm. We have witnessed hundreds of civilizations vanish - whole societies vaporized or processed. We have been dying to prevent the Trochinids from spreading to other worlds. To your world."

"Mara, I'm -."

"We have an early briefing. I had better get some rest."

"Yeah. Early briefing."

"Thank you for the dinner invitation," Mara-jul said. "It was . . . interesting. There is no need for you to get up to see me to the door. I can find my way." With that, she turned and a moment later, Ridley heard the hiss of the airlock door.

Ridley looked up at the sealed door. "Nice going, shithead. Your record still stands."

Ridley sat morosely at the table for a time, his forehead supported by his hands. He replayed the last hour or two over and over in his mind. This was probably the worst first date he had experienced since high school. Everything that could have possibly gone awry had done so in the grandest of fashions. He wondered if Mara-jul would ever speak to him again.

He cleaned up the dinner plates. He considered downing the rest of the ceremonial liquid by himself but decided against it. He felt bad enough as it was right now. There was no need to compound his misery by adding a Delfinian hangover the next morning. Besides, too much was riding on the upcoming mission. He needed to keep his wits about him.

Mara-jul got undressed and tossed the alien garb into a floating chair in her quarters. She donned a long white robe and sat to review the logistical analysis for the mission. Try as she could to maintain her focus, her mind was drawn back to the disastrous evening she had just spent in Ridley's quarters.

She found herself wondering if all human interactions were that volatile. It was a wonder that humans had survived this far. Were she and Ridley all that different? What did she say that caused him to assume such a defensive posture? Contrary to what Azrnoth-zin had told her about intimate human dinner gatherings, the evening was not a relaxed, pleasurable experience, but a nerve-wracking, edgy, confrontational affair.

She wondered if her choice of words was the key to Ridley's agitation. What had she said that had triggered his response? Her scientific mind wanted to know. But the female Delfinian in her also wanted to understand. Their relationship had always been one of subtle competition, and some verbal parrying. Perhaps that was where their relationship must reside.

The com link at Mara-jul's door sounded. She walked over to the airlock and activated the door. The door slid open and there stood Ridley, holding the two glasses of wine in one hand, her ill-fitting pumps in the other, and the decanter of ceremonial liquid cradled under his right elbow.

"You forgot your shoes."

"Oh. You can keep them."

"Mara, I don't want to fight with you. There's a good chance that I - that we may not make it back from this next mission. On Earth, we have a saying. It begins with, "I'm sorry for being such a jerk"."

"How does the rest of it go?"

"It varies from there. I don't want to go into battle and have you mad at me. Right now, I need all the friends I can get."

Mara-jul looked directly into Ridley's eyes. Slowly, a smile spread across her lips. "Please come inside."

Mara-jul led Ridley to the dimly lit bedroom. She was wearing a white dressing gown, the thinness of the material revealing the contours of her breasts and the indentation of her navel. Ridley's eyes consumed Mara-jul's curved lines and then met the blue-green of her penetrating gaze. He felt his pulse race, his face flush.

"Mara, we don't have to do this. I know what the -."

"I do not care what the Water Council thinks. This is what I want." She dropped the dressing gown and slid onto the floating platform.

Ridley fumbled with his clothing, tripping over his pants before he finally freed them from his ankles. He looked up to see Mara-jul smiling at him. He grinned sheepishly as he slid in next to her. "Smooth, huh?"

"Yes. Smooth."

Mara-jul ran her fingers lightly over the raised white scars on Ridley's shoulders and back, tracing the arc of the tase-whip across his skin. She studied the scars, then studied Ridley's face for an explanation.

"Like I said," Ridley said quietly. "Big, stupid and mean."

The look on Mara'jul's face softened. "I am sorry, Ridley. Tell me who did this to you. I will make sure they are brought before the Water Council and duly punished."

Ridley shrugged. "He was called Gort. A Drolong. He won't be tasing anyone soon."

Mara-jul pulled back, regarding Ridley with a questioning intensity in her blue-green eyes.

"You killed him?"

"Let's just say that Gort's head had an unfortunate accident with a piece of metal pipe I just happened to be holding at the time." Ridley raised his eyebrows and ran his fingers through his hair, giving him the look of a mischievous boy. His face became somber. "Besides, Gort was just the messenger. Someone put him up to the beatings."

"Who would do that?" demanded Mara-jul.

"Someone who thinks I'm a threat." Ridley stared directly into Mara-jul's eyes.

Mara-jul met Ridley's gaze, then gently touched his cheek with the back of her hand. Ridley closed his eyes at the exquisite touch.

"It must be difficult for you, being so far away from your people," she said after a moment.

"It's a tough job, but someone has to do it."

In the next moment, Ridley and Mara-jul came together and embraced. They stayed in that position for several moments, listening to each other's breathing.

Ridley felt the electricity of her body pressing against him. He leaned his face toward Mara-jul's and pressed his lips lightly to hers. She recoiled and stared at Ridley. Her gaze was more than a little distracting.

"What is this gesture that you do?" Mara-jul said.

"Oh, I'm sorry. It's called a kiss. Was it unpleasant?"

"No. Not an unpleasant sensation at all. Different." Then, she said after a moment, "I remember Azrnoth-zin telling me briefly about the human mating ritual. Is this part of it?"

Ridley smiled. "Yes. It is the beginning of the ritual. The man and the woman touch lips. Then they touch each other over different parts of the body. With their hands and their lips." Ridley pressed the hardness against Mara-jul's thigh. "Eventually, we become as one."

"What is the sequencing of this ritual?"

"There is no sequencing, Mara. You are free to be as creative as you dare. Only your imagination sets limitations."

She leaned into him. "Then teach me."

Mara-jul was a quick study. By asking her what she found more pleasurable, Ridley was able to map out her erogenous zones. She, in turn, with a slightly more scientific approach, was able to determine Ridley's zones of pleasure.

One thing Ridley discovered to be especially disconcerting. After a long passionate embrace and kiss, Ridley opened his eyes to see Mara-jul staring at him wide-eyed, the deep azure filling his field of view.

"You don't have to keep your eyes open all the time if you don't want to," said Ridley, smiling.

"If I close them, it will be difficult to learn the technique," she said.

"Try feeling it. This time keep your eyes closed. Let your other senses take over."

Ridley thought that he was going to lose the moment because of Mara-jul's somewhat clinical approach, then felt the arousal build within him as she pushed her body firmly against his. His mouth found hers and they began exploring.

"To boldly go . . . "

"What?" she breathed into his ear.

"Nothing."

Yes, Mara-jul was a quick study.

Ridley was greatly relieved to discover that he and Mara-jul were anatomically compatible. He lay on his back, half dozing. Mara-jul's head rested on Ridley's chest, her webbed hand moving gently over his skin.

Ridley found his focus drawn to the nearly transparent membranes between her slender fingers and toes. She had the innate ability to fan her feet outward to almost twice their normal size. He'd give anything to see her swim the four-hundred freestyle.

"Are you staring at my feet again?" she said drowsily. "I am beginning to feel self-conscious."

"Don't. I think they're beautiful feet. Sometime, I'd like to go swimming with you. That's all."

She moved her hand through the hair on his chest. "It is hard for me to imagine that humans can move through the water at all. There is so much . . . "

"Resistance? Well, we manage to flounder about. Did you sleep?"

"A little. I think it is not long before we have to report for the briefing."

He kissed her on the forehead. "Don't remind me. I can't believe that in a few hours we're going on a mission that I wouldn't give odds on any of us returning. What in the hell was I thinking?"

"It is a good plan, Ridley. We will survive."

"I wish I had your confidence."

"Azrnoth-zin says that you possess the thought transference ability."

"I don't know, Mara. That stuff makes me nervous."

"Why?"

"I guess it's like you no longer have a place to call your own. Once you give access to your thoughts, you've lost all privacy."

"You can learn to control the process," said Mara-jul, "just as you can learn to control the movements of your body."

"Yeah, but Mara, my mind goes in places that I wouldn't want to visit, let alone give someone else a guided tour."

"We all have thoughts that are not always desirable or pleasant. Some are painful and ugly. Think of this as an exercise that will help you to filter your thought processes. Is it not the same thing you spoke of when you instructed me in the close combat?"

"That's different, Mara." Ridley turned onto his side and looked at her. "That's tuning into yourself, not another being."

"Among Delfinians, the ultimate form of intimacy is to join through the mind-water link."

"Aren't you worried about getting in deeper with the Water Council? I mean, doing the mind link thing with an offworlder is like having sex with your pet, or something like that. Isn't it?"

Mara-jul gazed into Ridley's eyes. "I have already defied the taboos of my people by lying here next to you. I have made that choice willingly. Besides, I was a willing participant in the terran mating ritual."

Ridley sighed. "You're right. You're right. Fair is fair. Just go easy on me, okay?"

Mara-jul kissed Ridley lightly on the lips and pushed him onto his back. Her body felt cool and warm at the same time. Her eyes burned with an intensity that Ridley had not seen before. He felt himself falling downward into twin deep holes, the cool waters swirling around him.

"Don't we . . . put our fingers on each other's temples, or something?" he said, slightly nervous.

She looked at him. "This will not work if you continue to make humor."

"Sorry. What do you want me to do?"

"I want you to think of something pleasurable. Concentrate on that thought."

"You and me?"

"If you wish."

Ridley closed his eyes and focused his thoughts on Mara-jul. In his mind's eye, he pictured every curve of her face, the curves of her body, every detail. He saw her face even through closed eyelids.

He saw a young Delfinian child, black hair flowing in a turquoise sea. She was swimming with other children. They moved through the water as if they were in a slow ballet.

Images flashed before Ridley's closed eyes. He saw underwater cities. He saw Mara-jul, a few years older now, studying in some type of classroom, the background being the cerulean blue of some Delfinian sea.

Then she came to him, naked, walking slowly in clear ankle-deep water. Two suns burned behind her in a cloudless but brilliant blue sky. They were alone on a stretch of beach, the sand orange-flecked with purple.

"Let go of your thoughts," Mara-jul said to him, and pulled him deeper into the water.

Ridley relaxed and watched Mara-jul's body draw closer to him in the turquoise waters. Their bodies pressed together. Ridley watched in amazement as Mara-jul's body was drawn into his. Suddenly, a burst of intense pleasure resounded through Ridley.

He allowed his mind to scroll through thirty-three years of life. Ridley watched clear images of himself as a child engaged in play. He saw himself sitting at a table with his mother and father. His parents were having an argument. He remembered how alone that made him feel. Mara-jul stood behind, slightly out of focus as the memories poured forth.

The memories were so crystalline that Ridley found tears forming in his eyes. The image of his mother's face had long since faded from his conscious mind.

Images of dolphins and whales appeared in the water all around him. Among the dolphins were Charlie and Dali. They swam around Ridley playfully. Suddenly the dolphins disappeared in a burst of bubbles. Ridley cried out.

Mara-jul walked with him. They were in the chamber again. The tubes began to open and the yellow gas poured onto the floor. Ridley heard the scrabbling of talons. He mouthed the words for Mara-jul to run, but he could not see her.

Ridley found himself swimming in a deep blue sea. Next to him were the strange, blue dolphin-like creatures. Their prehensile flippers opened and closed. They were speaking to each other, but Ridley could not make out what they were saying. Their flippers turned into long webbed hands, and feet began to metamorphose from their trident-like tails.

Mara-jul gasped. Ridley felt himself jerked back to reality.

"How is it that you have memories of the Delfids?" Her voice was tight. "No one has seen them alive for over a thousand years."

"Don't ask me. After the neural reorganization those images were in my head. It seems to be the same dream sequences each time. There's always that weird chamber with the Trochinids and there's always the blue delfids."

"Ridley, I think it is very important that we determine where these images came from. I know of no other Delfinian who possesses these memories. Yet, they are Delfinian memories."

"Mara, if it's okay with you, I'll take a raincheck. I just saw some things up close and personal that I've not seen in a long time. I need a break before we go back there again."

Mara-jul looked exceedingly perplexed. "Of course," she said after a moment. "This experience must be overwhelming."

They were silent for a time, lying against each other. Ridley felt his heartbeat finally return to normal. Ridley thought he might have drifted off to sleep for a while.

"The first part was great," he said in a voice above a whisper.

"Which part?"

"Where you and I swam together in the sea. I felt like every cell in my body was exploding with pleasure. It was like no orgasm I've ever known."

"In time, you will be able to control those other thoughts. You will be able to pick random thoughts out from my mind and explore them as if you were there when they occurred," said Mara-jul.

Ridley propped himself up on one elbow. The furrows in his brow indicated to Mara-jul that he was still uneasy.

"So you were guiding me through what you and I saw?" asked Ridley.

"I asked certain questions in my mind," Mara-jul replied.

"Was it . . . pleasurable for you?"

"Yes. Very much so. But, I too, found the other images most disturbing. I want to explore the mind link with you further, but we will when you are ready."

"Thanks, Mara. I'd like that. But for now, let's go slow below the surface."

She kissed him lightly on the lips. "You must sleep, now. Your mind has undergone a great deal of stress. And I need you with all of your faculties operating at optimum in a few hours." With that, she hugged Ridley fiercely.

Ridley wrapped his arms around her waist. "Thank you," he said. "This was the best evening I have had in a very long time."

"I, too, enjoyed this evening, Ridley."

Ridley fell into a deep sleep. For the first time in a long time, he did not dream of blue dolphins or Trochinids.

CHAPTER TWENTY-FIVE

The largest open area on the *ZOO* besides the landing bays was the dining area. The briefing room had proven to be too small. Everyone was present for the meeting, strike force participants and technical support alike.

In the back of the room, Ridley, along with Azrnoth-zin, Mara-jul, Kelun, Trahg, Ryk, Tikah and META IV, sat or hovered at a long dais. Quillen-tok and Phon-seth sat off to one side, observing.

Ridley stole a glance toward Mara-jul. She was involved in a discussion with Kelun. She noticed Ridley looking at her and a faint smile passed between them.

He was amazed at how good he felt on so little sleep. The idea had been to get as much rest as possible over the three-day furlough. Ridley may have slept for ten hours in the last seventy-two.

Mara-jul stood and faced the roomful of warriors and technicians. "Let us begin. We will go through the group assignments first. Following that, each team will meet separately for the final briefing."

"A Trochinid processing station has been located by deep space probes in the Rizorian Cluster. One of the META units transmitted the information received via the probe after following what appeared to be a Trochinid battle cruiser equipped with the stealth device."

A small octagonal column appeared from out of the floor in front of Mara-jul. A holographic image appeared on top, showing a series of planets orbiting a solitary star. It zeroed in on the fourth planet in the system. The planet and its three moons grew until they almost filled the front of the room.

Mara-jul activated the control and separated one of the moons from the others. It was the smallest of the three and appeared reddish. The surface was barren rock and sand. A plateau was magnified; the Trochinid installation appeared to be growing out of the rock.

"As you can see, the processing depot is located on the top of this plateau. The planet has already been laid to waste. Reports indicate the Trochinids are in the final stages of processing the ores and minerals from the planet. Initial reconnaissance reveals the installation to be heavily fortified. The approach to the area is precipitous. The Trochinids do not expect an assault from here." She indicated a series of steep escarpments that formed a natural barrier to the plateau.

"That is why two ground assault teams," she continued, "one led by Commander Ridley, the other by Commander Azrnoth-zin, will approach from opposite directions and converge on the center. The goal is to gain access under the dome shield."

"The fighter squadron will attack the dome shield in an effort to draw the Trochinid's attention away from the ground assault and at the same time weaken the dome defense," Mara-jul said. "Because of the tracking system placements, the last three kilometers will be on foot. No hovercraft will be utilized." She turned to Azrnoth-zin. "Commander?"

Ryk and Tikah chattered at Ridley as Azrnoth-zin rose to speak. Ridley waved them off and shushed them. Azrnoth-zin cast an inquisitive look at Ridley. Ridley held up his hand. "Sorry, Commander. Please proceed." He glared at the two Mawhrbahts reproachfully.

"We expect to meet with heavy resistance," said Azrnoth-zin. "At the designated time, both teams will converge on the landing port where the ships are being refitted and refueled."

A Delfinian male in the front of the room raised his hand. "How will we know which Trochinid ship possesses the stealth device?"

"The META probe that was following the fleet was able to attach a sensor tag to the ship that had demonstrated the stealth technology. Unfortunately, the probe was destroyed shortly after it placed the tag. We have the frequency of the tag and will locate it once we are inside the dome shield."

Ridley leaned back in his seat and whispered to META IV hovering behind him. "Friend of yours?"

"META I-A served with distinction," replied the metallic. "It will be missed."

"Sorry, META," said Ridley.

"Once the dome shield is disabled, Commander Mara-jul's squadron will strafe the facility," Azrnoth-zin continued. "The shuttles will be launched from the *ZOO* and will rendezvous at the location determined for retrieval." Azrnoth-zin looked around the room. "If there are no further questions, I will turn the briefing over to Commander Ridley."

Ridley stood and walked around to stand in front of the holographic base. "The atmosphere on the third moon is highly toxic. All members of the ground forces will be issued personal force fields, plus emergency backups should failure of the primary systems occur. The grav force is almost two and a half times the standard, so the going will be slow. I want all members of the assault teams to experience the effects of heavier G in the simulators before we land. Adjust your PFFs accordingly. We need to be traveling with only the essential equipment. We're counting on the element of surprise to pull this one off."

Kirin-rah raised her hand. Ridley nodded toward her. "Go ahead, Kirin."

"We have been hearing of new weapons development specifically designed for this mission. What is the status, if any, of such weapons?"

"I'm glad you asked that question. The Mawhrbahts and Kelun have been working together to come up with some firepower that can be handled in a double G environment and still pack enough of a punch to send the nearest Trochinid to the roach motel in hell. When we break into the individual teams for the final assault briefing, we'll also go over the new weapons. The basic operation, from my understanding, is the same as the traditional plasma rifles and phase guns that we have been using all along, only with a few modifications. It should be a quick learn."

Ridley scanned the room for more questions. No other hands went up.

"If there is anyone in this room who is having second thoughts regarding this mission, well, now is the time to speak your piece. No one here will think ill of you if you decide you want out. Please let your team leader know as soon as possible so a suitable replacement can be found." The room remained silent; all eyes were focused on the offworlder.

"Okay, then." Ridley turned to walk back to his seat, stopped, and pivoted about. Scanning the room, he viewed an assembly of beings that he would never have thought existed six months ago. Now, he gazed across a sea of alien faces, many of whom had become friends.

"I just wanted to say that I feel privileged to have been able to work with all of you."

A single foot stomped the floor. Another followed. And another. The room resounded with the clamor from hundreds of stomping feet. Red-faced, Ridley made his way back to his seat.

"Teams Alpha, Delta, and Omega along with support personnel, will now convene for the final briefings," Azrnoth-zin said standing up. "Upon finalization of the assault plan, your team leaders will provide you with the deployment sequence. Good luck to you."

Ridley moved toward the area of the room designated for the ground assault teams when he was intercepted by Quillen-tok. Direct eye contact with the stately Delfinian leader was always a bit disconcerting to Ridley. This time, Ridley thought he caught a glimpse of concern behind those eyes and along the prominent brow ridge.

"Thank you for coming to this gathering, First Order," said Ridley, performing the formal Delfinian bowing gesture. "I have never truly expressed my gratitude for all of the help you have given us. Without your well-timed assistance, we would have never gotten this endeavor off the flight deck."

"You owe me no debt of gratitude, Ridley. All that transpired was the supply of necessary materials to develop an extension of the Delfinian fighting force. Your crew has proved itself beyond all of my expectations." Quillen-tok forced a wry smile. "Although, there were times when I thought I would lose the wager to the other members of the Council. Phon-seth is still bitter over his loss."

"I'm glad I didn't know about your wager, First Order. I would have really been sweating it then."

Quillen-tok's mood turned somber. "Be careful of what you seek out there, Ridley. There are things in the universe that are best left alone."

"I'm not sure I understand your meaning, Excellency."

"I know you have questions. It is evident in your thought patterns and your speech. I have observed how you watch and study all around you. Make sure that you are truly ready for the discoveries that you may find out there."

Ridley shook his head. "What discoveries, First Order? I'm sorry for being so ignorant, but I'm confused."

Quillen-tok nodded. "It is not a simple matter. When the time is right, we will speak again."

Phon-seth returned from his inspection of the new weapons array the Mawhrbahts and the Yhrynen were demonstrating.

"Farewell, Ridley," said Quillen-tok. "May your mission be successful and your return safe."

Phon-seth nodded toward Ridley. "Good luck to you and your team. The Delfinian people are proud of this crew on this day."

"Thanks, First Order," Ridley said, still trying to glean some meaning out of Quillen-tok's cryptic warning. "We'll try not to disappoint anybody."

Ridley turned and walked over to where Azrnoth-zin was standing with the other members of the ground assault teams. The teams were being introduced to some of the new additions to the arsenal.

"You look troubled," said Azrnoth-zin. "Is there something wrong?"

"No. I don't know. Quillen-tok just gave me the weirdest warning."

"What did he say?"

"He said that I should be careful about what answers I seek in the universe, or something like that. Some things are better left alone. Got any idea what he was talking about?"

Azrnoth-zin contemplated this for a moment. He shrugged his shoulders and went back to listening to the demonstration.

Kelun and Ryk were demonstrating the newly modified phase cannon or "Troch-blaster" as it had come to be affectionately named. It was less than half the size of the unwieldy Trochinid weapon, with the advantage that the power-pack could be worn by the same person wielding the cannon.

"There is a booster sequence that can be activated here," said Kelun, indicating a small switch near the trigger. "It can boost the charge by two or three times the normal output. It is very effective for concentrations of Trochinids. You cannot operate in this mode all of the time, however, as your power supply will be depleted quickly."

"How is the recoil?" asked Groten-dah. He was young, probably the youngest Delfinian warrior on the assault team. In training, he had been one of the most tenacious. A bit cocky at times, thought Ridley, but it was clear the young Delfinian looked up to Azrnoth-zin and to him.

"The dampeners in the rear portion of the weapon will offset any recoil," said Kelun.

"This thing hardly bucks at all," said Ridley. "Even on max boost sequence, it's still no problem."

All members of the assault team were issued weapons and each began to check the mechanisms and feel of their weapon.

"Make sure you can take that apart and put it back together before we get to the Rizorian system. We'll have plenty of time." Azrnoth-zin said.

Ryk brought out a metal box and presented it to Ridley. Ridley opened it and held a small, metallic disc that was nearly flat. The multiple jagged edges were sharpened to fine points, tipped with a strange green color. Ridley held one up to the teams.

"This little beauty is Ryk's idea. He came up with these after I told him about a group of warriors on Earth called Ninjas. They employ these throwing stars as a means of subduing their enemies quietly and efficiently." A life size, three-dimensional model of a Trochinid was wheeled out by members of the Displaced Work Force and placed twenty-five meters from Ridley.

Ridley turned and faced the target. "We call these Silent Incendiary Devices, or SIDs. With a flick of his wrist, he sent the disc spinning toward the Trochinid mannequin. The SID found its mark and sunk into the chest cavity, leaving only a small, smoking black hole. A second later, the mannequin exploded from within. A cry of surprise erupted from the team.

"They're good up to thirty-five meters, depending on your technique. Kelun designed the explosive charge. The Mawhrbahts developed the nanotechnology that would pierce the body armor and get the device inside of them. By the time the Trochinids realize they've been hit, it's too late. All that from a little flick of the wrist."

"During the flight, we will practice aboard ship with unarmed SIDS," continued Ridley. "Check in with Kelun, Azrnoth-zin, or me if you have any questions."

Each team went over the final assault plans once more. Departure for the mission was scheduled for the next morning. After Ridley and Azrnoth-zin dismissed the ground assault teams, Ridley looked around for Mara-jul. She was still over in one corner of the flight deck finalizing battle plans with her squadron. Ridley could see by the looks on their faces that every one of those pilots would fly through the fires of hell for their commander. Looking at her now, Ridley figured he'd do the same.

Finally, the squadron meeting broke up. Mara-jul came over to where Ridley sat with Azrnoth-zin. "My fighter squadron is ready," she said.

"Good," said Azrnoth-zin. "So are the ground assault teams. Would you not agree, Ridley?"

"Huh? Oh, I think they're ready. Do you think we laid too much new stuff on them with the weapons modifications and all?"

"I would wager that all of them will be able to take apart and reassemble the weapons, as well as fire accurately before we leave port tomorrow," said Azrnoth-zin. He looked at Ridley quizzically. "Are you all right?"

"Yeah. I'm fine. I was just thinking about what old Quillen-tok said to me earlier."

"Do not dwell on that, Ridley. You must remain focused on the task at hand."

"What did he say?" said Mara-jul.

"It was nothing," said Ridley. "I'll tell you about it later."

"I suggest you both get plenty of rest before we leave for the mission," said Azrnoth-zin.

Ridley winked at Mara-jul. "Never felt better, Arn."

Azrnoth-zin snorted in feigned disgust. "Plenty of rest." He turned and walked out of the room.

"How do you feel?" said Ridley.

"Fine. I am not fatigued in the least."

"Me, either."

Mara-jul smiled at Ridley, touching his hand. "I have more questions about Earth culture and customs," she said.

"You know, I was just thinking about a little intercultural exchange right about now myself."

Mara-jul touched Ridley's cheek. "Azrnoth-zin was right."

"Oh? About what?"

"Humans do grow on you after a time."

CHAPTER TWENTY-SIX

Ridley felt the waves of pleasure wash over him as he and Mara-jul connected physically and telepathically. Sweat glistened from both of their bodies as they lay entwined, both of them craving the physical contact that had been lacking for so long.

Ridley found the mind-water link to be less daunting the second time. He was able to control his thoughts and discovered he was able to access more of Mara-jul's thoughts and deeply hidden emotions. It was as if he were wandering in a great hall with a thousand doors. Each time he opened another door, images from Mara-jul's life flooded his mind. With a little practice he learned to let go of his own pre-conceived notions and embrace the memories for what they were, part and parcel of the fabric that made up this beautiful and complex woman with whom he lay.

He discovered that some of those doors were not open to him. Mara-jul was purposefully blocking access to those recesses of her mind. Ridley, feeling like a kid newly released in a candy shop, persisted. Playfully, he prodded at Mara-jul's psyche, attempting to gain access to several of those secretive nooks. Mara-jul responded in kind at first, then began to withdraw. Ridley gently continued his persistent probing.

Sarn-ula's face came to his mind.

"No!" Mara-jul pulled back suddenly and looked away. She turned away from Ridley and faced the bulkhead, breathing heavily. Ridley lay on his back, staring at the ceiling of her sleeping quarters.

After several uncomfortable moments, Ridley spoke, his voice a hoarse whisper.

"I'm sorry. I shouldn't have done that."

So softly spoken, he almost didn't hear her response. "It was not your fault."

Mara-jul rolled and turned into Ridley, pulling him closer. They continued to lie there for several minutes, each groping for the words that would soothe and forgive.

Abruptly, Ridley sat up in bed, his arms folded around his bare knees.

"How long have you been playing me?"

Mara-jul sat up and placed her arms around Ridley's shoulders. He shrugged them off. Mara-jul looked away, then spoke, her voice strained.

"I have been reporting to Sarn-ula for several months. Mostly giving her information concerning the missions. She wanted more. She said you knew things. Things that were dangerous to the Delfinian people. She ordered me to access your mind through the water link. She said you would not block me."

"Well, she was right about that," Ridley said tersely. He turned angrily to face her. "Did you find what you were looking for?"

"Ridley, I have not divulged to Sarn-ula what has transpired during . . ."

"But you were going to!" Ridley stood up and faced Mara-jul, his face a mask of rage and confusion and pain. Mara-jul inadvertently winced and withdrew slightly, seeing the raw emotions in Ridley's face.

"Ridley, I was doing what I thought to be best for you and the Delfinian people. At first, I had my suspicions about your intentions, as did many of us. In knowing your mind, I came to know another aspect of your being. I could not go back and tell Sarn-ula now, knowing the connection we have achieved."

Ridley stood and in the dim light of the sleeping chamber, gathered up his clothes and dressed. He did not look at Mara-jul. Pulling on his boots, he walked to the entrance of Mara-jul's quarters. She followed closely behind, hastily donning a dressing gown.

"Ridley, listen to me! I couldn't tell Sarn-ula. I could no more betray you than I could betray myself."

The door slid open, Ridley's back to her. "I don't know what the hell I was thinking."

"I told Sarn-ula nothing!"

"Good luck on the mission, Commander."

The door slid closed behind Ridley with a soft swoosh.

The shuttlecraft was bathed in darkness. They were traveling along the equator of the second moon, keeping well concealed from the Trochinid surveillance sensors. They had gone to com silence several hours ago. The next communication would be when the dome shield went down.

Ridley and Kelun manned the controls. Ridley had come to admire the delicate looking Yhrynen. His soft-spoken manner coupled with his childlike inquisitiveness made him instantly likeable, despite his ungainly appearance. Of the three billion Yhrynen that had once flourished on their homeworld, only one survived among the Displaced Work Force. Kelun believed more of his people had survived. Like him, there must be others who had been away from Yhrys surveying distant parts of the galaxy when their home world was attacked.

The other members of the team included two Mawhrbahts, Tikah, and a younger one named Osik. At the moment, Osik was fast asleep in one of the corners. Ridley was envious of the Mawhrbahts ability to sleep just about any place, any time. Tikah was aft, helping one of the Delfinians with last minute weapons calibrations.

The remainder of the team was made up of three Delfinians. Ridley was glad Kirin-rah had been assigned to his team. Time and again, she had proven herself to be dependable when the going got ugly. Her tenacity in battle and her ability to keep a cool head while under fire bolstered Ridley's confidence.

Duhan-ben and Boren-rhan were the newest additions to the *ZOO* crew. Both of them were tenth order warriors, recently come of age, and now able to join the Delfinian fighting force. There appeared to be an air of competition between the two, Ridley noticed, during training and drills. Neither of them lacked for enthusiasm. It was interesting how they had asked Ridley for the data logs about Earth. In their spare time, they devoured any and all information they could get their hands on regarding Ridley's homeworld.

Earlier, aboard the *ZOO*, Ridley almost ran into Mara-jul as they both rounded a corner on way to the command center. For a moment, their eyes met. Ridley fidgeted awkwardly, then turned away and resumed walking.

"Excuse me," he said.

"Ridley, it is important that I speak with you," Mara-jul said sharply to his retreating back.

Ridley turned around tiredly. "If it's about the mission, go ahead and talk."

"It is about us."

"Wrong answer. See you in at the final briefing, Commander."

"You will not allow me the opportunity to tell you what happened?" Mara-jul looked stricken.

"Funny thing about those water links," Ridley said. "A little too much information."

"I told Sarn-ula nothing of value. I could not bear to see harm to come to you."

Ridley glared at Mara-jul, his jaw muscles clenching. "You should have told me! You were the last one I would have thought . . ." His voice trailed off. He held up a hand. "I need to focus on the mission right now."

Ridley turned and walked to the command center without looking back.

In the closed quarters of the command center, the air was so thick with tension even Trahg noticed something was amiss. Mara-jul spoke with Azrnoth-zin, Kelun and Trahg, then spun abruptly on her heel and left the command center to join the members of her squadron. Azrnoth-zin watched Mara-jul exit, then turned to observe Ridley.

"Ridley, shouldn't you go -?"

Ridley turned sharply, pointing a finger at Azrnoth-zin. "Leave it alone, Arn."

Azrnoth-zin looked questioningly at Ridley, then turned back to his calculations.

Ridley checked the flight plan again, frowning over the readouts that scrolled across the flat screen in front of him. Kelun turned his slender, snake-like neck and regarded Ridley impassively with his large pink eyes.

"Ridley, are you not feeling well?" the Yhrynen asked.

"Huh? I'm fine," Ridley snapped. "Why?"

Kelun cocked his smallish head curiously. "Because, I have noticed that you have checked the flight trajectory seven times in the past two hours. You seem distracted."

"I'm fine. Really. Just a little nervous about the mission, that's all."

"No. There is more than that. I have seen you go into battle before. This is different. Is something wrong?"

"Damn it! The last thing I need is someone asking me how I feel. Stick to what you do best, designing weapons and flying this crate!"

Kelun tilted his head again, looking at Ridley. Emitting a strange gutteral sound from deep in his throat, he turned back to the controls.

Ridley sighed, then placed a hand on the slender shoulder of the Yhrynen he had befriended.

"I'm sorry Kelun. Nerves are a little raw right now."

In an effort to force thoughts of Mara-jul from his mind, Ridley stood up and decided to check in with each member of the crew again. He looked back to see Kirin-rah having some difficulty with her weapon.

"Your stick for a while, amigo. I'll be right back."

Making his way to the rear of the shuttle, Ridley sat down next to Kirin-rah. "How's it going, Kirin?"

"I wish I had been given more time to learn these weapons," she said. "I feel as if it is not an extension of me yet."

"Go through the activation sequence for me," Ridley said.

"First, you . . ."

"With your eyes closed. Don't look at the weapon."

Kirin-rah's hands moved deftly over the weapon. The pulse cannon came to life, humming as the power cells fed into the activator chambers.

"Looks to me like you got it wired," said Ridley. "I think you'll like this better once you get a chance to use it. You are more ready than you may think you are."

"Commander Ridley, may I ask you a question?"

"Sure."

"Do you ever feel . . . fear? I find that I have a strange feeling inside of me. Almost like I am ill. Why is that? I have gone on many missions, yet the feeling is still there."

Ridley ran his hand over the top of Kirin-rah's. "Feel that dampness? That's genuine, hundred-proof, scared shitless. And that's a good thing. Because, if you don't feel that in this type of situation, you're either stupid or dead. That bad feeling in your stomach will keep you alive."

"I am unsure about this ascent that we are going to make to approach the installation," said Kirin-rah. "I have never before experienced this thing you call rock climbing."

"You'll do fine. Tikah, Osik and I will define the routes. You all just have to follow our leads. You'll be tied in the whole way. Did you spend some time in the simulator in heavier G?"

Kirin-rah nodded. "Have you ever climbed in a heavier atmosphere?"

"No," said Ridley, forcing a smile. "I haven't. But there's a first time for everything."

"Azrnoth-zin told me that you had to climb to get away from the people that wanted to capture him."

"Yeah. Old Arn took to it like a Delfid takes to water. What did he tell you about it?"

"He said it was one of the most frightening things he had done in his life."

"Oh. Well. Don't believe everything Azrnoth-zin tells you. He has somewhat of a flair for the dramatic."

"I want to serve well, Commander Ridley."

Ridley shook his head. "If I live to be a hundred, I don't think I'll ever get used to being called "Commander"." He touched her on the shoulder and smiled. "I have no doubt you will."

Ridley walked back to the command seat. "What's our ETA, Kelun?"

"Two hours, forty-seven minutes at present velocity."

"If I weren't so damn nervous, I'd nod off like Osik back there."

The shuttle emerged from behind the planet's's veil of darkness two hours later. Ridley found himself holding his breath as the third moon came into view.

Using a low flight approach and following the system of deep ravines and canyons that criss-crossed the third moon, the shuttle was able to avoid detection. They landed five kilometers south and east from the Trochinid installation, shielded by a deep cut in the moon's surface that angled toward the escarpment in the distance.

Before he stepped out into the alien atmosphere, Ridley and Kelun activated the two metallics that would bring the ship to the rendezvous point. META IV was aboard the *ZOO*, preparing the med-surg section to handle the wounded. These metallics were of the same design as those that had manned the recon ship that picked up Azrnoth-zin and Ridley.

Ridley adjusted the personal force field and stepped through the airlock. As his feet hit the dusty, reddish soil, the first sensation he experienced was of being sucked into the ground. His body felt like he had gained in an instant an additional 220 pounds. There was no way they could have prepared adequately for this. For a moment, Ridley's only desire was to get everyone back into the shuttle to try to get a little closer to their objective. He knew, however, that would only jeopardize their already precarious position. A moment later, the metallics manning the shuttle lifted off and left the teams standing on the hostile surface. It was the most isolated Ridley had ever felt in his life.

The team followed the coordinates and made their way slowly through the maze of ravines in the planetoid's surface. It would be a longer and more arduous approach, but the chances were better of not being detected than if they had chosen a more direct route.

"What's the atmosphere made up of here?" Ridley said, his breathing suddenly more labored.

"It is primarily composed of nitrogen," replied Kelun. "There are smaller concentrations of argon, sulphur, carbon monoxide and xenon gases. I suggest you do not deactivate your personal force field."

"Thanks for the safety tip. How the hell can the Trochinids breathe this crap?"

"One of the reasons they have been so successful is their high level of adaptability. They have evolved in such a way that their bodies can withstand many toxic environments."

"Do you think they're slowed down by the G force here?"

"That is uncertain," said Kelun. "To my knowledge, this is the first time the Trochinids will be engaged on solid ground."

"I hate being a pioneer," said Ridley.

The terrain became progressively more rugose, slowing their already plodding pace. The ones who appeared to be least affected by the heavier G force were Tikah and Osik. They moved from boulder to boulder with no hint of fatigue in their movements.

At first, Ridley and company trekked for almost an hour before they stopped. Their rest intervals increased to every thirty minutes, then every twenty, then fifteen. Ridley felt as if he were wading through waist deep mud. The effort caused him to sweat profusely inside of the PFF, creating a mini-greenhouse effect. As uncomfortable as it was, it beat the alternative residing on the other side of the shield.

Ridley called a halt to the march and unshouldered his pack. Duhan-ben was breathing in gasps. Rummaging through his pack, he produced a handful of small whitish pills. Ridley adjusted the frequency of his personal force field to match that of the young Delfinian's. The two PFFs shimmered as they contacted each other, forming a shimmering bubble. Ridley placed the pill in Duhan-ben's palm. The Delfinian looked up at Ridley and attempted to speak.

"It's a little concoction of META IV's," Ridley said, opening a bottle of water and handing it to Duhan-ben. "She calls them oxygenators. They're supposed to increase the efficiency of oxygen uptake during times of extreme exertion."

Duhan-ben swallowed the capsule. Within thirty seconds he was almost breathing normally. "That is much better."

Ridley handed the young Delfinian warrior several pills. "Use them sparingly. We're really going to need these once we make the climb and attack the compound."

He then systematically distributed pills to the members of the assault team. After the team had rested for several minutes, Ridley motioned for them to continue moving. They followed a convoluted series of wind-blown rifts, slowly edging closer to the plateau. After taking the pill, Ridley felt a resurgence of energy. His feet didn't feel as leaden: even the packstraps weren't digging into his shoulders as much.

Ridley thought about the two explosive charges he carried in his pack. Azrnoth-zin carried two identical devices. Between the two of them, they possessed enough explosive capacity to blow the plateau into fine dust particles once the stealth device was recovered. Which was exactly what they planned to do.

Ridley felt a presence. He looked over his shoulder in expectation. Around him in this stark environment, the other members of Delta Team went about their duties. He realized it was coming from within. Mara-jul's image came to his mind. It was faint at first, but when he focused his energies, he could feel her thoughts.

Azrnoth-zin is delayed. The approach is slower than anticipated. Ridley, be careful. Come back to me.

Ridley did his best to remain focused. Mara-jul had said she did not betray him to Sarn-ula. But she must have divulged something. What was it that Ridley had in his mind that Sarn-ula

OFFWORLDER

so desperately desired? And how had she convinced Mara-jul that
Ridley posed a threat?

He was surprised the connection between them was this
strong for him to receive her thoughts over such a distance. Part of
him wanted to project to her, but he could not. Not now. The deep
cut of her betrayal was still too fresh. Besides, he needed to focus
on the task at hand. If he made it out of here, they would speak
again.

He attempted to project his thoughts out to Azrnoth-zin.
He cleared his mind, focusd his thoughts, then awaited an answer.
Azrnoth-zin did not respond. Ridley hoped his friend was just
focusing on the approach and had not run into early resistance.

The team struggled through the rifts, hardly noticing the
wind-sculpted red rock formations on all sides. There were areas
where large sections of ferrous rock had collapsed into the ravine,
making progress more difficult. The assault team was now forced
to scramble over the top of these slabs or crawl between stacks of
tumbled boulders.

Ridley finally called a halt under a huge, ancient slab that
had broken free and slid into the canyon, leaving a space beneath
that twenty people could stand under comfortably.

"We'll rest here before the final push to the plateau," said
Ridley. He grimaced as he removed his pack and set it near his
feet. "Tikah. Osik. Once you've gotten some rest, scout ahead
and see what we're facing."

Tikah chattered at Ridley.

Ridley took several deep breaths to fill his oxygen-depleted
lungs and said to her "No. Don't engage them. Just get back here
pronto. And above all else, be careful."

The two Mawhrbahts nodded, then disappeared quickly
into the boulder field.

After twenty minutes, Ridley was getting worried. Tikah
and Osik had not made it back to the designated rendezvous
point. He hadn't heard any exchange from weapons. The heavier
atmosphere should transmit sounds better here. Time was growing
short.

247

"Okay everyone, let's keep moving," Ridley said, pulling his pack over his aching shoulders.

Suddenly, Tikah and Osik appeared from behind a large reddish boulder, which was streaked with black striations. Tikah indicated that two Trochinids were posted at the base of the plateau where the ravine dead-ended. The plateau was less than a kilometer away. No. She didn't think they had been seen.

Word was spread quickly among the team. They moved out in single file, Ridley and the Mawhrbahts in the lead. A short time later, with the top of the plateau looming before them, they came to the place where the Trochinids had been spotted. Ridley and the team crouched behind a large slab jutting out at an angle from the side of the ravine.

The two sinister aliens sat perched on a slab of rock, facing each other, their heads almost touching. They did not appear to be moving. Ridley almost assumed they were asleep. Upon examination through the binoculars, Ridley saw that they appeared to be in somewhat of a trance-like state. Good. They hadn't been detected.

A small hovercraft sat idle several yards from them. The engine compartment was open, various nondescript parts lay strewn about the ground. The Trochinids must be awaiting assistance or relief. Obviously, the insect-like aliens lacked the engineering expertise of the Mawhrbahts. Ridley hoped the craft could be salvaged. It would be a lot easier to ferry the team to the top instead of making the climb.

Ridley signed a messsage to the other members of Delta Team. "Don't damage the hovercraft." A firefight was sure to bring reinforcements. Another tactic had to be employed to neutralize the two sentries.

Ridley turned back to the team and said quietly, "I need a volun -."

Tikah and Osik were standing in front of him before he could finish the sentence. Ridley nodded and produced the throwing stars from his pack. Tikah and Osik removed stars from their small packs. Silently, they moved out among the boulders.

The going through the boulder field was agonizingly slow. Each of them had to make sure their passage stirred up no dust clouds. When they were within fifty yards of the Trochinids, they split into three directions: Tikah was to approach from the left, Osik from the right and Ridley was to go at them straight up the middle.

Ridley crouched behind a low-lying boulder that barely concealed him. Unshouldering his pack, he prepared to stand up and throw the small detonating stars at the nearest Trochinid. He set the force field to intermittent discharge and jumped to his feet.

His movement caught the immediate attention of the Trochinid sentries. Snarling, they lurched to their full eight-foot height and lifted their weapons. Ridley let one of the throwing stars go with a sharp flick from his wrist. The sentry in front caught the star in the upper thorax. It stuck but did not immediately eat its way into the chest cavity. The Trochinid looked at it with a malevolent curiosity. Suddenly, two more stars appeared in each Trochinid's chests. They attempted to pull them out, but the chemicals had already taken effect. The smoldering stars dissolved into the thoraxes, the Trochinids screamed and clawed at their chest cavities.

The first Trochinid disappeared in a muted splatter of greenish-yellow gore. A second later, the other one exploded. Their body parts littered the ground, but the only sound Ridley could distinguish in this atmosphere was a sickly, wet slap at the time of impact.

Ridley looked at the two Mawhrbahts and gave each of them the thumbs up sign. With both hands he pointed to the downed hover craft. A minute later the rest of the team had joined him.

"Do you think they got a com signal out?" said Kirin-rah.

"I don't think so, " said Ridley. "Kelun, see if you can help the Mawhrbahts get that hovercraft operational. The rest of us will start preparing for the climb, just in case."

Ridley and the Delfinians pulled the ropes from the packs and began uncoiling them at the base of the rock wall. Several minutes passed before Kelun lumbered up to Ridley.

"The drive system is fused," he said. "It appears these two were stranded after they burned up the drive unit. Tikah says it would take hours to repair the damage."

"We don't have hours. Sooner or later someone is coming to get them." Ridley looked up at the series of vertical cracks that disappeared from his line of sight. "Oh, hell. Looks like we do this the hard way."

Within minutes, all members of the team had donned harnesses and were awaiting Ridley's orders.

Ridley dumped the oddly shaped metal pieces on the ground in front of him and organized them by size.

"What is that?" said Boren-rhan.

"It's lead protection. I'll stick these pieces in the rock on my way up. It's to keep me from taking a long fall. Second one up, pull it out so it can be used again on the next pitch."

The Delfinian looked uneasy.

"Don't worry, Boren-rhan. The Mawhrbahts and I will go up first."

Osik, Tikah, and Ridley split up the gear and each headed off to find an accessible crack to begin the climb. Ridley instructed Kirin-rah in the belay system, then walked over to the face and located small rocky projections to begin his climb.

"Here are the rules," said Ridley. "Keep at least three appendages on the rock at any given time. Focus on what's in front of you. Don't spend time looking down. Keep well inside the crack system unless you absolutely have no other holds. Once we move out onto the cliff face, we're easy targets."

Ridley climbed up several feet. "Oh. One more thing. Breathing is essential."

The Mawhrbahts moved twice as fast as Ridley and had already secured the first ledge before Ridley was halfway up the crack. Ridley placed the protection sparingly, but with enough spacing that he could survive a fall. Moving vertically in this gravity was exhausting; Ridley was gasping by the time he reached the first ledge, two hundred feet above the ground.

Once Ridley was able to assume a sitting position, he anchored himself to the rock and tugged on the rope to let Kirin-rah know he was ready. He reeled in rope until he felt the steady pressure of Kirin-rah on the other end. She gave two tugs on the rope, indicating she was commencing the climb. Twenty minutes later, Kirin-rah's strained and sweaty face appeared above the ledge. She flopped down beside Ridley, her breathing coming in great heaves.

Once she had regained her breath, Kirin-rah pulled herself to a sitting position next to Ridley, who was in the process of organizing the gear for the next pitch.

"You humans do *that* for pleasure on your homeworld?"

"Yeah. Members of my species are gluttons for punishment."

"I think I prefer large bodies of water to this."

"On Earth, some people would pay a fortune to come to a place like this and do exactly what you're doing right now."

"Why?"

"For the right to brag about it," said Ridley. "Are you okay to belay me again? I think I'm all set here."

Kirin-rah nodded and attached herself to the ledge and the rope through her harness. "Ready."

"See you on the second floor. Next stop, housewares, appliances and ladies' lingerie."

Kirin-rah glanced up at Ridley, an odd look on her face. Ridley stepped up, then jammed his fist into the crack to lever himself up.

It took nearly three hours to reach the summit of the plateau. By the time Ridley had dragged himself over the last ledge, he had consumed two more of the oxygen boosters. Tikah, Osik and Kelun were already on the ledge. Kelun and Osik were belaying the other two Delfinians. Tikah organized the packs.

"Well, at least we don't have to carry the climbing gear any more," Ridley said, between gasps. "Whose idea was this anyway?"

Tikah chattered a barrage in Ridley's direction.

"Okay, okay. Don't rub it in."

A faint humming sound brought Tikah to attention. Before he could react, Ridley saw the hovercraft cruise overhead and disappear over the edge of the plateau. Ridley hoped the last of the climbers were not exposed.

"Do you think they saw us?" Ridley said, peering over the edge into the gathering gloom. The outline of the hovercraft soon faded from view, descending toward the valley floor below.

"I think we're okay," said Ridley. "I don't think they know we're here. Let's hope the darkness will hide our footprints."

Tikah chattered at Ridley.

He pulled himself up to his feet and peered over the top of the ledge. The horizon was lit up with an eerie orange glow. He wasn't ready for the immensity of the sight before him.

In the center of the great plateau was a vast spaceport. It appeared more like a city than a processing depot. Smaller, dome-like structures surrounded several taller spires. The Trochinid base was a hive of activity. Support vessels moved between several immense battle cruisers, which stood moored to the taller spires. A gigantic, box-like behemoth that Ridley knew could only be a processing ship was stationary at one end of the spaceport. Even from this distance, Ridley could see the black maw of the huge loading bay and ramp. Shuttlecraft moved back and forth between the squat freighter and the battle cruisers.

"Holy shit!" Ridley said in a loud whisper.

Tikah looked at Ridley, made a small sound almost like a whimper, then returned her gaze to the spectacle on the plateau.

Ridley turned away and slid down to a sitting position. "Next time I come up with a hair-brained idea like this, I want you to hit me with something, preferrably something very heavy."

A tug from the rope brought Ridley back to the problem at hand. Kirin-rah was ready to make the final ascent. Finally, Kirin-rah's fingers followed by her face appeared above the lip of the ledge.

"Did you take some time to admire the view?" she said, grunting with the effort of pulling herself onto the rock ledge.

"Sorry, Kirin. I got a bit overwhelmed for a minute."

"They could not see us when they passed over. We were all well hidden in the crevice."

"Good. Let's hope they're not smart enough to investigate the area around the hover craft."

Soon, the rest of the team was assembled on the narrow outcropping below the level of the plateau. Using the high power imagers, Ridley scanned the terrain between them and the depot. The image in the viewfinder revealed a brightly lit landscape, even in the approaching darkness. A series of fissures branched out like an enormous spider web from the center of the processing facility.

"That large structure near the center," said Kelun, "is the central processing center. The Trochinids offload their cargoes into the structure from the ships. Once processed they distribute the materials throughout the fleet."

"So, is our stealth ship in among all those others?" said Ridley.

Kelun activated the sensor tag from an instrument he produced from his pack. The instrument began a low-pitched beeping. "Yes. The ship is there. It is the large battle cruiser on the far side of the processing depot."

Ridley looked at Tikah. "There's a series of crevices that run from here to the base. I want you and Osik to scout ahead and see if we can use them to get closer. We don't want a direct approach across the plateau if we can help it."

Tikah and Osik scampered over the lip and disappeared into the nearest depression. All of the climbing gear was stowed against the ledge. Delta Team checked their weapons again.

Ridley fretted about where Azrnoth-zin was right now. His mouth felt dry and his legs were leaden. What seemed an eternity passed before the Mawhrbahts finally clambered back over the ledge, their PFFs bearing a fine coating of red dust.

Tikah and Osik had found a way through one of the cuts. The small ravines were set with electromagnetic sensor arrays to detect movement. Above the ravines, the surface defenses appeared impenetrable. The Trochinids had concentrated most of their surveillance along the most obvious approach. In the narrow ravines, two sentries were posted about every three hundred meters. It seemed the Trochinids liked to work in twos.

Ridley explained what the plan was to be. The ravines were their only option. After a few final words, the Mawhrbahts crawled out into the darkness once more.

"Okay, everybody. Safeties off, full charge, quiet as you go. Let's get to that rendezvous point." Ridley was the next to go over the lip and crawl into the nearby shallow cut.

One by one, the rest of the team disappeared into the night.

CHAPTER TWENTY-SEVEN

Azrnoth-zin looked down from the small rise toward the lights of the processing facility. The central spire was a flurry of activity; Trochinid transfer ships moved up to the processing station, picked up their cargo, and then flew back to the battle cruisers docked nearby. He counted fourteen battle cruisers. That meant there would be thousands of Trochinids swarming around the complex.

He signaled for Ryk. The furry little Mawhrbaht with an attitude scurried over to where Azrnoth-zin was crouched. Azrnoth-zin had the distinct feeling that Ryk perceived himself as being much larger than his actual stature.

"Did you locate the tag?" Azrnoth-zin asked.

The diminutive alien nodded and held up a small receiver and adjusted the controls. An orange light blinked on one of the diagrams. Ryk pointed to a warship that was currently maneuvering into place at the vertical processing station. Azrnoth-zin nodded.

"Take Mistra and scout ahead. I want to know what kind of resistance we are facing. See if you can locate the quickest route through those ravines to get us under the dome. Do not engage the enemy."

Ryk whistled softly to Mistra. The two Mawhrbahts disappeared over the small rise of reddish sand and were swallowed by the darkness.

Turning to the other members of his team, Azrnoth-zin conveyed his orders. All were Delfinian except Ryk and Mistra, the two Mawhrbahts, and Bauk, the Markanian.

Azrnoth-zin stepped away from the others for a moment. He projected his thoughts outward in the direction where he thought Ridley was. Earlier he had unsuccessfully attempted to connect with the man from Earth and Delta Team. He wondered if Ridley's squad had encountered heavy resistance; the possibility loomed that Ridley's entire group may never have reached the summit.

An image came to his mind. He could see a shallow ravine in front of him. Behind him in his mind's eye, was Kirin-rah and as he concentrated his focus, he saw Kelun. Ridley and Delta Team were on the move. Azrnoth-zin projected his status to Ridley, then terminated the link.

When Azrnoth-zin rejoined the others, he saw that the Mawhrbahts had returned from their reconnaissance.

Ryk chattered a staccato series of chirps and trills. Azrnoth-zin still had difficulty following everything the Mawrbahts said. It seemed only Ridley's ears could pick up the subtle nuances of Mawhrbaht speech. Ridley had, after all, spent a great deal of time learning the language while working in the hulls of the ships. They had found a direct route to the dome.

Ryk barked a series of truncated guttural noises. The ravine was guarded by several pairs of Trochinid sentries spaced at intervals of a few hundred meters. The two Mawhrbahts had not been seen. Time to see if the new assault weapons worked, Azrnoth-zin thought casually. He turned to face his team.

"Ridley's team has made the summit and are advancing. So far they have escaped detection. They are using the ravines to access the facility. The surface is heavily laden with sensors."

"What did they see?" asked Khar-aul, a young Delfinian Fifth Order.

"The route to the dome is well guarded," said Azrnoth-zin. "Trochinid sentries are stationed in pairs every two hundred meters. We will have to subdue them quietly. Prepare your throwing stars and activate your phase weapons."

Ryk spoke again. Azrnoth-zin nodded. "Yes. Proceed. Use the throwing stars at close range. Bauk, ready your crossbow."

Khar-aul spoke up. "Commander, I would request to accompany the Mawhrbahts forward."

"Not yet, Fifth Order. They will scout ahead. Their ability to move quickly is their advantage. Our reactions are slowed by this gravity and I will need your expertise once we are inside the dome."

"Commander, I am ready to give my life for the glory of this mission."

Azrnoth-zin fixed the younger Delfinian warrior with a hard stare. "I have a much better suggestion. You can serve the Delfinian people best by recovering the device *and* living to tell about it."

Azrnoth-zin smiled inwardly at his statement. A year ago, he would have spoken the same words as Khar-aul. Damn that Ridley and his terran morality. Azrnoth-zin was worried about his friend.

Turning back to Khar-aal, Azrnoth-zin said, "Make it back to the rendezvous point alive and I will sing your praises across the sectors."

The younger Delfinian relaxed for a moment, the features on his face softening. "I have been reviewing the data logs from Earth. I have heard that you are planning to go back there, to deliver Ridley to his people."

"Where did you hear that?"

"It is spoken among Delfinians and the Displaced Work Force alike," said Khar-aul. "I would like to see this place called Earth. I would like to speak with the Delfids."

Azrnoth-zin nodded. "If and when I decide to go back, you will be under consideration to accompany me. For now, I want you to keep this conversation between you and me."

"Thank you, Commander."

"Inform the others that we are to move out immediately."

Khar-aul gave a brief salute, then moved off in a crouch, passing the word among the rest of the team. All were struggling against the relentless drain of the gravitational force of the dense moon. The strike force moved slowly through the low-lying ravine and followed the cut as it grew deeper. Of all the factors Azrnoth-zin had worked into his calculations, he wondered if the heavier atmosphere of the moon would be the one variable that would ultimately affect the outcome of the mission.

A short time later, the two Mawhrbahts scurried up to Azrnoth-zin. Ryk and Mistra gave their latest reconnaissance report. Ahead was a series of sensor relays, each guarded by two Trochinid sentries. There were five stations to be bypassed before they reached the dome.

Azrnoth-zin quietly issued orders. The Mawhrbahts scampered ahead of the rest of the team and disappeared around a bend in the ravine. It was not long before Azrnoth-zin and the others came to the first sensor relay. Two smoldering Trochinid corpses lay on the ground, evidence the Mawhrbahts were successful in quietly dispatching the first two sentries.

The rest of the mission depended on split second timing. Azrnoth-zin hoped that Ridley and his team were in place and that Mara-jul and the light fighters would be able to create the diversion allowing them to slip under the dome. Once the dome was deactivated, Mara-jul's team could attack the vulnerable ships.

"Keep moving," he said. "We don't want to keep Ridley and the others waiting."

CHAPTER TWENTY-EIGHT

Though the thought transference was limited to a series of brief images, Ridley was able to piece together the location of Alpha Squad. Ridley was relieved to learn that Azrnoth-zin's team had made the summit and was also advancing across the plateau.

Ridley gathered Delta Squad around him. They had made it through the fourth sensor relay station without detection. Eight Trochinids were now part of the arid landscape. The looks of quiet determination and resolve from the members of his team met Ridley's gaze. All except Kelun's. Due to poorly developed facial muscles, the Yhrynen's countenance reflected constant placidity.

Ridley downed another oxygenator pill and washed it down with a swig of water. Wiping parched lips, he said, "Okay, people. Four down, four to go. Kirin-rah, I want you to bring up the rear. Make sure we don't get a Troch attack from behind. If anything happens to me, it's your show." Ridley took a deep breath, then exhaled. "Any questions?"

No one spoke.

"Well then, let's go ruin their day."

They hadn't traveled far when Tikah and Osik bounded up to Ridley, informing him that at the next sensor relay station there was no cover and too much distance to effectively use the throwing stars. Ridley moved up ahead with them and peered around the wall that angled toward the Trochinid sentries.

One of the Trochinids was adjusting the relay system. The other cast a malevolent gaze back in their direction. Its large gray-green head swiveled slowly back and forth. The bulging yellowish eyes gave the impression that the creature could detect movement from both great distance and peripherally.

The Trochinid at the sensor station needed to be taken out first. Tikah and Osik were correct in their assumption. A throwing star wouldn't do here.

Reaching inside his pack, Ridley found the small, folded Markanian crossbow. He snapped it into place and loaded a fusion dart into the sling. The crossbow was good up to fifty meters. Ridley sighted in the Trochinid at the station. He inhaled a breath, took careful aim, and let the dart fly.

The fusion dart landed in the sand three feet short of the Trochinid. Cocking its head, the sentry lurched over to look. It picked up the dart in its talons. In the next instant, the Trochinid was engulfed in a burst of blinding light. It screamed in agony.

Ridley was up and running. He took three steps, dropped to one knee and loaded another dart into the bow. The second Trochinid turned back to the sensor array. Ridley let the fusion dart go. The sentry was enveloped in a blinding flash. Tikah rose and flung a throwing star at the wounded Trochinid. It turned into a quivering mass of gore, flopping face down into the sand.

Ridley looked up at the diminutive aliens and gave them the thumbs up sign. Tikah, through her animated body language, told Ridley to shoot better next time. Ridley shrugged and rolled his eyes.

By the time the Delta Team reached the edge of the perimeter, sixteen Trochinids had been neutralized. The sensor arrays were disabled and Ridley's aim had improved significantly.

The assault team gathered at the bottom of the ravine. The personal force fields were operating at maximum output. The energy cells were working overtime to disintegrate the blowing dust that clung to the outer surface.

Ridley checked his watch. Ten minutes until Mara-jul would light up the sky. Ten minutes and two hundred meters to go once they cleared the lip of the ravine. From here on, Ridley was counting on the confusion created by Mara-jul's attack.

Ridley scrambled to the top of the ravine with the rest of the team, and peered over the edge. The translucent dome appeared like a huge inverted punchbowl, with ships docked at various levels as if suspended in a gelatinous mass. The dome would shimmer and disappear momentarily to allow a ship to pass through.

Ridley drew the Troch blaster from the sling on his pack. "Final systems check," he said. "Ten minutes to showtime."

CHAPTER TWENTY-NINE

The force field on the landing platform was the only thing that separated Mara-jul's fighter from the black void of space. Twelve light fighters were crowded into four landing bays. She opened a channel to address the other pilots.

"Prepare all fighters for final launch sequence," she said. "Final systems check for com links and holo-emitters."

Each fighter had been retrofitted with a holographic imager in the nose section. Once in space, the pilot could project as many as three images of his or her ship. The images could be programmed to maneuver independent of the mother ship. The ruse was Ridley's idea. The Mawhrbahts had engineered the emitters and installed them in all of the ships. Mara-jul still remembered the image of her fighter as it appeared, then dissolved into the bulkhead of the cargo bay.

The sleight of hand, as Ridley had referred to it, was designed to distract the Trochinids away from the real assault taking place on the ground. So far, Ridley's and Azrnoth-zin's teams had managed to avoid detection. With images of three times as many ships attacking the dome, the chances for Mara-jul's squad were even better. The twelve real fighters would dodge and weave, forming up for an all-out assault once the dome was destroyed.

Mara-jul flashed back to her childhood. She remembered lying on her back in the water, her father next to her, watching the images appear and then fade overhead. She always looked forward to the Water Festival. The holographic displays used during the festival were designed to entertain and educate. Today, the holo imagers were to be used for a much different purpose.

She thought of Ridley. Unable to pick up his thoughts, she found herself wanting to project even harder across the void. She wanted to tell him she was sorry. She remembered the stricken look on Ridley's face when he discovered the truth. She did not realize the magnitude of how much the reorganization had changed him, expanding the powers of his own mind control. She wished she had told him about Sarn-ula. She wished she had told him about her feelings for him. The connection between them was strong, yet she did not know why. The rational part of her being told her that she was going against all that Delfinians considered part of the strict code for living. The other part, the part that was speaking the loudest now, felt the exhilaration and anticipation of a newly discovered passion. This feeling was stronger than anything she had ever experienced.

Suddenly, Mara-jul felt the gnawing anxiety of not knowing whether she would ever see Ridley again.

She squeezed her eyes shut and shook her head as if she were ridding herself of an unpleasant memory. Mara-jul turned back to the task at hand.

She scrolled through the fighter's computer one more time, then checked the holo-imager and com link. Satisfied, she donned the virtual image headset and switched to open com.

"All ships, prepare to launch. Fighters one through four on my mark."

Mara-jul's fighter group was to spearhead the attack. Once they were away, the squadron would fly in three groups of four.

"Rendezvous at these coordinates." She punched the numbers into her computer. Instantaneously, the readouts appeared in the other eleven fighters. She fired the igniters on her ship and made the final launch check.

"Fighters one through four away."

Disengaging the force field, Mara-jul blasted out of the flight bay. She felt the visceral clench of acceleration, her body pummeled against the padded seat. Even with the momentary discomfort, this was still her favorite feeling, that feeling of raw acceleration and power, and that she was in control of it.

"Fighters five through eight away," she said, as she set the formation, the other three ships falling in beside and slightly behind hers.

After the last four ships had safely blasted off from the *ZOO*, Mara-jul signaled the main ship. "Prepare to launch assault team recovery shuttles. Proceed to designated holding area until signaled."

"Yes, Commander," said the voice of a metallic. "Shuttles are away. We will await your signal."

"All units, prepare for the jump to star drive." The jump was to be brief but tricky. A miscalculation would land them past the dark side of the small moon and ruin any chance of a surprise attack. Mara-jul hoped the data from the long-range sensors were correct. There had been no indication of any Trochinid activity on the small moon.

Mara-jul engaged the star drive. Instantly her body was plastered into the cushion. The sleek fighter vibrated as it overcame the inertia and smoothed out as it settled into SD9. Within minutes the warning sensors indicated that it was time to disengage the star drive. She decelerated along with the other eleven ships. Before her was the dark side of the small moon that shielded them from the Trochinid base.

Instinctively, Mara-jul activated forward shields and began a scan of the moon's surface as, one by one, the other fighters came out of the jump flanking her.

"Fighters two through six move into position," she said angling her fighter toward the horizon. "Seven through twelve take your positions." The first six fighters followed Mara-jul; the second six flew to the opposite side of the moon. Their attack would come from either side of the darkened moon.

"From this point on, the com link is off. Voices will only lead them to a real fighter. Use subspace band or thought transference." Mara-jul checked the computer. Twelve minutes.

Mara-jul glanced to her right and then her left. She felt a great swelling of pride as she watched the warriors flying formation with her. Many of the squadron she had trained personally. These pilots were considered the best in the entire Delfinian fleet.

She thought of Ridley and tried to get a sense of where he was. It was troublesome; she could not get a feeling for him now. She hoped they both lived to see each other again. To hell with what the Water Council thought. To hell with Sarn-ula. *Damn you Ridley,* she thought. *Stay alive so I can tell you myself.*

Her thoughts were interrupted by the computer beginning final countdown. Mara-jul activated laser cannons to full charge. Next, she initiated the holo-projector. Instantly, she was flanked by three other fighters, each with a perfect replica of her sitting at the controls. It was slightly unnerving as one of the images turned to her and saluted. The computer controlled all of the functions of the holo images from now on, down to the hull signatures designed to confuse the Trochinid sensors.

As she entered the light, Mara-jul accelerated the ship into attack speed. Looking around her, she saw a full squadron of fighters screaming toward the Trochinid depot.

CHAPTER THIRTY

It was too good to be true. The assault team was within striking distance of the depot. From their vantage point behind a cluster of boulders, Ridley saw six Trochinids perched in front of the dome. They squatted before a large doorway that led to a flight of steps into the main part of the complex. Unless they were taken out in the next four minutes, the dome would be sealed after Marajul's fighters attacked. Ridley doubted the explosives strapped to his back would be of much use then.

The Trochinids, unaware of the intruder's presence, were gathered around what appeared to be a huge slab of jerky. They would lean in and vigorously shake a hunk of the material loose with their fangs, squabbling over the choicest pieces. Ridley thought shark feeding frenzies were more pleasant to watch. He didn't want to know what they were eating.

Ridley turned to the others. Without speaking, he motioned for Tikah, Osik, and Kirin-rah to follow him. Tikah and Osik were to disable the last relay, while Ridley and Kirin-rah took out the Trochinids. Suddenly, the two Mawhrbahts were gone in a flurry of sand. Ridley watched two small ripples in the ground as the Mawhrbahts closed in on the dining Trochinids.

Ridley motioned for the other members to come forward. "Pick a target. Watch out for the Mawhrbahts," he whispered. They inched forward.

The Trochinids were too busy devouring the slab to notice the twin bulges of sand move toward them. Suddenly, Tikah and

Osik burst from the sand, weapons leveled. They opened up on the Trochinids. Two disappeared instantly in the phase cannons deadly crossfire.

Ridley and the others were up and running toward the door, weapons firing. Ridley saw his fire splatter a Trochinid against the wall. Kirin-rah took out another one. One of the Trochinids leapt for the relay station, but was cut down by Kelun.

The sixth Trochinid fired off a series of bursts at the Mawhrbahts. The ground in front of them exploded in a cloud of red rock and sand. When the dust cleared, Tikah was bounding for the relay station. Osik lay in the dust.

Ridley hit the Trochinid square in the back before it got off another shot at Tikah. Suddenly, the air was ringing with the high pitched sound of alarm. Overhead, the dome was under attack. Laser cannon charges from Mara-jul's fighters hit the dome and dissipated.

Ridley ran to where Osik lay. He turned the Mawhrbaht over. Part of Osik's chest cavity was gone. Ridley felt the intense heat of rage consume him. "I'm sorry, Osik," he said. Looking up at Tikah, he shook his head.

Tikah motioned to him that the relay station was disabled and that the door would remain open for ten seconds.

Turning to the others, Ridley yelled, "Go! Go! Go!"

Ridley was the first one onto the platform and ducked quickly behind a grouping of metal alloy cannisters. Kirin-rah ducked through the arched door as the dome shimmered and sealed the arch.

"Kelun, I need a reading on that ship!" Ridley said. "How close are we?"

"Twelve hundred meters in that direction," Kelun replied, his slender finger pointing the direction.

A series of blasts occurred at the opposite end of the compound.

"That would be Azrnoth-zin and company," said Ridley. "Right on time. Let's see if we can let them know we're here."

The assault team advanced through the alien complex. A long, low-slung building lay before them. It was quonset hut shaped, but made of a shimmering material Ridley did not recognize. Delta Team skirted along the side of the long temporary building. Touching the sides of the structure, Ridley's hand came away sticky. Ridley and his team hunkered against the side of the structure. Everywhere, Trochinids lurched and hopped toward the fire fight on the other side of the depot.

"Azrnoth-zin's team is in trouble," said Ridley. "They'll never be able to fight through all that resistance."

"What do you suggest?" said Kelun.

"See if you can locate a munitions or weapons storage. I think we need a distraction."

Kelun scrolled through the data on the hand scanner. "Fifty meters off to the left of this long structure."

"Time to light things up a bit." Ridley swallowed another oxygen pill and took off at a dead run toward the building. He noticed it was a little easier moving inside the dome. The Trochinids must have gravitational dampeners that were activated when the dome shield was up.

He reached the building as three Trochinids emerged from around one end. They saw him and began firing. From their position, the rest of Delta squad laid down a deadly fire, dropping the three Trochinids in their tracks.

Ridley located the sealed entrance and stood off to one side. The only way in was to wait for the next Trochinid to come out. From the pack, he pulled the first of the charges. He didn't have long to wait. The entrance shimmered, then a Trochinid lurched through. Ridley rolled the charge behind the Trochinid into the entrance. Catching movement, the Trochinid turned its weapon on Ridley. A star suddenly appeared in the Trochinid's thorax. It clawed wildly at its chest for a moment, then disappeared in a cloud of greenish-yellow tissue.

Ridley ran for the safety of some large cylindrical structures. The blast lifted him off his feet and sent him face first onto the platform. Ridley felt the shockwave from the blast pass over him. If not for the PFF, he would have been a cinder.

Azrnoth-zin loaded another cannister into his spare phase rifle while the Troch blaster recycled. Things did not look good. At the perimeter, the Trochinids had detected their presence and were mobilizing to their position. It was going to be meter for meter from here.

He turned to look at the team. They had already lost one of the Delfinian warriors. Two others had sustained wounds, but they were still able to move and fight.

Peering around the corner of the building they had taken, Azrnoth-zin's heart sank. At least twenty Trochinids were gathering to overrun their position. The Trochinids had already closed off any escape from where they had come. Nearby, three dead alien soldiers lay smoldering.

"How will we know where to find Ridley?" said Khar-aul. The wound to his right shoulder was still oozing blood, but no major arteries had been hit.

"He will announce his presence shortly," said Azrnoth-zin. "Right now, there are about twenty-five Trochinids standing between us and the command center, and I don't believe they're going to allow us to walk through."

Azrnoth-zin considered using one of the charges from his pack, but he had to get closer to make it effective.

Suddenly, the compound shook with a deafening blast. Fiery debris rocketed skyward and rained down all around them.

Azrnoth-zin turned to Khar-aul and the others. "That's him. I'd know that signature anywhere."

The Trochinids, momentarily distracted from the frontal assault on Azrnoth-zin's team, turned their attention to the destroyed munitions center. Azrnoth-zin saw several flashes, then Trochinids began flying in all directions as laser blasts tore into their ranks.

"Ridley's team has them in a crossfire! Move out!"

Just then, the remaining Trochinids started leap-running toward Azrnoth-zin's position. Flushed from their hiding places they advanced on the assault team. Azrnoth-zin and the others dropped to one knee and began firing into the advancing ranks of Trochinids. The Troch blasters belched out flame and death. Everywhere, Trochinids were on fire. The stench was overwhelming. Out of the smoke, Ridley's team materialized and added to the volley. The remaining Trochinids were torn apart in the firestorm.

"You okay?" said Ridley, running up to where Azrnoth-zin and the others stood.

"We lost one warrior. Two are wounded, but can still fight."

"Osik," said Ridley, his mouth taut. "We lost Osik."

"Have you located the ship with the stealth device?"

"That way," said Ridley. "About six hundred meters."

"By the size of that explosion, you must have found the munitions storage," said Azrnoth-zin. "It's fast becoming your trademark."

"I like big noises." Ridley looked up to see a contingent of Trochinids moving toward the blast area. "I think we need to split our forces. One team goes for the gold and grabs the stealth device, the other blows the dome. Mara's taking a beating up there."

"Agreed. What's your preference?"

"Like I said, I like big noises. We'll take out the dome."

Azrnoth-zin unshouldered his pack and set the explosive charges on the ground in front of Ridley. "I think these may be useful."

Ridley scooped up the charges and loaded them into his pack. "Guess I'll see you all at the pickup point. Good luck, Arn."

Azrnoth-zin nodded. "And to you." With that, he and Alpha Team took off at a trot toward the docked Trochinid ship.

Ridley turned to the Delta Team. "Let's go give Mara-jul some targets to hit."

Mara-jul and her fighter squadron were in a bad way. One of the Delfinian fighters had already fallen under the fire from the Trochinid cannons. The holographic ruse had worked for several minutes. The Trochinids had quickly wizened and began targeting their weapons on the thermal signatures of the light fighters. The fighters were forced into evasive maneuvers to avoid the deadly surface guns. Out of the periphery of her vision, Mara-jul caught movement at the surface. A full squadron of Trochinid short-range fighters had been launched from the moon's surface.

"Evasive maneuvers!" She said, breaking the com link silence.

The Delfinian fighters broke from the attack to evade the Trochinids. Although slower than a Delfinian light fighter, the Trochinids made up for this in sheer numbers. They pursued the Delfinians relentlessly in threes and fours. The juggernaut of Trochinid fighters poured forth from the great ships.

Four Trochinid ships screamed past Mara-jul, their weapons hammering her forward shields. Mara reacted and fired rear guns, taking out one of the ships in a fiery ball of metal and exploded gases. She banked hard to starboard and came to bear on the three remaining vessels that had also turned.

"Shields at seventy percent," indicated the computer. Mara-jul knew the shields wouldn't hold for more than another head on pass. She performed a scissors maneuver over the Trochinid ships. Two of their bursts went wide, the third caught her starboard side. Mara-jul fired while spinning and caught another ship with a blast directly into the cockpit.

"Shields at sixty percent. There is a stress fracture at the starboard stabilizer," said the computer voice.

The two remaining Trochinid ships were on her tail. Mara-jul reversed shields and accelerated away. The gap between her ship and the Trochinids increased, yet they kept coming.

She pulled an outside loop and activated the holo imager. Now, four fighters appeared to be aimed at the two Trochinid vessels. Momentarily confused, the Trochinids targeted the two outlying images. It was all the time Mara-jul needed. She fired forward cannons and the Trochinid ships mushroomed into starbursts.

Her heart racing, Mara-jul turned back to the battle at large. She saw another of her squadron being pursued by three more Trochinids. Angling her ship in for a shot, she let out a cry of rage as the Delfinian ship disintegrated in a yellow ball of flame.

"The dome is still intact!" one of the pilots said over the com link. "I don't think they made it down there!"

"Maintain your positions," Mara-jul said. "We need to give them a few more seconds."

She hoped Ridley and Azrnoth-zin deactivated the dome soon. She and her fighters were living and flying on borrowed time.

CHAPTER THIRTY-ONE

To reach the central part of the complex, Ridley and Delta Team had to skirt several more of the odd-shaped structures. The elongated quonset huts were arranged in rows, that looked like a series of slime-encrusted barracks. Due to the pall of smoke that now filled the inside of the dome, Ridley could not tell how many of the buildings lay before them.

The smoke provided one distinct advantage. Trochinids scrambled from building to building, yet it was difficult to recognize an intruder in the haze and confusion. Ridley surmised that most of the Trochinid's efforts were being directed at locating the interlopers. He had counted at least fifty Trochinids in various groups searching through the complex.

A group of six Trochinids lurched past the team just after Ridley pulled everyone back into the shadows of one of the structures.

"How much farther?" Ridley said, peering around the corner of the organic building. In front of him, between the storage centers was a large reddish-brown rectangular slab. It was at least fifteen feet long and close to ten feet high. It appeared to be bound by some translucent, gelatinous substance. Along the ground next to it, congealed reddish-brown fluid pooled.

"One hundred meters," said Kelun.

"Do you smell that?" Ridley brought his hand to his nose to ward off the stench. "Something is permeating through my PFF."

"I smell it, too," said Kirin-rah, swallowing hard to avoid gagging. "It smells like . . ."

"Rancid meat." Ridley said.

They had to pass by the slab to get to the next cover. Crouching next to the slab, Ridley fought back the gag reflex. The smell was overpowering here. He looked down at the sticky puddles of fluid near his feet.

"What in the hell is this stuff?"

He heard Kirin-rah gasp behind him. Turning, he saw her face a mask of horror and revulsion. She pointed up at a place about midway up the slab. Ridley tracked to where she was pointing. At first, he saw only contorted shapes. As his eyes adjusted to the haze and smoke, he realized what they were standing next to.

A face, twisted in a death grimace was staring out at him. Another was soon discerned, now a gargoyle's face. The heads belonged to Delfinians. They looked as if they had been caramelized into a fetid square of jerky. Ridley felt the bile rising in his throat as his eyes picked out other body parts, some recognizable, some alien.

"Processed," said Kelun. "This is where they store the processed. This is what became of the crew from *Burok-gahn*."

"Whatever happens, please do not allow me to be taken by the Trochinids," Kirin-rah said, her voice still shaky.

Ridley had a nagging feeling about this place. He knew he had never been here before, yet something in a dark corner of his mind seemed oddly familiar. Beyond the loathing and death he felt all around him, there was something else. He tried to define the feeling for several seconds. It was like a painful itch he couldn't scratch.

"I'm going to take particular pleasure in blowing the hell out of this place," said Ridley. "Come on, you all, one hundred meters to go."

By moving along the sides of the structures and using the smoke for cover, Ridley and the Delta Team soon reached the center of the complex. Standing alone in the middle of a cleared area, the central control building for the processing station rose to nearly twelve hundred meters, its sharply pointed roof with sensor equipment almost touching the top of the dome. Ridley observed occasional flashes above the dome through patches in the haze; Mara-jul and her squadron were in up to their ears.

The structure itself resembled a series of inverted bells stacked one on top of the other. This effect created a platform where hovercraft and small shuttles could dock. Ridley thought the control center resembled a series of vertical beehives.

The smoke lifted slightly off the ground and Ridley's hope spiraled downward. A detachment of Trochinids had formed a living circle around the base of the building. They stood two to three deep, weapons held at the ready position.

Ridley turned and slid against the wall of the storage center, managing to avoid the slimy coating "Well, we're not going in by the front door."

Kelun peered around the corner with his long flexible neck. "This is where they were mobilizing. They knew to protect the control center."

"I hope Azrnoth-zin is having an easier go of this," said Ridley. "Any suggestions?"

Suddenly, a hovercraft appeared over their heads, and sped off toward one of the platforms. Ridley noticed the two-occupant flying sleds were coming and going with some regularity.

"I think I have an idea," Ridley said, looking skyward toward the hovercraft. "Kelun, can you drive one of those things?"

The Yhrynen looked at Ridley in its childlike way. "A simple matter, to pilot one. I think acquiring one would be a much greater problem."

"I think I know how to acquire one. Here. Give me a boost up."

Members of the team lifted Ridley until he was able to scramble over the top of the storage building and plaster himself against the roof. Ridley was covered in the vile, sticky substance that formed a thin layer on the roof. Reaching into his pack, he produced the small crossbow and loaded an incendiary dart into the mechanism. The haze was clearing even more. If he didn't get a shot off soon, he was going to be a sitting target on the roof.

From the fourth level of the dome control center, a Trochinid got into a hovercraft and moved away from the platform. It descended slowly, banked, and then accelerated when it was several feet above the tops of the storage buildings. Ridley steadied the bow and waited, the whirr of the hovercraft's engines growing louder in the smoky haze. He knew he had one shot.

Steady, steady. The craft disappeared momentarily in a swirling cloud of smoke. It materialized almost on top of Ridley's position. Ridley took aim and fired, then ducked his head as the skid plate barely missed his head. The hovercraft disappeared into the haze.

The next sound Ridley heard was the soft splatter of exploded tissue, then a grating crash beyond that. Ridley jumped from the roof and ran in the direction where the hovercraft went down. The others were just ahead of him.

They found the downed hovercraft about thirty yards away leaning against the side of one of the storage buildings. It was covered in a glaze of greenish-yellow slime.

"It appears to be intact, other than minor exterior damage," said Kelun. He wiped some of the entrails away and restarted the vehicle.

Ridley turned his pack around so it lay across his chest. He pulled two of the charges from the pack and held one in each hand.

"Let's go tell them they've got mail."

Kelun worked the controls and the hovercraft lifted unsteadily off the ground. "I think there is some damage to the forward stabilizers," he said. "It will be difficult to maintain a proper attitude."

"This will have to do," Ridley said. "Shoot for level four through seven. We set the charges there, the whole thing comes down like a house of cards."

Suddenly, Tikah leapt onto the hovercraft and chattered at Ridley.

"You think you can fix the stabilizer?" Ridley asked.

Tikah nodded.

"Just keep your head down."

Tools appeared in the Mawhrbaht's hands and she crawled over the stabilizer section and began to enact repairs. The rest of the team watched as the hovercraft disappeared into the dissipating haze.

Kelun attempted to stay within the smokescreen as they ascended. From his position on the hovercraft, Ridley peered into the third level of the command center. The inside from here looked to be a tangle of wires. Inside, Trochinids stood behind objects that Ridley could only guess to be some type of command consoles. The consoles appeared to be made of a kind of organic material. Ridley caught independent movement from snake-like tentacles emanating from the structures. He shivered involuntarily. He felt as if he were on the inside of a rotting corpse.

Breaking through the haze on the fourth level, the hovercraft faced the expansive landing bay. The area was busy with Trochinids. Several other flying sleds were at the wait near the living consoles. Tikah looked up and announced the stabilizers had been temporarily repaired.

"Goose it!" said Ridley.

The hovercraft lurched forward, speeding into the bay. Realizing their security had been breached, the Trochinids opened fire. Ridley activated the two charges. He caught glimpses of some substance like dark spaghetti strands that actively interlaced across the ceiling and walls. Kelun accelerated toward the rear area and suddenly banked to avoid a barrage of weapons fire. Ridley let the charges sail. They broke through the other side of the bay and shot out into space. Kelun banked the hovercraft around again and headed for the seventh level.

The Trochinids were ready for them as the hovercraft screamed through the seventh level. Microbursts were all around the hovercraft. Kelun wrestled with the controls attempting to maintain their course as the vehicle shook violently.

Ridley reached into the pack, activated the two remaining charges and let the pack fly. A blast from a Trochinid phase cannon struck the rear of the hovercraft. The craft dropped hard, bounced twice on the flooring, then careened out the opposite landing bay. Flashes of light sparked off Ridley's personal force field.

The roar of the explosion was deafening. It began below them and crescendoed with the sixth, then the seventh level becoming consumed. The conflagration spread upward and downward simultaneously, engulfing the platoon of Trochinids massing at the base.

The effect of the detonation had a cascading effect. Each level was consumed in the blast and contributed to building the force of the explosion. Shattered pieces of metal and debris were flying out in all directions. Chunks of metal glanced off Ridley's and Kelun's personal force fields.

Ridley slapped Kelun on the back. "Nice driving!" He looked back to see Tikah desperately clinging to the shredded tail section. Ridley turned around and grabbed the Mawhrbaht and pulled her forward. The fur on her back was singed and smoldering, but she was unhurt.

"Brace yourselves. It is not going to be a pleasant landing," said Kelun.

The Yhrynen had a gift for understatement. Perhaps it was because of his soft, lilting voice or the placid features that tended to lull the listener into a sense of well being.

The Hovercraft hit the platform with a bone jarring crash. Kelun pulled it to the left and attempted to lay it on its side as they slid toward one of the storage silos. The craft slammed into the wall. Ridley felt a jolt of pain shoot from his head to his tailbone.

Now there was firing overhead. Through the fog that addled his brain, Ridley recognized the familiar report of weapons fire from the Delfinian light fighters. There was scattered phase bursts around them. The rest of Delta Team held off several Trochinids that had followed the hovercraft to where it crashed.

Ridley rolled out of the damaged craft and checked on Tikah and Kelun. Both were shaken. Ridley noticed that one of Kelun's arms was hanging at an odd angle.

"Can you move?"

The Yhrynen nodded. "I walk with my legs, not my arms."

The Delta Team continued to lay down cover for Ridley, Kelun and Tikah. Overhead, fighters from both sides rocketed through the haze. Ridley heard detonations that could only be large ships becoming engulfed.

"Tell them where you come from, Mara, " Ridley said, looking skyward.

"I have activated the retrieval beacon," said Kirin-rah, rushing up to Ridley. "The shuttles are on their way."

Ridley stood up stiffly. "Let's start moving in that direction. We should be hearing from Azrnoth-zin any time."

Ridley heard more firing in the distance, near the docking station. Azrnoth-zin's team must be making the final push toward the ship and stealth device. Ridley activated the com link.

"How ya doing, Arn? We've worn out our welcome over here."

All he heard was static. Then, "- heavy resistance." More static. "- attempting to board now."

"Do you need assistance?"

"No time . . . Trochinids between positions . . . to retrieval zone."

Ridley looked at the others. "He says he'll meet us at the pickup area. Kelun, I need the shortest distance between points."

Kelun pointed the navigational receiver in the direction ahead. "That way." He looked from the display back to Ridley. "Two large groups of Trochinids are converging on this position. One stands between us and Alpha Team. They have homed in on our coordinates."

Ridley noticed his PFF was beginning to flutter. It had been operating at full power for too long. He saw some of the other force fields showing the same signs of wear.

"Too long at the carnival, folks. We need to haul ass!"

Ridley downed the last of his oxygenator tabs and took off at the best sprint he could muster. Kelun, Kirin-rah and the others followed, moving between the storage facilities. Rounding a corner, they came under a barrage of fire from the first of the Trochinid units.

"Shit! They've got us boxed in." Ridley pulled back just before a volley erupted on the other side of the building.

"The others are closing in from the rear," said Kelun.

Ridley activated the com link. "Mara, honey, please be there."

Static. Ridley's heart sank. Mara-jul did not respond.

"Oscar fighters! This is Delta Squad. Do you copy?"

More static. Then, "Ridley, I'm kind of busy right now. What is it?"

"Mara!" He was joyous and relieved she was still alive. "I don't mean to be a pain in the ass, but we're in a hell of a mess here. We're pinned down and there's a whole lot of Trochinids between us and the shuttles."

"I'll be with you in a moment," came Mara-jul's even reply. Ridley heard more static. Mara-jul came back on the com. "Sorry to keep you waiting. Now, feed me their coordinates."

Kelun sent the coordinates. A moment later, Mara-jul's light fighter roared over their heads, delivering two phase cannon blasts to the advancing Trochinids. The leaping aliens were thrown in all directions as the explosions ripped through their ranks.

"Nice shooting, Mara. How about one more pass to emphasize the point?"

The storage building where the Trochinids were mobilizing exploded in a brilliant red ball of flame. "Thanks, Commander. We can take it from here," Ridley spoke into the com device.

Mara-jul's fighter looped around and passed low over their heads. She tipped the wings once each way, before heading back into the battle.

"You're welcome. Now, make it safely home, Ridley. I'm going to check on Azrnoth-zin."

"You watch your beautiful behind," said Ridley.

"I would rather watch yours." The com link went to static.

Ridley and the rest of the team moved as quickly as they could through the complex, past the burning structures and scorched and twitching forms of Trochinids. Ahead of him, Ridley saw another low-lying structure. The front of the building had been partially collapsed from one of Mara-jul's blasts. As Ridley started to run across the open ground in front of the entrance, he saw two forms suddenly appear from out of the shadows.

The Trochinids were not armed, but upon seeing Ridley, leapt out toward him. Ridley caught the first one in mid-air, hammering it back into the building. The second one disappeared in a spray of yellow-green gore. Tikah, Kelun and Kirin-rah had zeroed in on it simultaneously.

Ridley was having more difficulty catching his breath. His eyes stung and he felt a prickling sensation on his skin. He knew his PFF would not last much longer.

Something inside that building pulled at Ridley. He went to the entrance and peered in. By the time the others had caught up to him, Ridley turned around and waved them off. "Keep moving. The shuttles will arrive beyond this next set of buildings."

"I have lost contact with the shuttle, Commander," said Kirin-rah. "What should we do?"

"Stay on plan," said Ridley. "If you can't raise them in the next two minutes, call up the other shuttle."

"What are you doing, Commander?" said Kirin-rah. "There's no time for this."

Ridley felt the intangible pull of a force inside that building. "There's something in there I have to see. I can't tell you why or how, but I have to see what's in there. I dreamed about this place."

"There are still advancing Trochinids, "said Kelun. "They will overrun this position soon."

Inside, the eerie, greenish glow both repelled and beckoned Ridley at the same time. "Get back to the rendezvous point. That's an order." Ridley turned and faced his team. "I'll be along shortly."

He stepped inside the building and instantly felt the sticky dampness. The smell was almost unbearable. Ridley heard movement behind him. He turned and saw Kirin-rah with the others just behind her.

"I'm sorry, Commander. But Azrnoth-zin has taught me that a certain level of civil disobedience is necessary in order to fully develop oneself as a warrior," Kirin-rah said.

"This isn't your nightmare. Get out of here."

"We go to the shuttle as a team or we go through here as a team. It makes no difference to us," said Kelun. "I, too, am curious to see what this place is."

Ridley let out a long breath. "That's what I get for picking a group of free thinkers. Watch yourselves. This was not the place of pleasant dreams."

They advanced slowly through the building, their weapons held at ready. Once his eyes adjusted to the gloom Ridley found himself looking at a scene from his nightmare.

Before them were row upon row of upright, eight-foot, opaque cylinders. Each cylinder cast its own sickly greenish light, which appeared to pulsate from within. The gas within the chambers swirled and billowed, obscuring whatever lay behind it. Along the sides of each cylinder was a metallic frame that bore strange markings. The top of the cylinders had a series of color-coded signals that read across the top like a ticker tape.

"That's odd," said Kirin-rah. "These chambers resemble Delfinian reorganization tubes." She stepped closer and examined the symbols on the chamber. "Ridley!"

Ridley stepped back to where Kirin-rah was examining the strange hieroglyphics.

"This symbol here is a root for a very old Delfinian word," she said pointing. "But what could it be doing here?"

Ridley looked at the symbols. His mind was reeling. He stepped forward and traced his fingers along the lines of the strange runes. Where had he seen symbols like this before?

Suddenly, the realization hit him like a punch to the stomach. Earth! He had seen these symbols on Earth. These were the same inscriptions as on the metal shard that Enrique had given them when they arrived in his village at Punta Chueca. Azrnoth-zin still had that piece somewhere on the *ZOO*.

Ridley felt blind rage well up inside of him as he came to the grim realization. Tears welled in his eyes. He tried to brush them away, but to no avail.

"Commander?" said Kirin-rah. "Are you all right?"

"No. I will never be all right."

"What does all this mean?"

Ridley turned quickly on Kirin-rah, staring at her increduously. "You mean you don't know?"

Kirin-rah shook her head.

A sound near the entrance caught their attention. It was the sound of claws scrabbling over metal. Ridley looked up to see several Trochinids at the entrance swaying back and forth, staring balefully at them. The Delta Team began stepping back slowly, deeper into the chamber. One of the Trochinids let out a shrill scream. It stepped closer to the wall and placed its clawed hand over a protruding disc. Momentarily, the disc glowed bright green, then disappeared into the writhing wall. The Trochinid lurched back, squatted on its haunches, and watched.

Ridley heard a series of soft hissing sounds all around him. Glancing around, he saw a tube slide open, the greenish gas spilling across the floor. Behind the green fog, something stirred. Another tube opened, then another. And another.

"They're all opening!" said Kirin-rah.

"Run! Run faster than you've ever run before! It's a birthing chamber!" said Ridley.

Delta Team attempted to make for the entrance, but stopped short after several feet. The front entrance was a mass of snarling Trochinids waiting for the spectacle to unfurl. The last of the Troch blasters were spent; phase rifles were all they had now - no match for the numbers at the entrance.

"Get to the back of the building. Now!" Ridley yelled.

Ridley heard another sound as he ran between the opening chambers. He heard the sound of talons raking across the floor. Lots of talons.

CHAPTER THIRTY-TWO

Just when it looked as if Mara-jul was going to have to recall the light fighters, she saw the dome flutter and then dissipate.

"The dome is down!" announced one of the pilots.

"Move in and target the large cruisers," said Mara-jul. "Avoid the ships on the lower levels until we receive word from Alpha Team that the stealth device is secure."

The light fighters banked downward and flew through the complex of moored cruisers, leaving a swathe of burned and ruined ships in their wake.

Mara-jul attempted to reach Azrnoth-zin through the com link. "Alpha Team, report."

"We are in position now," said Azrnoth-zin.

"Do you require assistance, Alpha Team?"

"I believe the ship is powering up, Oscar Leader. Can you target the drive engines?"

Mara-jul brought the image up on her computer. The ship that bore the tag signature was near the lower portion of the station. It would not be possible to engage its shields until it had pulled away from its mooring.

Mara-jul banked her fighter around for another pass. Two Trochinid fighters came at her from her flank. She spun in a three hundred sixty-degree turn to avoid their fire. Activating aft guns, she vaporized one of her pursuers. She turned vertical to pass through two tall refueling stacks, barely clearing. The second ship could not make the turn in time. It exploded into fragments against the metal columns.

Mara-jul brought the fighter around and made the fast approach toward the lower level of the refueling station. Down here, the number of Trochinid fighters was less, but now she had to deal with ground troops firing up at her. Explosions bounced off her shields from the small weapons fire below.

Ahead she could see the tethered ship attempting to power up and break free from the mooring. Mara-jul targeted the engines and closed the distance, firing two bursts from her forward cannons. The rear drive engines erupted in a fiery flash. Mara-jul aimed for the mooring area. She let loose a barrage that took Trochinids and equipment in a conflagration of photonic energy.

The Trochinid ship attempted to engage its remaining thrusters to maneuver away from the platform. Mara-jul took out the main drive engine with her fourth shot. The Trochinid ship shuddered, then pitched downward to the floor of the complex, crushing dozens of Trochinids under its weight.

"I do not think I could have made it much easier for you, Alpha Team," she said. "I put the ship virtually at your feet."

"Thank you, Oscar Leader. We were having some discussion as how to reach that level of the ship," said Azrnoth-zin. "You just solved our dilemma."

"Please finish your task as quickly as possible. The Oscar Squadron is standing by to blast the rest of this complex into the next sector."

She is beginning to sound like Ridley, thought Azrnoth-zin. Maybe we all are.

"We'll be in and out in a few moments," he said.

It was then Mara-jul received the incoming com link from Ridley. She reversed the fighter and accelerated toward the other side of the plateau.

As soon as the Trochinid battle cruiser hit the main platform, Azrnoth-zin and Alpha Team were on the run. Many of the Trochinids left standing were burned from the engines or dazed from the impact. The Alpha team advanced, firing steadily into the confused Trochinids. Moments later they were alongside the downed cruiser.

Ryk chattered at Azrnoth-zin indicating the best entry was forward. They moved along the charred and burning hull, leap-frogging their way. Azrnoth-zin moved out in front, just as three Trochinids emerged from an airlock just ahead. He crouched and fired, taking care not to cause any aberrant detonations this close to the command center. The three Trochinids were blown backward from the blast, landing in grotesque positions several meters away.

Azrnoth-zin was the first to go through the shattered airlock. The chamber was dark except for the occasional spark of shorted-out systems. Acrid smoke hung in the air. Moving cautiously, he soon found the next airlock. He saw dead Trochinids everywhere, the casualties of Mara-jul's phase cannons.

Once inside, Alpha Team moved toward the control center of the ship. Azrnoth-zin maintained the point position with Ryk and Mistra behind him. Next was Bauk, the Markanian. Bauk had lent his expertise earlier with a sure hand on the small crossbow, a weapon native to his former homeworld. Dygar-zahl and Anwar-tet, two Delfinians of the Fourth order, followed next, with Khar-aul bringing up the rear.

The Alpha Team found the control chamber in shambles. Small fires sputtered along twisted pieces of machinery forcing them to navigate a strobe-like maze.

Ryk and Mistra chattered at Azrnoth-zin, indicating the stealth device would be located in this chamber. Azrnoth-zin nodded for them to proceed and motioned for the rest of the team to set up a perimeter defense and guard all entrances to the chamber.

The Mawhrbahts dug through the wreckage and soon located a floor grate that looked promising. The grate was too heavy for them to lift by themselves, so Azrnoth-zin, assisted by Khar-aal, managed to slide it out of the way. A cylindrical object, roughly two feet in length, was attached to conduits running underneath the floor. The device had a series of flashing lights located on either end. The center of the metallic cylinder glowed a reddish color.

Ryk chattered excitedly to Azrnoth-zin, indicating they had found the stealth device. The pitch of the furry engineer's voice grew increasingly shrill.

"You can't remove it unless the system's are shut down?" said Azrnoth-zin. "Where is the main control center?"

Ryk and Mistra pointed across the chamber and engaged in yet another lively exchange. Azrnoth-zin shined his lamp across the chamber. On the far wall was a metal panel. Ryk jumped and danced about Azrnoth-zin, indicating that the main systems control for the ship needed to be overridden there before the stealth device could be removed.

A blast occurred behind them. Someone screamed in agony. It was Bauk. Turning, Azrnoth-zin saw the Markanian being dragged through the airlock, a Trochinid's jaws clamped on his head. Other shrieks were heard, this time they were coming from Trochinids attempting to come through the airlock. Anwar-tet moved to counter the assault from the airlock. In the next instant he was engulfed in a photonic blast.

"Get ready to pull that device," Azrnoth-zin said, jumping up. He fired once into the airlock, then took off running toward the far wall of the chamber.

Small arms fire ricocheted off Azrnoth-zin's PFF as he sprinted across the room. He could tell that the force field generator was wearing down. He reached the opposite wall as two photon blasts arced into the bulkhead, sending metal flying everywhere. The PFF sputtered with the impact, but held.

Tearing the panel from the wall, Azrnoth-zin beheld the intricate circuitry that powered the central command center of the ship. He dared not shoot out the controls, as that might cause the device to overload. The detonations burst all around him. Azrnoth-zin focused all of his concentration on the panel before him. Finding what he thought to be the main circuit, he took a deep breath and pulled the circuit breaker from its socket.

There was a sound of machinery humming, then abruptly, it stopped. Ryk signaled that the device was off line. Azrnoth-zin turned his attention to the airlock. Half a dozen Trochinids were attempting to gain entrance into the chamber. Dygar-zahl was laying down a deadly barrage of blasts from his position behind a twisted section of the metal superstructure. He was pinned down. Khar-aul was firing from another area of the chamber, trying to give Dygar-zahl time enough to retreat to the rear of the chamber. Due to the angle of fire, he did not have a clear shot at the Trochinids just beyond the airlock.

Ryk and Mistra signaled that they had freed the stealth device from the coupling. Azrnoth-zin was up and sprinting across the floor to cover their position. A blast caught his force field full on. The impact sent Azrnoth-zin backward landing him in a pile of scrap.

Winded from the impact, Azrnoth-zin realized his PFF would last only a few more minutes. He opened up a channel on the com link and gave the coordinates to the shuttle metallic. Getting back on his feet, Azrnoth-zin's eyes were stinging and an acrid taste filled his mouth.

He zig-zagged his way to the center of the floor and fired as a Trochinid launched itself from the airlock toward Dygar-zahl. The shot caught the Trochinid off center and sent it spinning against the bulkhead. It attempted to come to its feet, but a well placed shot from Khar-aul splattered its head like a rotten melon.

"Get to the shuttle!"

Khar-aul began firing a continuous burst into the airlock. "Run, Dygar-zahl!"

Dygar-zahl, realizing it was now or never, fired once more, then stood up and began sprinting across the chamber. He almost made it to the rear airlock when a photonic blast ripped through his PFF and into his back. Azrnoth-zin saw the expression of confusion and pain as Dygar-zahl's body arched and then went to his knees. Azrnoth-zin knew he was dead before he hit the ground.

They quickly reached the outside of the ship. Azrnoth-zin found his breath coming in gasps. The shuttle touched down fifty yards away, firing at a group of advancing Trochinids. Azrnoth-zin motioned for the rest of Alpha Team to go before him. He fired as the pursuing Trochinids emerged from the airlock, dropping another one of the creatures in the opening.

He ran across the last few yards holding his breath. The personal force field was gone. He hit the ramp and rolled as a Trochinid blast knocked him off balance. The ramp was drawn up just as Azrnoth-zin inhaled a lungful of the noxious atmosphere.

He lay on the floor of the shuttle gasping until a med-surg metallic placed an oxygen nebulizer over his face. He felt the thrust of acceleration. Within a minute, he was breathing easier. The META unit piloting the shuttle turned around and addressed him.

"Commander," it said, "Commander Mara-jul wishes to know if all personnel are clear from the station. She wants to lay down incendiary bombs."

"Tell her to proceed," said Azrnoth-zin. He looked around the shuttle, still semi-dazed from the effects of the toxic atmosphere. "Wait. Where's Ridley and Delta Team?"

"They have not reported in. The other shuttle was shot down during the retrieval."

"Tell Mara-jul to hold back. Delta Team is still not secure."

"Commander, may I remind you that we determined if any team member was not present at the pickup coordinates at the designated time, we were to proceed with the demolition."

"Sometimes you have to break your own rules. Turn this ship around!"

CHAPTER THIRTY-THREE

Shapes emerged from the chambers like wraiths shrouded in a sickly green haze. The sound of scuttling grew nearer, louder. Ridley had his back to Kelun; he was flanked by Kirin-rah and Tikah. Boren-rahn and Duhan-ben stood on either side of Kelun, completing the determined circle of fighters. Without a word, they synchronized the frequencies on their PFFs to bolster the waning power from the depleted cells. They faced outward, waiting for the final deadly charge.

"Get the most for your shots," said Ridley. "Set for wide dispersal."

"They seem unsure of themselves," said Kelun. "They appear to be milling just beyond our line of sight."

"It's probably because they're infants," Kirin-rah said, snapping her last canister into place. "They will wait for the boldest one to attack, see what happens, then rush us as a group."

"Where's that goddamn shuttle, Kelun?"

"I cannot raise them on the com. Either there is too much interference from this structure or the shuttle has been taken out."

"I'm sorry I got you all into this mess," Ridley said, pointing his phase rifle at movement in a swirling patch of fog. "This wasn't supposed to be how this mission ended."

"It has not ended yet," said Kelun. "We needed to find out the truth just as much as you did, Ridley."

Ridley perceived a new sound coming from the mists. It took him only a second to realize that what he heard was the sound of small jaws snapping open and shut.

"Here they come . . ."

A form burst through the fog in a spring-loaded leap, its jaws open wide. The miniature Trochinid spat and toxic spittle hit the PFF, then sizzled. Ridley fired and the infant Trochinid was catapulted backward, a huge smoking hole where its thorax used to be.

There was a moment of confusion as the four-foot tall Trochinids retreated and scrambled after the remains of the first attacker. A moment later, another one flew at Kelun. It bounced off the shield, screaming as the shield discharged. The confusion afterward lasted only seconds. The baby Trochinids came at the Delta Team, all claws and teeth.

Ridley fired continuously, the phase weapon growing hot in his hands. The Trochinids were about half the size of their adult counterparts, but they were harder to hit. They swarmed toward Delta Team's position at the back of the birthing chamber. Trochinids were everywhere - climbing the walls, clinging to the ceiling, only to drop onto the force fields. At this rate and intensity, the PFFs would not hold out for long.

As one birthing chamber hissed open, Ridley caught a glimpse of a wriggling mass encased in a slimy, yellowish-green cocoon. Ridley watched in horrid fascination as the head chewed through the egg case, the miniature Trochinid glaring with the same yellow-eyed malevolence as the adults. Ridley fired a burst into the chamber, igniting the infant Trochinid and exploding the birthing tube. He began taking out birthing tubes anytime he saw one nearby beginning to discharge the greenish-yellow gas.

"Kelun! I need another canister!"

The Yhrynen reached into his pack and handed Ridley a plasma canister. Ridley ejected his spent canister and snapped the new one into place.

"What do you have left?" Ridley said, blasting another Trochinid hatchling off the shield.

"One more," the Yhrynen said with little emotion, and shot two Trochinids as they attempted to gain purchase on the fluctuating shields.

The juvenile Trochinids were hurled away each time they contacted the invisible dome of the PFFs. By grouping together, the Delta team was able to increase the net protective effect of the force fields for a while. Now, the Trochinids were no longer being repelled by the PFFs. They clung to the invisible barrier, clawing and screaming as discharges of energy occurred all around them. Suddenly, the shields shimmered like a disturbance on the surface of a flat pond as a Trochinid reached through the shield, clawing at Ridley. The shield responded more slowly this time before it scorched the talon. The Trochinid screamed and retracted its talon.

"Shields are failing!" Kirin-rah yelled, as she ducking out of the way from another Trochinid's reach.

The body count of mangled Trochinids piled up around the Delta Team. As soon as one was blasted off the PFF, two more would leap into its place. The shield diameters had already shrunken to a third their normal output.

Ridley heard a scream to his right. Duhan-ben's shield collapsed from the weight of the Trochinids. In an instant he was covered with swarming mass of fangs and claws. Blood spattered against Ridley's PFF, then ran in rivulets down the shield.

"Duhan-ben!"

Duhan-ben's screams gave way to the crunching sounds of jaws connecting with bone and sinew.

Ridley blasted the Trochinids off the shield directly over him. The phase rifle was almost too hot to hold. The weapon ceased firing and Ridley ejected the spent canister. Without hesitating, he reached for Duhan-ben's pack, found another plasma canister and snapped the last one into place. He fired a volley at a series of chambers opening to his left. The chambers and their occupants exploded in three brilliant flashes of light, shards of the chambers raining down all around them. Near his foot, Ridley noticed one of the pieces had some of the symbols he recognized earlier. He shot another Trochinid and picked up the hot fragment of the chamber, bouncing it in his hand to keep it from frying his fingers. He hastily stuck it inside his jacket pocket.

The blast had momentarily illuminated the chamber. The floor of the structure was a sea of baby Trochinids, clambering over the dead, leaping over the chambers. Others stood atop the debris, snarling and weaving back and forth. Concentric circles appeared in the shimmering shields, followed by rapier-like claws. A small, triangular head suddenly appeared, snarling as it tried to wriggle through the waning shields. Ridley pulled his phase pistol and fired point blank at the Trochinid's face.

Kirin-rah's PFF buckled. In the next instant, she was on her back as a Trochinid dropped down onto her from above. She fired as the Trochinid clawed at her. The Trochinid was blown backward against the last of the shield. Another one came at her. She attempted to club it with her spent phase rifle. The Trochinid backed away, sizing up its prey, then lunged forward. She screamed as it bit into her shoulder.

Ridley took his phase rifle and clubbed the Trochinid across the head. He hit it repeatedly as hard as he could. The Trochinid went limp and rolled off Kirin-rah. Ridley dragged Kirin-rah into his own flagging PFF. It would not be long now. Tikah was already sharing her PFF with Boren-rahn, who had sustained a ripping slash across his abdomen. Kelun was reduced to clubbing the Trochinids as they forced their way through the remainder of his waning shield.

A fiery pain erupted in Ridley's back as a talon raked across it. Turning to face his attacker, Ridley saw a Trochinid fighting its way through the remainder of his PFF. The creature clawed at him again, but Ridley was able to duck out of the way. He spun and caught the Trochinid in the jaw with his foot, sending it sprawling backward, its neck broken. Another came through the shield with jaws dripping saliva. The rotten breath from the small alien made the bile rise in the back of Ridley's throat. Ridley brought the rifle up and fired into the Trochinid's mouth. The head disintegrated, the body thrown backward into a group of Trochinids who jumped on it and began devouring.

One of the members of Delta Team screamed. Through blurred vision, Ridley saw Boren-rahn dragged off into the mists by a band of juvenile Trochinids. Ridley could barely lift his weapon to fire anymore. His breath came in gasps. The metallic taste burned his mouth, his nostrils, and windpipe.

Above the sound of Trochinid shrieks was the ear-rending sound of metal tearing behind them. The rear wall of the chamber buckled inward and then shattered in an explosion of metal and organic parts. The mob of infant Trochinids scattered as the shuttle landed nearby what was left of the Delta Team. The shuttle laid down a steady stream of fire, vaporizing any Trochinid within striking distance.

Ridley's PFF failed. Inhaling a breath of noxious air, he picked up Kirin-rah and clumsily draped her over his shoulder. Reeling, he stumbled toward the ship's ramp. Like a strangely disjointed dream, he vaguely registered Azrnoth-zin at his side, firing into the crowd of Trochinids, then assisting the both of them into the shuttle. Ridley and Kirin-rah collapsed in a bloody heap onto the floor grate. He felt the pull of acceleration as the shuttle blasted through the roof of the birthing nest.

"Oscar Team, Delta Team is home," Azrnoth-zin said, as the shuttle accelerated away from the depot. "Blow it to hell!"

Mara-jul's voice came over the com link. "Is Ridley with them?"

Azrnoth-zin looked down at the bloodied Ridley, who now was receiving oxygen from one of the metallics.

"Ridley is alive."

A moment later, there was a blinding light as the plateau evaporated in a chain reaction incendiary detonation from Mara-jul's fighters.

All of the treatment beds were full in the med-surg section aboard the *ZOO*. META IV moved quickly and efficiently, triaging the wounded. Delfinians and members of the Displaced Work Force acted as field medics, treating where needed. Most of the remaining members of both Alpha and Delta Teams, as well as two from the Oscar Team were here. Most were suffering from various stages of asphyxiation.

Ridley sat on the edge of the floating bed, his shirt off. A nasty laceration crossed his back just below the shoulder blades. META IV hovered behind him treating the wound with the same horse shoe-shaped device Ridley had seen Azrnoth-zin use back on Earth.

Ridley tried hard to concentrate on memories of his home world. *Earth.* He needed to find an image to replace what he had witnessed earlier today. He knew if he closed his eyes right now, he would go insane. Ridley stared ahead stuporously. He winced occasionally from the surgical device.

"Ridley," said META IV in her best chiding voice. "There is only so much scar tissue that your body can assimilate."

Ridley continued to gaze straight ahead, his eyes unfocused. "How's Kirin?"

"Her wounds from the bite itself were not serious, but the infection is. The analysis of the Trochinid saliva reveals some of the most virulent strains of bacteria I have ever seen. That is why it is necessary to hyper-dose you. Your wound is already becoming infected." META IV moved around to the front of Ridley. "Are you all right?"

"Stupid, stupid bastards," Ridley said under his breath. "I'm okay, META." The tone of his voice was less than convincing.

Azrnoth-zin and Mara-jul entered the med-surg section and walked over to Ridley's bed. Ridley's gaze drifted from Azrnoth-zin to Mara-jul. Even from his poor state of focus, Ridley could see that both Azrnoth-zin and Mara-jul looked wan and haggard. Mara-jul's brilliant blue-green eyes were rimmed in red and swollen. In his hands, Azrnoth-zin carried two pieces of metal, both with inscriptions etched on their surfaces. Ridley recognized the shards. One piece was from the birthing chamber. The other came from Enrique's village back on Earth.

"How are you feeling?" said Mara-jul, touching Ridley's arm.

He grabbed her hand. "Right now, I don't know how I feel. Arn, you look like shit."

"Thank you. May I say that you have never looked better." Then, Azrnoth-zin's facial features tightened. He looked down at the floor, as if he were unsure what his next words would be. He shifted his gaze to the two metal shards, then up at Ridley.

"I had the computer run a compositional analysis on both of these pieces. I do not know how or why, but structural configurations on these fragments are nearly identical. The symbols are ancient Delfinian. They also are a match. Both pieces date back to the same time of manufacture, give or take a few years."

"How could you know and we did not?" Mara-jul said, almost accusingly. "How did you know that the Delfinian's created the Trochinids?"

"I'm still not sure. It was in my dreams. Somewhere, in the re-wiring of my nervous system, I guess I acquired information that most Delfinian's are not privy to. Either way, your Water Council has been selling you a bill of goods for a long time. Ouch! Dammit, META! That hurts."

"This wound will have to be cauterized. I am afraid you will bear this scar for the rest of your life. However, I think the deleterious effects of the atmosphere are starting to wear off," said META IV. "That is good."

"I . . . I still can't believe it could be possible," said Mara-jul, trying hard to maintain her composure.

Ridley looked directly into Mara-jul's eyes. For the first time since he had met her, behind the anger, Ridley saw a combination of confusion and fear. He wanted to comfort her, but couldn't bring himself to move. All he felt at this moment was a great hollowness, almost a detachment, the likes of which he had never experienced before. *So this is what post-traumatic stress syndrome feels like,* he thought.

Azrnoth-zin's gaze remained on the two nearly identical shards in his hands. "I have had suspicions, but could never draw this conclusion. Delfinian history always had an element of vagueness about it, especially before the Trochinid wars began."

"What will we do when we get back to the fleet?" said Mara-jul.

Ridley's head whipped up, glaring at Mara-jul, his eyes narrowing. "We're going to get some answers from the Water Council."

"They will admit to nothing," said Azrnoth-zin. "The ramifications of divulging this information would be catastrophic to the fleet. All order will be lost. Sarn-ula would never allow this to happen."

"I want the entire crew of the *ZOO* to have access to this information," said Ridley. "I think the Displaced Work Force more than all of us, have the right to know what and who they have been fighting all along."

"Ridley, I don't think that -."

"Tell them!" Ridley's and Azrnoth-zin's eyes locked in hard stares. It was Azrnoth-zin who broke his gaze, never having seen so much rage in his friend's eyes. Under the bruised and worn exterior, Ridley looked like he might explode.

Azrnoth-zin shifted his gaze to Mara-jul. She was staring off toward the rows of wounded Delfinians and the Displaced Work Force, all who earlier had been fighting a clearly defined enemy. Now, the lines had all but been erased, Azrnoth-zin thought. He noticed that Mara-jul's cheeks were wet.

"I must insist that Ridley get some rest," intervened META IV. "His neurological and musculoskeletal systems have been strained to their limits."

"I will inform the crew," said Azrnoth-zin. "Everyone."

Ridley nodded weakly, then painfully eased himself down on the floating gurney.

"Today, because of me, ten members of this crew died. And right now, I'm having a hard time justifying those deaths."

Azrnoth-zin rolled the two shards over and over in his delicate fingers, then nodded at Ridley. He turned and exited through the airlock. Mara-jul remained bedside continuing to hold Ridley's hand. For several moments, neither spoke. Ridley felt the pressure on his hand from Mara-jul as she squeezed tightly.

It seemed like a long time before either of them was able to speak, the sounds of trauma permeating the air of the med-surg section. Medical personnel hurried from one treatment area to another. Against the far wall of the medical bay, lying in a neatly arranged row, Ridley stared at three smaller cylinders. In those cylinders were the lifeless remains of Osik, Bauk and Anwar-tet, the only ones recovered before the plateau was detonated.

Ridley heard a strange noise emanating from Mara-jul's throat and turned his gaze back to her. She was looking at him. And she was crying.

"When I heard your shuttle had been destroyed, I thought I would never see you again. Such pain I felt in my chest, I thought I would never be able to draw a deep breath again."

Ridley grimaced from the pain rippling across his back. He attempted to breathe deeply, but was wracked with a coughing spasm that brought his knees to his chest. After the coughing subsided, he looked toward the ceiling.

"The whole time I was out there, I was thinking about you," Ridley said finally. He drew the back of his hand across his face. "I wanted to water-link with you. I wanted to know you were okay. Funny, huh?"

Mara-jul put her head down. Ridley watched an opaline tear run down the end of her smallish nose, hang briefly at the tip and cascade onto the floor.

"I betrayed you," she said, almost a whisper.

Ridley cleared his throat. "You were following orders. You were being a good soldier."

"Somehow, I find little solace in being a good soldier." Mara-jul raised her head and was now looking at Ridley. "There are things that are more important than duty."

Ridley ran two fingers across Mara-jul's wet cheek.

"Yes, there are."

Tikah and Ryk entered the med-surg section. They approached the treatment platform tentatively. Ridley motioned them forward.

"It's okay, you two. I'm alright."

The two Mawhrbahts stepped up to the platform and looked plaintively at Ridley and Mara-jul.

"I'm sorry about Osik." Ridley said, running his hand through the thick fur on Tikah's back. "I'm so sorry."

Mara-jul and Ridley heard sounds coming from the Mawhrbahts. So different than any of the other chirps, whistles and chatter in their repertoire, Ridley could only assume they were the sounds of Mawhrbahts mourning.

After a moment they reported to Ridley, informing him in their staccato fashion that the stealth device had already been disassembled and analyzed. It was now ready for replication.

"Hell of a note, isn't it?" said Ridley. "We steal something from the Trochinids that for all we know, the Delfinians may have given them a long time ago."

The Mawhrbahts, not understanding Ridley's meaning, cocked their heads at him inquiringly. Then they jumped down from the treatment platform and ambled over to the smallest of the draped cylinders. They stood quietly over the cylinder containing the lifeless form of Osik for several moments, then left the med-surg section.

As Ryk and Tikah exited through the airlock, Kelun ducked his long slender neck through the door and entered. Even with his delicate arm broken, the Yryhnen insisted on returning to his station in the command center. He strode over to Ridley and Mara-jul.

"No more visitors! I want this area cleared of all non-essential personnel," said META IV forcefully. "Ridley must have time to recuperate."

"I beg forgiveness at the intrusion. I am sorry to disturb you, Ridley," Kelun said, glancing first at the metallic then at Ridley. "I thought it important to tell you this news in person."

Ridley propped himself up on one elbow, grimmacing with the effort. "What is it, Kelun?"

"Our most recent sensor reports tracking the Trochinid fleet's movements reveals the main part of the Swarm has altered their course. It seems even their outlying ships have corrected and are all now on the same heading as well."

"Where are they going?"

"Within the last cycle, our long range sensors picked up a weak signal from the Twenty-ninth system. The one you refer to as the Sol System. The Trochinids appear to have intercepted the same signal."

Ridley sat bolt upright, ignoring the stab of pain in his ribs. "Oh, my God. They're heading toward Earth."

CHAPTER THIRTY-FOUR

The Water Council was submerged deep within the aqueous link when the airlock doors slid open suddenly. Ridley, Azrnoth-zin and Mara-jul, followed by Kelun, Ryk, Tikah and several crewmembers from the *ZOO*, strode purposefully toward the water cylinders containing the remaining six members. The elite guard moved quickly and stepped up to intercept the intruders. Before they had a chance to draw their weapons, Ridley and the others were pointing phase pistols at them.

The members of the Water Council broke their link and stared at the intruders with great solemnity. Sarn-ula motioned to the rest of the Water Council and simultaneously, they surfaced, long robes trailing in the bluish water like fins from some exotic fish.

"What is the meaning of this?" demanded Sarn-ula, her webbed hands clinging to the edge of the large upright cylinder. "How dare you enter these chambers bearing arms."

"We're here for some answers, Sarn-ula," said Ridley, tossing the two identical metal pieces onto the crescent-shaped table in front of the link tubes. "That one is from the Trochinid birthing chamber. The other is from Earth. Maybe you'd care to enlighten us as to why the symbols are both Delfinian."

"Summon the rest of the elite guard!" Sarn-ula said. "I will not tolerate such insolence from this rabble. How dare you draw weapons on members of the Council. Guards! Shoot them. All of them."

One of the guards brought his weapon to bear. Kelun shot it out of his hand. The other guards looked stunned at how quickly the response had been. They lowered their weapons.

"Drop them on the floor. Now!" said Ridley.

The elite guard complied, their weapons clattering resoundingly throughout the chambers as they fell to the floor.

"Ryk, Tikah, seal the door," said Ridley.

The Mawhrbahts were at the door in a flash and soon had the mechanism jammed. Ridley turned back and glared at the Water Council. "Now, you were about to say?"

"This Council has nothing to say to you, offworlder."

Ridley's sidearm whipped up and fired a single shot at the base of the water cylinder. The chamber shattered in a burst of fragments and fluid. The water cascaded over the platform, dumping Sarn-ula onto the floor, sodden robes heaped about her.

"Talk, damn it!" Ridley pointed the phase pistol at another cylinder, the one that Phon-seth floated in. "After I take out all the tubes, I'll start on each one of you."

"Wait."

Ridley turned to see Quillen-tok pull himself from the link tube and descend the spiral stairs that led from the top of the water cylinder.

Sarn-ula drew herself to her knees. She looked shrunken and miserable. Ridley had an image of the Wicked Witch from the Wizard of Oz melting into a pile of clothes on the floor.

"Do not talk to them! They are not Delfinian."

"We are Delfinian," said Azrnoth-zin defiantly, stepping forward. "How long did you think you could conceal the truth from the Delfinian people?"

Quillen-tok attempted to help Sarn-ula to her feet. She pushed him away. "I told you keeping the offworlder alive would be disastrous. Now, do you see what he has brought upon us?" Her words came out in almost a hiss.

Mara-jul stepped forward, looking down on the sodden form of Sarn-ula. Mara-jul's face was one of stony resolve. She looked defiantly at Quillen-tok. "How many more have to die before the truth be told?" she said angrily.

"Everyone has grown weary of the lies, Sarn-ula," said Quillen-tok, gathering his wet robes to keep from tripping over them. "The time for truth has been a long time coming."

The elder Delfinian stepped toward Ridley holding both hands outward. "Please," he said softly. "No more violence. I will tell you what you want to know."

The elderly Delfinian statesman stared at the two matching pieces of metal setting on the table, as if imploring them to give him the words to continue. Under the sopping robes, Ridley saw Quillen-tok's shoulders heave, as if a great weight had been placed on them.

"A very long time ago," he began, "the Delfinians were explorers and scientists. We had passed through thousands of years of peace. In that time, we amassed data from all over the galaxies, charted new planets, expanded the arts on our home world. Our civilization thrived. The rate of new technological and scientific discoveries was difficult to keep up with, so rapidly did they occur. There was no disease, no hunger, no wars."

Quillen-tok's arctic gaze took in everyone in the chamber. "Since Delfinus was a water planet, our ancestors had some travel logistics to overcome in order to explore the vast expanses of the universe. You see, Delfinians several millennia ago did not look like we do today."

"What do you mean?" said Ridley.

"We more resembled your Delfids on Earth. We swam through the waters of Delfinus with powerful tails. Our hands and arms were incorporated into flipper-like appendages, except we did possess opposable digits for manipulation."

Ridley's eyes went wide in realization. "So, you're the big blue dolphins in my dreams!"

"You lied to all the people," said Mara-jul. "There never were the Ancient Ones after all."

"Oh, there were the Ancient Ones," said Quillen-tok. "They were the original Delfinians. They were what we looked like before the Genetic Transformation and the Great Separation."

"What Genetic Transformation?" said Azrnoth-zin, his face troubled. "I do not remember any of this or the Great Separation being taught."

"None of you do. Please let me continue and I will illuminate all matters."

Several attendants approached from beyond the darkness bearing fresh robes. Quillen-tok stopped, shed his wet robe, which was replaced by a dry one from one of the attendants. The other members of the Water Council changed from their wet clothing as well. All except Sarn-ula, who stood on the floor in a puddle, glaring at the proceedings. Her attendant, not knowing the proper protocols to maintain during a siege, draped the robe over her frail shoulders.

"As I said, our physical restrictions to a watery environment limited our mobility during exploration of the sectors," Quillen-tok continued. "Our scientists had long been renowned for their expertise in genetic manipulation. We began traveling throughout the expanse, harvesting genetic material. At first, we designated metallics to do our collecting for us. Later, we were able to harvest it ourselves. It took us a very long time before we were able to decide on a morphology that would allow us access to most parts of the systems."

"Earth," said Ridley. "You took human DNA from Earth."

"That is correct, Ridley. Earth was a veritable living laboratory. Nowhere in all of our travels had we discovered such a rich biomass. We harvested genetic materials from many of the species on your planet, not just humans. So you see, the Delfinian-human link is a very close one indeed. That is the reason why the Water Council wanted you put to death. I knew that once you walked down that ramp, the Delfinian way of life would never be the same."

"And what of this Great Separation?" said Azrnoth-zin. "What happened to the Delfids?"

By now, the remaining members of the Water Council had exited the Water-link cylinders, descended the stairs and were standing on the floor, each one flanked by a robed attendant. Quillen-tok looked at the Council, drew a deep breath and was thoughtful for a moment. He walked back slowly to the crescent-shaped table and again picked up the two shards, examining them in the light. The runes glowed as the light from the cylinders reflected off their surfaces. He placed the shards back on the table, turned back to face Azrnoth-zin, Mara-jul and Ridley.

"At first," he said, "only the scientists and exploration crew members were allowed to make the transformation. Over time, more and more Delfinians chose to assume this new form. The Ancient Ones decried this as an abomination and blasphemous to their teachings. As the numbers of bipedal Delfinians increased, the tensions between the two factions grew. This new strain of Delfinian had developed another trait, one not present before in the aquatic species." Quillen-tok's gaze turned to Ridley. The elder Delfinian's deep blue eyes were intense.

"We became aggressive. Our scientists did not realize the extent this trait pervades humanity. For the first time in our history, we began to persecute our own simply for being different."

"I think I'm beginning to understand," Ridley said sourly. "Don't let the Delfinian people know they got a batch of flawed genes from Earth."

"When did this take place?" demanded Azrnoth-zin.

"Seven thousand years ago."

"What became of the Ancient Ones?" asked Mara-jul.

"That part of our history is correct," said Quillen-tok. "Or at least most of it. The Ancient Ones, fearing more reprisals from the Transformed, decided to leave. They left in the last of the great aqueous ships, the ones they had originally explored the expanse in."

"So how come I knew about the Ancient Ones while Azrnoth-zin and Mara-jul didn't?" said Ridley.

Quillen-tok paused, closed his eyes, then reopened them. "At birth, each Delfinian has a small implant placed in their brain. This processor prevents the assimilation of certain information. In essence, it blocks out specific memory engrams. While you underwent neural reorganization, you received the entire history from the Delfinian data banks. We were monitoring you to see just how well you had assimilated the information. At first, we seriously doubted your system could withstand the neural inputs. We did not think you would survive, let alone recollect. Apparently, we misjudged you, Ridley."

"Apparently. Why did you need to censor your own people's memories?"

Quillen-tok turned his gaze to Azrnoth-zin and Mara-jul. "The Thousand Years of Peace came to end. We went to war with Dalgoor, a neighboring planet in our system. Their planet was an arid place with limited water resources. A gradual shift in their polarity caused the limited water supply to dwindle. They saw Delfinus as their salvation."

"Did we share water with them?" said Mara-jul.

"No. The Delfinians sent a contingent of representatives to Dalgoor. The negotiations did not go well. The Dalgoorians sent the delegates back to Delfinus, all dead and mutilated."

"So you went to war," said Azrnoth-zin.

"Not directly. We did not possess a standing armada. All of our resources were dedicated to exploration and scientific investigation. Our leaders conferred and decided to create an army to defend Delfinus. So, on a small moon in the Trochos system, our geneticists began developing the ultimate warrior."

Ridley's jaw dropped. "You invented those damn things? Jesus H. Christ on a bike!"

Quillen-tok nodded. "The Trochinids were to be the consumate soldier. They could withstand the harshest of environments. They could eat on the move and could be programmed to fire weapons, even follow simple commands."

"What happened?" said Azrnoth-zin.

"Something went wrong at the facility. As you have seen with other life forms we have created over time, the Trochinids developed a sentience unbeknownst to their creators. The geneticists missed this mutation and before they could respond to it, the compound was obliterated. All Delfinian scientists were killed and presumably consumed. The Trochinids managed to learn the programming sequence to the birthing chambers and not long after, were able to find transport off Trochos. By this time, there were enough of them to form an assault. The nearest planet was Dalgoor. It was the first of many worlds ravaged and consumed by the Trochinid swarms. Over the millennia, they have become more efficient at attacking and processing planetary systems."

Mara-jul stepped forward, cold rage in her eyes. "All of these years. My family. Your mate. Everyone on Delfinus has lost someone. All these millions of lives lost because of a horrible act committed by our scientists. When was it going to stop?"

Quillen-tok suddenly looked very old. He stared for a long moment at her. "In the beginning, we thought we could contain their spread," he said sadly. "Resilient and resourceful, they were able to modify and improve their replication sequence. We did not understand the capacity for their numbers to grow exponentially. It was not long before they spread like a plague to all parts of the galaxy."

"Maybe you should have talked to someone on Earth first," Ridley said sarcastically.

"But why keep us blind to the truth?" said Azrnoth-zin.

"Because of what just has transpired here in these chambers. A decision was made by the Water Council to commit ourselves to the eradication of this menace from the system, no matter how long it took, no matter how many Delfinian lives it cost. The Trochinids must be stopped. The leaders knew compliance and support from the people would be difficult if not impossible, given the harsh reality. So, processors were implanted in all newborn Delfinian children. Both of you, Azrnoth-zin and Mara-jul, have those micro-processors in your cortices. The only ones who do not possess the chips are the seven members of the Water Council. The processors of newly chosen Council members are removed when they ascend to their positions."

"So you committed the Delfinian people to a war they could never win at the expense of not only their own civilization, but the destruction of entire planetary systems as well," Azrnoth-zin said bitterly.

"They had no other choice," said Quillen-tok. "The Transformed believed the Delfinian people were a condemned race. They were more than willing to commit the Delfinian people to rectify the situation."

"Yeah, too bad they neglected to inform several billion others of what was coming down the pipe," Ridley said angrily. "What in the hell were your ancestors thinking? How could anyone who calls themselves civilized or sane conjure up a living cancer like the Trochinids?"

"Even your people are not above the development of organisms that could wipe out all life on your planet," said Phon-seth accusingly, stepping forward.

Ridley faced off with Phon-seth. "It's not even close to the same thing. If we blow ourselves up, we have only ourselves to blame. We didn't create something that would wipe the entire slate clean."

Quillen-tok let out a long, ragged exhalation. The chamber was quiet except for the background humming of the ship's drive engines. Finally, it was Ridley who broke the silence.

"I just got word that the Trochinid fleet has changed course and is drawing a bead on my home town of Earth. I'll be leaving on the *ZOO* as soon as possible. I'll be taking anyone from the Displaced Work Force who wants to go along for the ride."

"You cannot leave!" said Sarn-ula. "You are treasonous deserters. Our ships will destroy your puny vessel the moment it leaves space dock."

Sarn-ula advanced on Ridley pointing an accusing finger at him. "You and all of your alien filth will be terminated!"

"You can't terminate me, lady, because I quit!"

Ridley glared at Sarn-ula, then at the rest of the Water Council. His knuckles were white, his forearm muscles tensed on the phase pistol he still held pointed down at the floor. Ridley looked at the phase pistol, shook his head and holstered the weapon.

"Oh yeah, one more thing. I kinda figured you were going to get a bug up your robe, so I had the Mawhrbahts hardwire explosive charges in various locations on this ship. Very sensitive locations, if you catch my drift. All it takes is the activation frequency from me. You launch even one fighter after us and I can

promise you we'll arrange for a meeting with your Ancient Ones
- in the next life."

"Take the *ZOO* and any other ships or supplies you
require," said Quillen-tok. "You will receive safe passage. You
have my word."

"No!" Sarn-ula said, her voice almost a shriek. "They must
not leave!"

Ridley noticed the elite guard was no longer paying
attention to the rantings of the once great Delfinian leader. They
stood at their positions, heads bowed as if someone had pulled the
plug on their obedience. Ridley thought they looked as if they had
been cast adrift on a deserted moon.

"Go in peace," said Quillen-tok. "No one will follow you."

Ridley stood, barely able to control the shaking in his legs.
He nodded to Quillen-tok. "Once we're away, I'll transmit the
location of the charges. Oh, we're leaving you with a little parting
gift - the stealth device we acquired on the Razorian moon. Seven
Delfinians and three DWFs died to give you an extra edge. No big
deal." Ridley spun on his heel and started to walk away.

"You will die, offworlder!" Sarn-ula shrieked. "Your
miserable world and all who inhabit it will perish. Without our
help, you cannot survive the Swarm. You are all fools!"

Turning around, Ridley cast a hard look at the fallen leader.
"Maybe, Sarn-ula. But who's the bigger fool? The one who hides
from the truth or the one who confronts it?"

He turned and walked out of the Council chambers without
looking back.

Ridley went back to his quarters on the *MENTOR* and
gathered together his meager belongings. He hadn't arrived
with much and now he was leaving with little more. He shed the
Delfinian tunic and donned the faded leather jacket, his father's
flight jacket. The familiar leather felt heavier, yet more supple than
the Delfinian uniform he had worn for the last six months.

Making his way back to Landing Bay Seventeen, he noticed
how the looks from the Delfinians had changed. Many would
not meet his gaze. Nervous looks darted from one Delfinian to

another. Word traveled fast here in the vacuum of space. Ridley kept his eyes focused ahead and walked briskly toward the cargo bay. He wondered if someone still loyal to Sarn-ula and her minions would think this was all his doing and decide to take him out with a well-placed shot between his shoulder blades.

He moved through the crowded corridors, the mass of personnel parting like a Delfinian sea to allow him passage. No one spoke to him on his way back to the *ZOO*. That was fine by Ridley.

Upon entering the landing bay, Ridley was unprepared for the sight that greeted him as he strode through the airlock. Before him stood the entire Displaced Alien Work Force. Among them were at least fifty Delfinians. All eyes were focused on Ridley. The large room was silent.

"What's this?" said Ridley, looking at the sea of alien faces that filled the expansive hangar.

Azrnoth-zin stepped forward. "I told them that you were buying the first round on Earth. This is most of us. Some of the work force in the outer parts of the fleet received the word late. They're coming in now."

Azrnoth-zin noticed that Ridley's eyes were glistening with tears.

Mara-jul stepped forward and embraced Ridley, then kissed him. "I want to be where you are," she said.

Ridley hugged her fiercely and kissed her again. "I was hoping you were going to say that."

"Besides, you require my constant vigilance to guard your vulnerable posterior."

Wiping his eyes with his sleeve, he saw Kelun step forward.

"I am pledged to the protection of your homeworld," Kelun said. "Earth will be saved or we will die trying."

"We'll probably all end up as the catch of the day for the Trochinids," said Ridley. "Thank you. Everyone."

The huge throng moved in closer until Ridley was surrounded by a sea of bodies. Kirin-rah, still recovering from her wounds hugged him.

"I have not finished my training in disobedience," said Kirin-rah, smiling.

Ridley laughed. "Oh, I'd say you have it down pretty well, Kirin." He nodded at her. "I'm glad you're here."

Khar-aul fought his way though the crowd and stood before Ridley, performing the salutory bow. Ridley gently lifted him from the shoulders until they were eye to eye.

"Looks like you're going to get that grand tour of Earth after all," Ridley said, smiling broadly.

The young Delfinian warrior looked like he would explode from enthusiasm and pride.

Ridley noticed several of the elite guard present among the Delfinians. And there were the Mawhrbahts, hundreds of them. Ryk and Tikah were at Ridley's legs, clinging tightly. If he tried to move now he would topple over and probably be crushed to death.

META IV glided over the tops of the alien's heads and positioned herself over Ridley. "I respectfully request assignment aboard the *ZOO* as primary med-surg unit."

"META, you are the med-surg unit," said Ridley.

"No longer. Five others are volunteering for this mission. They are all multi-functional as well."

"It's going to be a long, cramped trip."

The room began to vibrate with the sound of hundreds of feet stomping the floor. The din escalated until Ridley could barely hear Azrnoth-zin speaking next to him.

"Explosive charges?"

He noticed Azrnoth-zin was grinning. Ridley shrugged. "My Uncle Jake used to say," Ridley found himself yelling, "If you can't dazzle them with brilliance, baffle them with bullshit."

"I want to meet this Uncle Jake," said Mara-jul.

"You will." Ridley interlocked his arms with Mara-jul's and Azrnoth-zin's. Nodding to the crowded room, he said, "Time to go home."

About The Author

John R. Gentile is a marine mammal naturalist and researcher, physical therapist, sea kayaker, SCUBA Divemaster, and nature photographer. John, with his marine biologist wife, Katie Iverson, has been conducting a photo-identification study of bottlenose dolphins (*Tursiops truncatus*) in the upper Gulf of California since 1997. To date they have well over 100 dolphins identified as permanent or part-time residents of the waters around Puerto Peñasco, Sonora, Mexico.

John is currently putting the finishing touches to *Siren's Song: Book III of the SOFAR Trilogy*, due to be released in the Spring of 2006, as well as working on a screenplay revolving around Arizona-Mexico border issues.

John and Katie live in Tucson, Arizona with Marley, a chow with a sense of humor.

Printed in the United States
43858LVS00004B/94-153